The
SATIN
SASH

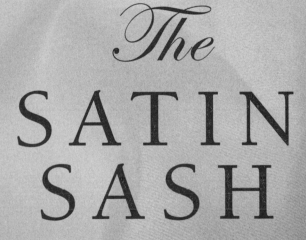

The SATIN SASH

Red Garnier

HEAT

HEAT

Published by New American Library, a division of
Penguin Group (USA) Inc., 375 Hudson Street,
New York, New York 10014, USA
Penguin Group (Canada), 90 Eglinton Avenue East, Suite 700, Toronto,
Ontario M4P 2Y3, Canada (a division of Pearson Penguin Canada Inc.)
Penguin Books Ltd., 80 Strand, London WC2R 0RL, England
Penguin Ireland, 25 St. Stephen's Green, Dublin 2,
Ireland (a division of Penguin Books Ltd.)
Penguin Group (Australia), 250 Camberwell Road, Camberwell, Victoria 3124,
Australia (a division of Pearson Australia Group Pty. Ltd.)
Penguin Books India Pvt. Ltd., 11 Community Centre, Panchsheel Park,
New Delhi - 110 017, India
Penguin Group (NZ), 67 Apollo Drive, Rosedale, North Shore 0632,
New Zealand (a division of Pearson New Zealand Ltd.)
Penguin Books (South Africa) (Pty.) Ltd., 24 Sturdee Avenue,
Rosebank, Johannesburg 2196, South Africa
Penguin Books Ltd., Registered Offices:

80 Strand, London WC2R 0RL, England

First published by Heat, an imprint of New American Library,
a division of Penguin Group (USA) Inc.

First Printing, December 2009
1   3   5   7   9   10   8   6   4   2

Copyright © Red Garnier, 2009
All rights reserved

HEAT is a trademark of Penguin Group (USA) Inc.

Library of Congress Cataloging-in-Publication Data:

Garnier, Red.
The satin sash/Red Garnier.
p.   cm.
ISBN 978-0-451-22803-1
I. Title.
PS3607.A7655S37   2009
813'.6—dc22   2009024620

Set in Bembo Regular
Designed by Alissa Amell

Printed in the United States of America

This book is dedicated to—
The agent of my dreams; a most savvy, fantastic, knowledgeable woman, Roberta Brown.
To Tracy Bernstein; a *gem* of an editor, whose brilliance, support, and enthusiasm are not the only reasons I dote on her.
And to my husband. I love you with every bit of my being. After all these years, you still make my heart flutter.

Acknowledgments

A huge, heartfelt thank you to my friends who read it first—and threatened in the most convincing way to kill me if I didn't show it! Your advice, your support, your countless hours on IM and e-mails, have kept me excited and inspired. So thank you, Sierra Dafoe, for sharing your amazing knowledge with me; Wylie Kinson, for your insightful critiques and witty observations, which I can't live without; Lilli Feisty, for your awe-inspiring faith and talent; R.G. Alexander, for your support and friendship, which mean the world to me; Robin L. Rotham, you know I will continue to beg for your amazing advice!; and Karen Erickson, my daily brainstorm gal and woe buddy—you are the best.

Also, I am entirely awed by all the terrific people at NAL/ Penguin, and want to thank each and every one of them for their terrific job in this book and for making it happen.

And to all of you readers who like to cuddle up to a story. I hope you enjoy mine.

The
SATIN
SASH

Chapter One

"Your woman wants me."

Grey Richards froze, then lowered the glass of wine and turned to look at the man facing him. Heath's jet black eyes gleamed with a disconcerting mix of devilment and concern.

Grey glanced over the crowded room to where Toni stood, smiling among a group of women. His gut clenched in a knot. "Come again?"

"Your woman. She wants me."

For a stunned moment, Grey gazed into the crimson depths of his glass, his sixth of red cabernet, and decided if he wasn't drunk, then his friend and partner *was*.

"Toni?"

"Do you have another woman?" Heath replied.

Grey could only stare at him.

Underneath the black tuxedo he'd borrowed from Grey, Heath Solis was still the rough-edged daredevil he'd met twenty years ago, and while his social skills could use a little polish, Grey had always appreciated his bluntness.

No one cut through the bullshit like Heath.

Together they'd been through good times and bad, but unspoken between them lay a quiet understanding. They worked well together. Grey the brain; Heath the muscle.

Having jointly built RS Corporation from scratch, making the company Chicago's most successful commercial development firm, Grey managed the corporate offices in the city while Heath handled their businesses abroad. Where Heath liked to keep his private life to himself, Grey had to face the press. Grey enjoyed living lavishly, while Heath preferred frugal surroundings.

Despite their differences, they were united by dedication, wills of steel, and a fierce loyalty and trust.

Heath's childhood might have been far from the ideal foundation for a hero, but Grey would put his life in no one's hands but his.

Heath was the brother Grey never had. Grey was *all* Heath had.

He couldn't believe he was hearing this.

"You're serious?" he asked.

Heath's jaw was set, his expression somber; Heath's face could send people scrambling when he scowled, and lure the ladies when he smiled. "I wouldn't kid you about this," he said, shooting Grey a sidelong glance. "You haven't exactly taken her off the market, have you?"

Head reeling, Grey looked back at the group of women to find Toni gone. The room was alive with music. Glittering chandeliers hung from a vaulted ceiling, fountains spouted champagne, busy waiters circulated among the guests.

He and Heath stood a good distance from the dance floor, amid dozens of vacated tables at what had been a five-thousand-dollar-per-seat mediocre dinner, but it didn't take him long to spot her.

She was on the dance floor, whirling in the arms of Senator Louis. A pretty flush stained her cheeks as she let the energetic man twirl her round and round.

Without even realizing it, she'd had Grey's nuts in a twist from the instant he set eyes on her. Now at the sight of her petite, graceful body draped in shimmering fire-engine red, while she smiled

one of her million smiles, Grey was a ball of lust waiting to be unleashed on her.

Her little bottom jiggled, her bosom heaved, and her eyes sparkled like gems. She was all fun, all life, all sweetness and spice. The
large diamond studs he'd given her for Christmas peeked through
the glossy chestnut waves tumbling past her shoulders, catching the
light.

His blood thrummed in his veins with the desire to press his
mouth to one ear and tongue her. Eat up that sweet, feisty baby, his
juicy-lipped baby, nibble by nibble. His chest swelled, a sensation
that had become painful of late and all too real.

He was in love with her.

Irrefutably, indisputably in love with Toni.

It was a place he'd never imagined himself to be. A place where
all thought centered around her, all actions aimed to please her. A
place where Grey could hardly think.

All he could think of was her.

What had started as a passionate fling had turned into a full-
blown relationship, to the point where Grey's penthouse had been
empty for months. The closet in Toni's apartment was now crammed
with his expensive suits and endless racks of ties. Their bathroom
looked like a war zone. His schedule was continually interrupted
with unexpected but delightful "situations."

And he wouldn't change any of it for the world.

You're not wearing panties tonight, Toni.

Why not?

*Because every time I look at you, I want to know your pussy is bare under
that dress, and I'll think of nothing but taking you home and licking you.*

She'd been a sight to behold, leaning over the bathroom mirror, creaming those pouty lips with a glittery red substance. "Will I
get a prize for surviving an entire night without panties?" she had
playfully asked, setting the lipstick down and twirling around to fix
his collar.

Her eyes gleamed appreciatively as she took in his tuxedo-clad figure. She fitted her body up against his and fingered the black bow at his throat. "Will I get to take everything off but this, Mr. Richards?"

"Give me some of that," he murmured huskily as he ducked his head to run his tongue across the plump bottom curve of her lips, "and I'll show you how I plan to suckle the lips between your thighs."

At thirty-five, Grey had seen and done it all. As teenagers, he and Heath had had dirty, raunchy sex with the dirtiest, raunchiest women they could find. Prostitutes and kinky widows and women who seemed so high and drunk they'd do anything with anyone. They'd done things to women that the girls in high school and college would never in their wildest dreams let a man, much less a boy, do. That had been sex for Grey at sixteen, seventeen, eighteen.

Later, through the years, while he and Heath went their separate ways, he'd acquired a connoisseur's taste for it, like fine wines and cigars. He'd sought pretty women much as he sought out the finest cars; he'd had them all.

And not a single experience compared to being with Toni. No orgy or threesome or plain-vanilla sex could capture a fraction of the intensity of his feelings for her, his *wanting* of her. She was so passionate, her eager receptiveness to his touch consumed him. He was addicted to memorizing her noises, testing her responses, discovering where to caress, to touch, to bring her pleasure. Her face as it bloomed in orgasm brought him to his knees; he'd never seen anything so beautiful.

He wanted her now. Here, at this wretched party. In front of Heath, in front of everybody.

He burned under his suit, itched to take her into a nearby hall and remind her who it was she wanted, who it was she fucked all day, every day, and she *begged* for more.

He did no such thing.

Instead he averted his eyes and studied his friend and business partner once again.

"What would have given you the impression she wants you?"

Heath took a step to stand shoulder to shoulder, his midnight gaze tracking Toni. Grey did not like the hot, possessive way Heath looked at her. Or the slow, knowing smile stretching his lips. "Do you honestly think I don't know when a woman wants me?"

"Did she tell you so?"

"Nah. She's too fine to tell me in words."

Oh, she was fine all right. More than fine. Perfect.

Unlike the models Grey had preferred for years, Toni was no tall, bosomy Amazon. She was a small, sprightly thing—a little fire to Grey's ice. A whirlwind of smiles and surprises that made his heart ache with how freaking adorable she was.

Her eyes—the vibrant energy of her entire being simmered inside them. A chameleonic green of shade undeterminable, susceptible to her emotions like mood rings. Grey got dark forest with her passion, emerald with her smiles, mossy green with her silence.

What color does Heath get?

Struggling to remain calm, Grey raised the fluted glass and contemplated his beauty above the rim, engaged in yet another lively dance. Song after song blasted in the room, but Grey heard nothing but his heart pounding.

Your woman wants me. . . .

Toni was a sensual, sexual, highly emotional being. Sweet in nature; deliciously responsive in bed. Her lusty appetite was unsurpassed by that of anyone Grey had ever met before, and her responsiveness to the barest touch was addictive. She wasn't afraid of anything and would always try something once. She liked it dirty, a little naughty, and seemed to get a thrill when he got rough. But never, *ever*, had Grey considered she might crave more. More sex, more lust. *More.*

"If she didn't say so, then why would you be telling me this?"

"We danced." Heath bent to whisper. "I touched her."

"And?"

"And she let me."

While Grey had been listening to Carlton earlier, specifically to the retired accountant's monotonous dissertation on the economy, Toni had been in Heath's arms. Sans panties, because he and Toni had thought to play a little game of anticipation tonight.

She let Heath touch her?

Stomach churning with bile, he set the empty glass on a passing tray. "Toni is a sensual woman, but she responds to *no man* like she responds to me." He fixed his friend with a cold smile—the same he used across the boardroom when the meeting was adjourned. "Whatever it is you're thinking, you can forget it."

Heath snorted, a primitive sound Grey recognized as having multiple meanings. His partner jammed his hand into his inner coat pocket and produced a long, shiny red sash.

Grey's eyes slimmed to slits. "That looks familiar."

"She wore it around her neck." Heath grasped the back of Grey's hand and slapped the sash into his palm. "Tie it to my door if you change your mind. I leave Wednesday."

Grey fisted the flimsy fabric in his palm and glanced up at Heath's retreating back. "Wait."

Probably unused to Grey's most glacial tone being directed at him, Heath stiffened, hands fisting at his sides before he turned around.

Their gazes met with no antagonism, but with a calm, collected watchfulness.

"You're saying . . . you want. . . ?" There was little that differentiated Grey from a statue.

"You know what I'm saying." The broad white smile Heath shot him was the devil's own. "Think about it, Grey."

⌢

Through the top of Mrs. Jennings's coiffed white hair, while the elderly woman told one of her numerous dog anecdotes, Toni watched the two men. Grey. And that wicked, bold, dark-headed creature. Talking. Very seriously. About something.

Grey's hard-boned, chiseled blond face was inscrutable, but Toni had noticed he had not glanced at her in a while. Her tummy contracted with nerves. Whatever his partner was speaking to him about, Grey did not seem pleased.

She wiped her hands on her sides, hating the pebbles of moisture on her skin, hating that she was almost cowering by the curtains. She did not want to see that black-haired man again. She didn't even want to *think* of what had happened, yet the memory was there, flickering in her mind, mocking her.

He'd stood with Grey throughout most of the evening, and the moment Toni had set eyes on him, she'd known it was him. Grey's overseas business partner. A man Grey respected, admired, and spoke of so often Toni had sensed the man somehow—invisibly—played a part in her and Grey's burgeoning relationship.

The enigmatic Heath Solis.

They made a riveting picture, side by side. Grey with his sleek blond-streaked hair; Heath his antithesis with a head of tousled black silk. Like day and night, ice and rock, both equally mesmerizing, both oozing masculinity and power. Grey with his imposing presence seemed more intimidating somehow, but Heath was dark and rugged.

Danger had never looked so tempting.

As she made her way to them from across the room, people interrupted to draw Grey away—people always sucked up to Grey—and the dark-eyed menace was left alone. He eyed the crowd with the air of one who didn't want to be there. Then his gaze collided with hers.

Those eyes assessed her in a single sweep and left each inch they covered tingling. Toni hadn't realized she'd stopped walking until someone bumped into her as she continued to stare.

An older woman in blue silk paused to speak to him. He ducked his head to listen and nodded, his lips forming a lazy smile.

Her heart hammered while other things inside her moved. Should she introduce herself?

She stole a glance at Grey, surrounded by a group of older men and women. He'd promised to introduce her to his partner tonight, but judging by the avid conversation around him, it didn't seem like it would happen soon.

Her gaze slid back to the tanned, tall stranger as the woman patted his broad, square shoulder and continued on her way.

Heath lifted his head, his eyes returning to her—as dark and tenebrous as what Grey had said of his past—and for a moment everything faded except that aggressive black stare.

Her heart thundered in her ears, drowning all music, all sound. This had happened before. Across an office desk, when Grey had leveled that cool amber gaze on hers, Toni had been taken. Was *still* taken by Grey. Absolutely. Completely. Damn it. Why couldn't she breathe?

He advanced. So slowly she might have made an escape if she'd had an ounce of inclination. As it was, faced with six feet three inches of testosterone approaching, she could barely drag in air. Her pussy gave a little spasm, and her throat closed as she tried to swallow.

His jaw was all square bone; his eyes glimmered under the somber slashes of his eyebrows. The arrogant slant of his nose was barely softened by the plump sensuality of his lips. And those lips were curling slowly, almost sarcastically.

The cruel sexiness of that smile blasted her with a shot of pure, unadulterated lust. A lust Toni had felt for no one but Grey. Until this moment, *this* man. He was awesome. Bad and primal and *animal*.

There were whispers. People noticed him as one would notice a storm, a hit man, danger. Yet she could not take her eyes off him for long enough to turn and appease the gossipers around her.

His scent reached her before his hand did. He smelled of earth and rain and tree bark, and the aroma made her head spin. Without a word, he engulfed her hand in his hot one and dragged her through the throng of people with single-minded purpose.

Almost stumbling on her dress as she tried to keep up, she was shocked that he didn't release her when she tried to pull free. "What—what are you doing?"

He paused once they were safely in the middle of the dance floor, flanked by dancers.

"You wanted me to ask you to dance." His hands slid to the small of her back, drawing her to the incredibly hard wall of his body. "So I'm asking."

Toni had heard his voice over the phone. Sometimes milky and soothing like Baileys, other times rumbling like thunder. The thunder now skimmed over her skin like the very satin of her evening gown. He could've been Grey for the effect he had on her—and no one made her feel like Grey did.

She felt a moment of panic when his thigh slipped between hers. Their bodies touched from knees to chest; his rock-hard, hers malleable. Flames licked her on the inside, her pussy watering between her legs, naked under her dress.

The moment the top of his bulging thigh brushed her clit through the material, she thought she'd burst. "I-I don't think you understand. I'm—"

"I know who you are." With a dangerous smile, he slid his hands to the small of her back, the tip of his long fingers resting on the top of her butt. "You're Grey's girl." And in her ear, "His record."

The obvious bait brought a smile to her lips as she raised her eyes to his. "And am I supposed to know who you are?"

"You should." He cupped her rear intimately and an odd little sound escaped her, more like a whimper than a gasp. He grunted, as though pleased, and raised one hand to tug at the satin sash around her throat. The sinuous glide of fabric teased the back of her neck as he bent to whisper in her ear, "I'm your worst nightmare."

And maybe he was

When a large, possessive hand curled around her elbow, jolting her back to the present, she knew it.

Even before she heard Grey's voice. "We need to talk."

⌒

We need to talk.

He said nothing else after he dragged her aside at the benefit to utter those hushed, spine-tingling words. They'd been accompanied by the most glacial stare Toni had ever seen, and Grey wasn't known for his warmth.

The ride to her place was rife with tension, and the piercing looks Grey sent her way made her all too aware of her missing sash.

Her throat had never felt so bare.

And Toni had never felt so miserable.

Staring out at the sea of headlights dotting the street, she fiddled with her hands above her lap and wished she could find it in herself to entertain him the way she usually did after these events.

She could tell him how the senator had asked her name five times tonight, her age another seven. How the pepper steak had caused the old woman at their table to turn a particular beet red. But her throat felt too tight and her stomach knotted.

Tonight . . .

Nothing about tonight was funny. Least of all the thought, the mere possibility, of losing Grey.

She'd never been in love before. She'd been dedicated to her studies and career for what felt like forever, with a few sparse dates to spruce up her weekends. And then came Grey. And falling in love with Grey had proved as mystifying and overpowering as the man himself.

The last two years had been lush with passion, her happiness so great that sometimes she thought she'd burst from the sensations in her chest. That amazing high she felt, the adrenaline, the dizziness of loving Grey. She was so addicted to it . . . to *him*. For the first time in two years, the fear of having a future without it—without Grey Richards—began to gnaw her raw.

He drove his fine black Porsche toward her apartment in silence, but every once in a while, his eyes would rake her breasts, her waist, the place between her legs that felt so wet.

He'd been sleeping at her place for months, and Toni wondered if that would change tonight. She couldn't bear it if it did.

A drop of rain fell on the windshield, and she gathered her courage and turned in the leather. "The senator called me Tori all night," she said lightly.

Grey didn't seem interested.

"By the fifth time, I didn't even bother to correct him." Her smile quivered on her lips, but Grey wasn't interested in it, either. "He was nice though," she added, wiping her sweaty palms on her lap. "He certainly knows how to dance."

Grey said nothing. *Nothing.*

His incredible strength of character made it difficult to imagine he could be susceptible to human emotions like fear or rage, but Toni knew a Grey no one else knew; one who laughed with her, who tucked her against his body at night, whose gaze was warm and affectionate and not the cool amber he turned on others. *Her* Grey. And she sensed the tempest in him—simmering under his skin.

We need to talk.

Oh, god.

When they finally reached her apartment, the air between them was charged and carried in it the unmistakable sizzle of lust and the dense fires of anger.

Toni's heart gave a tight clench of dread as she followed him inside.

By the reckless way he threw the keys on the console by the entrance, she knew exactly what he wanted to discuss.

Tonight in a room full of people, she had been captured by one thing alone: another man. He'd made her shiver, her heart race, her pussy wet even when it had already been drenched.

I'm your worst nightmare. . . .

Now, hours later, witnessing the granite set of Grey's features and the steely proprietary look in his eyes as they walked into her bedroom, Toni couldn't help but agree.

She didn't know why she'd experienced such a powerful attraction to his partner, but she knew with all her heart that she loved Grey.

She couldn't stand the mere thought of being apart from him.

And she hated having felt this.

Wildly, she wondered what she could say, what excuse she could give him for having wantonly draped her body against Heath's as they danced. Had Grey seen them? Had he noticed she no longer wore her sash? Was he disgusted with her? Repulsed by her? Would he not be able to forgive her?

Close to splintering under the pressure, she leaned back against the wall, weak-kneed as he shut the door and shrugged out of his jacket.

The soft drum of raindrops hit against the windowpane. Through the lulling sound, she could hear Grey's deep, even breathing and her own quickened breaths.

The very air seemed to crackle with the suppressed energy of his presence.

His motions were painfully slow as he set his jacket aside and started for her. Her heart raced. Her stomach twisted in need and desire and dread.

Without the benefit of light, his eyes glowed eerily. She got the distinct impression she was about to be devoured.

"Have fun tonight, Toni?"

He pinned her between the wall and his hard body. Emotions lit up his gaze like flashes of thunder, and she could see one in particular taking her breath away. A new breed of desire. Raw. Carnal. Taking her breath away.

"Yes, I did, Grey."

She rubbed against his slab of a body, and god! His cock felt huge against her stomach, the familiar form perfectly delineated through his pants. His balls were high and tight, the width of his shaft broad, the turgid head stretching the material tight. She pressed her body into his, undulating suggestively, but he didn't move. Didn't do anything but stand there.

Moaning softly, she clawed at his shoulders, buzzed her lips up his neck, filled her lungs with the citrusy scent of him.

Cream coated her pussy, and her nipples pinged as she pressed them to his chest. She wanted to show him she wanted him inside her, filling her pussy with his hardness, but he remained impassive.

When he finally moved and lifted one hand to cradle her cheek, she went utterly still. His touch was so very gentle. That simple, tender cup of his hand sparked a wildfire in her.

As she had danced with the thrillingly frightening Heath Solis, she had pictured falling to her knees and opening his fly, filling her mouth with that part of him she'd sinfully craved. Her tongue had tingled with desire to taste him, to discover what kinds of sounds he made when he was sucked.

At this moment all she craved was the salty, delicious taste of her Grey. Whom she adored, whom she could never get enough of.

As the silence stretched, she stared deep into his eyes and tried a smile that couldn't quite make it. "Grey, say something."

He didn't.

Only stared at her as though he was seeing a stranger.

His golden eyes trekked across her face; her nose, her cheeks, her lips, her eyes.

"You." His voice was a terse rasp. "Have been a naughty girl."

Toni melted back against the wall, parting her legs. "Yes. Oh yes, Grey, I'm so bad."

He cupped her sex over her dress and pressed the heel of his palm to her clitoris. The heat of his skin seeped through the satin, searing her. "You let another man touch you."

Fire streaked through her as he massaged and she rocked to his hand, seeking to assuage her aching pussy. "Yes, but I'm sorry. So sorry."

"Are you, now?"

His hand opened wider on her cheek and his palm nearly swallowed her face.

The pad of his thumb bit into her lips and with one brusque swipe, he smeared her crimson lipstick all across her cheek. "Who's this for, Toni?"

He repeated the move, smudging her face with the glittery substance, arousing her beyond measure with his roughness. "Tell me. Who's this for?"

Toni doubted she had any red left on her lips, but Grey continued to scrape, leaving the flesh of her lips puffy. "Who's this for, Antonia? Tell me."

Something thrilled inside her at the need in his voice, the jealousy. The fierce emotion was eating at Grey, and it only intensified her ache for him.

She slid her hands up his chest, every hard muscle palpable under his shirt. "Who do you think it's for?" When had she ever dressed for anyone else? When had anyone else's opinion counted? "I'm yours, Grey. All yours."

He nipped at her lower lip, his eyes hooded. "That's right."

Yanking up the skirt of her dress, he burrowed one hand between her legs, cupping her moistness. She whimpered, and a wash of cream flowed into his palm.

"You promised to make love to me," she whispered, and twined her hands around his neck. "I've been waiting for this all night."

With two deft fingers he fondled the pink lips of her sex, watching her as her features melted. "I keep my promises." He eased two fingers into her creamed cleft and let out an anguished groan. "God, you're soaked."

She moaned and clasped him tighter. Her fingers bit into his shoulders as she gyrated her hips, coaxing him in deeper. "Take me."

He pushed in deeper against the needy flutters of her pussy, and his face, such a stoic beauty most of the time, was etched into a landscape of need.

"I don't trust myself right now."

Toni framed his strong jaw with her hands and pulled him to her mouth. "I trust you. I love you. Fuck me hard."

A sound got strangled in his throat as he captured her lips so hard her head slammed back against the wall. His flavor invaded her—wine and need and Grey. His tongue stabbed into her, once, twice, moving up to the roof of her mouth, over her tongue, beneath it.

He hulked over her, framing her face as he deepened the kiss, ravaged her lips.

His hands moved down her ribs and curled around her ass, gripping her to the slab of his hot, aroused body. He groaned into her mouth, the sound purely male and gratifying. It exhilarated her to know she pleased him, made her feel feminine and powerful.

She tugged his shirt out of his waistband with awkward hands. Grey slanted his mouth over hers and jerked the top of her dress down her shoulders so roughly she heard a tear. Her breasts popped free and he instantly covered them with his hands.

Toni shivered as he caressed. She parted his shirt and examined every dent and ridge of his chest with her fingers. The warm silk of his skin delighted her. Grey had the most amazing body. Athletic, hairless, tan, and hard.

"Take your pants off, Grey."

Something flashed in his eyes; then they were both rushing to yank off what remained of their clothes.

His body returned to hers, skin to skin. Flush against her, he bent and rubbed his cock against her pelvis, the taut head grazing up to her belly. "Love," he rasped, rocking against her, "how you feel against me."

His body almost made love to hers with those brazen, undulating moves. A carnal dance of bodies, brushing to the echo of their panting breaths.

Clutching him against her, Toni nipped at his chin, whimpering from the stimulation of his chest brushing her nipples. She curled one leg around him, opening her sex to him.

"Is this what you offer?" he demanded.

He slipped a hand up to brush her pussy so lightly she keened in despair when he retrieved it.

"Yes, please, yes."

He crushed her back against the wall, grinding his hard cock against her distended lips. "I want it."

He jammed her breasts into his hands and massaged the flesh, and Toni greedily swiveled her hips, trembling with the need to feel his cock against her.

Through silky, blond-tipped lashes, he watched what he did to her, his face dark with carnal desire. He grasped the tiny points of her nipples between two fingers and plucked them like petals. Pluck, graze, pluck. Currents of electricity ricocheted through her. He rolled the beads expertly between his fingers and pinched, just like she liked it.

Her nerve endings sizzled. "Ooh!"

"Like that?" He pushed them in with his thumbs then tugged them out, causing her overheated body to buck in reaction.

She panted hard, the tightening sensation deep in her core almost unbearable. "You *know* I do."

"More?"

Toni arched her spine, her breasts surging up to him. "More."

He ducked his head. The heat of his mouth enveloped one puckered nipple. He suckled and lightly grazed it with his teeth, nibbling. Hot, delicious pleasure feathered down her thighs.

Toni cradled the back of his head, keeping him confined against her, praying he'd never stop. "Oh, Grey, yes, yesss."

He moved to her other breast, her first nipple left red and raw. He soaked the other tip, swiping it with his tongue. Then his lips surrounded the pearl and suckled in his mouth. He suctioned, nipped, used his teeth to drive her wild. The tension in the center of her body threatened to tear her apart.

He tortured her. Sweetly. His hands, his mouth, the storm he caused in her; they were the most effective reminder of who owned her, commanded her passions, awakened her deepest longings.

The sex was always an avalanche of passion, earth-shattering in its intensity. Afterward it would be all love, a little banter, a burst or two of laughter. Then Grey would be cool again. The ruthless businessman the world knew.

He was ruthless as a lover, too.

He inched his head down her abdomen so slowly he had her writhing in anticipation against the wall.

Juice trickled down her thigh as the strong, satiny tip of his tongue nudged her clit. Her pussy gave a hot series of spasms when he repeated the caress, going deeper this time.

She tensed her muscles, screaming in her throat. Desperate, she grabbed a fistful of his hair and wrested him up. "Grey, I need you—"

He silenced the remainder with his rampant kiss. Toni clumsily wrapped her arms around his neck, her breasts compressed against his chest. She couldn't think, breathe. Every inch of her burned. She wanted closer. Needed closer.

He squeezed her thighs with his big hands. "Wrap both legs around me, dirty girl."

When she did, his massive erection prodded her sex. She let out a needy noise when he used the head to tease her clit.

He watched her with burning eyes, his chest heaving with each languorous move of his hips. The strong pulses in his cock vibrated against her pussy, making her quiver.

"Grey . . ."

"Want me in?" His voice was barely intelligible, rough as sandpaper.

"Yes!"

He drew his hips back, then rocked them forward. "There you go." Her sheath parted as the head entered. "Nice and slow." He dipped his thumb into her mouth.

Toni sucked on his thumb, her pussy easing around his shaft as he pushed deep.

His head fell back as he groaned. She moaned simultaneously.

He started a rhythm, a slow rock of his hips that made her painfully aware of each inch he withdrew and each inch he impaled.

Gasping, Toni bit down on his thumb and reared up, drawing his cock in as far as it would go. "Faster, Grey." She swiveled her hips, and a powerful tremble that seemed to affect the entire room rocked across his body. "Christ." He flattened her completely against the wall and took up a merciless rhythm, one that wasn't meant to please, but to take.

Toni grabbed his ass, glorying in each flex of taut muscle, urging him in deeper, meeting his thrusts with frantic swivels of her own. Each long, steely penetration had her writhing, the pressure mounting inside her, sending her toward an earth-shattering explosion.

The cup of his hand on her thigh tightened reflexively while the other still covered her mouth, letting her suck on his finger. "Is that how you'd suck his cock, hmm? Is that how you'd lick Heath's cock while I fuck you?"

She stiffened at the startlingly erotic image, her momentary rigidity betraying her to Grey. And then she purred in acquiescence because, yes, oh yes, that would be lovely.

Her sex rippled around him, massaging his length, milking his desire. Her eyes fluttered shut as she sucked and tasted his thumb. Soon she was crying out mindlessly, moan after moan rising up her throat, muffled by his hand on her mouth.

He sampled her neck, tasting her, then focused his attentions on her ear. The rough velvet of his tongue swiping across the sensitive shell ignited more electrifying sensations in her. "Tell me you love me. Tell me now."

"Oh, god, I love you."

He grunted and kept pumping and pumping, all power and stamina, all bad and wicked, all hers this moment.

Her body contracted, the tension escalating. She came with a quick, jarring jolt, sobbing out helplessly as the swift contractions burst through her. Grey clamped her hips with both hands and delivered one, two, three final plunges. And the man newspapers around the globe had dubbed Glacier dissolved. His body jerked, a roar tearing out of him.

Still thrusting, he kissed her mouth as he shuddered, a sloppy kiss full of tenderness. He murmured something hot against her lips, but Toni could not understand his words.

She was limp against the wall, receiving his semen, entranced as she watched him come. To have put that twisted look of pleasure on his face made her heart tremble.

He sagged against her once he finished, then surprised her by pulling out and setting her away from him. He rested his palms and forehead on the wall a few feet away and labored to recover.

Toni swallowed at the absence of his weight. She wrapped her arms around herself and slowly smoothed the goose bumps from her flesh. Grey always coddled her after they made love. He would hold her so tenderly, coo at her as if she were a baby, tell her how beautiful she was, how hot she made him.

But tonight Grey snatched up his clothes almost immediately and disappeared into the bathroom. She deserved no praise tonight.

Toni winced when the door shut behind him. She heard the water faucet, the scrape and brush of his toothbrush.

Guilt and confusion swamped her, but she knew one thing: Grey deserved more than her silence.

Her hand shook as she turned the doorknob. Inside the small bathroom, she faced his broad back and reflectively said, "We danced. I was attracted to him, and it surprised me. I won't deny it."

He didn't move, and when he did, it wasn't to sneer or mock or lash at her. It was to meet her gaze in the mirror and nod in somber understanding. "I know."

He didn't say more and left for the bedroom. How did he know? How *could* he know? Had he seen her making an idiot of herself, turning to putty in his partner's arms?

Distraught at the thought, Toni cleaned up and removed her makeup, scrubbing hard where he'd smeared her lipstick on her cheek. She brushed her teeth and slipped on Grey's old Chicago Bulls T-shirt, loving that even when she'd been the only one wearing it for a year, it still smelled like him.

She found Grey sprawled naked on his back, the bedsheets up to his waist. One sinewy arm covered his eyes. Toni lifted the covers and slid under the sheets, instantly seeking his body for warmth.

Without a sound, he curled an arm around her and pinned her to his side. Giving a silent prayer of gratitude, Toni draped one bare leg across his and cuddled even closer, peering into his face.

"Grey?"

"Not now, Toni."

Chapter Two

He couldn't talk to her.

He didn't know what he'd do or say or betray.

Sprawled in a chair by the window, Grey studied her sleeping figure while he tangled the cool satin strip between his fingers.

The clock on the nightstand read 4:36 a.m.

She'd been tossing and turning all night. And he'd been watching her. Loving her. Hating her. Wanting to selfishly use that body he cherished, take her hard and bury his anger into the depths of her. He remembered everything. Vividly. Every word, every look, her smell, her voice. Every moment with her.

She'd rocked Grey's world since that first time he'd seen her work: a personalized card from a man he did business with.

Through the echoing noise of what was yet another social evening, Grey had surveyed the sleek embossed logo and design, impressed with what he saw. Elegant, edgy. Totally unique.

"Sharp card."

He grew up in money. Recognized the importance of appearances. Bank loan agents, investors—they could all be swayed with an intimidating glare, a powerful stance, most of all a sharp tie. And apparently Grey could be swayed by a petite bit of a woman, strolling the next day into his office with a portfolio of her work.

Antonia Kearny.

His first impression, aside from a youth she couldn't manage to conceal in the rather insipid business suit she wore, was that she was little more than average, her hair tied into some sort of twist behind a pale oval face, a few coppery tendrils framing a high, smooth forehead.

She had a small, rounded nose and small, plump lips painted the color of raspberries. She was nothing extraordinary—certainly nothing to turn heads—but when she began talking, showing him her work with that lively glint in her eye and a quiver of excitement in her voice, Grey had been charmed. Totally enchanted by her.

He'd wanted to slip his hands under her skirt, spread her legs open, and see if the lips of her pussy glistened like her shimmering pink mouth.

Instead he'd glanced at his watch, unsatisfied by the thought of a quick romp atop his office desk. "I'm afraid I'm running out of time, but I'd appreciate it if we discussed this over dinner."

Time seemed to still as she looked up. "Dinner?"

He noticed his tongue would fit perfectly through the opening in her mouth. Just a little wider, and he could push his cock inside, see it rimmed by the pink of her lips. Stirred by the visual, he bowed his head. *Yes, love, dinner. I'll be having you.*

"Name the place, Ms. Kearny."

Although alarm skittered across her every feature, he sensed her determination in making the sale. She tucked her catalogues back into her briefcase, tentatively suggesting, "The Chop House?"

"Excellent. And your address?" He leaned forward in his swivel chair. "To pick you up?"

She hesitated, then rummaged through her things and scribbled down her address on a tiny yellow slip.

Hours later, tucking the note back into his breast pocket, Grey knocked on her door. His heartbeat had increased en route to her home; it pounded severely when he arrived. A lion's roar in his ears.

She opened with an exerted little gasp, wearing a navy blue dress that, although loose from her waist to her knees, exposed a delectable amount of cleavage and amply showcased two very pert breasts.

Flushing under his slow but discreet inspection, she quickly went back inside to retrieve the portfolio she was forgetting.

An invitation, if Grey ever saw one.

He followed her down a narrow hall, making no attempt to evaluate the simplicity of her home, intent on one thing only. *Mine. Mine. Mine.* He caught up with her in the bedroom as she bent to lift the briefcase. "Mr. Richards, do you want me to bring the—"

He wrapped her in his arms, roughly drawing her against him. "What I want is right here."

His glaring hard-on was cushioned in the cleft between her buttocks. She stood utterly still. Smelling divine, feeling divine. Her suppleness amazed him. Her shampoo drifted up to his nostrils, the scent as tantalizing as spring.

"I . . . don't sleep with my clients, Mr. Richards."

He eased her gently around and flashed her a wolfish smile. "All right. I won't buy."

The breath shuddered out of her lips, and for the first time in his life, Grey wanted lipstick smeared all over his mouth. Her eyes were bright with sexual energy and wide with innocence.

He found the combination irresistible.

Their kiss had been sex in itself. A mating of tongues, a fusion of mouths, souls. Cultivated and controlled as he was, he'd barely been able to rein himself in. Pins flew from her hair; his pants were at his ankles; her panties shredded across the floor. She was on the window seat, one breast poking out at an awkward angle from her dress, her pussy exposed to him like an open flower—and only then did Grey pause for a breath, for a condom, for a freaking grip on himself.

Then the tips of her heels dug urgently into his buttocks, and he snapped like a twig.

The sex had been no smooth seduction. It had been carnal, reckless, animal.

No one made him lose control like she did. For months he was all over her, insatiable, intent on feasting on her until he was sated. And while he waited for the loss of interest that never came, they began flirting, teasing, exchanging secrets, childhood anecdotes— a Pandora's box Grey had never opened before. Not to discover someone else's contents, not to share his.

One weekday morning he woke up in her apartment with a pleasant buzz in his head, a smile of contentment on his face. He caught sight of her quietly watching him, and it hit him; that knee-buckling, chest-expanding feeling he knew he'd never felt in his life.

He left for work as usual, but surprised her by storming back within minutes. She had her briefcase in one hand, the other reaching to unhook her coat. "Did you forget something?" she asked, blinking in surprise.

He meant to *tell her* he adored her, tell her she was his everything, that he wanted her, needed her. Instead he growled, "This," hooked two fingers into her belt, and hauled her forward until he latched on to her mouth. And he kissed her and kissed her and kissed her, and the words wouldn't come.

They were there. In his heart. Quiet, burning words he couldn't speak even while she framed his face with her hands and whispered, "I love you, Grey Richards."

He felt stripped of his skin, defenseless, because this fiery little creature could speak those achingly beautiful words he couldn't. This sweet and saucy girl, with her reckless chestnut hair and big, innocent green eyes, loved Grey.

He'd never felt so vulnerable in his life.

And he watched as her face went pale when she realized he wouldn't, couldn't, say them back.

She laughed. At herself. Maybe at him.

She mumbled something indiscernible, pivoted around as she

shook her head, but he clutched her back to him with force. "Say that again."

Her next laugh couldn't quite hide her unshed tears, but even then she gazed into his eyes and softly, stubbornly said, "I love you. With all my heart."

And when he couldn't find it in him to speak, he used the tongue that felt stiff and dry in his mouth and loved her with it.

Money did not teach you how to care, how to show you care, or how to deal with the discomfort of expressing it. While Grey's parents had traveled the world, money had been Grey's nanny. Countless maids, chefs, chauffeurs, and toys had been his. None had made up for the absence of his parents.

His mother had the bearing of a queen, and Grey remembered touching her little. She'd never been much for hugs, though she had been free with her smiles, plastic as they were. As for his father, Lucien Grey Richards didn't give anything for free.

But he sure had a lot to say about character. No tears. No weakness. No sniveling. No neediness. Grey had gotten it all down to a T by the time he was ten.

Still, nothing he did seemed good enough for them.

Toni had been raised differently. Her mother baked. Her father worked to put money on the table. Toni talked to them regularly. She was affectionate, compassionate. Warm.

She was strong-willed, but the fact that she could bend to accommodate made her so much stronger in Grey's eyes. People like Grey were make-or-break, but Toni flowed like a river—calming or destructive as only water could be. Her capacity to love humbled him. Her excitement for life, her thirst for new experiences, that impish humor that came at the oddest moments.

And her passion . . .

If he'd thought she was enthusiastic about her work, she was even more so about Grey. She gave him her all, freely and unquestioningly. And now this woman who'd turned his world upside down, who called him to his face all the words nobody dared, whose first impulse once she got into bed was slipping into his arms to be held, wanted Heath Solis.

And Grey would not forget that. He could not live with that. And what most ripped at him, most infuriated him for making himself this vulnerable, was that no matter who else she wanted, he still wanted her.

⌒

Toni woke to find the bedroom empty—after an eternal, unsettling night. As she lay in bed, batting her eyes open, yesterday's events crystallized in her mind with a suddenness that made her jolt.

She jerked upright and looked around, an ache spreading through her chest. "Grey?"

Faint light from the hall filtered through the tiny slit at the bottom of the door. She sighed as she got out of bed, brushed her teeth, combed the tangles from her hair, then padded out into the kitchen.

He was bent over the dining table, the newspaper splayed across the table before him. Covering his long, muscled legs was a pair of cotton drawstring pants that rode low on his hips. His bare torso revealed each of the tautly marked muscles on his back—every ridge, dent, plane. All a woman could think of at the sight was touching. His blond-streaked hair was mussed, and she ached to tousle it even more.

Would he pull away if she did? Was he angry, shocked, disappointed?

Her stomach gripped. "Want some eggs?" she asked.

For two years they'd shared breakfast in companionable silence, but now Toni needed to gauge him, and the need to talk was eating her raw.

Grey lifted his coffee cup, but not his head. "Got all I need."

She puttered around the kitchen, opening and closing cabinet doors. "Toast?"

"Later."

Her back to him, Toni nonchalantly dropped a slice of wheat bread into the toaster.

"So. Anything interesting?"

She glanced past her shoulder to find Grey checking her out, particularly interested in her ass. He caught her watching him and cocked a brow at the amusement in her eyes before turning his attention back to the paper. "Not really," he said.

Her smile was sheepish. "You mean, not really as interesting as my ass?"

The rich, rumbling sound of his chuckle made her knees weak. "That's what I meant."

Her smile widened as she turned back to pull out a plate from the cabinet. She loved it when she caught him staring at her. She loved . . . him. Every bitty thing. Even his annoying arrogance.

Her toast popped up the second her groggy mind registered something important, and she pivoted around to stare.

Her satin sash was wantonly draped around Grey's thick wrist, and as he calmly read the paper, his fingers were playing with the tip.

Panic seized her, and she went deathly still. How on earth did he . . . ?

He raised his head and caught sight of her rooted to the spot like someone about to be beheaded. The two little creases at the corner of his eyes deepened.

Toni could almost see the wheels in his brain spinning, twirling like the shimmering fabric coiled around his wrist.

Struggling for calm while her lungs were twisting, she quickly crossed the kitchen and slipped between the table and him, settling on his lap.

"Grey." She was swamped with love for him. Desperate to comfort him. If she didn't get this out in the open, there was no telling how it would tear them apart. "It was one dance. It doesn't mean anything."

His rich whiskey eyes slid away from hers, and he reached around her to fold the paper in half. "It does to me."

She rubbed her hand up the muscles in his chest, pausing over the place where his heart beat steadily. "Surely it has happened to you—a beautiful woman catching your attention, even if you're with me."

His face was beautiful; the sensual lips, the patrician nose, the stubborn jaw. Beautiful and impassive. "It hasn't happened to me."

Desperate, Toni edged closer to him, gingerly kissing the corners of his lips, so plump but disappointingly unmoving under hers. "I wanted to be truthful with you."

The red sash fluttered to the floor. One hulky arm went around her, securing her against him as he tipped her chin so she would meet his gaze. "I don't want anything between us, much less lies."

She gave him a weak smile. "You and I have our faults, but lying isn't one of them." She sought his jaw with her fingers and tenderly traced the faint shadow of stubble. "I'm sure it will go away."

"No, it won't go away. It will hang like a shadow over me. I'll obsess whenever he calls and you answer, and wonder when I fuck you if you want me to be him."

She gasped. "That would never happen! How can you say that?" She gave his jaw a firm, meaningful squeeze. "I'm crazy about *you.*"

He held her face between his hands and covered her lips with his. She had been kissed a thousand times by Grey, and a thousand times she had been caught up in the storm of his kiss. But this kiss . . .

Was a tempest.

Through the dark, rich taste of his morning coffee, his kiss carried his power, the simmering energy he kept inside him, every need he gave no vent to. His lips moved commandingly over hers, his tongue swirled, his heat seared her.

She was left quaking. And then he was squeezing her jaw, dragging his mouth roughly across her lips, pouring his words into her.

"I'll give you everything you need, everything you want, Antonia Kearny, and when I'm done giving, you will think of no one else but Grey Richards."

He stabbed her mouth with his tongue in a kiss that was almost painful in its intensity. She met his avid thrusts in kind and at last broke free to catch her breath, her lips achy and swollen.

"Grey—"

"Shh." He rubbed his hands up her back, caressing her with every ridge inside his palm. "Quiet now."

She swung a leg to his other side and straddled him. She had never known such a violent need to be close to him. She had never ached for such a wild, reckless reassurance of his love for her. Feeling his rigid sex between her legs suffused her with an odd sense of relief.

She moved anxiously on his lap, longing for a connection to him, proof that what they shared stood strong and stable. Did he love her? Did he *care*?

"I'm sorry if I hurt you," she whispered. "I never meant to."

His erection swelled under her, the distinct column pulsating like something breathing, living, reassuring her of his desire. His hunger.

Grey dropped his head to her chest, slipped his hands under her T-shirt, and kissed the valley between her breasts through the worn cotton fabric. "Suppose . . ."

He opened his mouth over one breast and gingerly licked once, twice. Wetness seeped through her shirt and into her puckered tip. Her other muscles quivered with envy.

"Suppose I fuck you." The hot breath against her breast filtered through cotton to her skin. "Suppose he fucks you." He raised his hand to cup the other globe and expertly thumbed the rigid nipple. "Suppose we both fuck you. You'd like that, wouldn't you?"

His words excited her, made her wonder if a woman existed who would *not* like that, but at the moment she couldn't even attempt to make sense of what he said. Every pore was Grey's and every one of them sang to his touch.

Inflamed from skin to bones, she rocked over him, delighting in the friction of his shaft under her wet cleft. Beneath her T-shirt she was nude, her sex and his hardness separated only by his pants. She could actually feel the heat of him as though there were nothing between them. That nearness, the awareness of how rigid he was—how ready to take her—made her pussy contract with need. He smelled of Dial soap and Grey, his hair a thick, luxuriant mane in her hands.

"Where did he touch you, Toni?" He spoke in a husky rasp, his eyes half-covered by his lids as he glanced up at her. "Here?" Both hands caressed her breasts.

Toni remembered Heath's touch, the playfulness in his hands, and she couldn't suppress a shudder.

Her breasts heaved in rapid pants as her hands sought support from his firm, square shoulders. "H-he grabbed my ass."

"This ass? My ass?"

He palmed her ass, and a rumbling sound erupted from him. Her shirt had lifted as she changed position, bringing Grey's hands in direct contact with her skin. He tugged the cheeks apart, then pressed them together.

"Oh, Grey."

"Where else did Heath touch you?"

Ribbons of lust flittered inside her when she heard his name. "He . . . he rubbed his thigh against me."

"Oh, really." He brought one hand forward and slipped a finger between their bodies. She hissed and trembled as he rolled her clit in sharp little circles. "Did it feel like that?"

Her head fell back on a plea. "Yes."

At his newly gained access, he swirled his tongue up her throat to her jaw. She lowered her mouth and parted her lips for him. He groaned and slipped his tongue in, kissing her.

He pinched her clit—not too hard, but just right; right enough to send shocks of pleasure across her body—and she gave out a squeak.

He chuckled at her reaction, his words soft and indulgent. "Do you want him to do that to you, darling?"

He wore the most amazing smile. Each was like a little trophy to her; Grey smiled so rarely. Now his teeth glinted white against his tan and his eyes glowed like sunset. Another trophy for her. Another delightful feeling of satisfaction because she pleased him.

"Do you?" he insisted. He pressed her clit in with his thumb.

She bucked and grabbed his shoulders, gasping as she said, "Yes!"

"Ahh."

Honey oozed out of her pussy, spreading moisture across his pants. Inside she was a firestorm, sensations ricocheting within her womb. "Grey, you're making me want to come."

"So." He slipped his finger farther under her, into her slit, and watched her as he delved in. "Come."

He found her favorite spot, buried deep within her, surrounded by wet tissue and cream. He pressed and stroked it expertly, burying his finger to the base. She keened and started to ride that finger as she would ride his shaft.

"Yes, yes."

The abrupt, continual ringing of the kitchen phone took a moment to filter through her haze.

"Ignore it."

She groaned and inwardly wished she could. "It might be a client of mine," she gritted, trying to get off. He seized her waist with both hands and held her back.

"Ignore it."

As she hesitated, he pitched his hips up and scraped the column of his cock against her. Toni whimpered, riding that move with a to and fro of her hips.

"This is all you need right now," he rasped.

"Yes."

"This is all you want, all you need. A big, hard cock."

"Please."

"Will one do, darling, or do you want two?"

He was humoring her, maybe even mocking her, but she was still seized with tremors as the answer popped into her mind.

Yours . . . Heath's.

Oh, god, she was out of her mind, turning into a wanton, thinking only of coming, of being fucked and fucked and fucked.

Grey spread his thighs wide apart and angled her back a bit so he could grapple with the drawstrings of his pants. When his cell phone vibrated on the table behind her, they both went utterly still.

"Fuck." Grey reached around her and pressed the answer button, his tone clipped, cold. "Grey here."

A silence.

"Friday will be fine."

More silence.

Breathless to continue, she slid part of her body between his legs and lowered her mouth to his chest. He caressed her back with one hand as she circled his nipples, teasing them with her tongue. The little pulses in her pussy seemed to come at the same time as the jerks in his cock pressed firmly against her lower belly.

"The numbers are at the office—tell him you'll fax them over tomorrow morning."

He stroked her hair with heavy petting motions as her mouth ventured lower.

Once she was a breath away from the bloated head of his penis, he fisted a hand in her hair, hampering her progress. She squirmed in protest and raised her lashes in time to catch the twitch of a smile on the corner of his lips.

"I appreciate it," he grumbled as he clicked the phone off and set it down on the table with a resounding thump. "Christ, don't do that to me."

She shot him a smile full of wicked intent. "Was that Louisa?"

"Yeah." His hands returned to her head and gently rubbed her scalp.

"How's she doing?"

"Other than calling me on Sunday and asking if she may move a pen?"

She laughed. "She's new; give her some time." She surged up to kiss him and sultrily whispered, "Have I told you how wonderful you are for hiring her? She was so desperate."

"*I* was desperate. Which explains my hiring her."

She smiled, letting her hands drift down his taut arms, every inch of them like rock.

Louisa had been Toni's friend forever, and though she didn't have much experience in the corporate world, she'd been in sore need of a job. Grey's assistant had recently married, and Toni had asked him to consider her friend for the position.

Toni couldn't remember a single time Grey had denied her anything. She couldn't even ogle anything in a store window for fear Grey would haul her inside and flick out his American Express black Centurion.

He was cold when it came to business, and out of necessity, cutting to strangers who approached—Grey was too smart not to realize when someone had a hidden agenda. But he'd strip the shirt off his back for the people he loved.

Toni was passionately in love with him, but she'd thought that would mean she was passionately and exclusively *in lust* with him, too.

"Come here." He swiped the newspaper aside and boosted her up, setting her rear on the table. "I can't take it when you look like this."

She lifted her arms so he could tug off her shirt and squirmed delightedly when he rained slow, loving kisses on her shoulders, her nose, her forehead.

"So sexy," he cooed. "Groggy and tousled."

"You look very sexy yourself. Naked and—"

He stepped out of his navy drawstrings and she completely lost her voice.

She sizzled at the sight of him, glorious, nude, *hers*. She licked her lips as he came forward, his long erection perfectly angled toward her entry. She parted her legs and wrapped them around his hips. He entered, hot enough to melt her.

They moaned together. Her body arched to receive him, her thighs clenching around him.

He shut his eyes. "So good." He started pumping without haste, each leisurely stroke searing her with pleasure. "So tight, baby, so good."

Her spine arched instinctively as she fell back on the tabletop, writhing with sensations. Their bodies touched solely in the spot where their damp, burning sexes joined, and that singular contact intensified the pleasure. Every nerve in her body seemed to home in on Grey's powerful inward strokes, and she swore she could feel each up to her heart.

She braced up on her elbows, her breasts heaving as she watched the massive shaft move in and out. Glistening and corded with dark veins, it stretched her wide, reached down to the depths of her.

She watched his gorgeous face, every ripple of muscle in his body. Every flare of his nostrils and flex of his abdomen, every crease added to his face as he grimaced with pleasure. She watched it all. And when the pleasure became excruciating, she could watch no more.

Her eyes drifted shut, a profound warmth unfurling within her. She made flimsy, throaty noises of encouragement so he wouldn't stop.

He didn't. He kept pushing in so slowly she could savor every inch as he entered.

"You coming, darling?" His voice was as dense as his plunges.

"Yes." She bit her lip, tensing her muscles, trying to prolong the ecstasy. "You?"

He rasped, "I'm there."

"You there?"

He gripped her hips, tendons straining in his neck as he began a series of rapid thrusts that sent her teeth jarring and her breasts jerking. "I'm there."

"Grey . . ."

"Come with me."

Toni's head thrashed, her body convulsing over the table—coming as though at his command. Grey grunted as he continued to fuck, his balls slapping against her rear until one final delve lodged him in deep and he spilled with a deep, gruff sound.

She cradled the back of his head when he settled his cheek against her stomach and curled his arms around her waist.

"Hmm. So good." He nuzzled her abdomen and kissed her just below her navel. "Want a bath?"

She sighed. "I'd love a bath."

She stared thoughtfully at the fixture on the ceiling, listening to his retreating footsteps.

Within seconds he was back, waving her sash before her eyes—a bright red reminder of her wantonness. He studied the expression of uncertainty on her face, and tonelessly asked, "Did you give it to him?"

"Of course not," she scoffed, struggling to sit. "Why would I do such a thing?"

He glanced at it with combined annoyance and indulgence. "He told me to wrap it around his door if I decided he should fuck you."

Toes to her scalp, she blushed bright red. "Oh?"

He bent over her and whispered, in a voice that was frighteningly low and erotically dangerous, "Say *ménage*, darling."

She could not recover her breath. "What?"

"You might just get one."

Hair wet from a recent bath and a towel wrapped around his hips, Heath dropped down on the bed and clicked the TV remote off. The tray from room service stood near the door, his burger and fries untouched for hours.

He sighed and rubbed his face with his hands. No use trying. He couldn't get her off his mind. Grey's girl. No. Grey's *woman*.

Toni.

For two years it was all he'd heard from Grey.

Leaving for Cabo with Toni; will give you the new location update on Monday.

Moving to Toni's; here's the number.

Worse were the times Heath had called him at *Toni's* only to hear his partner panting, and the unmistakable flirtatious purrs of a woman who, no doubt, seduced him while he spoke on the phone.

The first months, Heath actually didn't give a damn about Toni. Grey's women came and went, though admittedly not as quickly as Heath's. But after a while Heath began to respect the woman who could keep Grey so . . . well, frankly, so goddamned happy. And then came the worst part. To his shock, Heath started to wonder what it would be like to have a Toni for himself.

The first time he heard her voice over the phone, he swore he'd just been kicked in the nuts. He didn't remember what she said or how he replied, but he remembered the instant, painful throb in his dick. Her silky, I've-just-been-fucked timbre followed him for weeks. Heath began to fantasize about her. Toni. Wanton sex goddess. Toni. Seductive siren. Toni. Elusive, faceless Toni.

On his subsequent trip to their Puerto Rican offices, he'd found a pretty little twenty-year-old at a bar and taken her up to his hotel room. Burning for weeks that had felt like years, he kissed her, groped her body over her clothes and whispered her name.

"But . . . that's not my name."

Heath drew in a deep breath, jarred from the fantasy. "Let's play a little game," he said in a husky tone as he sat her on the bed and slowly started to undress her. "You call me Heath, and I call you Toni, hmm?"

"But Heath *is* your name."

"It's Heathcliff, baby, but tonight I am Heath just for you, and you are Toni just for me. Understood?"

"O-okay."

He kissed her lips again, caressed her little breasts with the dark, beaded nipples. "You like that, Toni?"

"I-I feel weird."

"Don't." He stroked her nipples with his thumbs, tonguing her mouth as he went deeper into the fantasy. "I really want you, Toni. It's all I can think about."

"Heath."

"Oh, baby, yes, say my name."

Heath groaned at the reminder. So many nights wanting her.

Now he had a face to go with his fantasies, and it was lovely. Unforgettable.

He predicted coming to it, alone at night while he worked his pained cock, thinking of that lovely face—over and over.

He'd never doubted Toni would be special. Grey wasn't one to be easily impressed. His partner's fine taste was legendary. The woman to win him over had to be perfect.

But what had struck Heath most at the benefit was discovering that Toni wasn't one of Grey's long-legged models. She was petite and lively, and the second those large catlike eyes had risen to his, bringing to view lips wide and plump enough to rim a man's cock, Heath's mouth had run dry.

She was no duchess. She was no porn star. She was your average girl next door, out on a special evening in her knockout red dress. And he wanted her.

He couldn't begin to describe the way she'd felt against him when he'd had her in his arms and she angled her head back and smiled. . . .

And am I supposed to know who you are?

The heat of that smile poured through him like sunshine. He'd have taken those lips with his if she weren't Grey's.

Grey's girl . . .

Either the bravest woman Heath had ever met, or the biggest, sweetest, most beautiful little fool.

Grey's talk of her had gotten him excited, aroused, titillated by the faceless woman who made Heath *want* something. But staring down at those eyes, he'd been slammed. In the chest and in the groin. And with every ounce of his being, he'd wanted her. He'd wanted that fruity, peachy-scented woman with the impish smile wrapped all over him.

If she were anyone's woman but his partner's, nothing would have stopped Heath from having her. He'd have her right here, sprawled under him.

He'd make her laugh. He'd lick her up. He'd stroke the inside of her creamy thighs and move slowly inside her. He'd make her forget to breathe.

The way she'd responded to him . . .

She'd blushed and squirmed as he held her, but she'd been melting in his arms. Heath didn't know if Grey spoke to her about him or not. He didn't know if she, like him, was affected by the mere sound of his voice. Lately just the mention of her name. But he knew she was affected by his presence.

Toni wanted him.

Heath wanted her.

Grey had been informed.

He was going crazy with combined dread and anticipation. Would Grey do *any*thing about it? Grey was so hard to read, so intensely contained to the world. . . .

The thought that his partner could at this moment have a naked Toni in his arms made Heath ache for a prostitute. Both his heads hurt.

He was more than a little cranky.

And damned fucking tired of looking at the food tray.

Slicking back a few damp strands from his forehead, he crossed the room and wrenched the door open, pushing the wheeled cart out into the hallway. No cold burger and fries for him, thank you.

He popped a pumpernickel roll into his mouth before abandoning the cart when a flutter of white caught his attention. He straightened, swallowed back the lump of bread, and stared at the door.

Covering the PRIVACY PLEASE sign Heath left out permanently, a long envelope dangled from the doorknob, the logo at its center unmistakable.

RS CORPORATION. His heart began to pound. His stomach moved and not from hunger.

Wrap it around my door. . . .

In slow motion, as though the thing were a viper—as though he would find that shimmering red sash inside it—he reached out and yanked it from the door. Tearing it open, he found a note carrying Grey's unmistakable sloppy handwriting, the only thing that wasn't perfect about the man.

Dinner.

A barely legible restaurant address followed, and underneath it, four words. Boldly underlined.

My office first. Monday.

Heath chuckled. "Ahh, Grey, you've got your balls in a knot, haven't you?"

He shoved the note back into the envelope and strolled into the room, fisting his hand around his towel to keep his boner from causing it to unravel.

He snatched up his cell phone. Heath had very little use for gadgets, but when business called, business called. In this case it wasn't business, but pleasure.

Ahh yes. Pleasure.

Pleasure with Toni.

Falling back on the bed, he texted a short message. Just four words. Four little words that any second now would pop up in Grey's cell phone.

I want the sash.

Chapter Three

". . . Yes, Mr. Hawkins, I will deliver before Thursday so you can make a prompt decision. . . ." Puttering around the bathroom in her bathrobe, Toni tucked the phone to her ear and frowned at her reflection.

Setting aside the towel she'd been drying her hair with while Mr. Hawkins repeated his wish list for her upcoming design, she braced a hand on the sink and leaned closer to the mirror. A red oval colored a patch of skin between her neck and shoulder. It was sensitive to the touch, triggering a not-unpleasant burn. A warm, delicious pleasure washed through her as she realized how it got there. Grey.

"Elegant and bold. Make it clear we're taking on the world. I'm counting on you to deliver," Mr. Hawkins was saying.

She brushed her damp hair, shifting the phone to the opposite ear. "And deliver I will, Mr. Hawkins," she assured. "I'm certain you'll be extremely pleased with it. I'm mixing gold, black, and a deep royal blue, and playing with a combination of fonts that will absolutely delight and shock you. Oh, and a very catchy slogan I'm working on." *If my lover can get his hands off me, that is . . . and if I can concentrate enough rather than think of him, his friend, and the possibility of fucking both of them. . . .*

"Good. Good," she listened to him say. "And I hear you have a shot at Viscevis. That true?"

Viscevis.

Her stomach gripped. She set down the brush, admitting, "It's true."

She still could not comprehend how that happened. A multimillion-dollar merger, where the merging companies wanted to combine their existing logos into a new one.

A task Toni continued to find daunting. A task she secretly suspected should be handled by a large firm, someone with more experience. A task that might just be a wee bit too much for her.

One existing logo was sharp and elaborate; the other heavy and solid. Combining them in a harmonious fashion seemed impossible, and yet she desperately wanted to land Viscevis.

Your work has heart, Miss Kearny. I like that. . . .

"The old man said your work had heart. He's been promoting you."

"Well, I'm . . ." Shocked. "Pleased to hear that."

And dearly hoped "old man" Mr. Preston—already promoting her while she still had forty days to deliver her proposal—wouldn't have reason to regret it.

As soon as she and Hawkins finally hung up, she caressed her neck and got a fuzzy feeling in her stomach. *Grey.* She sauntered into the bedroom to rummage through her closet. His side was predictably in perfect order. Pants lined up by color, shirts and coats lined up by color, ties lined up by color. Her side was a mess, but somehow among that mess Toni had full knowledge of where she kept everything, and she refused to feel guilty about being a tad disorganized.

In fact . . .

Reaching into his side with a wide smile, she switched a black pant to the area of his gray ones, then brought a shirt from the top and stuck it between his jackets. "There we go, baby. Let's get you a little messy."

She anticipated what he'd do tomorrow morning. The same

thing he'd done yesterday and the day before. He wouldn't say a word and quietly set his clothes back in order.

When a morning came when he said something about it, *any-thing* about it, she'd celebrate.

Moving to her tangled section, she rummaged through her tops, thinking he was up to something. Something . . . wicked. Grey worked that way. He plotted and schemed and planned, and Toni knew, without a doubt, he had some plans for her sash.

She didn't know what to do.

She knew he'd turned the possibilities around in his head while he'd twirled her sash around and come to a decision.

There was no moving Grey from a decision, just as there was no moving a wall.

The man was so confident in himself Toni had yet to see a day when he felt challenged and didn't step up to the plate. That episode in Aspen when Toni had been determined she could snowboard with him, Grey had asked, only once and in amusement, "Are you sure about that, Toni?"

"Of course, Grey. I can ski, can't I? I can snowboard."

She'd landed in places she hadn't even imagined the mountain had. It had been awful. And she wouldn't even get into the time they went horseback riding in Cabo. Damn.

If he dared give her sash to Heath Solis . . .

Pushing the alarming, tantalizing thought aside, she threw on the first pair of jeans she found and a downy cashmere pullover, then strolled down the hall.

After pouring herself some coffee, she maneuvered around the couch to her workspace. Light filtered into the living room through the window overlooking the street, enough light for her to work with during the day. Setting her cup on her small, cluttered desk, she took her chair, lifted her laptop lid, and scanned her flagged e-mails from clients.

Unable to concentrate, she eyed the screen, and found her finger rising almost of its own volition, caressing Grey's mark. Tempted to see if he was out of his usual morning conference, she logged into an online messenger and typed him a message.

> designgirl78: I have the oddest bite on my shoulder. I think I was ravaged while I slept.

Nothing returned for a couple of seconds, so she answered one more e-mail and opened her work files. Then the orange screen popped up.

> RICHARDSGREY: You were.

She bit her bottom lip, her smile widening as she typed.

> designgirl78: So there must be a werewolf in the neighborhood, 'cause it doesn't quite look like a vampire's.

> RICHARDSGREY: It's mine.

> designgirl78: Ahhh!! Then maybe you'll indulge me with a repeat when I'm awake.

> RICHARDSGREY: I will

Her hands paused on the keyboard. She gathered her courage, drew a long, tremulous breath, and typed . . .

> designgirl78: Grey, about the sash . . .

> RICHARDSGREY: It's done.

It's done? What the hell did that mean?

> RICHARDSGREY: I know you want this.

> designgirl78: I was hoping we could forget the whole thing.

> RICHARDSGREY: We're doing dinner tomorrow.

A second screen popped up.

MADONNAFAN123: Toni, are you there?

designgirl78: Hey, Louisa.

And to Grey . . .

designgirl78: Dinner?

RICHARDSGREY: I promised to introduce you. So I will.

designgirl78: But that was before.

RICHARDSGREY: We're doing dinner.

designgirl78: What FOR?

RICHARDSGREY: Trust me.

Louisa's window turned orange.

MADONNAFAN123: So where are you going this weekend?

designgirl78: I don't know— is Grey kidnapping me?

MADONNAFAN123: He just said to rearrange his meetings. Mr. Solis's site
visits, too.

Toni felt the blood leave her face. A weekend to where? And
dinner!

She clicked the mouse and brought up Grey's window. She
tapped a finger. *Dinner.* Was he testing her?

Of course he was.

He was cunning, he was ruthless, and he was Grey Richards.

She wanted to tell him to take his dinner and shove it up his
behind, and at the same time, she wanted to storm into whatever
restaurant they were going to, ignore that presumptuous handsome

bastard Heath Solis, and prove to Grey he had nothing to be concerned about.

Did he feel he couldn't trust her?

Dread spread through her at the thought. Because she trusted
him in a way she'd never trusted a soul.

Not because of his MBA from Stanford, his ruthless business instincts, the empire he'd built almost single-handedly, or his
knack for accomplishing anything he set his mind to. Not because
when he opted to turn on the charm, he could very possibly ne-
gotiate world peace, but because he was fair and intelligent and
amazing.

With him, she'd discovered herself. Plus a world she hadn't
known existed until Grey.

She'd never known sex could be so pleasurable, that she could
feel so desirable, so comfortable with herself, her body. All her res-
ervations and fears seemed to be ebbing away, spurred on by Grey's
blatant, overwhelming desire for her. But when did you stop exploring? When was enough sex enough?

This puzzling, powerful attraction to the fascinating Heath.
Where in the world had it come from?

It's been there for months, years, from the start, a little voice answered.
That enigma of Heath. The one person her lover thought so highly
of.

A threesome . . .

Grey had been mentioning it during sex. He was gauging her,
she knew, seeing how much she wanted it. And embarrassingly, she
got so *wet*!

A part of her wondered why he insisted on it. Kept teasing her
with the ménage. Did he want one just to please her? To prove to
her and himself he was truly the only one for her? So she would
not be curious anymore? Or did he believe she would stray like his
mother, having all those lovers under his father's perfect, arrogant
nose?

While deep down she craved to keep things between them just

as they were, she couldn't deny the excitement the prospect of a threesome gave her. Sex with Grey and Heath Solis. *Awesome* sex with Grey and Heath Solis.

But if they did this, would it be the best sex of their lives or something to regret forever?

Shaking her turmoil aside, she typed . . .

designgirl78: Dinner's fine.

RICHARDSGREY: I'm moving things around the office. If we leave for Cabo this weekend, can you move your Friday appointments to next week?

designgirl78: When have I said no to Cabo OR you? I'll arrange it.

RICHARDSGREY: I might be late tonight, T.

designgirl78: Aw. *sad, weepy face* I'll try not to mope around. Maybe I'll go see Mom and Dad, unless I get caught up here with a proposal. Then maybe not. I'd hate it if they started on me. If I hear the word marriage one more time, I'll sock them.

RICHARDSGREY: What is wrong with the word? Other than your mother using it in every sentence?

Toni blinked, dumbstruck. Marriage was an institution that created false expectations between two people and . . . she sighed, and shook her head dejectedly. There was *nothing* wrong with marriage.

Except being in love with someone who did not believe in it.

RICHARDSGREY: Do you need anything? I've got a line beeping.

designgirl78: Go get it! I'll see you later.

RICHARDSGREY: Dinner tomorrow at 8?

designgirl78: 8 is fine.

RICHARDSGREY: Be a good girl

designgirl78: But you like it when I'm bad! ☺

RICHARDSGREY: *Yes*

Afterward, she chatted a bit more with Louisa and then rose to sift through her designs at her corner workstation. But as she settled down in her old comfy chair and shuffled through her material, there were no thoughts in her mind but of *sex between three* . . .

An image of that handsome bastard Heath Solis sprang to her mind. Those glimmering black eyes. The hands . . . god! His *smell*. And the cruel, decadent way he smiled . . .

Her pussy gave a furious clench at the memory, her nipples beading eagerly under her sweater. A slight tingle in the pit of her urged her to touch herself. Delve into her jeans with her fingers and fondle where it hurt and imagine it was Grey. And right there on the chair in the corner, or maybe by the front door, Heath watched them. And Grey would be so hard and hot and moving inside her, and she'd be riding him with all her might. . . .

She halted her hands before she could fondle her breasts, shaking her head in disgust. *Work.* She had work to do.

Viscevis, I'm going to get you.

⌐

"Here we go, just as you requested!"

Seated behind his desk at the far end of the wood-paneled office on the nineteenth floor of the RS building—where he regularly spent ten hours a day, with the exception of Sundays—Grey took the files Louisa handed him and gave them a quick scan as she sank into the seat across from his.

"These are the Carson City files, Louisa. I asked specifically for the Columbus, Ohio, ones. The Four Stars shopping mall."

Rather than rise to fetch them, she licked her red lips, blinking. "You said Carson City."

Grey frowned. "Carson City? We finished our building last year."

"You asked for Carson City," she insisted.

He leaned back in his chair, let the papers fall on the desk, and pinched the bridge of his nose to stifle an oncoming headache. "I apologize. I'm not myself today."

"Don't worry. I'll get those for you." She rose to her feet, tugging her skirt back to her knees, and Grey snatched the file from his desk and held it up for her. He was not *in the mood* for her fumbling today.

"You can take this one, Louisa."

"Oops. Yes. Thank you."

He picked up a financial report on his desk and skimmed it. "Toni's rent is due Friday. Pay it before she does."

"Of course."

He turned the page. "The Cabo San Lucas arrangements I asked for?"

"Pilots all set for Friday, and your housekeeper has been notified. Oh, and Mr. Solis is here to see you." She pointed a thumb at the massive carved double doors. "He's just outside."

"Mr. Solis can come right in," he said, dropping the report as Louisa flung open the doors. Heath immediately stalked past her.

"Well, do come right in, Mr. Solis," she said cheerily.

"Heath." Grey slid their latest contract across the surface of his desk. "Since you're here."

Propping his hips up on the edge, Heath grabbed the papers and plucked a pen out of the leather stand. He was clad in torn jeans and a solid black T-shirt that bulged around his biceps—his usual attire, one that gave voice to the phrase *I don't do suits*.

"I made two amendments, pages five and nine," Grey said, settling back in his chair. "A few clauses on payment and discretion on the deal. If they break it, we walk."

"It's all good." Heath did not read them, but initialed them all and signed the last page before slapping it down on the desk. "What else?"

Grey tossed down a pen as he rose. "You know what else."

Heath sank down in the recently vacated chair and stretched his legs out before him, watching as Grey came around.

Grey leaned back against the desk, crossing his arms and tucking his hands under his armpits, his voice deceptively soft as he said, "I'm thinking of tearing your head off."

While the words might inspire any, *any*, of his employees and collaborators to genuine fear, Heath merely crossed his arms, leaned back in his seat.

"You *knew* she was mine, and you still came on to her."

"Yes."

"Why?" he demanded. "You're suddenly in the city. At a party, which you hate, and then you deliver your whopper of a news flash."

Distracting himself, Heath followed the curl of his fingers into his right palm. "I don't want to play house with her, so you can relax."

"You fuck with her, Heath, and you're fucking with me."

Heath loosened his fist. "I know better than to fuck with you."

"Then don't."

The narrowed black eyes Heath leveled at him held anything but contriteness. "I would have had her right then if it weren't for you."

The tomblike silence that followed was disturbed by a chirpy "Here we go, the files you requested, Grey."

Grey didn't bother to look at her. "Thank you, Louisa. Just set them on the desk."

"Are you sure you don't want me to—"

"No, that will be all."

No sooner had the click of the doors sounded when Grey spoke. "Do I have to tell you how conflicting I find this?"

Soundlessly, Heath rose to his feet, directing himself to the wall, which held dozens of framed photographs of buildings in progress. "You love her?"

"I'm going to marry her."

Heath snorted in derision. "Pull the other one, Grey."

Snatching the glass of brandy next to his computer, Grey emphatically said, "I am."

The look on Heath's face when he turned couldn't have been more comical. "Should I start picking up silverware, then? A gravy boat?"

Grey merely smiled. It wasn't often he had Heath at a disadvantage, but he found himself enjoying the sudden uncertainty on his partner's face.

An ivory carpet covered the room, and the distance between the doors and Grey's desk was immense, as he well liked his space. He took full advantage of the area now as he circled. "I mentioned a threesome, and she's excited about it."

"It's been a while," Heath mused.

"Sixteen years."

"That long?" Heath whistled, scraping his hand along his shadowed jaw as he tracked Grey pacing across the room. "I must be getting old."

Toni *quivered* every time Grey had mentioned the threesome. Her body flushed and she got all loving on him. She rode him, licked him, kissed him, came all over him. God.

His cock was a perennial pain inside his trousers. He couldn't blank out the images that tumbled through his brain. Images that made his chest constrict, his stomach twist, his heart *ache*.

Toni undulating . . . giving out those little purrs of hers, Heath feeding her cock, Grey rocking in her tight, syrupy pussy . . .

It would kill him. It would drive him out of his ever-loving mind.

Grey returned behind his desk and added, "We'll have dinner. I'll confirm for myself if she wants you. Then we'll see."

"She wants me. That woman of yours is made for passion. You deny her, and she'll be looking somewhere else."

"Where did you read that, *Glamour*?"

Heath linked his hands behind his head and shot him a look full of impatience. "I don't read that shit."

"Then where does this brilliant advice come from? You haven't been in a relationship your entire life."

"Neither had you before Toni. And I once fucked your driver and *he* was in a relationship. He gossiped like a girl. Shit, he *whimpered* like a girl."

"And you like that?"

Heath considered, the verdict coming out a bored, "Whatever."

"If we decide to do something about it, we're not doing it here. We'll do it in Cabo, give her a weekend where there are no prying eyes and she can let go."

"Is that an invitation?"

Grey shook his head. "It's a maybe."

"I want the sash."

"The sash is mine until I know for sure." Tipping his glass to drain the last of his brandy, he assessed his friend as the liquid burned a path down his throat. "How do you feel about kissing?"

Heath shrugged, and Grey set the glass back down with a thump. "Good. So you wouldn't mind not kissing her. On the lips."

Heath cranked his head to Grey's and both his eyebrows shot up in surprise. He was the only human being Grey knew who could laugh in silence. It had never bothered Grey before, but now he evaluated Heath with new eyes.

New, wary eyes.

He was as big as Grey, less controlled perhaps. Everything about Heath was black: his hair, his clothes, his eyes, most of all his humor. At work he was tireless, dedicated, steady as a bull, but Grey wasn't certain how far he could be pushed on a more personal level. He respected Heath; he'd never even *tried* to bend him to his will before. There wasn't a doubt that now he had to.

"Toni . . ." he explained. "She likes to kiss for hours. When she wants to kiss, she goes on forever. . . ."

And she poured her heart into those kisses. All of her soul. Those kisses were Grey's.

Heath raised his hands in a placating gesture. "Agreed. No tongue tangles."

"And her derriere," he added, setting a few pens back into the leather cylinder beside his computer. "That would be off-limits too." Rather than take his chair, he braced his hands on the edge of his desk and leaned forward. "I don't want us to hurt her, you understand."

Heath's eyes glimmered with interest as he rose to his feet, rammed his hands into his jean pockets. "How would we do this, then?"

"Other than that, what the lady wants."

"Would I get to fuck her by myself?"

"No," Grey growled, "you *would not.*"

"I'm supposed to say no if she asks?"

"She won't."

"Won't what?"

"Won't ask, Heath." If she did, if she so much as tumbled around with Heath without Grey . . .

"But if she does?"

No. She would not. Having a threesome was one thing. Toni and Heath alone together was something else entirely.

"*If* she asks," Grey stressed. "Which she won't."

Heath accepted with a nod, and Grey rubbed the tension from the back of his neck. His thoughts were in a tangle, and the feeling had him on edge. He was burning for her. He'd been aroused all day, in the car, the shower, the office. He was *still* in pain.

Heath halted midstep. "If it's eating at you, why are you doing this?"

Grey met his gaze head on. "Let's just say I'm humoring her." He narrowed his eyes. "Have you been tested recently?"

"Of course."

A slimy, icky dread slithered through his blood at the thought of anything going wrong. Out of control. Out of his hands. "This is a woman I'd die for. Do you understand me?"

Heath's lips curled. "You *do* love her."

"You hurt her, and I'll crush you, Heathcliff. I don't care what we've been through."

His partner seemed thoroughly amused as he hauled the chair back with his ankle and sank down. "And you've told her how you feel, Romeo?"

Grey considered not responding to his jibe, then admitted, "She knows how I feel."

"But you've never told her."

"I don't have to."

"Women like to hear it."

"Heath, your advice is starting to irritate me."

Heath stacked his hands behind his head, his brows drawn up. "Women like those words. Even I know that."

"You don't know what you're talking about." When Toni said the words to him, it didn't feel all that amazing. He felt powerless. And she said them all the time, so easily, so unselfishly. It killed him not to say them back.

Shaking his head, he strolled to the window that made up the entire west wall of the office. "She wouldn't be with me if she thought I didn't love her."

"Why not?"

"She's proud."

"No more than you are."

Grey gazed blindly out at the city, seeing Toni in his mind.

"Her coffee's practically water." He didn't know why that came out of his mouth. Apparently Heath didn't, either, because he just sat there staring at him.

"She's a reckless driver," he continued restlessly. "This is the second time this month she's gotten a low tire. She rubs them against the sidewalk all the time."

"Parking tickets?"

"I can name at least five officers she knows by name." Grey would have smiled ruefully if he weren't still fighting the urge to tear Heath's head off. "She rumples my hair before I leave for work. She draws her name on my files. She messes with my clothes."

Damn. She was adorable. An adorable, mischievous, sweet little mess. When Heath remained silent, Grey turned and pinned him with a look. "I want to drown her in pleasure until she can't remember her name, and I want us to go on for hours. Hours. I don't want her to breathe or think or do anything but feel what we're doing to her. All day, all night. Can you do that, Heathcliff—think of someone else's pleasure other than your own?"

"I'll have her writhing."

"What I want to hear is that you'll be careful. Thoughtful. She's not like you and me."

He smiled lazily. "It's obvious she's a woman, Grey."

"That's not what I'm talking about, and you know it." Grey thought of that lively imp he knew, of how he liked to take care of her, to take from her in bed and then coo and coddle and spoil her. "She's never done anything like this," he said.

Toni wasn't cold or jaded, but lively and warm and excitable. Grey would never forgive himself if that was taken from her.

Heath's smile faded, his jaw bunched with tension. "If you need the words, I'll say them. I'd cut off my arm before I hurt a hair on her head."

Deep down where it most counted, Grey knew this. He knew it with every cell of his being; Heath would give her all the pleasure she could handle, but no more. And he wouldn't stick around after sex. He'd be gone before anyone knew what happened, his current obsession forgotten, and never, ever, come back for more.

"I'm in control," Grey said with steely finality.

"I'm not complaining."

"Good. We're clear, then." Relaxing at last, he sank into his chair and flicked open the button of his jacket as he leaned forward, all business. "About dinner . . ."

Chapter Four

It gave her a heady feeling, driving Grey's manly, rumbling car. An unnerving one, too, because she feared she'd scratch it or flat-out smash it up like she'd done her old Ford.

Drivers glanced at her as they sped past her, probably thinking, *Why is this person in such a sporty car driving at forty miles an hour?*

Pointedly ignoring them, Toni kept her eyes on her own lane, trying not to consider the fact that she might be needing glasses to drive. All that time over her papers, the computer . . . not good for her eyes.

She absorbed the fancy car interior—shiny chrome, glossy wood, yummy-scented black leather. Turning on the radio, she scanned the stations until she found a favorite Madonna song playing, then cranked it to a loud blast and guided the sleek black car to her parents' small home at Old Town. Every time she turned, the wheel slid inside her fingers like butter. She loved this little car.

Old Town was a curious neighborhood, its architecture ranging from cozy cottages to modern high-rise buildings. Her parents' home was among the smaller ones, but with its green lawn and baskets of flowers flanking the front door, Toni thought it was the most inviting. Or maybe it was just her childhood memories that made it seem so inviting. The corner stand where she and Janice, aka Pippi

Longstocking, had sold lemonade to their neighbors. Planting her very first tree, the top of which she could no longer see, it had overgrown the house so fast.

Finding a spot for the Porsche under that tree, she parked and strolled into the two-story brick home. The scent of baking cookies expanded her lungs. Mouth watering, she followed the familiar sound of her mother's humming down a narrow, shadowed hall and into the brightly lit kitchen.

"What's for dinner?"

The slim, silvering woman by the oven jumped in fright. "Antonia, you scared me to death!"

Laughing because her mother never called her Antonia unless she was serious, Toni snatched up a thick glove and helped her pull out the cookie sheet, setting it atop the stove. She tried plucking one up, but her mom slapped her hand. "Hot! And wait until after dinner."

Toni groaned and moved over to her customary position at the kitchen island to help chop the vegetables.

She hadn't yet positioned the tomato, and Mom was already telling her all about her friends' daughters who were getting married, had gotten married, or were happily expecting, and Toni frowned down at the cutting board, knowing what was to come.

"So how are you and Grey?"

Yes. There it was. She stifled a moan and sliced. "Fine, Mom. How are you and Dad?"

"Well, you know your father. Got that crazy hunting thing in his head. I swear if I'd known he was going to start killing all these animals, I'd never have married him."

Keeping her hands busy, her mom moved around the kitchen island. The place was bright and cluttered, with colored pots hanging from the ceiling. Mom's knitting sat in a nearby basket, her gossip magazines tucked into a corner.

"So when are you and Grey going to tie the knot?" she asked, wiping her hands on her apron.

Toni sighed drearily, her temples beginning to throb. She had to set the knife down and rub. "We've talked about this, Mom."

"And I'm sure any day now you'll both change your minds."

"If two people love each other, they don't need papers to stay together," she mumbled.

"Hell, yes, you do." Appearing through the door, her father smacked her cheek with a sloppy kiss; then the large, rowdy man proceeded to investigate the food they were preparing. "I love your mother, but she can drive a man so crazy, I'd be long gone if divorce weren't such trouble."

"See." Her mother beamed, oblivious to having been just insulted.

Toni should have stayed home and tried to tackle the Viscevis logo.

And her mother went on, because, really, there was no stopping that woman once she was on a roll.

And Dad was on her side now.

"Sweetheart, when you find The One, the most natural thing to a woman is to want to secure him. Especially a man like yours. Daddy and I love Grey, darling, but those men just aren't long-term. They're too exposed to temptation. All that money and the women and the power. First wrong step you make, sweetie, and that man is out the door. After all, what's holding him back?"

"There's me," she said in an unsteady mumble. Did he care for her enough? Would he stop caring one day? Maybe he just *thought* he felt something but wasn't certain enough to tell her. Why didn't he ever say it?

And Mom worried that Grey was too much for Toni. Grey knew people her parents could only read about in magazines. His name was among the most influential in the city, while the Kearnys were simple people.

Her father had been manager of a small air-conditioning business for fifteen years; her mother a caring, loveable woman dedicated to her home. They did not have servants or jets or houses in

Marrakech and Mexico. And their daughter was no Miss Universe either. Though why they thought Grey wanted one, Toni had no clue. Stereotypes, maybe.

"If Grey walks out on our Toni, he's a fool. I still wish you'd *ever* looked at me with those moon eyes she gives that man."

Her mother's scowl was murderous as she swiveled round. "Just maybe, Homer, you should think of what to do to deserve those moon eyes. I see no fancy sports car in our garage," she argued. "Plus, Grey can never keep his hands off her, and I haven't gotten even a morning kiss lately."

Eyes twinkling, he squeezed her mother's rump, and his hand got a slap for its daring.

"As I was saying, Toni," her mother continued, a blush tinting in her cheeks, "if you want to keep him—"

Toni buried her face in her hands and groaned. "Can we please veer off the topic of marriage? Ask me something else. Anything else."

"Grandchildren. There's a topic for you. Your daddy and I want some."

Anything except that.

"Mom, my career is just picking up. I can't think of having a kid now. I wasn't even able to take care of Daffy." She pointed to the surly old furball eyeing her from his permanent place on the living room couch.

"But you and Grey talk about it?"

She snatched a glass from inside a cabinet and poured herself some water. "No. We do not, because neither of us wants one right now." And because nobody could truly understand how difficult it was to talk to Grey. He listened, he wasn't judgmental, but he was just so . . . so . . . *logical.*

It was practically impossible to get him to talk from the heart.

"Let's talk about something else and stop torturing me. Dad, that deer over the fireplace looks miserable. Tell me about him."

Her father's chest expanded an inch or two. "Ahh, that's a ten-point piebald whitetail deer. A really big buck, by anyone's standards. Now I'm planning to go bear hunting to Alaska. I'm growing a beard and . . . well, speak of the devil and he appears! Good evening, Grey. How are you?"

What Toni felt hearing Grey's distinct, low-pitched voice was indescribable. Like being swamped with whipped cream, covered in melted chocolate fudge.

"Homer."

Even at this hour, his suit, the Hermès tie, everything about him was perfect. A smile curved her lips as she watched him pat her father's back and move to her eagerly awaiting mother.

"I hope you don't mind I let myself in, Beth, I stood out there for quite a while."

"Grey, darling, that's one crazy chime out there and half the time it doesn't work. You're always most welcome here." Mom pulled him down to kiss his forehead, and Toni noted he no longer stiffened when she did.

When Grey popped a chocolate-chip cookie into his mouth, he didn't get a slap. Her mother's grin covered her entire face. "Take more, Grey—take all you want! I made those just for you."

And then he was coming over to Toni, and her legs went rubbery. In his eyes she saw that glimmer he had for her, a mirror to the delicious emotion she felt every time she saw *him*.

"Aren't you going to say hello to me?" he huskily murmured. The next second she was wrapped in all steel, all heat, all him. He brushed his lips across hers, their breaths mingling.

When he pulled away, he riveted her with eyes that smoldered with emotional intimacy.

Tilting her head farther back, she raised her hand to undo his tie like she always did. She draped it across the back of the couch, undid his two top buttons, Grey docilely letting her, and then she plunged her hands into his hair, playfully fussing it. "Wrapped up early?"

He gazed at her lips with a distinctly famished expression. "Seems like."

"A good thing, too," Mom chimed in. "I'm just about to serve."

The next minute, they were sitting at the round oak table by the window. Once dinner was under way, their first bites were taken in companionable silence. Toni had always suspected that Grey secretly loved spending time with her parents. They said anything that came to their minds, but for the most part, it seemed to amuse him. No one ever listened with such quiet attention to her mom's boring anecdotes of Toni's childhood.

Toni could not stop eyeing her lover. The effortless way his hands moved. His *lips*. He was an Adonis, and he was *hers*. It was an intoxicating thought.

As he listened to her father's hunting stories, she noticed how Grey, with his youth and sophistication, was so opposite of her dad. Her father was open and talkative, while Grey was reserved and contained. There was just something innately controlled and interesting about Grey she'd never seen in another man. With the possible exception of his father.

Grey's father was the most handsome, compelling, sixty-five-year-old man Toni had ever seen. The man seemed immune to time, he was so attractive. Full head of luxuriant silvering hair, powerful square face, plus those same golden eyes she had fallen in love with.

He was also the biggest bastard she'd ever met.

All she'd needed to understand why Grey didn't talk of his parents had been that one formal dinner, where they'd treated Toni like some lowly life-form out for Grey's money—not that Grey's money was theirs, because RS was Grey's and Heath's alone.

Grey had endured no more than two or three of their thinly veiled insults before calmly setting down his napkin and saying, "Mom. Dad. Enjoy your dinner."

He'd pulled out Toni's chair, so solid and composed when she'd been mortified at leaving the table so abruptly, and led her to his car. He said nothing on the way home. Nothing when they arrived. Nothing when they made love. The following week, while she was e-mailing a new proposal to one of her clients, he'd surprised her by whispering, "I wouldn't change a hair on your head, do you know that?"

Stunned, she'd stopped typing and gaped.

"I know how much you wanted to impress my parents, and when you saw them for what they were and refused to play into them, you impressed *me*. All the money in the world couldn't buy them your class." He feathered his mouth across hers, and his lips twitched, forming a crooked smile. "Aren't you glad fourteen nannies raised me rather than them?"

Toni had pictured a blond, gorgeous little boy trying valiantly not to care whether anyone showed up for his soccer practices. And when she tried to remember if he'd ever showed her a birthday picture where his parents were actually in it and found that there were none, she disliked Mr. and Mrs. Richards all the more. But oh, she loved their son.

"Toni was just telling us about your plans," her mother was telling him.

"Was she." The lack of a question in his voice told Toni he knew full well what was coming.

"Yes." Her mother's face furrowed as she wiped her mouth with a linen napkin. "Homer and I can't say we agree. Antonia is thirty already, and she's not getting any younger."

Under the table, Grey's hand went to her thigh, drawing her eyes to his. "Fill me in, sweetheart?"

Smiling, she patted his leg under the table, resisting the urge to do some other kind of touching, which was tempting with him near. "It's not what you think. Sweetheart."

Her mischievous grin brought a twinkle to his eye.

"Marriage makes people compromise," her mother went on. "Toni would compromise for you as much as *you* would for *her*. Homer, I brought the meat loaf; could you bring more gravy?"

Her father grumbled a protest but promptly rose to fetch, and her mother beamed.

"See? Compromise."

"Mom and Dad have been talking marriage and babies all afternoon, Grey," Toni said, rolling her eyes and spearing a carrot slice
from her plate.

Grey opted to fork something up from his plate, too.

"Well?" her mother prompted, pinning him on the spot with a
direct look.

Grey faced Toni. "I'd say no more than two."

She almost choked. She snatched up a glass, took a long sip of
water, and plopped it back down. "Two what?"

"Kids."

She sent him a puzzled look, her heart fluttering wildly, unexpectedly, and then she managed to steer the conversation to other,
safer topics.

Grey listened to her father's hunting tales, praised her mother's
new cookie recipe until she flushed, and Toni was left imagining
what a little Grey would look like. She'd never thought of Grey in
a fatherly way. He was too . . . proud and too . . . worldly. And yet he
was so gentle and protective of Toni, it brought to mind how he
would look lifting a little girl up high in his arms.

How could Toni not want that?

And why did she have a feeling Grey would give her a threesome a thousand times over a family?

The rest of the evening she fought bravely to push those
thoughts aside.

⌒

Once they said their good-byes and crossed the walkway toward
the street, she said, "Did you mean it, what you said in there?"

"What? About children?" He steered her toward the Porsche
when she'd instinctively started for her own car. "Let's take mine.
I'll have yours picked up tomorrow." He waved her keys in the air,
his eyes glinting. "Your tire's fixed."

"I didn't know there was anything wrong with it until I saw you'd left your Porsche." Stopping, she gazed into his beautiful eyes, filled with awestruck admiration. "But you don't miss anything, do you?"

There was an almost imperceptible softening in his gaze. Tenderly, he ran his knuckles down her cheek. "It's fixed," was all he said.

"Thank you. My hero. And I'm happy to report your car is intact!"

He walked her over to the passenger's side, but rather than helping her into the vehicle, he flattened her against the door so fast she gasped from the shock of his weight. "I need to have you; I need to be inside you."

Heart thundering, she stroked her hand lightly across the prominent bulge on his crotch, watching his face tighten. "And I want . . . this. You. Inside me."

He pressed his forehead against hers. "God, take me. All of me."

Her throat hurt at his plea. Rising up on tiptoe, she slid her hand around the back of his neck, loving the thick, muscled feel of it as she drew him to her lips. Her nostrils tingled at the dark coffee scent of his breath, and then she tasted. The shock of the cool flavor blended with the heat of his tongue shot a rush of electricity through her.

Pebbles on the gravel crunched beneath the wheels of a car as it passed by. It didn't stop her, didn't stop him from pressing into her.

Their mouths moved languorously, sampling, enjoying, the simple connection of their bodies, their tongues, moving her to her soul. She was him. He was her. His arm curled around her waist, dragging her closer.

"You're in my head." One hand sifted through her hair and tugged her back, his lips sliding along the curve of her jaw, up to her temple. "In my head. All. Fucking. Day."

"I was so anxious for you to get home to me." Her voice was a husky whisper breathed against his chin. "I was this close to touching myself."

His deep-throated groan rolled across her skin like a caress. "You know that drives me insane. Why didn't you?"

"I had to work, even if I didn't actually get anything accomplished. I'm . . . a little nervous about my sash, Grey."

Receiving no reply, she grew nervous and tried to draw away. "We should get going," she said, but he caught her hand and halted her.

Tension rolled off him in waves. "It's your sash, Toni. You make the call."

"And what call would that be?" she questioned, playing with the fingers of the hand that held hers.

He seemed reluctant to speak, and equally as reluctant to let her go, but then he drew back and opened the door. "Get in the car. I'm taking you home."

Home.

He'd made her home his.

He was in every organized compartment of her little place. He'd maneuvered somehow to pay the rent despite her emphatic protests, and all her expenses prior to Grey had suddenly, magically, become nil. He took care of everything.

She'd always thought maybe she'd feel less like a kept woman or some sort of mistress if he'd say those three important little words to her. She'd prepared herself to wait, and though she'd been accused of being proud, she'd swallowed back her pride and opened her heart to him, told him what she felt, praying he'd follow. She'd been so disappointed when she failed. She'd gambled with her heart, saying *I love you* to a man like him. . . .

Over a year and a half later, she was still waiting to hear it back.

Stubbornly waiting for him to be ready.

And one lesson in humility had been enough. She'd chew off her tongue before she had to beg for the words. Do something desperately needy like ask him. God! What suicide that would be. Putting him on the spot in that way. Would he feel forced to say yes? Or would he say the answer she thought was most obvious: *I don't know.*

I don't know was, simply, not good enough when you were head over heels for someone. In fact, it wasn't merely not good enough; it was depressing.

Disheartened, she glanced out the window as he drove up to Lincoln Park. The night was dotted with gray clouds that seemed ready to burst open and cover the city with a deluge of rain.

After hushed moments, Grey said, "I spoke to Heath."

She could feel his eyes boring holes into the back of her head. "Oh?" she said lightly, turning after three reckless heartbeats.

"We're on for dinner tomorrow."

"Dinner." Her stomach churned.

His gaze shifted between the road and her. "We're civilized people; we can do dinner."

"Yes, of course."

How to survive it was another matter.

But then maybe—and she dearly hoped so—by taking a second look at Heath Solis, she would realize he wasn't such a powerful black force pulling at her, that he was just a . . . man.

⌒

"Relax."

"I am relaxed!"

"You're pale and you're going to make that little lip bleed."

"Let's get *you* relaxed," she countered, plunging her hands into his delicious blond hair, leaving it tousled as he pulled open the glass door of the small, upscale French restaurant. The moment Toni stepped inside, she eased her hold on her lower lip and tried for an appearance of elegance and relaxation. She'd chosen a simple black cocktail dress with a high neckline for the evening, her hair done in a loose twist at her nape. A sleek gold necklace hung around her neck, falling down to her navel.

Grey spoke to the maître d' in a hushed tone, and the woman blushed. "Why, yes. Yes. Of course! Mr. Richards." She fumbled for the menus. "Your table is ready, if you'd both follow me."

In the willowy redhead's wake, he guided her toward their usual booth at the far end. Lovely jazz music drifted in the background, the space graced with sleek, dark wood tables and edgy, colorful Warhol pieces. The booths against the walls were upholstered in chocolate-colored suede with striking white stitching.

As she walked through the scattered tables, some boasting sleek, tall arrangements of pussy willow shoots, her legs felt so stiff she marveled that she did not stumble on her heels.

They reached the dark corner booth, and she quietly commended herself when Heath rose to greet them and she did not gasp. He was as overwhelming as she remembered. Swarthier. More beautiful. God. He should be locked somewhere. In a bedroom. With her and Grey.

With enviable calm and self-assurance, Grey urged her forward. "I'd feel extremely ridiculous if I had to introduce you two."

Her cheeks burned as she stretched her hand out.

"We've met," Heath said, his voice masculine and deep as he shook her tentative hand. His grip was firm, his palm dry and rough, sending prickles of awareness up her arm.

She'd thought, many times throughout the day, that this dinner would serve a purpose. That she would realize that no, Heath Solis wasn't some god of the underworld intent on eating her heart.

It wasn't working.

Her heart felt like someone had taken a bite out of it, and it cost an inhuman effort to tug her hand free and slide into the booth. Her stomach muscles contracted as the men greeted each other. Grey wore a loosely buttoned black dress shirt that highlighted the blond streaks in his hair; Heath, blue jeans and a black crewneck that molded around his shoulders. They were so stunning, so blatantly male.

Any moment now, she expected the heads in the restaurant

would swivel their way and people would wonder what she—five feet four, not very bosomy, and not blond—was doing with the two of them.

She took the menu the waiter handed her and studiously eyed each of the offerings as though she'd never read them before. On her right, Grey scrutinized the thick, velvet-covered wine menu. On her left, Heath was scrutinizing *her*.

"I'm thinking red wine?" Grey remarked. "An Hermitage?"

"I'll have white," she quickly said. She'd have a bottle, thank you. This was so *awkward*.

"White. Excellent. Would Les Chaillets—"

"I love it. And a bottle will do nicely."

His eyes sparkled as he gazed at her, and the corner of his lips lifted in amusement before he returned to the menu.

She risked a glance at Heath, and his attention was on her hair. His eyes slid along the gathered strands in slow, thorough inspection, then down to linger on her nape.

When he pulled his gaze back up, his eyes positively smoldered. "What did you do to your hair?" he asked. Thickly. Like a lover would murmur in the dark.

"I'm . . . nothing. It's just tied back."

"The oysters here are excellent, Heath."

"Oysters." Heath reclined in his seat. He did not stop staring at her. All of her. As though he were thinking of dinner and she was *it*. "I might have those."

"The lobster is good, too."

Your woman is good.

Heath didn't say it, but she felt the words buzz through his mind. Buzz through her body. His eyes weren't black, she now noticed, but a brown so dark you could barely make out his pupils.

"Toni? You're having your usual?"

"I think so, yes." She swung her gaze back to the offerings, a finger busily sliding down the list. "Though maybe I'll try something different. Your salmon last time was delicious."

"Ah yes, I think I'm having that." Grey folded his menu. "Do you want to order something else and we can taste both?"

She slapped the menu shut. "Deal. You pick."

Grey signaled with his hand, asking the waiter something about the wines.

"What do you do, Toni?"

"Pardon?"

"What do you do?" Heath repeated, stroking a finger down the length of a spoon. "When Grey isn't taking up your time, I mean."

The way his finger stroked . . .

She pulled her gaze back up, gathering her thoughts. "I'd say I take more of his. I love kidnapping him from work."

"And he likes it?"

"Yes!"

He snorted, that great chest of his jerking as he did. The glimmer in his eyes was so playful she could not quite pull her lips back into place.

"I'm a graphic design artist," she said, to answer him. "I used to work at a very prestigious firm, but I'm afraid I'm a bit . . ."

"Unpunctual," Grey offered as soon as the waiter had left.

She spread her napkin on her lap, wrinkling her nose at Grey. "Yes. More or less. I don't seem to thrive on nine-to-five hours. So I'm on my own. I'm not doing all that badly."

"She's doing wonderfully," Grey proudly said. "Do you know Foxtrack, the motorcycle gear company?"

"Of course."

"She did that one. Then there's—"

"Why haven't you done RS?" Heath interrupted.

He was unnerving her. She looked into his eyes and that bad-boy smile and presumed he was imagining her naked, which made her want to imagine him naked, which made it difficult to speak. He had a smooth, intelligent forehead that furrowed when he listened to her, and a nose that was shy of perfect. She would not even get into the small, intriguing scar on his chin.

"I'd intended to make a fabulous design for RS before Grey and I got involved. That's how we met, actually."

"She doesn't sleep with clients. She won't do anything for me." Grey set his hand over hers on the table, his fingers caressing her knuckles. "I've offered her the world for a design and still get nay."

"It's just that I'd hate to bring business between us," she explained to Heath.

"I see." He was staring at them holding hands, and she did not know why she felt guilty. Maybe because of the brooding expression on his face.

Within minutes the wine was uncorked, their glasses filled, hers with white and theirs with red, and the conversation steered to the big, busy world of RS Corporation. Properties, buildings, zoning commissions.

The men's voices felt like touches, and goose bumps rose along her flesh. Grey's low-pitched and clear. Heath's the rumble of a motorcycle. The nearness of those large, tanned, overwhelming bodies was fatal to her imagination.

Rather than focus on the conversation, her mind flicked with images of them. Together. Naked. Not engaged in polite conversation but in sinful, highly erotic acts of lovemaking.

Her breasts throbbed as she imagined being in a clinch between them, feeling both their cocks, her flesh covered by theirs. She took a sip of her wine, and another. The burn sliding down her throat did nothing for the one between her legs. *Oh, Grey, take me somewhere. . . .*

As the men spoke about someone named Parsons, peppering their sentences with *not very competent* and *troubles of a personal nature* and *dickwad*—this one from Heath—the waiter appeared with their appetizers. A plate full of ice decorated with tiny toast points held a small bowlful of black sevruga caviar; a second similar one was topped with puffy white cream.

Stopping their conversation abruptly, Heath signaled at the offerings once the waiter left. "Do you like caviar, Toni?"

"As a matter of fact, I do," she said primly.

Before she could pluck up a toast point, Heath dipped his middle finger into the plate full of crème fraîche and lifted his creamed finger to her mouth.

"Lick."

She fought the staggering impulse, remembering Grey's test, how she was fully determined to pass with flying—

"Lap it."

She gazed into burning amber eyes when he spoke, the urge to please him intense. She'd liked to think it was mutual, the way Grey seemed intent on pleasing her, the way she craved to please *him*.

Into her ear, he poured his hot whisper. "Baby," he purred, "I said, *lap it*."

Her cunt squeezed. And she found herself trembling with eagerness as she turned her head and snaked out her tongue, tasting the cream, feeling it melt against the roof of her mouth.

Heath rammed his finger inside her mouth, making her suck it. The pleasure was so great, so shocking, her eyes fluttered shut. Giddy sensations trickled through her as she explored with her tongue, tried to separate the man from the cream, isolate the taste of Heath Solis.

She was loath to stop once she licked off the last drop from his long finger. He stroked her tongue with the pad, awakening little nerves she'd never known existed. Her heartbeat elevated to alarming speed. She'd never been so thrilled, so aroused in public.

Heath pushed his face so close she inhaled his sweet, fruity breath. "That's going to be my cock."

Thrown into a daze by his bold, entirely too thrilling words, she watched him sink two fingers into the caviar like a spoon. Before she could pull herself together, he dipped his fingers into her mouth. The salty sevruga spilled over her taste buds. And she pretended it was his cock—that surely massive, velvety thing he could pleasure her with.

Tongues of fire licked her insides as she suckled. She reached under the table for Grey. Nothing could get her so excited, so damp, than feeling him aroused. Her pussy wept when she found him with her hand. His swollen cock pushed his pants up into a tent, and she created friction by sliding the heel of her palm up and down the length. His entire body was utterly still except for his hips, slowly moving with her, dancing to her hand.

A perverse bliss flitted through her as she watched Heath's expression as he fed her. His thick-lashed eyes were barely open, and his features were stretched taut. Then she turned to Grey. Never had she seen that carnal eroticism on his face. She could feel his arousal like an incoming tornado. He was ready to *take* her. She gazed at his mouth, hungrily wanting.

He had such sensually curved lips, lips to pleasure her, love her, and god, how good that scorching mouth felt on her nipples, her lips, her pussy. Desire raged through her bloodstream. Dangerous. Reckless. He could take her right here, and she might not even care that they would be watched.

She reluctantly let go of Heath's thick, luscious fingers, and licked a stray drop of cream from the corner of her lips. Grey's eyes caught the move and his irises transformed to the color of twenty-four-karat gold.

He set his wineglass aside and circled her nape with his hand. "Your mouth drives me crazy." When he drew her forward and his scalding mouth covered hers, ecstasy ripped its claws into her. His tongue worked hers, suckling, pleasuring, taking with such force, she realized this play had ignited him. Then he was biting at her bottom lip, nipping at her jaw, roughly nibbling on her earlobe. "Say it and it's yours. Tell me what you want and it's yours."

"No."

He stabbed her with his tongue again, and she latched on to his mouth and sucked him deeper into hers, shuddering uncontrollably as his passion roared through her.

He broke away. "Open to me." She tensed as his hand brushed up the length of her bare thigh, his expert fingers sliding under the hem of her dress.

His thumb skated across her cleft, and she turned her head to his shoulder, burying her face there with a wanton whimper. "People can see."

"Nobody's looking at you but me and Heath."

She muffled her haggard breaths in his collar, helpless against the delicious, tight press of his thumb into her clit. "Take me someplace else."

Where he massaged the hardened clit through her panties, the tissue flared. She clamped her thighs together and gritted her teeth to fight the soaring sensations.

But he would not take no for an answer, his hand digging into the crevice of her legs with single-minded purpose. "Let me in. Let me touch you. Show me how wet you are."

His words vibrated through her in a lust wave, and she pulled his head down to her lips and plunged her tongue into his ear. "I'm drenched. So drenched."

He dropped his head to her shoulder as though he couldn't hold it up anymore, reverently saying, "Baby."

And just like that her thighs spread apart, craving what he would do. Once he found the source of her moisture, he tugged the fabric aside and eased his longest finger inside the welcoming sheath. She felt her spine arch against the backrest, her entire body wanting to buck up for more.

Their booth was mercifully secluded, but she occasionally caught sight of busy waiters that passed. Thoughts of being seen like this had her coiled like a spring.

The ruthless, powerful thrusts of Grey's finger triggered a chain reaction in her, sent her galloping to the very peak of bliss.

His stubble chafed the skin of her throat as he rubbed his jaw against her like a lion, breathing on her, licking. "Ask me for what you want, Antonia."

Stubbornly, she didn't. His finger left her weeping cleft, and she dazedly brought her head up. Grey pushed his finger into her mouth. "Suck. Taste yourself. Tangy. Sweet." She tasted, felt his groan vibrate around the booth. "It tells me all I need to know," he rasped through his throat, "but I want your mouth to say it. I want to hear how hot, how wild, my lover is."

Oh, god. She was wild. Unashamedly wild. "Why?"

"It turns me on."

His devastating words, combined with the knowledge that the mouthwatering Heath Solis was watching, caused fire tornadoes all over her. It took all her effort to squirm away from her blatantly tempting lover, struggling to compose herself. "This isn't the place for this. This is . . . We came here to eat and . . . talk."

Yes. Eat and talk. Like civilized people who did not do . . . threesomes.

"No, we didn't." Grey leaned back in his seat, his jaw set at an obstinate angle, his breathing not quite back to normal as he searched inside his pocket. "Heathcliff?"

"Grey?"

Grey slammed his palm on the table, his long, tanned fingers sliding across the linen, up to the center. The startling second he uncovered the shiny red sash tightly balled beneath them, her heart flew up to her throat.

Her eyes flicked up to Grey's, and her chest hurt so intensely she thought she'd expire. "Why are you doing this?" she whispered.

She thought he wouldn't answer. He stared at her lips, and she expected him to kiss her, but instead he quietly raised his eyes. What she saw in them made her heart leap. "You want it. And I want to give it to you."

I love you.

The words blasted into her mind, shocking the breath out of

her. Words unspoken between them, but a fulmination in his eyes,
rushing with his touch when he ran his knuckles down her cheek.
Her insides jelled, the muscles in her body quivering.

"You want it," he repeated, his voice throbbing with emotion.

Toni's heart vaulted in her chest. He was in love with her. He
was. Somehow she had slipped into his heart; that cold, hard heart
to which her own seemed to beat. The knowledge burst through
her in an explosion, beautiful, earth-shattering.

She jerked her eyes back to the sash and sent her hand flying.
She crushed the satin under her palm, reclaiming it as hers.

A cryptlike stillness spread.

And Heath. Wicked, sinful Heath Solis set his enormous, callused hand over hers. "Toni." He stroked the back of her fingers
with his and her pulse hitched. "Grey wants this. I want this. You
want this, too."

She looked into his eyes. The dark eroticism in his gaze skimmed
through her blood. Oh, god—she wanted sin, ecstasy, bliss. She
wanted Grey; she wanted Heath. A part of her demanded that she
clutch her sash protectively to her chest, and a part of her wanted
Heath to have it. The part that screamed, *Yes, yes, you're a hot, wicked
devil of a man and I'm not in a coma, and I want you* and *my luscious,
delicious lover to take me until I scream.*

Her mind raced. She hauled her gaze back to the molten gold
of Grey's. She wanted a bedroom. A closet. Somewhere she could
tear off the dress chafing her skin, rip the clothes off Grey. Heath.
She would scream when they entered her. She would feel relief.

When she spoke, her voice hummed with arousal. "You've done
this before, haven't you? Threesomes?"

Grey seemed ready to smile. "I have."

Her lungs hardened like stones in her chest as she pictured him
with two beautiful women. "With whom?"

"Heath."

A shock of excitement burst through her. The image of these
two breathtaking men, naked and surrounding fortunate little her,

made her insides knot. But she could still not seem to let go of her sash. "Heath, and who else?"

"Women."

Of course.

Toni would not expect a handsome, successful, powerful man like Grey to have the sex life of a choirboy, but the realization, the reminder, of how experienced, how worldly he was made her stomach grip. "How many women?"

"At a time? One."

"And overall?" Three? Ten? Fifteen? Why did she feel like her heart was being wrung?

"Many, Toni."

Many. Her lover had had—her lover had *shared*—many women with Heath. "Ten?" she ventured.

"I didn't count."

"At least ten," Heath offered.

She didn't turn, instead studied Grey with the same intensity with which he seemed to be gauging her reaction. In a quiet, cottony voice, she asked, "Did they like it?"

He reached for her mouth, this time running the pad of his thumb across the quivering flesh of her lower lip. "They loved it," he said in a thick whisper.

The idea of Grey with those women, with anyone but her, had an unprecedented jealousy surging through her. Violent. Painful. She fisted one hand tightly on her lap. "Did you care for them?"

If he said yes . . .

Damn him if he said *yes*. . . .

A fierce, eerie light flashed in his eyes, and she thought he would say something about his feelings for her. Three full heartbeats passed. Then she realized it was too much to ask of Grey. He gave her anything. Everything. Except that.

"No, I didn't care for them. And I was a boy, Toni. Now I'm a man."

My *man,* she thought furiously.

She let go a shaky breath, but it was as though nothing could pull their gazes apart.

Her voice dropped to a whisper. "And did you enjoy it?"

He nodded.

The gesture built a staggering, overwhelming desire in her to override all those many others from his mind, drive him out of control, out of his mind, as madly and deeply in love as she was. The words screamed in her head. *Thrill him. Excite him. Surprise him. Make him love you.*

Arousal swam in her veins . . . tantalizing thoughts of Grey loving her with his hands, his hungry mouth . . . Heath inside a moist, throbbing part of her . . .

Raising her free hand, she cupped the thick back of Grey's neck and drew him forward. "Come here, baby," she pleaded, amazed when he easily complied. Against a mouth that was opening to take hers, she sensually whispered, "I'm going to drive you wild, Grey Richards. So wild that you will think of nothing else, no one else, but Toni Kearny."

He groaned into her mouth, not a groan of protest, but a gruff animal sound emitting his approval. And he closed the hairsbreadth between them and took her mouth voraciously.

⌒

Voyeurism had never been Heath's thing. He was either an active participant or not interested. Not that a kiss could be considered voyeuristic. But then that was one hell of a sensual kiss.

From his seat across the table, he tightened his hold on Toni's hand as she continued kissing Grey. No way in hell would he release it.

He wanted that sash, and she was holding it.

The restaurant continued to move in the slow, discreet way fancy places did. Waiters passed by the secluded booth. No one gawked or paused. But Heath could not drag his eyes away.

No wonder Grey didn't want him to kiss her. The delectable Miss Kearny was eating Grey up with that killer mouth, and damn, Grey was worked up in a way Heath had never seen him. If that man opened his jaw a fraction more, it would crack.

His hands were guiding her face, tilting her this way and the other, and their kiss was so mouthwateringly sloppy it was painful to watch. If Heath were closer, he had a mind to push his head in there and find a spot for his own tongue somewhere deep in the recesses of Toni's mouth.

The kiss tingled across his entire havoc-wreaked body. It made him ache in his seat. He'd never thought a man as unmoved, as impenetrable as Grey could ever be so hungry. Hell, he'd never thought *he* could be so hungry. For a kiss. A woman.

Toni. Kearny.

With that beguiling combination of innocence and sex, the sound of her name screamed in his head like a siren call. Damn, he was almost tempted to beg her to make that same husky vow to him, too.

No man is an island. . . .

He'd heard this from a retiring construction worker who spent his lunchtimes with a book.

Heath had snorted. *I'm it, buddy. Lunchtime is over.*

He didn't like emotional entanglements and he didn't like messy good-byes, which made his relationship with Grey so easy. Grey wasn't sentimental; his partner was forthright and the most level-headed man Heath knew. They worked. Heath elbowed him. Grey let himself be amused sometimes. They were themselves.

Heath pretty much didn't give a shit about anything else.

But watching Grey and Toni kiss . . . fuck, just the way they stared at each other . . . damn, even watching Grey fondle her little hand . . .

Some kind of creepy, unwelcome loneliness gripped at his chest. Maybe the knowledge that his partner and best friend was as emotionally isolated as he was had kept the feeling at bay, kept him from feeling like an oddity. But something in Grey had cracked, and something in Heath envied it.

He was torn with wants. He wanted to rise from the table and find something to do other than watch them. And he wanted to slide up to crowd her from behind and plunge into her silken depths. Most of all, he wanted to bend her over the table and fuck her until they both passed out.

Instead he raised his wine—the Hermi-whatever—and tossed back the liquid. He desperately craved a beer. Once they drew apart, Grey left Toni's hair in a delectable, thoroughly touchable mess, and she brought a pair of glazed forest green eyes to Heath's.

His mouth ran dry. He'd never seen a more kissable, more fuckable pair of lips, no bullshit. Her pupils were dilated with arousal. The black almost swallowed the gold-speckled green of her irises. Sweat glistened across her small forehead, and that fine-sized chest of hers rose and fell heavily with each breath. She smelled of woman in heat, and if he didn't have her soon he'd . . . he didn't know. But it wouldn't be good.

"This fire . . ." he gruffly told her, caressing the inside of her wrist as he turned her hand to stroke its smooth center with his thumb. He liked that part of a woman, the dent in her palm, and he liked fucking it with his thumb. Slowly and sinuously, until the meaning of what he was doing became clear.

Her eyes widened almost imperceptibly.

"This fire isn't just Grey's." He watched the color rise in her cheeks as her lust heightened. "It's mine, too. I fed it and stoked it, and I want it." In a bold, unequivocal move, he brought her hand under the table and almost groaned when she held him. "This one's for you."

Beneath the light touch of her palm, his crotch was rock. Fire. Hot male dick pulsing against her—*for* her. "That's your fire. And I promise you no one's putting it out but you."

He'd tried, and nope. He wanted Toni.

Withdrawing her hand with notable hesitation, she gave one last wistful look at her sash.

And Toni pursed those pretty lips just so, and he could see the steel in her eyes when she swung her gaze to his. A challenge. The sweetest challenge he'd been issued in his thirty-five years. To take that shimmering red material. And then her body.

This little she-cat wasn't fooling around.

With a smile he couldn't quite suppress, he reached out and enfolded it in his grip. He imagined he was closing his hand around something more intimate of hers. The satin was cool and flimsy, begging him to lift it up to his nose and take a whiff of her perfume. Tonight he'd wrap it around his cock, and he'd play with it, and *this* weekend . . .

"Cabo?" he asked, the word for Grey.

Grey directed his reply at Toni, with a look so carnal Heath seriously envied the sweaty, headboard-banging, animal-sex session those two had coming.

"Cabo."

Chapter Five

Ménage . . .

It sang like a chant in her brain. It sang this morning when she slipped into the shower. It sang when she e-mailed her clients to notify them of her three-day absence. It sang when she turned off her computer, tucked her cell phone in her desk drawer, and hauled her suitcase out the door, following Grey.

Ménage . . .

It kept clamoring when Heath Solis, his jeans, his smile, and his plain black T-shirt joined them at the airport, and it screamed in her head as they flew forty thousand feet above the ground in their fine little company jet, a Citation X that soared smooth as a bird and flew faster than any other private aircraft.

Ménage . . .

Grey wanted it. She wanted it. Craved it. The looks they had shared the entire week were charged with it. The knowledge that they would do this. *Together.* It had been with them all week, in their sex, their looks, their touches.

Ménage.

He had her primed. He had her ready. He had touched her all week, and every time her orgasm approached, he'd halt.

With Heath's sinfully sexy body lounging at her right and

Grey decadently gorgeous facing her, it was difficult not to turn liquid.

As soon as they'd boarded, Heath had popped two pills into his mouth, guzzled an entire liter of water, and propped his head on his hand. Noticing that he seemed to fall instantly asleep, she and Grey had each picked up a book to read quietly.

Every time she peeked at him through the tops of the pages, he glanced up, too. In tan Dockers and a white polo, jaw rough with earthy stubble, hair slightly mussed, he looked rugged and unkempt today. A golden Midas fallen from grace.

She wanted him.

She wanted Heath Solis.

She still could not *believe* Grey had only yesterday mentioned the man was bisexual.

Snuggled on the couch as he watched the football game, he'd made a casual remark about Heath being bi, and Toni had jumped. *Heath is bisexual?* Grey had waved it off as if he were discussing the most boring, most inconsequential topic ever. But Toni could not think of anything else all evening. Oh, she'd known that man was bad. Bad, bad, bad. She'd pressed her legs together so, so tight at a visual her mind suddenly conjured. "I didn't know."

"Now you do."

"Did you and he—"

Grey had chuckled softly. "I'm not bisexual, baby. He is."

Now Toni continued to wonder what kind of confused woman found a bisexual man attractive.

The same kind who'd have a threesome.

As soon as they landed, Grey stored his Harlan Coben in a glossy wooden plane compartment, and Toni slipped her Jodi Picoult into her tote bag. Anticipation simmered in her veins. Her nerves were wild and awake, sensitive to a glance, a whisper, the faintest brush against her skin. She wouldn't let Grey know that.

"Don't think I've been playing your little game, Mr. Almighty Richards," she whispered to Grey as she unfastened her seat belt and gathered her things. While he helped her out of her sweater, she lightly added, "I've been touching myself all week in the shower, and it's been wonderful."

"Is that a fact?"

"Yes." She nodded somberly, tying her sweater around her waist. "It's a fact."

He extracted her bag from her grasp, still whispering for Heath's sake. "So why are your panties in a twist?"

"They're not in a twist."

His smile was full of carnal male knowledge. His heavy-lidded gaze made her nipples throb. "I know for a fact that they are."

"Ha. I can take care of my own panties, thank you." She added a flippant toss of her hair as she slipped her feet back into her sandals.

"Can you, now?" He flattened her against him so fast he knocked the breath out of her. With a grinding move of his hips that presented his need to her throbbing cunt, he had her gasping. "I want your pussy. I want your breasts in my mouth. I want you creaming all over me." Her body responded to his erotic words, her muscles clenching with anticipation. "You need me inside you, Toni. Three days without me and you're going insane."

"Dream on. B-by all means, let your imagination fly."

He kissed her with the force of an avalanche, pouring his passion into her, his tempestuous need having built up for seconds, minutes, hours, days. "I'm so hard for you I could break marble."

She could barely pry herself free. "Good; I hope you have fun with it." In a nonchalant gesture that took a miracle to perform, she shouldered across him, down the aisle. Turning, she watched him slap Heath's shoulder.

"You coming, Heath?"

Heath pushed himself off the seat. "Yeah, I'm coming."

"He hates small airplanes," Grey told her. "Motion sickness, I don't know. He takes drugs even in the larger planes."

Heath raked a hand through his hair and shook off his daze.

Even in such a state, the dangerous aura around him made her insides thrill.

"Big, bad Heath is afraid of flying?" she said almost to herself, smiling at the notion.

Grey squeezed her rump before she climbed down the stairs.

"He heard that."

⌒

Her veins thrummed as she descended the stairs, strode into the small airport and went through the long line at customs, where a group of armed soldiers inspected their baggage.

A frowning young man with a weapon slung around his shoulder rifled through her bags—his hands were all over her bras, her thongs, to the point that she was beginning to feel violated—while the three of them stood statuelike across the table and watched. Grey was simmering with impatience.

Heath bent to her ear. "I think Grey has a mind to strangle that man," he muttered.

"Watch a man putting his hands on your woman's panties and see how you feel," Grey said, his words belying the coolness with which he spoke them.

When the man glanced up, Toni smiled brightly and tried to pretend they weren't discussing him. Or the fact he wore no gloves while he messed with her clothes.

Lifting a hand to smooth away Grey's frown, she rose on tiptoe and placed a kiss on his jaw. "I can always not wear them. I know you like that."

Like that? She knew for a fact he *loved* that.

When a second man came over to "aid" in the inspection, the entire process became ridiculously intrusive and began to annoy *her.* Grey finally stepped forward, his voice authoritative. "Are we done here?"

The men tucked her red La Perla back into the suitcase with a grave nod, and Grey zippered it up. He snatched her hand, linked their fingers, and together they made their way through the rustic halls of the airport, each hauling his or her own suitcase.

"Cat, I'll get that."

Before she could protest, Heath, carrying only a small travel duffel around his shoulder, grasped the handle of her suitcase and hauled it on. She smiled, wondering why the gesture seemed . . . so nice. "Thank you. Why did you call me Cat?"

She was in such a sexually deprived state, his drug-induced drawl had the effect of a vibrator on her. "I'll have you purring like one."

The airport was a small one-story building, noisy and crowded with tourists. The scent of food and sweat permeated the air. To one side of the hall, an array of colorful Mexican *tiendas* displayed T-shirts and dolls and sombreros. The other side was occupied by revision tables, waiting areas, flight check-in, but the area was so limited in tables and chairs that people were actually scattered on the floor as though at a picnic.

As they pulled their suitcases down a long ramp, Grey's housekeeper, Señor Gonzalez, a kindly brown-eyed man with laugh lines around his mouth, waited next to a shiny black Lincoln Navigator. All of Grey's cars were black, something Toni didn't get; she'd learned from experience that the tiniest scratch was always most visible on *those*. She'd given a few to his Porsche that fairly screamed "Toni was here."

While the men flung the suitcases in the trunk, she hovered nearby.

The heat pounded atop her head, but a hushed breeze played with her hair. Not a sharp Chicago breeze, but a flimsy one that made the nearby palm trees gently sway. She could smell the ocean in the air and couldn't resist dragging in a good lungful before she slid into the back of the car.

Heath rode up front with the reed-thin Mexican; Grey and Toni in the back. Grey slipped an arm around her waist and hauled her across the slippery leather. He flattened her cheek to his chest. "Stay right here with me."

He was so infuriatingly sexy. She'd been so sure he wouldn't last at his play. So certain he'd lose at his own game and take her one evening, one morning. He hadn't. The man's will was iron, and now she was steeling herself to punish him. A little. If she could manage.

They rode for thirty minutes through desert landscape dotted with cacti, a landscape that looked lonely and barren and beautiful.

Once they reached the picturesque small town of San José, the scenery changed, with the endless blue of the ocean visible to their left.

Grey and Señor Gonzalez had a bit of a language issue—neither spoke the other's—so they didn't communicate through the entire ride. Heath occasionally spoke to him in Spanish, but his voice was still thick. She assumed he was still groggy. It was kind of adorable.

His T-shirt stretched taut over the roundness of his shoulders, and his glossy black hair looked played-with. During the ride, he ran a heavy, tired hand through it, and she suppressed the urge to reach out and do the same.

This weekend, they were both hers.

The car climbed up a narrow road. They passed gates and long stretches of manicured gardens, and then the house came into view. White and grand, it sat atop the rocky cliff, with sweeping terraces and massive archways, surrounded by lush green palm trees. Up the wide steps and inside the sunny foyer, they were greeted by an array of fresh flowers Señor Gonzalez had set atop the central round table. The tall windows in every room had been opened to let in the breeze, and the marble floors shone like mirrors.

Grey showed Heath to the guest room before following Toni to theirs. Their room at the Cabo house was three times bigger than their bedroom at Toni's.

A fluffy lime green rug covered the floor, while the walls were cheerfully decorated with two rows of framed beach drawings. A plush duvet was spread across the bed, an assortment of soft-hued pillows propped on the massive oak headboard. The glass door windows covering one wall opened to a sprawling terrace that boasted a variety of teak furniture and a perfect view of the Sea of Cortez.

The great crash of waves, even with the beach a 120-stone staircase away, echoed in the stillness.

Toni started unpacking.

On the small forged-iron table by the window, Grey unloaded their passports, his iPod, her home keys, then propped his shoulder against the wall, ankles crossed as he fiddled with his cell phone, scanning his messages.

When he tucked it back into his pocket, he pushed himself off the wall and lazily sauntered around the room. So nonchalant. So unaffected by this abstinence that had her in a frenzy.

On the bed, he found a lacy black pair of panties she must have overlooked. Absently, he fingered the crotch, and she felt the touch on her sex and tensed against the sensation. She gritted her teeth, angry at herself.

She had been like this all day. So sensitive to the merest look, touch, scent.

Smiling, he crushed it into a ball and tucked it into the pocket of his tan slacks. She wanted to clamp her mouth over his and devour him.

Instead, she feigned indifference and went to the window, remembering the whales they'd seen the last time they visited. Soaring into the air, crashing back into the water. The water lapped at the jutting black rocks, and she marveled at how calm the sea looked. How she would like to feel it against her. How Grey would feel against her . . . and Heath , , . And then she forgot the sea, the whales, the past and the future, when Grey drew up behind her.

"I'm dying to make love to you."

Shivering, she wrapped her arms around herself, clutched tight. "I'm dying, too."

He drew nearer, the heat of him infiltrating her clothes. Was he stroking her hair? "Are you wearing some? Panties?"

Her breathing pattern changed. "Why do you want to know?" The words were faint; inside them, a silent scream for him to touch her. Make love to her. Take her before she went up in flames.

He seized her wrists and brought her arms up, flattening her hands against the window. His weight pressed into hers as he caressed her sides, his voice the very sound of desire. "I'm going to strip you down to your skin, and I'm going to take every little inch of you with my tongue."

It took an effort to say, "Hah."

He nudged her legs apart with his knee, seized her long skirt with both hands, and crept them up to her waist. Air rushed across her bare bottom. "I'll make you come for all the times you haven't come, and then I'll have you coming some more."

A tremble shot through her, and she fought for it not to show, her palms sweating against the glass.

His hand slipped between her ass cheeks. A shock of excitement ripped through her as he groped her. "Pussy." His terse whisper passed through her in a current of electricity. "My hot, wet, juicy pussy. You've been walking like this all day?"

His fingers tunneled into her cleft, stroking the outside, startling her to a cry when he pushed in. She threw her head back, parting her legs wider. "Yes!" She was frantic for him, for *this*.

"I feel starved, Antonia." The words were whispered against her neck as he expertly rolled her clit under his thumb, his zipper scraping her buttocks as he rubbed his arousal against her. "I'm starved for the sounds you make, the sight of your face as you come. I'm starved for your nipples, your tongue, the things you say to me when I'm inside you."

"I miss you, too." Her eyes drifted shut, her body rocking to his moves, their unchecked passion soaring through her. "Three days, and I can't stand more."

He chuckled. "In three more days, you won't be able to stand, period."

She threw her head back and laughed, and he covered one breast with his free hand, massaging the flesh. "Do I amuse you, Miss Kearny?"

Her lingering laugh drifted to a moan when he twisted his wrist, a second finger joining his long middle one inside her channel. Her hips moved to his hand, seeking more.

The click of the bedroom door faintly penetrated the cloak of their desire. One word leapt into her mind, and her eyes sprung open.

Heath.

Grey slid out of her. "We've got company."

Taking her wrists in his hands, he gently lowered her arms. He was breathing as fast as she was, his face close to her ear. "We're going to strip you naked, and we're going to lick you like candy, and when you're squirming and begging for cock, we're going to fill you up until you can't breathe." His sweltering tongue did erotic things to her earlobe, gingerly fucked the crevice. "We're going to do this all weekend, Toni. Night and day. Until all you can think about is getting more tongue on your pussy, more dick in your mouth, more getting lapped at like a wet, juicy lollipop."

She'd come if he kept speaking, plunging his tongue into her tingling ear.

"Turn around for me, baby."

She did. Flutters exploded in her stomach at the sight of Heath. Not a dream. Not a thought. But real. Flesh-and-blood man.

Definitely not her worst nightmare.

His eyes came at her across the room, heavy lidded, shining with lust. He wasn't smiling.

Grey drew her protectively to his side. "Breathe."

But she couldn't. Not when Heath fisted his hands on the front of his shirt and tugged it over his head. The chest he revealed was ridged and muscled, every rib delineated, his abs marked with taut muscle.

Black hair reckless atop his head, his muscles flexed as he carelessly tossed the shirt aside, and then his hands went to his waistband. God, she felt like an innocent. *A virgin.*

Her legs turned rubbery as he flicked the button of his jeans, his fingers deft as he lowered the zipper. Heat pulsed between her thighs, fast like her heartbeat.

She couldn't help closing her eyes as Heath started shoving his jeans down his hips. But she *heard* the slide of denim, heard her heart thundering, heard the fabric whisper down his legs.

Grey gathered her blouse at her sides, sliding it up. *This is it, this is it, this is* it . . .

In her wildest imaginings, she'd pictured herself as a beach temptress—not coy, but a brazen goddess driving two gorgeous males to uncontrollable lust. In reality, she was just Toni Kearny, and she was overwhelmed. She could hardly breathe, much less move or act sexy.

Grey gripped her waist, his fingers digging into the side of her hip. "Open your eyes, Toni. See what you do to him."

She pulled her eyes open and gaped. Heath was wearing the longest, biggest erection she'd ever seen. He stood with his feet braced apart, his arms at his sides, his fingers curled into his palms. And something hummed. Inside her. In her blood, coursing dangerously through her veins.

Her eyes ran along Heath's strong cheekbones, the plump curve of his mouth, the golden tan across his body. Silky hairs dusted his chest. An arrow of thicker hair started under his navel and fanned out to a dark thatch from where that enormous penis thrust out. Her fingers tingled at her sides, alive with a need to touch him, compare him to Grey, discover their differences and their similarities.

"You see Heath?"

"Yes." God, yes, she *saw*. Felt. Sensed. Smelled them both.

Grey captured her earlobe in his teeth. "We own you tonight."

"I . . . I own you both."

The admission made Heath's eyes flash, like a bull at the sight of red, a green light, a yes.

Grey buzzed her ear with his nose and his hands were roaming, caressing up her hips. "Let's get naked, Miss Kearny."

Jolted into action, she clenched her fingers in the fabric of his polo and struggled to wrench it off him. He helped her, then shucked off his Dockers, his underwear, until she beheld six feet three inches of glorious, bare-assed, mouthwateringly naked Grey.

Looking down at her, he caught her wrist and tugged her forward. "My turn."

He'd undressed her a thousand times. When he did it leisurely, he always kissed bits and pieces he revealed. Now he kissed the swell of one lace-encased breast as he reached behind her to undo her pink bra. "So beautiful . . ." He pulled the straps from her shoulders and let it fall, raking his tongue across one elongated nipple. "Oh, sweetheart, you're so sexy. . . ."

She wanted to eat him up with her mouth, to swallow his beautiful words into her.

Her bra dropped at her feet, and her breasts sprung fully free. He kissed both.

Gently he turned her around to unhook her skirt while Heath came to her, smelling of earth and rain and a rich, balmy musk. Her skirt swooshed down to her ankles. A gust of air cooled her before Heath's proximity reversed her body to heat.

She felt so naked. But his face . . .

His face was ravaged with need. His nostrils flared. Suddenly, she felt as though she were the only woman he'd ever seen; so alive were his eyes on her, so greedy, taking in the perky swell of her breasts, her clean-shaven pussy.

His fingers skimmed up her cheek as he ducked his head. His tongue glided up the corner of her lips, teasing her with the tip.

"I'm so fucking turned on," he growled. He turned his head to lick at the other corner of her lips, harshly whispering, "Say my name."

"Heath." It felt too good to say it.

"Ahh, Toni." His head went down, and his tongue swept gently across the puckered bud of one nipple, his fingers enclosing the flesh around it.

A melting sensation spread through her thighs as she mapped his arms with trembling fingers. She stopped exploring and sunk her nails into his shoulders when his mouth opened around her, covering her with heat. The power in his mouth combined with the soft sucking noises felt like jolts of lightning.

Silently winding around her like a panther, Grey came to watch.

His sculpted bronze torso, his neck, his muscled arms—her heart pounded at the sight. Her breath became ragged as he wrapped a hand around his pulsing flesh and stroked up. She'd never seen him touch himself. He did it so expertly, almost casually, the unmistakable scrape of flesh singing in her ears. He was marvelous. A god. Touching himself.

Their gazes met over Heath's hunched shoulders. Gazing deep into her eyes, he stroked himself a second time—deliberately slowly, so it took him two full seconds to go from base to head and back down again. She licked her lips, loving that cock, that long-fingered hand, that man. A spiral of wanting whirled inside her tummy.

"Do that again," she mouthed.

He shook his head, eyes glimmering as he let go of himself and took another step. She watched him bob as he walked, and her pussy rippled with wanting that cock just as it was; marvelously red and fully extended.

A tender heat mingled with lust shone in his eyes as he came within touching distance. He reached out to pet her free breast, smiling as he plucked the nipple with two fingers. "This one's mine." He lowered his head, his eyes on hers, and against her flesh, breathed, "You're mine."

She clutched the back of his head and drew him to her breast. "Yes."

When he covered her nipple with his mouth, she threw her head back in bliss. "Yes."

Wow wow wow wow . . .

She'd never thought it would feel like this. She'd worried she would discover this had been a bad idea, but no, no, it was so good. Felt so maddeningly *good*.

There wasn't a single breath she took that wasn't spiced with their desire. Sensations assailed her, one after the other, following their touches, their sounds. Her nipples had never felt so hard, so hot. Grey's mouth was sure and loving on her nipple, and the breast Heath suckled grew raw and fiery. He was not a gentle lover, and his roughness excited her, his hands not so careful as they went around her and squeezed her ass. She yelped in surprise, and his gruff sound was muffled by her sweaty skin.

He moved, and a thick, blunt-fingered hand slipped between her thighs. She bucked when he found her and pressed the tip of a callused finger into her clit. Her breath hissed through her teeth.

Grey looked up from her breast. "You like that?"

"God. Perfect. *Yes*."

"She likes that, Heath."

And Heath did it again. And again. He caught the flesh and pinched, pressed, plucked. She screamed, her head rolling loosely on her neck, her breath soughing out of her chest. Grey moved around her, became her wall, and raw, hungry screams welled up in the back of her throat as she let her weight rest on him, let Heath do things to her.

Their combined panting breaths were like a dark, endless song in the room, punctuated with Toni's cries as Heath made bold, wicked movements on her clit.

Grey's chest jerked roughly against her back as he breathed. "Toni?" His murmur throbbed in her ear. "Tell us what you want, baby."

"She wants me to eat her."

Her mind spun with Heath's dirty talk as he knelt before her, drawing her legs apart.

His eyes bored into hers for a heart-stopping moment, and smiling a lazy, sexy smile, he ducked his head. "Don't you, Toni?" A moan caught in the back of her throat when he tasted her. A soft, wet flick.

"Yes." *Please please please please*.

His tongue came so long, so strong, giving deep, velvety strokes up her entrance. She'd never been licked like this. He licked like a *dog*, using only his tongue, and it was maddeningly erotic.

Grey's breath whispered across her hair, his mouth nipping at her shoulder. "You're awfully quiet, my love."

She smothered a sound. She'd imagined she would ravage them, both of them, take them like a wild woman, but she could hardly move. Only feel. Feel *them*. Against her. Doing dirty things to her.

Instinctively, her hands came up, burying in Heath's soft, thick hair, drawing his mouth against her clit.

"Don't you want me to know you're enjoying it?" Grey pressed.

Heath laved the bud with his tongue, his thumb driving inside her. Her body surged up hungrily, but she kept from moaning still. Embarrassed. Embarrassed that she was ready to come.

"Give me your moans, baby, purr for me." Grey's strong, elongated erection dug into her bottom, intensifying her yearning as he played her nipples to an ache. "Purr for Heath, Toni."

She turned her head, ashamed that she would come with another flick of Heath's mouth. Her parted lips scraped across Grey's jaw, silently asking, begging for his participation with each sultry breath she poured on him. "Grey."

He was tense, just standing with her as she was tongue-fucked, and there was a moment when she could no longer contain her sounds of need. The little circles of her hips, craving Heath's mouth.

Grey's fingers pinched her breasts. She pushed her chest up to him, pitched her hips wantonly to Heath's face while she licked at Grey's, lust shooting through her. "Grey." Heath drew back and fondled the moist petals, and Toni panted against the stubble of Grey's jaw. "Grey."

He dragged his eyes from what he'd been hotly, darkly watching and seized her mouth, kissed her with passion and heart and emotion. He drowned her whimpers with his mouth, rubbing himself against her fevered body as Heath curved his hands around her ass and raised her to his mouth, probing lightly, expertly into her.

She detonated with a muffled cry; her climax racked through her, waves and waves of shudders seizing her like earthquakes.

When she thought her legs would buckle, Grey caught her, kissing her lips as he scooped her up and carried her to the bed. The aftershocks of her orgasm made her tremble as he set her down. He brushed her wet hair behind her shoulders, and his hand remained on her face, his eyes following his thumb as he ran it along her cheek. "I can barely stand the sight of you like this."

She smiled breathlessly up at him. "How is 'this'?"

He was sober, his face tight with heat. "Dewy-eyed, aroused, a little scared. It makes me want to hold you, and it makes me want to spread you open for me."

She smoothed a strand of hair back from his forehead, flooded with love for him. "Do both."

His skin glistened, light from the setting sun giving it a bronze hue as he bent over her and touched lightly between her legs. "I'll spread you open." He skated two fingers across the glossy pink mound between her legs. "I'll make you come for me." He nipped her shoulder, his cock brushing against her thigh. "I'll hold you all night if you let me."

He was saying all kinds of sweet things she'd never heard before, like wanting to hold her, and it made her a little emotional. Her lust raged, and the combination weakened her, had her nerves quivering.

Grey adjusted her to her side, aligning himself behind her as Heath plopped down on the bed, his eyes glimmering as he reached for her hand.

He raised it to his mouth and licked the center of her palm, swirling his tongue around. She'd never realized she had so many nerves there. At each moist swipe of that tongue, her pussy quivered, her breasts, her toes.

Once he was finished, he lowered her arm and forced her fingers around the long, veiny length of him. His pulse beat in her fist, his cock too long to completely hold even with both hands. He was as big as Grey. A trickle of bone-white liquid rose to the slit, gathering at the tip like a milky raindrop. Toni greedily licked her lips, scooting over to kneel between his thighs.

Heath's hand came to the back of her head, urging her down on him. She could barely decipher his dark, smoky words.

"All of it, kitten."

In answer, she lapped at that juicy cock, adjusting her back so Grey could move behind her and cup and touch her ass as he liked. She wanted his touch, needed it. When his hand stroked the curve of one supple cheek, she moaned appreciatively.

She dove for Heath's flesh, taking the entire stalk, until the tumescent head met the back of her throat. Grunting, he rolled his hips, watching her pleasure him, taking in the visual in with his eyes. The slide of her lips up and down the glistening column, her hand fastening around the base, her free hand sweeping out to stroke the heavy sac gathered so closely to his body.

Gray stole a hand between her ass cheeks, sliding two fingers up the wet cleft to find her throbbing clit and give it a circle. "Just seeing you with your mouth full has me dripping."

His words poured over her like lava, stirring up her blood, inflaming her senses.

Trembling, she parted her knees farther, opening up to him, his touch, his love. Grey nuzzled her cheeks as he fondled her, the scrape of his whiskers burning her skin. "So soaked, darling."

"Grey," she gasped.

"Oh, fuck, I want you."

He buried his mouth in her pussy from behind and lapped all the way up to her clit, then stabbed inside her waiting vagina. Pleasure shot through her. His mouth worked her, tongue lapping and sipping up her musky cream before he sunk two fingers right in. He swirled them inside her, seeking, caressing, pushing her to the edge.

Delirious with sensation, she rocked her body back and forth, her nostrils flaring wide as she hauled in air while Heath's immense penis crammed her mouth. She extended her tongue to lave every steely inch, inhumanly aware of every twitch of his cock, every flex in his taut abdomen.

A tiny spurt of cream dripped to her tongue, tasting of salt and milk, and she wanted more, wanted his cum gushing in her mouth, tumbling down her throat.

She heard his voice then, dense but carrying a note of helplessness. "Toni." It did things to her, the way he said her name.

She worked him faster as Grey continued toying with her pussy, twisting those two fingers inside. All the way in. Screwing them in.

Heath grabbed a fistful of hair. *"Toni."* He started pumping into her mouth with fast, erratic jabs. "Are you going to eat me, Toni?" he demanded. "Do you swallow, Toni?"

The mattress screeched as he stabbed her mouth again and again, his neck straining, his entire face twisted with pleasure. Oh, god. He was perfect. Reckless and powerful and out of control.

She reached between his splayed legs and grazed her thumbs across the hair-roughened sac of his balls. He flung his head back. "Fuck, that mouth does wonders, Toni."

The heavy rod slid in and out of her mouth. Grey grabbed her hips and fitted himself to her entrance as Heath grunted, groaned, thrashed on the bed. "Eat me up, Toni. *Eat me up*—" His desperate words turned to a gravelly groan as his cock jerked inside her, a spurt of warmed, spicy cream sluicing into her mouth.

He convulsed so powerfully, a tremble of her own jolted through her. Feverishly she drank the rich liquid, but it was so much that some of him trickled out the corner of her lips. Her own orgasm felt poised in her clit and she knew if she touched herself just lightly, she would burst. But instead her hands were on his thighs, feeling those contracted muscles loosen as he went lax.

And Grey roared and stabbed inside, long and fat and rabid for her, fucking right there where she was wet and open. She screamed. Her pussy rippled, clamping onto the scalding length that stroked her insides. The fronts of his thighs were flush against the backs of hers, his body draped over hers like a blanket of fire.

A sensory overload threatened to assail her. She began to tremble, sizzling shivers running all over her. The musk of Heath's feverish skin, his shaft—still fully erect against her chin and neck—most of all the animal vibrations rumbling up his throat as he watched.

Rapture gripped her as Grey stabbed her with a teeth-jarring thrust and hissed, "Touch your little pussy for me." She exploded. Grey clamped her waist in his hands as her walls contracted around him, milking all nine inches of that raging cock.

With an expletive, he rammed his hips to hers, deepening his thrust, and let out a fiery groan while his large, magnificent body trembled against hers.

Seconds after the lingering tremors receded, Toni cradled Heath's testicles in her palms, tracing the head of his cock with her tongue.

"You're still hard," she whispered, licking more of the driblets of cum that seeped through the slit. He seized the back of her head and gently pulled her up until her face was a whisper from his.

His eyes positively burned. The blunt side of his thumb swiped across her lips, gathering his moisture. He dipped it into her mouth, smeared her tongue with the flavor of him. She purred with hunger, and he rasped, "Fuck me, Toni Kearny. Fuck me until we can't breathe, until we pass out, until there's not a drop left in my body."

The words—dirty words spoken with fervid need and on such a

poetic note—brought a sluggish smile to her lips. "A poet, are you, Heath?" she teased.

He gathered her in his big arms and rolled on top of her, setting her down on the length of the bed. His face lax with desire, he reached down and trailed two fingers across her wet pussy. "I want to come here."

She trailed her fingers down his furrowed chest, so tempted to feel the little hairs there, caress the damp, glistening flesh underneath. "Yes."

He adjusted her under his body, fleetingly glanced past his shoulder. "This all right with you, Grey?"

A second passed. Then the sound of a foil slapping flesh. "Use a goddamned rubber."

Toni was well protected. She and Grey never used a condom, and it hadn't occurred to her how necessary one was. Because Heath fucked a lot, and he fucked everyone; he loved fucking. *God.*

Heath eased his weight off her and Toni scrambled up to help him, wanting to touch his penis again, feel it against her fingers. He surrendered the foil quietly, his gaze tracking her moves, watching her slide the thumbs of both hands as she sheathed him. He touched her cheek in a tender gesture that surprised her. "Thank you."

Swamped with an emotion she couldn't place, she cupped his jaw in her hands and tilted her head up to his, but before their lips could touch he sank his face into her neck, giving her throat a blistering, openmouthed kiss—unlike any the area had known before.

She linked her hands behind his neck and took him down with her. She fell back on the pillows, her thighs parting as he lowered himself above her, long and excited.

He drew back to watch her, shielding her view with his broad shoulders so that all she saw when their sexes touched was Heath and those glowing black eyes, the straining shoulders, that rugged face. His shaft slid back and forth against her swollen nub. She squirmed anxiously when he did not enter, and he smiled.

"I know you want me. Here"—he pressed his head to her—

"take this." He eased into the slick sheath, and simultaneously they moaned. The deep slide of him inside her awakened all her inner nerves. He sank in deeper. Heavier than Grey, making deep, rumbling sounds that were different and arousing.

The bulbous head of him stretched her slowly, the steel column advancing inch by inch inside her. She burned with it, burned for more. The tissue was swollen, sensitive, ravaged by Grey but still dripping in moisture for Heath. She moaned in her throat and locked her ankles at his back, arching.

Grey was at her ear, sounding so aroused he made her flesh pebble. "You look gorgeous when you're being fucked. The way your body moves. I could film you like this." Her heart fluttered at his words. She reached out to touch him and he snatched her hand and brought it up to his mouth, nipping at her wrist with his lips.

That this was pleasing Grey made her so wet, so fevered. *Watch me, Grey. Watch me come; watch me love it.*

But Grey wasn't content to just watch. He pulled her arms back, pinioned them behind her head for the invasion of Heath. He nibbled her fingers while Heath slowly, lazily fucked her. Her breasts, so exposed in this position, bounced a little, and Heath watched them with glee, eyes glimmering.

Heath flattened his palms on her stomach, pushed up the mounds with the heels of his palms. His callused hands felt dry as paper, and her senses reeled at the new sensation of him squeezing, groping, kneading.

She responded eagerly with sounds that told him just how delicious she found his touch, most of all his licks. He licked her everywhere, using only his tongue—no lips, no nibbling—just licking, leaving a moist path all over her skin. He circled his hips, withdrew, and stayed out long enough for her to mewl in protest.

He impaled her again, and she tensed, a sound leaving her lips. Tendons in his neck strained against his throat as he plunged to the depths of her and withdrew. Then her hands were on the firm flesh of his ass cheeks, gripping the rigid muscle, urging him to go on.

He stroked so deep this time, triggering a wave of ripples in her pussy. His head fell back, his face clenched with passion. "Christ."

She was there. So there. Lifting her hips up to him, dragging her nails up his back. "Come, Heath."

"Fuck, yeah." He surged up on his knees, slipped his arms under her and lifted her up in a taut, trembling arch until their upper bodies were flush. Grey's hands came to her ass, a finger idly stroking the rosette as Heath held her against him with one unyielding arm. Heath inserted the blunt tip of his thumb between their bodies, feathered it up and down her clit.

Then a tentative fingertip pressed into the untouched dent at her back. And Grey huskily asked her, "You like this?"

Before she could answer, that long finger intruded into the tight passage, creating a peculiar, sweet, jolting pain. He slipped and slid the finger in unison to Heath's huge cock, rocketing her pleasure to new heights. It undid her. Her orgasm wrenched through her, thrusting her into a tailspin of shudders, where all she could hold on to was Heath.

And he moved even slower, prolonging the earth-shattering tremors, sliding his hands up her back while she clung to his neck as he pumped. Then she felt him, just a bunched, controlled shudder, his arms flexing around her, his head burying in her hair with a muffled "*Fuck.*"

He jerked inside her, and her womb tightened around him. When his rocking stopped, they fell still. A blush crept over her.

He remained inside her. They were panting. The slick coat on their skin glued them together. Then his hands covered her cheeks, and he kissed her forehead almost reverently, as if in gratitude for receiving him.

She knew Grey was behind her, but she was embarrassed to turn around. She couldn't look at Heath, either. He was *still* inside her.

Face lowered, she pushed at his chest. He drew out reluctantly, helping her off the bed. Almost in a frenzy, she scanned the scattered clothing on the floor for her skirt.

Grey stood, and he was positively long and aroused. His voice was tinged with amusement.

"You're blushing, Toni."

She snatched her shirt up once she found it. "Am I?"

"Heath's blushing, too."

"Shut up, Grey," Heath snapped.

He was also getting dressed. He plunged his head into his shirt, his neck crimson red. He got dressed so fast, Toni realized how sex must be to him, how quickly he always left afterward.

She couldn't bear to look up at Grey and she did not know why. "I'm taking a shower," she murmured, pushing a tangle of hair back.

Grey caught her wrist as she made to go, his eyes glowing like lightbulbs. "I have a better idea."

Chapter Six

From the door of the vast, shelf-lined closet, Grey watched her slip on her zebra-print bikini, his eyes brimming with male appreciation. "I said skinny-dipping."

Whirling around to fully face him, she let the thin straps of her bikini bottom slap against her hip bones. "And I said, dream on, lover."

Leaning an elbow negligently against the doorjamb, with the barest smile threatening to appear, he said, "You skinny, we dip."

She adjusted the two small triangles of her top over her breasts and raised her arms to tie it behind her neck. "Nice! You should take my job. You can be quite creative when you set your mind to it. Did you know that, baby?"

"You make my mind race."

He stepped up and reached around her neck, his fingers grazing the little hairs at her nape as he tied one string, then slid sinuously down her back to knot the other.

She did not miss the fact that she made his mind race. Not his heart.

Trying not to dwell on it, she went up on tiptoe to kiss him, and his hands splayed on her back. "Zebras are carnivores' favorite prey," he murmured, and lightly caught her lower lip between his teeth.

"It's the coloring. They fairly scream to be eaten." She was ready to be devoured by a devastatingly gorgeous, golden-eyed carnivore when he slapped her fanny. "Let's get you fed."

They raided the kitchen, and found inside the fridge trays of sliced fruit, fresh salmon, and shrimp cocktails prepared by the artful hands of Señor Gonzalez. Carrying the food out to the pool area, they set it on a round table, and nibbled and sipped martinis and wine.

Skinny-dipping, Grey had said.

The men were an awful temptation as it was. Her gorgeous lover wore sexy 007 trunks—of the hunky new Bond type—that Toni had purchased for him last year at Neiman Marcus, and he looked ready for a campaign shoot for Hugo Boss. Heath wore electric blue trunks in a surfer style that reached his knees, and he looked ready to join the cast of *Lost.*

When they migrated to the sleek, upholstered chaise longues lined up along the left side of the infinity pool, Grey discreetly plucked the bow at the back of her bikini top and Toni ended up lying the better part of the afternoon topless, nipples pointing up, chilly and pebbled in the refreshing air.

Palm leaves stirred. In the distance, the waves crashed and rolled along the sand. A crescent moon made its way into the darkening sky.

Inside the pool, his arms on the ledge, Heath could not seem to tear his eyes off her. He'd done laps around the pool, his powerful arms slicing the water. Now his hair was slicked back behind his head and glistening rivulets slid down his tanned neck and shoulders.

Grey was sprawled on the lounge chair next to hers, those awesome, muscled, hair-dusted legs of his stretched to full length while he ate a fresh mango slice.

She thought she might doze off when she caught a movement around a corner of the house, past the neatly maintained grounds of the pool enclosure. She frowned. "Grey, I thought Señor Gonzalez had left for the day already." Three gazes followed the little man as he came around, carrying a large black plastic bag with dry palm fronds sticking out.

"How much do you pay that guy?" Heath asked.

Grey's lips curled. "Apparently not enough."

"The last time Grey and I were here, he fell off the ladder and dropped right into those bushes." Toni pointed, but Heath didn't drag his eyes away from her; instead he flashed her a smile. A fast, wicked, dazzling smile that might have made her knees buckle if she'd been unfortunate enough to be standing.

"I've told him to back off, but he won't listen." Grey settled back on his chaise and waved a hand at the house. "He likes looking after her. You forget that's his lady."

"A high-maintenance lady," Heath said with a grimace.

Grey ran a hand through his damp hair. "He's such a hard-working bastard. He spends days washing her. Then it rains, and he's at it again."

"I dig that," Heath said.

"So do I."

Toni thoughtfully tapped a finger to the corner of her lips, scrambling to remember the last time Grey had washed *her*. "See, I remember being someone's lady, but I don't remember being washed so diligently."

"I wash you diligently."

She wrinkled her nose. "Like, fifteen months ago? Hey, think we would fit in the tub, the three of us? You can *both* wash me diligently." The wanton words came out so unexpectedly, she was shocked. Aware of two pairs of eyes on her, she bit the inside of her cheek and glanced down the length of her legs at her bare toes.

"Heath's allergic to soap," Grey said.

Very vividly Toni remembered how clean he smelled, what his skin tasted like. A little of water and salt and maybe . . . grass. But how much did she really know about Heath Solis? "Do you read, Heath?"

"When I'm bored enough."

"What do you do during all those flights, all that time traveling?"

"I sleep."

"He hates to fly. Has to be drugged." Grey stretched his long legs farther out, his arms flexing as he crossed them over his chest. "What would a therapist say about that?"

"I don't know, Grey. Ask yours."

Grey chuckled, obviously the last man on earth who'd pay someone to make him *talk*. With a fading smile, Toni scrutinized Heath's rugged features while seriously wondering why he didn't have anyone. He was a little primitive, and the intense look in his eyes might seem frightening, but she had to admit that *she* found that riveting. Like discovering a mystery, a complicated puzzle, or submerging herself into an ocean where both danger and treasures lurked.

"Do you ever get homesick?" she asked.

He brought an arm up and swiped his forehead with a dripping forearm. "I don't have a home." She couldn't detect any hint of self-pity in his voice, but somehow his words were sad. "What I meant was," he amended, covering for his curtness, "I like moving around."

"But if you found someplace you loved more than others . . . would you stay put?"

"I won't."

He said it with such certainty, she bit back the only reply that came to mind, a strangely disgruntled, *Oh.*

"No high-maintenance lady for Heath," Grey said.

"Sir Richards, *teléfono!*"

Grey wearily scrubbed both hands over his face. "Oh, for god's sake."

Toni snatched one big hand down and peered into his eyes. "I thought you weren't working this weekend."

Grey bent to kiss her neck before he rose. "I'm not."

It had to be at least eight p.m. in Chicago. She thoroughly appreciated her friend's dedication, but if Louisa didn't rest, that meant Grey didn't, either, and he worked hard enough as it was. "What time does Louisa leave the office, anyway?" she asked, scowling.

"Apparently never," he called as he lunged up the three steps to the house.

"Grey has a new assistant," she turned to explain to Heath. "She's a friend of mine, actually."

"Do you have many friends?"

She couldn't tell if he was really interested or simply making idle conversation. Looking at the particularly impressive poker face he wore, she couldn't tell a thing—*she* ought to know about that, seeing as Grey had elevated it to an art form—so she kept her reply on the short side. "I have a few good friends. But I'd love to see them more than I do. You?"

He shrugged, like it didn't matter. "Just Grey."

She sat up straighter and folded one leg to tuck her toes under her opposite knee. Lights from the interior of the house threw a wide stream of light over the pool area, casting an interesting play of shadows on his face. If her gifts lay more in the creative arts, rather than the graphic, she'd have an urge to paint him. Draw the slanted lines of his eyebrows, capture the angle of his nose, the exact shade of shadow across that belligerent jaw. "Grey told me how you met," she said, wondering, *Why is Heath Solis alone in the world?*

His eyes fell to her breasts, her position fully exposing the globes to him, and something in her went liquid when his eyes began to glimmer.

"So his dad hates you?" she continued.

"Intensely." He wanted to suckle her. His jaw was working as his eyes took in her nipples. And she knew, *knew*, in every atom of her stirring body, he wanted to suckle her.

"It's mutual," he said at last.

"How old were you?"

"Sixteen."

"And what was a sixteen-year-old boy doing parking cars?"

"If you touch your breasts for me, I'll tell you."

His brazenness sent a river of heat pouring between her thighs. Even as she told herself she should make him work for it, even as she told herself to laugh it off and ignore him, she shifted her weight on one arm and obediently, coyly, found herself handling one perky breast. It swelled in her hand, grew heavy as she massaged with her fingers.

"All right," she said huskily, "now tell me."

True to his word, he said, "I did all kinds of stuff before Grey and I started working together." His ravenous stare turned her muscles to mush. "That was my first time parking cars, and wouldn't you know it? In roars Lucien Grey Richards in his shiny red Ferrari." He chuckled softly, his hair slapping against his temples as he shook his head. "He was lecturing this quiet young man who rode shotgun. . . ."

"Grey," she breathed, making love to the word, to her breast.

"Yeah. He had on that stony face of his. He was quiet . . . you know, *pissed*. His old man got out of the car and slapped the keys to my palm, saying something like, 'If I see a single scratch, you'll be working the rest of your life to pay for it, son, so I suggest you take good care.' "

She sat up, engrossed, and Heath narrowed his eyes when her hands fell to her sides. He paused for only a moment. "I stared down at those keys," he continued, "thinking how very much I'd like to test that threat, and then Grey came over and whispered so the old man wouldn't hear. I swear he was reading my mind. He said, 'Don't be shy. Take her for a ride.' Then he smiled that cold smile of his. 'Make her squeal.' He was so pissed and so cool about it, he gave me a laugh. So I thought, *I kind of like this guy*. And I took her for a ride, made her squeal." He grinned at her. "And made his father squeal, too."

Toni laughed, enjoying hearing the story again. "You two are so bad."

"You're beautiful when you smile."

She jerked in her seat, taken aback by his compliment.

"Don't," he whispered.

"Don't . . . what?"

"Don't stop. Touch your breast for me."

For a moment, she considered lying on the chaise, stroking herself to orgasm for Heath as she did for Grey, but rather than act on the tantalizing thought, she just gazed at him, her hand unmoving on her breast. He was blunt. He was rough. He wasn't supposed to affect her this way.

"Tell me how you and Grey met," he said. Almost every word he spoke seemed to crackle with authority. But then he smiled, and those smiles softened everything. Her legs, her insides . . .

She smiled warmly as her memories surfaced, dropping her hand to her lap. "I wanted to sell him a new image. A kick-ass design and a sharp new logo for RS. He actually came looking for me—can you believe it? He saw a logo and business card I did for a client."

Heath was quietly attentive, so she settled back comfortably and continued. "So I met with him in his office. And when I saw him . . ." She remembered the jolt she felt, being the sole focus of those sharp amber eyes. She remembered thinking, *Wow. What a man, what a presence, what a god.* "When I saw him," she said, her voice cottony, "I'd never wanted anything so much in my life."

And I still can't really believe he could be mine, she thought privately, and then waved a hand to disperse the thought.

"We were having dinner to continue discussing my ideas. I wanted to land RS so badly. Imagine what it would do for my reputation, to create an image for a company like that. But we didn't even get to dinner." She remembered Grey on her doorstep, remembered rushing back inside to get her briefcase, and she remembered Grey's hands on her his hot, sweet scented mouth against her skin, whispering, *What I want is right here.*

And what she wanted was there. In his eyes, in all of him, in the entire intimidating male package of Grey Richards.

"Love at first sight?"

Yes. It was love. Wild, complete, beautiful, vulnerable love.

She thought her voice sounded bizarre, airless, full of longing. "It's impossible not to love him. He's . . ." There were no words in the dictionary to describe him. "He's Grey."

And I desperately want him to love me.

She shrugged with a little smile to hide her insecurities, then held her breath, noting Heath was staring down at his hands. She had the distinct impression she'd made him uncomfortable.

"Are they wrinkled?" she teased as she rose to her feet, drawn to him by some unearthly pull she couldn't resist. "You've been in there for quite a while."

"They're soft," he said, rubbing them together, his damp, sooty lashes lifting up to reveal his eyes. The chilly air caused gooseflesh to rise along her skin as she walked to the edge of the pool.

The water glistened, its color the dark, rich blue of sapphires. As she walked down the steps, the shock of the cooling water on her skin made her suck in her breath. Dragging in more air, she impulsively plunged beneath the surface to get her body accustomed, then surged up and slicked her hair back, gasping. Heath had turned around to prop his elbows on the ledge and watch her. She smiled at him. Maybe because she was so susceptible to his charm, it was impossible for her smiles to affect him as deeply as his affected her. But still, she let it play on her lips and admitted, "I was getting lonely."

And somehow, suddenly, he looked very big and very lonely, too, standing there in the same pool but too far away to touch. And she thought perhaps she and Grey should set him up with someone, one of her single friends. Maybe Heath would like Louisa or Francine . . . and maybe *they* would like Heath. Toni certainly liked him, and this way he wouldn't be entirely alone in the world, and someone would get to enjoy him. . . .

For an electrifying moment, they stared, and all her matchmaking thoughts fled under the sheer flaming intimacy in his eyes.

The water sloshed against her, a sensual caress against her breasts, and she said the first thing that came to mind. "I'm cold."

He waded toward her, his muscled torso cutting the water around him. "I'll keep you warm."

Before their bodies met, his hands grasped her shoulders and drew her up along his body. Her nipples ended up flattened against his chest. Her pelvis flared up like a match when he thrust his erection against her in a bold move that unequivocally said, *Feel how hard I am for you.*

Lust radiated off him, scorching her skin, searing her nerves. Her upturned face was inches from his neck, and she impulsively inhaled his scent, the pungent and savory aroma of earth. Then she realized he was staring down at her in silence, inspecting her features one by one. His eyes traveled across her forehead, her eyebrows, her nose, her chin, back up to her eyes. The look in those black pools of wanting was gentle and admiring.

"Did you enjoy coming with my arms around you?"

Enthralled, she watched his lips move as he spoke; the pink tissue had such a provocative plumpness, she craved to feel them on hers. She wished on *any* of one of those blinking stars above, *Kiss me . . .*

"I enjoyed it very much. . . ," she admitted, a cozy whisper. "I was wondering when you were going to do that again."

Kiss me . . .

"Now." He buried his head at her throat the next second, and she purred feebly as those plump, wet lips dragged against her neck tendons.

"Daddy Gonzalez thought we might like some towels."

Startled and assailed with guilt over her lust, she arched her neck at the sound of Grey's voice and lifted an arm up high, her flesh going lax with his presence. "Grey, I need you."

He helped her out of the water and swathed her in a plush dry towel, planting a kiss on her forehead. "I need you, too."

She tipped her head up to Grey's as Heath surged out of the pool behind her. "Share the great office emergency?"

"Give me a kiss and we'll see."

Smiling at the somber look on his face, she fitted her lips to his, loving the warmth and strength of his arms as he enfolded them around her and scooped her up. "Come on, Miss Kearny, up we go."

"What happened? Did the building burn to ashes? Did someone quit, die, break a nail?"

He gave a put-out sigh as he carried her around. "It's foolish. She just wanted to assure me her job was done for the day. Baby, I don't think she's lasting that long."

"Patience, Grey." She palmed his jaw. "It *is* a virtue."

"Not mine, sweetheart."

As he lowered her on the chaise, she extricated her arms from the towel and lay back so he could dry her off. "Let's get you dry, hmm? I won't have my woman saying I don't take care of her. And I *do* wash you diligently."

She laughed, and her womb brimmed with liquid fire as his familiar scent swamped her. He was bent over, his hair darker in its dampened state, streaked with lighter golds and falling across his forehead as he dried her off in brisk, efficient moves she suspected he didn't mean to be sexual. But to her they were. Her heart was in love with Grey. Her body was in love with his body. She could not help the strengthening of her heartbeat, the lust pouring into her blood.

Heath was toweling off his hair a few steps away and paused when she took one of Grey's large, capable hands and pressed it between her legs.

"I'm wet here, too," she confessed.

Grey's eyes flicked up to hers. Something passed there, something that sizzled. He swiped her wet hair behind her forehead with his free hand, his voice deepening. "Right. Wet."

He hooked his thumbs under the strings around her hips. "Let's get this wet thing off you and we'll see." He peeled off her bikini bottom, and she gasped at her buttocks hitting the raspy, rainproof chaise fabric. He tested her pussy lips with his two longest fingers, his pupils dark and dilated, simmering with heat. "Is this what you wanted me to find, Antonia?"

The flesh distended as he inserted one finger, then swelled more for two. He plugged them deep into the heart of her. Her toes dug into the chaise while her hips rose, a shriek of ecstasy leaving her lips.

Heath dropped his towel and took a step forward. Over his shoulder, Grey said, "Want to take a look at this, Heath?"

She fell still as he approached. Her mouth dried up at the sight he presented with his erection straining his royal blue trunks to a tent. Staring brazenly at her tits, he crooked his shoulders and seized her inner thigh. She could feel the calluses in his palm as his dampened hand slid slowly upward.

Watching his intense expression, she licked her lips, tingling with the knowledge that Grey watched what Heath was doing to her with a matching intensity.

Heath's thumb touched one distended lip first, then pulled it aside so he could gingerly stroke inside. Against her right hip, the ridge and form of Grey's penis stabbed into her flesh. Huskily, he whispered something about licking her dry and ducked his head. His tongue laved one tightly pebbled nipple.

By the time Heath stuck a long, expert finger inside her, she reared up in need. "Yes," she said, her voice hoarse.

He slid over the crest of her clit, coating his thumb with her cream until it glistened, and with their gazes locked, he raised it to his tongue.

"She's soaked, Grey."

She trembled as Heath lapped hungrily at his finger, his tongue flat and long, triggering memories of having it in her pussy.

Her nipple vibrated when Grey spoke against it. "I know she's soaked." He kept her anchored against him as he rose, her toes touching the ground. "Cold, Toni?" he whispered.

She buried her lips in his neck, where she smiled in mischief. "Guess again."

"Just say when, and we're all over you."

"When when *when!*"

⌣

Damp swim trunks hit the ground with a splat. Then the three of them stumbled up the steps, through the terrace sliding doors, and into the lamp-lit bedroom, all while Grey was groping and squeezing and tasting any body part within reach. Delicious, all of her.

"You there, Heath?"

"I'm closing this damned thing," Heath answered as he tried to find the catch on the rolling glass door.

"Don't break it."

Toni's feet had barely touched the rug when Grey hauled her body up against his. His lips hung over hers for a breathless second. "Now say 'cock,' baby."

She had moist skin, moist hair, a moist mouth. "Cock," she breathed.

He pushed his hard-on authoritatively against her pelvis and flattened his tongue to trace the line of her collarbone. "You'll get cock. You'll get cock everywhere. You'll get it in your mouth, in your pussy; you'll get it down your throat."

As he backed her toward the bed, an arm loosely around her waist, she curled her fingers around his shaft and tugged him on like a dog on a leash.

"I want you inside me," she murmured against his neck.

His hand fisted at the small of her back. "Count to ten, and before you get to three, I'm there."

Her features were dewy with arousal, and no matter how light her hold on his cock and slow their progress, Grey would follow her to the bed with a crook of a finger.

He covered her with his eyes. He could trace the bikini she'd worn with his hands, but instead he traced it with his eyes. The start of a tan spread across her abdomen, her legs, her neck, her slender arms. The little globes of her breasts were burnished bronze like the rest of her torso, the nipples dusky and small.

New tan lines ran less than an inch above the two small rises of her hip bones, dipping to a delicate V between her legs. Between those toned, slim thighs, her pussy was the prettiest, pinkest, most beautiful thing Grey had ever seen. Her clit was tucked between two rosy, tender lips. He knew the inside by memory. He knew the folds they hid were the same shimmering pink of her tongue. He knew how those petals spread, how they moistened for his fingers, for any part of him that touched her. He knew her grip, her every ripple, how warmly she encased him.

"Get on the bed."

Squealing at the predatory look in his eyes, she spun around when the back of her knees hit the mattress. She climbed on the bed and made to cross when he caught an ankle in his grip and yanked her back to the edge. "I'm sorry, but you're not going anywhere."

Her surprised shriek turned to laughter as she struggled up to a sitting position and pointed a chiding finger at him. "Where's my lover? What did you do to him?"

"He's insane." He caught her waist in his hands, turned her over, and pressed her flat on her stomach. "You drove him wild."

She squirmed halfheartedly as he draped his body over hers, ass jiggling against his groin. "Wait! Wait!" she said. "You have to want it bad."

"I want it very bad."

She stilled her squirms, canted her head. "A-all right, then you have to make *me* want it bad."

"You said 'when' three times and you were ready to come; I'd say that's enough foreplay for you, don't you think, Miss Kearny?"

She twisted and pushed at his shoulders so he'd give her space to turn around. "I was only checking to see if you were paying attention."

He quirked a sleek blond eyebrow, then pointed at his ear. "Forgive me if I don't hear you—some wench was screaming in my ear just moments ago."

"And what, exactly, do you do to feisty wenches, may I ask?" Her cool hands settled on his shoulders. Behind the light of mirth in her eyes, a fire burned for him, weighting her eyelids.

His smiled faded, and his timbre dropped to a purr. "Let me show you."

He caught her elbows and heaved her up to her knees on the bed, facing him, her playfulness gone. She was at her most vulnerable. She was wanting, waiting for him to give it to her, and her eyes pleaded for it. He felt just as helpless, just as open. "Do you make them scream some more in your ear, Grey Richards?"

"Yes."

They were breathing heavily, both their chests rising fast. "And what is it, exactly, that you make them scream?"

His thumb and index finger slid up the side of her neck to caress the back of her ear. "They scream *Grey*, baby."

"And what if I don't—"

He spread his fingers across the back of her head, pulled her forward, and took her lips. He plunged into her, and she gave out a famished, fevered exclamation. . . .

And shivered when Heath came around to nip at her shoulder, his murmur against her skin barely discernable to Grey. "You're beautiful."

Toni disentwined from both of them and spun around to settle on all fours. When she glanced at Grey over her shoulder, her eyes were luminous. Heath moved to the foot of the bed and curled his hand around his lengthened cock, nudging her lips with the ruddy head. "Kiss me."

She opened her mouth, and Heath pressed in. Grey exhaled slowly. His body was ready, his senses soaring, preparing to mate. So he couldn't explain why, when a hungry sound welled in the back of her throat as she took Heathcliff, he felt robbed of it.

He could not isolate the despair he felt as he moved on his knees behind her. He had done this dozens, *dozens* of times. Taken the woman, pleasured the woman, had her writhing. But the fact that from behind he could not see her face—get lost in the forest green of her irises—distressed him. The laughter in her eyes, the lust that had enlarged her pupils moments ago, that had been his. *His.* Not Solis's. He'd done ménages with strangers; he should well be able to do this for Toni.

So he concentrated on the lines of Toni's back, on the tattoo the damp tendrils of hair around her shoulders created. And he thought, *Take me inside your skin, Antonia, and let me feel what you feel.*

His throat ran dry as he stroked the lush mounds of her ass and spread her open for a look. His gaze caressed the rosette above her juicy lips, a place he fantasized about possessing, a place he wished that wouldn't hurt her during the conquering.

He kept those cheeks apart and slid his cock in between them, caressing his length with their fullness. He was so fat, his balls drawn high against him, gathered tight.

This was good, not seeing her face, because she couldn't see his. He couldn't seem to control the slightly twisted, painful grimace on it, a grimace caused by the cramp in his chest, the burn spreading from his groin, the confounding, masochistic, torturous pleasure of watching her eat someone else. He wanted to stop it. He wanted to roar. He wanted to watch her love it and be able to love it in return.

Forcing himself to focus on the physical, he circled the outer rim of her lush ass with the pad of his thumb. She shimmied her hips, inviting his touch, and her scream was muffled by Heath's cock when Grey inserted his finger into the opening.

Her rocking motions, the slick coat of sweat on her body, her rosette clutching his thumb. Grey was dripping. His shaft jutted out of him, seeking her.

His hands skated around her waist to engulf her breasts, full and round and heavy, the nipples balled up tight and ready for his palms. He tweaked them between two fingers, felt them bead to hard little pearls.

She lowered herself to her elbows, the line of her back angled downward so that her delectable rear was in the air for Grey. Her widespread knees caused dents in the comforter.

Her head bobbed shakily up and down as she worked Heath's erection, which glistened as it slipped in and out of her mouth. The man was smiling down at her, his eyes sparkling with lust. "I love your little tongue on me," he said hoarsely, and his hand was motionless on the back of her head as he swiveled his hips to enjoy that tongue.

She trembled when Grey grabbed himself and caressed her body with the tip of his penis. Up the back of her thighs, around her pretty cheeks, lightly across the small of her back. He envisioned coating her with his seed, smearing it across her skin, flavoring her with him. He envisioned Heath with blood pouring down his nose, predicted the exact sound his knuckles would make crashing into the man's jawbone. He envisioned those other thousand times he'd taken Toni, when every cry and moan and murmur had been just his.

Pushing the thoughts aside, he hunched down and began to masturbate her pussy, doing things to her clit that she liked. Pinch it a bit. Push it. Tweak and pull. Circle. Her scent permeated his lungs, invigorating as an aphrodisiac. He went into her slit with one finger and closed his eyes at what he found, her moistness trickling down his fingers. The tight clench of her pussy made his erection jerk against his abdomen. Then she whimpered, taking in two fingers, so damned wet and swollen he was sure she could take three.

"Like that?" he said, stabbing those two fingers deep enough to tear a sob from her. "Like cock?"

She humped his fingers as he screwed them in with leisurely but powerful strokes, her head held up high for Heath. Past her shoulders and her moving head, he could see as she bit at Heath's balls, heard Heath curse as he grabbed his dick and stuck it into her mouth again, "Goddamn, you're gorgeous like this. I feel your teeth behind your lips. I'm in love with that little tongue."

Love . . . love . . .

It was Grey who should say this to her; it was *his* mind that screamed the thoughts of love, and *his* body that hurt containing it. . . .

Inwardly cursing, he lowered his head between her parted legs, pushed in a third finger with effort and sucked her wet nub into his mouth. She screamed, bucked, convulsed as she came with powerful contractions. He stoked her orgasm with his fingers and mouth, her tangy taste making him growl.

He came up panting. "Do it again for me." He nudged her with his cock, one hand on the flat of her back, keeping her still for his entry as she continued to convulse.

He parted her with the head, stroked his cock along her inner walls, still wet from her orgasm—and from the way she whimpered at each in stroke, maybe a little too sensitive. "Make us come," he rasped.

He watched himself slide into her, feasting on the sight of her turgid lips wrapped snugly around his width. Her pussy walls contracted around him and he screwed in deeper with a groan. When he'd been swallowed down to the root, her body clenching him, she took Heath's cock just as far inside her mouth, almost choking.

"Easy," Grey rasped. He dropped his hand on one plump bottom cheek and gave it a hard squeeze as he fucked her more deeply. She was so tight, her muscles malleable in his hands. He dragged his cock out, then used his grip to haul her closer to him and stabbed in deeper, loving the slapping sound of their bodies.

His every forceful push was met with the slap of their flesh, with her hips thrusting back, with a whimper. His prized control vanished when her teeth sank into Heath's cock and the man roared and began to pump.

Grey gripped her waist for leverage and pistoned into her rip-

pling grip with unbridled, almost clumsy jabs, demanding, "Let go.
Let go now."

She was delirious, meeting Heath's ramming stabs with an upward move of her mouth and making all kinds of noises that flew
straight to Grey's head. Her words were muffled but still discernable. *"Grey."*

He stopped plunging, closed his eyes, and let that single word
pour through him, and she began to come. Her pussy closed around
his cock, sucking him in, jerking at his cock. He resumed his rhythm
by pushing into her with several rough grunting sounds, his body
contracting as her vagina walls squeezed around all nine inches of
rigid male flesh.

"Fuck, *yes*," he growled as he held her body in place and gave
her a series of wild, desperate final thrusts that triggered his release.
He poured himself into her, one, two, three shots of semen blasting
into her so hard he hoped they'd reached her throat and heart.

And Heath came with a mute roar, his neck straining. He trembled, his eyes rolling upward as he gripped Toni's head and continued to rub into her mouth, whispering, "Shit, baby . . . oh, shit . . ."

When the three of them collapsed on the bed, their labored
breaths were the only sounds in the still room. Then Heath began
to chuckle, shaking his head. "What do you do when your back
aches after a wild session like this one?"

"Pray?" Toni ventured.

Grey's lips twitched as he disappeared into the luxurious marble
bathroom, washed his hands, cleaned up. He returned to tenderly
wipe Toni's red bee-stung lips with a tissue, then guided it between
her legs, the flesh coated with him.

She propped herself up on her elbows, raised a hand, and slid
her fingers up his stubbled jaw as he dabbed the moisture between
her thighs. "Grey?" She sounded uncertain.

Halting the hand massaging his jaw, he turned it around to press
his lips to the tender blue vein running up the inside of her wrist.
He couldn't seem to meet her probing green eyes.

Grey stalked back to the restroom to dispose of the tissue, and on his return, he narrowed his eyes. Heath was spooning her— on *his* bed—bending over to whisper something to her ear. Grey couldn't remember if Heath usually did that with his women, but then he realized it wouldn't have mattered. The sight had his gut twisting. Her hands were tucked under her cheeks as she lay on her side. Her lashes rested, crescent-shaped and long, against her cheekbones. A half smile stretched her lips, and Grey gave them a perfunctory kiss. "You all right?"

She burrowed her cheek into the back of her hand. "Fabulous," she purred, then slid that hand out to sift her fingers through his hair. "You?"

Without answering, he met Heath's prying gaze as he tucked Toni under the covers. "We'd better catch some sleep." And with an edge he couldn't quite suppress, "See you in the morning, Heath?"

"Yeah." Heath snatched up his clothes, ignoring the tone, smiling in amusement at it, in fact. "Watch for the monster under the bed, Grey."

"Just get out of here."

When the door closed with a faint click behind him, a tense silence fell. Toni studied him with tight white lips and daggers in her eyes as he climbed into bed and pulled the covers up to his waist.

"You didn't have to treat him like a male prostitute, Grey."

He wasn't expecting anger. For a moment, he glanced disinterestedly at the blank plasma TV screen across the bed, coldly silent. Finally he reached for his cell on the nightstand, clicked it off, and calmly explained as he set it down, "We have a deal. Heath understands that."

"You don't have to be so heartless. You might have tried not using that dismissive tone, but I guess that's impossible for you, isn't it?"

He could take the entire world calling him an android and more, but from Toni . . .

He felt his face go wooden, a pressure gathering at his temples.

Holding a teeth-breaking clamp of his jaw, he waited for her to come to him, create that little nest for herself in his arms like *always*. When she didn't, he said in a flat voice, "What do you want Heath here for? We're going to sleep."

"I'm not saying he should sleep here, only that—"

"I'm heartless," he finished for her.

He reached over and flicked off the lamp, a move that said firmly, *I'm not having this conversation.*

At that, she rolled to her side and pulled at the sheets, and when they didn't give, she wrenched harder. "Give me the sheet, you insufferable—"

"Jesus!" He let go.

She gathered it around her with a rustle and punched her pillow. Punched it again. After the third punch, she cried out in misery, "Poor guy!"

"Poor guy? Heath?" Disbelief warred with annoyance, and he rubbed his nose between his thumbs and sighed. "Toni, Heath is anything but a poor guy, and he doesn't need you to defend him."

"He's too nice to say anything."

"Nice. That's the first time I've heard *Heath* and *nice* in the same sentence. You should see him when he's pissed—that'll rid you of the fantasy. I've seen him beat a guy to a pulp. Maybe you should, too."

"Do you think that's funny? Maybe the guy's family thinks it's funny, too!"

"Do you hear me laughing?"

She gave a haughty sniff. The mattress squeaked as she squirmed farther away. "Good night, Grey."

Grey dropped back on his pillow. Heath was a tough bastard, but Toni was a woman. No doubt she thought Heath shared her sensibilities. How come she didn't care for Grey's?

Ahh, because he was Superman, He-Man, *Ice Man*. A freaking Achilles without the heel, and every bit what he'd been made out to be.

His eyes took a moment to adjust to the darkness. Moonlight spilled through the open drapes, silhouetting her body. On the other side of the bed.

He loosened his clenched jaw, turned over on his stomach, buried his face in the pillow, and closed his eyes. Restless movement continued on her side of the bed. His side was tomblike.

"Dammit, I don't want to fight with you!" she exploded.

He took a moment to reply, without a hint of emotion and very little interest, "What is it that you want now, Toni?"

She seemed to debate whether to speak, and when she finally did, it was with a tinge of anger. "Why did you fuck me like that?"

"Like *what*?"

"Like that. You weren't making love to me, you were . . . you were just fucking."

"And what was Heath doing?"

She stiffened. Then her voice gained a worn, bitter quality. "But I'm not in love with Heath, now, am I? I don't remember going around smelling his shirts like some idiot and thinking of ways to make him smile and buying lingerie I pray he'll like on me."

Glowering, he turned his head to her, steeling himself against the accusation in her green eyes.

It was *impossible* for him to just fuck her. It was impossible *not* to make love to her. Didn't she know that?

She drew in a long breath when their gazes clashed. "Do you want to stop this, Grey? I don't think I want to do this any—"

"*No*," he snapped. "I have a board of directors who won't so much as speak until I do, and two thousand employees whose families depend on me. I have never in my life said I'd do something and not done it. I can make money out of air and I can crush my adversaries in a single fist, and with all certainty, I assure you, I can do *this*!" And he could, goddammit—what was wrong with him?

"Don't ever fuck me like that again. I mean it."

He groaned and scraped his hands down his face. "What else

did you think we were going to do this weekend but fuck?" he gritted.

"I don't want just sex from you!"

Grey squeezed his eyes shut, hanging on to his temper by a thread, wanting to shout, *And I don't want* just sex *from you, either!*

"I don't want to be one of your gazillion . . . threesome . . . conquests."

One. Two. Three.

"Some meaningless chick you and your partner screwed!"

Four. Five. Six.

"You, putting all your moves on me. You didn't even call me Toni. I could have been anyone."

Seven. Eight. Nine.

"Sometimes I swear to god my vibrator has more emotion than you!"

Fuck!

"Grey . . ."

At the end of his rope, he was about to bark *"What!"* when she added, in a tiny, quivery voice, "Why aren't you holding me?"

A prickle of unease slithered down his spine, and he snapped his head up. He'd been deaf to the hurt in her voice, but suddenly it was all he was aware of. She was close to tears.

He'd seen her cry once, the time he took her to watch *The Pursuit of Happyness.* At those first few tiny, delicate sniffles, he'd frozen in his seat. No one had ever cried in front of Grey before. He didn't inspire tears in people. But when he'd squeezed the delicate hand laced through his on the armrest, she'd flung herself into his arms and those sniffles had become sobs. It was crushing to listen to them, and they'd made his own throat close, too.

He rolled onto his back. "Get over here," he muttered, dragging in a breath, "and I'll hold you."

"Not if you don't want to."

"Get the *fuck* over here. Now!"

When she hesitated, he cursed under his breath and immediately reached out. Grasping her waist, he tugged her over the sheet to him, his voice hoarsening. "Get in here. I need you here. In my arms."

She turned over as their hips touched. "I don't want to fight with you." Her voice shook even worse than before. "And I don't like you just having impersonal sex with me. Are you angry over something?"

"The last thing I want to do," he said in an odd, gruff voice, "is fight with you, Toni." Gazing down at her glistening green eyes while a wealth of love washed over him, he let two fingertips trace her face in the shadows. "I'm not angry at you. I just wanted to be with you for a while. Just us. I promise I'll play nicer with Heath tomorrow if it makes you feel better, hmm?"

"It does . . . ," she admitted, stroking his throat, "make me feel better." Her teeth caught her lower lip, and her voice again went strange on him. "I couldn't see you. . . . And your hands felt so different, like you were touching just anyone. . . . And you didn't say anything to me even when I was trying to look so sexy for you. . . . I wanted to hear your voice . . . but you were mostly quiet, and I felt so . . ."

She inhaled a tremulous breath, and he realized that while he'd been quietly pleading for a lifeline from her, begging to crawl into her skin and feel close to her, she had wanted to be inside *him*.

He swallowed through a dry, sandpapery throat and closed his arms around her. "Come here, come closer. I need you. I need this."

This was the kisses they placed on each other's faces. *This* was the whispered words, the breaths they took in unison. *This* was their sweat-coated bodies tangling together, growing warm where they touched. She seemed so small when he gathered her like this, his entire body swallowing hers up.

"Heath just seems so lonely," she admitted, her fingers fluttering across his shoulders. "I feel a little sorry for him."

He inhaled the aroma of sex and peaches at her neck, in her

hair, dragging her essence into his lungs. "He's alone because he likes it," he whispered against her throat. "I swear you're the first person I know who's sorry for Heath."

"We should set him up with someone, Grey."

He suppressed the urge to laugh. "And who would you suggest, that wacky cousin of yours?"

"I don't know. My friends are pretty."

"Heath hates dates."

"Well, he shouldn't!" she chastised. Then, running lazy figure eights on the back of his arm, "Nobody should be that alone, Grey."

He kissed her, let his lips enjoy hers; no tongue now, just their lips molding and absorbing the feel of the other. "I agree." He plowed into her mouth, and her sweet, hot cavern was a welcoming heaven to his tongue.

Her thigh slipped in between his as their tongues curled. Her hands linked behind his head, and her breath seeped into him, "Grey."

"Darling." He covered a whimper with his mouth when he deepened the kiss, and his lungs closed. He wanted her again. To make her his, just his, remind her she was *his*. He couldn't imagine being without her—without the mischief she got into sometimes, the smiles, the laughter, the love she gave him.

He wanted to give her the stars. He wanted to fight with her and have hot makeup sex with her. He wanted to shower her with gifts and love and devotion. He wanted to marry her.

The desire had been strengthening, gathering courage. Conviction. They'd laughed about marriage together, criticized the institution, had gone on and on about not needing it. It had all been Grey, trying to convince himself he didn't need her, love her, want her more than anything or anyone.

Now nothing would give him more joy than making her his wife. Slipping his ring on her. Vowing the world to her. Waking up every morning to the irrefutable fact that she belonged to him . . . and he to her.

After Cabo . . .

"Thank you for this weekend," she whispered, stretching under him and raising her arms behind her head in languor.

He palmed the sides of her thrusting breasts and pushed them together to run his tongue down the cleavage they created. "Hmm. You're welcome." The mounds brushed his cheeks, and his thumbs slid up to her nipples. They were soft at first touch, but responded after a second pass.

He heard her yawn, say something in a murmur. He lifted his head, giving a nibble on her chin as he came up. "Sleepy?"

"Deliciously, utterly sleepy, but please don't stop. You're heavenly."

He chuckled and fell on his back, dragging her against him, where she snuggled her womanly curves against his side. She brushed a kiss across his cheek. "I love you."

She didn't seem to expect a reply any longer. She was already settled, a cheek to his chest, her breasts rising and dipping evenly against his ribs.

He skimmed his mouth across her forehead, his arms unrelenting around her.

"Don't ever stop," he hoarsely whispered.

"Hmm? Stop what?"

Loving me. "Telling me."

She laughed softly. "I won't."

"I like hearing it."

She surprised him, kissing his chest right above his nipple—the place nearest to where she rested her head—and whispered, "I know you do."

Chapter Seven

Heath was moving around the guest bedroom the next morning, searching his duffel for a fresh T-shirt, when he spotted her out on the long, sprawling terrace. Straightening, he moved closer to the sunlit window, taking in that delectable rear as she leaned on the stone ledge. Her chestnut hair flew in tangles behind her as she took in the ocean view. The sun brought out the shades of red and a hint of gold in her hair, and he wanted to run a hand through it and inspect it up close.

Her profile was exquisite; her nose tipped up at the end, and her lips pouted beguilingly. Without makeup, her skin had a fresh peachy hue that appealed to him. Her small, curvy body appealed to him. Crap, *everything* of hers appealed to him.

Her dress today was emerald green and shaped like a tube. Heath was liking that tube. Seemed easy enough to pull down, or up, to reveal what Heath most wanted to see.

After a moment he realized she was mumbling, shaking her head, creasing that cute face into a frown. When he realized she was cursing Grey, Heath chuckled. God, he wanted to fuck her.

His jeans felt tight and his dick kept expanding. He was so primed for her, so *full* of hot, needy cum for her. And he knew she ate it—oh yes, she liked eating him up. And he'd heard her and

Grey last night. . . . Had it been around three a.m.? Maybe four a.m.
He wasn't sure, but he heard the cry she gave. He'd bucked up in
bed from that sound alone.

She rounded with a stomp of a pink-toed foot and her head
jerked back when she spotted him. She absorbed his gaze for a sizzling second, her chest rising and falling in hungry little pants. *Are
you thinking of me fucking you, kitten? Do you want my hands on you,
my hard dick inside you?*

He crooked his finger at her, watched her lips part in surprise,
and then he reached out to slide open the door. He almost groaned
when she pulled her eyes away and stormed back inside. He was
just not used to this pain. A boner was something to be taken care
of fast, and this one wouldn't cease. He'd had it for days. Weeks.
His need was so great that all he could think of was spreading her
legs again. He had been thinking of her hair last night, her shoulders; now it was just what lay between her legs that overwhelmed
his mind, promising him ease. When would he get there, *be* there
again? Damn.

He knew Grey was somewhere in the house, even if he hadn't
understood what the fuck the Mexican guy had said this morning about Sir Richards. Apparently, Grey was royalty around these
parts. But Heath wasn't caging himself in this big white room. He
enjoyed being alone, but not when he knew Toni was somewhere
in the halls and rooms of this immense house.

He came down the hall and found her cuddled on a couch, a
magazine open on her lap. Her emotions flickered across her face
when she spotted him; she was shocked, delighted, wary.

The living room was—surprise, surprise—white like everything
in the house. Grey knew how to spend his money, though; with its
solid dark woods and light fabrics, windows that spread from top to
bottom and side to side, this room and the woman sitting motionless at its center made Heath think of paradise. Eve and the apple.
His eternal doom. All that shit.

The low couch she sat on, with its stunning beach backdrop,

was wide enough to sleep two people comfortably, and accented with plump pillows in a green that was almost as striking as the eyes that were now watching him. That couch had been specially made for a man to fuck on it.

His shoes made no sound when they hit the carpet. "Aren't you going to say good morning, Toni?" he asked.

She seemed ready to bolt. "Hi, Heath."

His eyebrows flew up. This was not the merry welcome in the morning he'd fantasized about. "You don't sound so enthusiastic. Am I not wanted here anymore?"

Leave. His specialty. School, foster parents, friends. Before anyone could even ask him to, he left. He had never been wanted, and he'd never cared. But today he cared. Today he cared to be wanted. He remembered being inside her body, sucking those breasts, all of his cock massaged by those tight, wrenching ripples in her pussy. By her tongue, her lips, her mouth.

But maybe she wanted him to leave. "Do you want me to go, Toni?"

"We invited you here, didn't we?" Ah, she was surly. Well. He'd take care of that easily.

"Where's God?" he asked, taking a seat.

Her lips curved into a smile. *Ahh.* She'd liked his joke. "On the phone."

"He pissed you off?"

She shrugged. Okay, so she wasn't in the mood to confide. He got the message. He snatched up a magazine and flipped through the pages, pretending to be as interested in kitchen decoration as she was. He peered at her through his lashes.

"He's been on the phone all morning, and it drives me insane. The man doesn't know how to unwind. Why can't he just disconnect?" She studied him with narrowed eyes. "You don't seem to have that vice."

"I've got plenty of others." At her inquisitive gaze, he offered, "The only thing I like about phones is smashing them."

She smiled fleetingly.

"Maybe Grey wouldn't need to be on the phone so much if your friend were a better assistant," he told her.

She sighed. "She's just new to it, that's all. She's eager to please, and she needs that job." Then, face brightening, "Would you like to meet her? My friend? She's very pretty, and Grey and I were discussing the possibility of setting you up on a—"

"I've already met Grey's secretary," he said, frowning over the fact that Grey and Toni had been discussing Heath's future like they were lords of it. "And I don't do dates. But thank you. To know you both thought of me last night in your love nest makes my heart flutter."

Her eyebrows pulled low over her nose. "For your information, she's his assistant, not his secretary," she corrected. "And this wouldn't be just a date. She's very beautiful and dedicated and—"

"And she wants Grey to fold her over his office desk with her ass up in the air," Heath bluntly finished, propping his feet up and crossing his ankles atop the coffee table.

Toni met his gaze with a blank expression.

Heath quirked an eyebrow. "She wants to fuck your man, Toni."

She seemed incredulous at first, then shot him a furious scowl that made him smile. He could tell she didn't believe him, but he knew what he'd seen. Whatever-her-name-was wanted Grey to ram her against the wall and spill his guts into her. She'd been panting all over the place that time Heath had been at the office, looking down at her boobs to see if she had enough cleavage going on, swinging her butt when she walked away.

"You think everyone wants to have sex," Toni grumbled, slapping the magazine shut. "You have a dirty mind."

He folded his legs and straightened. "And in this case, I'm correct as usual."

Impatiently, she pushed back a strand of her hair. This particular way she wore it—loose and artfully framing her face—was by far his favorite. She just made his dick itch so bad.

"Grey and I . . . ," she began, lowering the magazine to her lap. "We have a good thing going."

Her eyes flicked up to his and away, and her shyness endeared her to him. Her skin was flawless. He could almost feel it on his finger tips. Silk. Like that red sash he'd stroked along his cock, down his balls—the sash that still smelled of her.

He set the magazine back on the table. "I'm not taking you from Grey."

He just wanted to rip that tube thing off her body and fuck her until she screamed, and he wanted to cup her softly and fuck her slowly, too.

The breath shuddered out of her with a heave of her breasts. "I love him."

"Grey's crazy about you." *And so am I, crazy with wanting you.* "He loves you," he added.

She couldn't have stiffened faster if he'd slapped her. "What do you mean?"

"He hasn't told you." Grey was such an idiot.

She squirmed and pushed her hair behind one shoulder, looking unsure whether or not to admit it. "What makes you think he hasn't?"

"I know my people." When she continued to stare in quiet expectancy, he sensed a tangible anxiety in her; she wanted to hear it. She *hadn't* heard it. "I know he'd do anything for you, Toni," he said truthfully. "I've never seen a man so devoted to his woman."

Grey was a good, solid, fair, dependable man. Which, of course, was why *he* had himself a Toni.

And her eyes were so pretty. So green. So very, very shiny. There was hunger there. Lust for him. For Grey.

She held her breath as he rose to approach. He caged her in with his arms, planting one hand on the back of the couch. His free hand ventured along a creamy, rounded bare shoulder. The tip of his middle finger traced the gentle curve, and as he caressed her, their noses almost touched. "Do you think of me?"

Her breathing gave her away; she had. Of course she had. She was getting wet just having him like this. And his cock was pushing into his jeans, throbbing to get into her.

"Is there a reason I should?" she asked.

Sassy. He liked that. "Oh yes, plenty. Do you want me to be specific?"

"Please. Enlighten me."

How about he shock her instead? Wipe that smug smile off her face? "How about you coming like a rocket whenever I put my hands on you?"

She smiled. "You're full of yourself."

Her lips as they smiled were a feast for his eyes. Shit, he wanted that mouth.

"Do you want me again?" he asked, circling her shoulder with that finger, listening to the increase of her breath.

She opened her mouth but nothing came out. She was panting, aroused. Then she said, "Maybe."

He sounded as breathless as she now. "Maybe yes or maybe no?"

She raised her hand and set a single finger on his mouth, feathering the tip across his bottom lip. "Maybe yes."

The whisper-light touch combined with the *yes* kicked him in the gut so hard that his legs nearly buckled. Her lips were parted, and he could see she expected him to bend his head and tangle his tongue with hers. Damn it. He'd never longed for a kiss until this moment, when he'd promised not to want it, not to take it.

His tongue felt restless in his mouth, wanting to swirl around her finger, her tongue. When she lowered her hand, his pulse thrummed inside him, his dick engorged to the point of pain.

The pitiful groan was his. "Touch me."

He craved to ram her back against the wall and sink inside her, pound her, but her mood seemed so fragile, he forced himself to be gentle as he reached for her hand.

"Put your hand on me."

She did. She had no other choice when he flattened her hand to the bulge in his jeans. And she swallowed up his cock with that hand. God. He wanted her to squeeze, to tug, jerk him fast. He wanted her to lower the zipper, delve in deep, grab him, make him blow.

Gentleness wasn't his forte, but he was gentle as he cradled her cheeks in hands that almost engulfed her face, cocked his head to one side and kissed her eyelids, the tip of her nose. Not her lips. Not those. But anywhere else, he could kiss . . .

"Tell me you'd like my hands on you again." He sounded desperate; he felt desperate. Twenty-seven. Twenty-seven women he'd fucked while thinking of Toni. There would be more after, he knew. He would fantasize about this weekend, of her cat eyes and her warm smile . . . how she looked when Grey was petting her . . . when Heath was plunging into her . . .

"Heath . . ." She didn't move her hand over him, but it trembled against the denim. Her neck was craned way back so her neck curved along the backrest.

He gave a circle of his hips, meaning it to be coaxing, but the move was fast and demanding. "It's okay. Do you know I made a deal with Grey? I'm allowed to fuck you with or without him present. Any time you want it. You can lift that dress for me and before you know it, I'm inside you."

A telling ripple went down her body, tangible in the air, in the center of his being.

"Grey wouldn't agree to that," she whispered.

"He did. He's repressed, that man is. He's a sex bomb behind the suit and he'd love for me to fuck you. We could do it right here, right now."

She wanted to. Yes. She trembled with the urge to. She licked her lips once, twice. She could almost taste his cock in her mouth, and Heath could almost smell her pussy. *Those* big lips, he was allowed to taste, and he would kiss there for hours. All day. All night. Grey or no Grey.

"You're lying," she finally said, dropping her hand to her lap.

"What you hear from me, always, that's the truth." He raised his voice, but did not take his eyes off her. "Isn't that right, Grey?"

At the edge of the living room, Grey stood with his arms clasped behind his back, his expression inscrutable. "Having a special time?"

Heath straightened. "We were."

Grey came forward, dropping his arms. "Baby, I'm sorry. I couldn't hang up; it was one thing after another." When she nodded grudgingly, he addressed Heath. "I was thinking we could have some horses brought up and we could ride down the coast near San José. There's a new resort, the Latin Blue? I want to show you something."

Heath perked up. "The spread?"

"Yes. It's rather interesting." He glanced at Toni and smiled warmly. "And there's a restaurant by the beach that Toni likes."

Bowing his head in agreement, Heath bent to whisper in her ear, "I'll have you riding my cock." He was cruelly pleased when she shuddered.

⌒

They were dressed in khaki shorts and shades; aviators for Grey, Heath in a sleek blue-lens pair. Heath's torso was draped in a plain cotton T-shirt, Grey's in a sexy navy blue polo with the little alligator on his chest. Toni wanted them in the bedroom, not out here in the sun, in front of this swarthy, wrinkled old man holding the two huge horses. But the men wanted to see land, so they *would* see land. And she, well, she would be checking out some nice, innovative hotel logos.

Striding across the sand in a pair of soft terry cloth capris and a ribbed white tank top she'd changed into, she sidled up next to Grey, cautious to maintain a good distance from the two large animals; she had developed a healthy respect for those beasts.

She'd dreamed of riding a horse on the beach ever since she was a girl. Naturally, Grey had made her dream come true. He'd asked if she could trot, and in her stubbornly determined, I-can-do-anything-*you*-can role, Toni had insisted, *But of course!*

She'd bounced like a Ping-Pong ball on the saddle, panicked, and pulled back the reins so hard the horse reared and went bronco on her. In the space of a second, she'd been tossed onto her ass in the sand, precisely a second before the horse planted a hoof a hairsbreadth away from her ringing right ear.

In those seconds of horror and shock and fear—of the hoof falling on her face, the horse trampling her—the only positive thing she could remember was Grey bounding off his horse, checking her for injuries, clutching her face, growling like a bear, demanding things while she was too stunned to speak. *Are you hurt? Damn it, are you hurt? Toni, answer me!*

Still, she hated to admit she was a coward and swallowed back her protest when she was swept up to the large chestnut mare by Grey's powerful arms. "Up you go, Miss Kearny," he said before he swung up behind her.

Of course, Grey *knew* she would be too cowardly to ride one by herself; he hadn't rented three horses, after all.

"Juicy."

His teeth gleamed white behind his smile when she swiveled her head and shot him a puzzled glance. "What?"

He peered down at her bosom and ran a finger across the logo arching up like a rainbow over her breasts. "Your shirt says Juicy."

Her eyes fell on her top, then returned to him. "You like it?"

A smile still curving his lips, he gave a slight inclination of his head.

She grinned. "You bought it for me," she reminded him.

Their ears almost brushed as he bowed his head. "Did I get you this, too?" His fingers played with the tinkling charm bracelet on her wrist, where he thumbed each of the charms as she twirled it around.

"You did. And some slippers and a bathrobe and a necklace and a sexy velour tracksuit in flashy neon pink. Don't you remember? You whipped out your black credit card, and I clearly remember the saleslady being as delighted as I was." She was smiling to herself, their heads bent as both their fingers investigated the enameled charms. "We have a purse here," she told him, aware that he had become distracted by a spot behind her ear he was brushing his lips up against, "and a lipstick and a bathing suit, a dog and a . . . a diamond ring."

Suddenly pensive, Toni fingered the tiny ring charm, the small zircon sparkling prettily in the sunlight. An awful pressure gathered in her chest at the realization that might be the only diamond ring she'd ever see from Grey.

"All right, kidlets, we're set to go."

Dispatching the Mexican man with a slap on his shoulder and an *adios*, Heath bounded up on the black gelding. The horse made to go, but Heath expertly yanked at the reins and shushed him, running a tanned, calming hand down the side of its gleaming black neck.

The instant Grey clucked the horse forward, Toni went ramrod straight in her seat, her clammy hands grasping at the pommel. He tightened his arm around her waist. "Relax. I've got you. I'm not trotting this baby—I'll just walk her, all right?" Her hesitation made him add meaningfully in her ear, "I won't let you fall, Toni, I promise you."

She nodded, and as the horses headed down the beach at the very edge of the ocean, precisely where the sea foam crawled up to the sand, she began to relax. The blue horizon was dotted with yachts. The chestnut's head swung easily, almost lazily, sideways, its ears resting behind its head. Toni's body rocked along with Grey's, and she was surprised to find how erotic that soothing motion felt.

Grey held the reins in one hand; the other was splayed under her top, flat against her navel. Her thoughts weren't so peaceful, though. She couldn't banish Heath's words from her mind.

She wants to fuck your man. . . .

She scowled at the memory as Heath, who had bounded out ahead, turned the glossy-coated black horse back toward them, smiling one of his *Die, girls* smiles. He looked one with the horse, and he looked damned, damned good riding. But it was still no wonder Heath didn't have any friends. Didn't he trust anybody? Louisa was her friend!

She was also very pretty. Prettier than Toni, or at least sexier. Blond and blue-eyed, with a flirty Marilyn Monroe voice and very ample boobs. What if Grey noticed? *Damn.*

Was this what Grey had felt when she admitted she found Heath attractive?

Now she quietly decided it would be best to plead a headache tonight and not go through with any more wicked threesomes. She could pull out a board game or . . . suggest cards . . . or just say flat out, *No, guys. Thank you, anyway.*

Because it felt horrible. She felt horrible to have admitted this to Grey. To even consider he might want or think of someone else was *torture.*

She shuddered at the mere possibility, and quietly, so that Heath wouldn't overhear, asked, "Would you ever want to do this the other way? With a woman?"

Immediately, she wished she could bite back the words. There was just no way on this earth that she could watch Grey touch a woman's—

"Do *you*?" He sounded incredulous.

But she was dead serious. "I asked you first," she insisted.

He laughed behind her, and she didn't know if she should feel relieved or foolish. "I don't want another woman. Why are you asking me this?"

She shrugged, her eyes fixed straight ahead. "Maybe this weekend will start giving you ideas."

He bent to cuddle his nose into her ear. Her skin warmed at the erotic touch of his breath against her. "The ideas in my head are all about you."

Her lashes became heavy and her entire being went supple, moistening for him. Her lungs tasted the scent of ocean and his morning shampoo, and she found the back of her head neatly contoured by his neck and chin as she sagged against him. He'd made love to her last night. The memory of those stolen, breathtaking moments stirred her lust to wakefulness.

She'd been so rattled by their threesome. While Grey wasn't regarded as the most approachable human being on earth, he was always warmest with her. Yet last night with Heath, his touch had been distant, perfunctory, no matter how exquisite his hands still felt.

She'd thought she would drive him out of his mind for her this weekend, but she feared that in agreeing to a threesome, she'd just become one of *those* women. Women he screwed with his partner and dumped within the month.

The thought that they'd made a terrible mistake tortured her, and worse was having Heath parading himself around the house with those challenging words and even more challenging black eyes. She couldn't sleep last night.

Even in her tired, groggy state, she'd needed Grey more than sleep. They'd lain tangled together for what felt like hours, and then it was as if they both knew they wouldn't sleep without being together. She'd turned in his arms, staring up at his shadowed features. The tone in his voice—thick, hoarse, full of emotion—still haunted her. "What is it?"

Before she could answer, he was shifting her, knowing instinctively what she craved. He'd sought her out with two fingers and eased them into her cunt lazily, tiredly, with a slumberous quality to his eyes. His voice made his chest vibrate against her breasts. "Do you want me?"

With all my heart, she thought yearningly as she coiled her arms around his shoulders. "Make love to me."

"How? Tell me how."

"I . . ."

"With this?" He held her hips and put his cock gently in her, and she cried out in ecstasy as though he'd rammed it to the depths of her. He moved slowly, but she writhed as though he were pounding her full force, she needed it so much. "How do I make love to you, Toni?" he demanded. "With my cock?"

"With all of you."

And his face was on her breasts, turning to nip at one peak, then the other. "With my eyes?" he asked silkily.

She pulled his head up by the hair and kissed his eyelids. "Yes."

"With my hands, my lips?"

"Yes and yes." She kissed his lips, his nose, his forehead. "With your mind," she whispered. *With your words,* she thought. Words he didn't tell her in sunlight. Words she tucked deep into her heart as though he'd told her he loved her.

She'd made an embarrassing amount of noise even though this was the laziest way he'd ever loved her; slowly and tenderly, as though he were determined to prove he could do more than just fuck her as she'd accused.

In the morning, it was difficult to relate the businessman barking orders over the telephone with the man who'd loved her last night.

"See that stretch over there, Heath?" he asked.

Heath's horse let out a gust of air through his nose, almost covering Heath's words. "I see it."

"That's troubled. We might do something with it if we can get around the legalities."

Heath let out a laugh and ran a hand across the top of his head. "Don't tease me."

"Pretty, isn't it?"

Both men seemed engrossed by the verdant sight, and Toni was privately amused watching them. On the beach side, they passed a mother wading into the water with two little kids. The children pointed at the horses, and Toni waved and mouthed *hi,* while Heath asked, "What is it that you see there?"

"I'll explain when I show you this other resort. What does your gut tell you about it?"

"It says yes," was all Heath said.

"You're getting hard, Grey," she teased, squirming to get a better feel of the bulge biting into her backside.

He stilled her with one hand. "You've been wiggling."

"I have not!"

"I've been suffering quietly for an hour."

She snorted.

"I'm serious."

"I've been utterly still the entire ride, waiting for the horse to make up its mind to gallop away with us until we're in California. Or the hospital."

"That would be in the opposite direction, I believe."

"Are you afraid of horses?" Heath asked.

"A little," she grudgingly admitted. Heath only smiled. His muscled legs straddling the horse were . . . an eyeful. He really did look amazing on that horse. Francine would fall head over heels for him. Louisa, too. Any woman who could appreciate a man who knew how to take control. Any woman who liked raunchy sex and . . . dominant men with . . . big cocks and . . . skillful mouths.

Jerking her eyes away from him, she gazed at the landscape, crowded up ahead with hotels. "So why haven't you done anything in Cabo?"

"Government," they both said.

Heath added, "Grey would need to kiss some serious governor ass."

Toni jumped in to champion her lover. "Grey can get anything he wants, can't you, baby?"

"That's right, pet," he cooed down at her, and raising his voice, "I'll kiss governor ass. The problem is, we need to wrap up in Canada if you're parking your ass here for a year. And apparently, some serious bribery would also be involved."

"I'll do the bribing; you just write the checks and kiss ass like you love to."

"He hates kissing ass!" Toni said in Grey's defense.

"Except yours," Grey grumbled quietly to her, and they both laughed.

"There aren't that many apartment buildings," she noted as she sobered, scanning the houses dotting the cliff, the hotels lining the shore up ahead. "There are either huge houses or hotels, but maybe buyers would like a place with an ocean view and not an entire house to maintain?"

She wasn't certain, but suspected Grey had just kissed the back of her head. "You're brilliant, my girl."

My girl.

She was still a little mushy in the thighs over that endearment when they reached the sprawling hotel Grey wanted Heath to see. The resort was acres and acres of magnificence, with glistening windows and slanted rooftops, surrounded by gardens. "Do you want to see it with us, pet?" Grey asked as he helped her dismount.

Oh, tough one. Either stay with the smelly horse or . . .

Watch them work together. Ogle them from afar. Privately drool over them while they, in turn, drooled over the architecture. The men were such opposites, yet so alike in their passions. Their passions for land, for construction. Talking business with Heath, Grey was animated in a way Toni had never seen. Their interaction was natural and effortless, and entirely mesmerizing to watch. Like a couple of gifted athletes who lift each other's game when they play together.

Both in the bedroom and out of it.

Chapter Eight

As they crossed the sand and walked up the steps leading to the lush green pool area, a crowd of people came into view, and the sound of live music carried in the air.

"Oooh, a Mexican wedding!" Toni said, noting the colorful floral arrangements gracing each of the tables on the terrace, a tattered piñata sitting lonely over a nearby stretch of grass.

"We're not invited, Miss Kearny," Grey warned.

Not caring that the men hung back, Toni made her way around, plopped an abandoned mariachi hat onto her head, and plucked shot glasses of tequila from a busy-looking waiter. She brought them up to the men, both their gazes palpable though shielded by their lenses. "We're on vacation. You both take yourselves too seriously. Especially you, Grey. We're going to have some fun, all right?"

Without checking to make sure they drank their shots, she strolled back into the crowd. More than fifty people circulated over the lush green lawns and walkways surrounding the massive pool. Square tables had been set up around it, each draped in a different color cloth.

Children mingled with adults, some splashing into the pool, another group peering under a table where a group of women sat in avid discussion. Smiling when she realized those three little boys were hoping to catch a sight of the women's panties, Toni glanced back to notice Grey and Heath were at the very fringes of the party. They were looking high above and past her, discussing their future project. Grey had an arm stretched out, and he was pointing at the building as he spoke, while Heath nodded in agreement. Grey loved his properties, the developing, everything from spotting the land to giving it more substance. She could tell Heath shared his passion.

Feeling stirrings in her stomach, she moved on to investigate further, smelling the blooms in the air, the food from the buffet, and finally located the mariachi group that was the source of the music.

She was drawn into the excitement of the party and found herself smiling widely as photographers made the rounds, one of them attacking the partygoers, another following the bride and groom. The groom looked to be sixty years old; his much younger bride was dressed in an embroidered linen frock that did justice to the festive theme.

When a couple skirted by, dancing and kissing to a merry mariachi tune, Toni wanted to dance, too. And she wanted to kiss, too. And she wanted . . .

They stood like bodyguards, tracking her with their eyes, Grey with his hands clasped before him, Heath with them clasped behind his back. She waved them over. One said something to the other. They smiled. They were making fun of her! She wrinkled her nose and stuck her tongue out at them. Grey smiled, then turned his attention over his shoulder when a wandering beach vendor tapped his arm to show him an array of day dresses.

A laugh escaped her when he gave a nod of consent and pointed in her direction. Grey must be asking the man what size she would wear. He was nodding. Smiling. Yes, of course. Now he was diligently selecting a dress for her. *Oh, Grey.*

When Heath sauntered forward, she noted a couple of children nearby begin to whisper, watching him closely from their seats in the grass. She wondered if their little imaginations were making up stories about Heath. Would he be an evil villain to them? A pirate or a smuggler . . .

"That is one ridiculous hat, if I may say so."

She tipped the brim back so she could actually see his face. "Grey seems to like it."

"Ah. Well, his eyesight is going."

"His eyes are perfect. Grey misses nothing. It's *mine* that are failing." And how utterly sad was that for a graphic designer?

"How many fingers am I holding up?"

She laughed and folded them back into his hand. "Two. And it's from afar that I have trouble focusing."

"Ahh." Clasping his hands behind his back, he glanced around fleetingly, then directly at her. "Did you miss your high school parties, Cat?"

She waved a hand and walked around him. The sun was at an angle, and where the shadows hit, the breeze was fresh. "Oh, humbug. You two are boring."

He matched her steps as she made her way around the tables. "Grey is a little concerned we weren't invited to this party."

"And you?"

"I'm hungry."

"Ooh. Then follow me, sir." She waved him over to a table that had two full plates of mixed nuts at its center.

When she bent over to gather a handful, his legs and hips came flush against the back of hers and her breasts were enveloped by two large, brazen hands. "I'm hungry for *these*, Toni."

Her nipples pushed into his palms and a rush of feminine power rushed through her when his bulging erection pressed into her tush. His sensual, deep-throated breathing was a guttural sound in her ear. "I want you, Toni. Right here, right now."

She licked suddenly dry lips. She had a feeling her dry throat had very little to do with nuts and everything to do with Heath's frame going taut with arousal. "We're in the middle of a party," she said under her breath, afraid to look up and find someone watching this hardly subtle advance.

But she knew, felt, sensed people passing nearby. Flashes. Murmurs. Her breasts were still covered by his hands and it took supreme effort to not just stand there and let him have his blessed way. She moved away, extracting her fingers from the nuts and wiping the salty coating on the linen.

When he took her hand in his and began to guide her toward Grey, she was so shocked at the gesture she halted midstride. She looked down at their hands, linked almost casually together, and Heath stopped, his features wooden and incongruous with his smile. "Does this bother you?"

"No." She squeezed him. "It's fine. I'm just surprised."

Still not comfortable, he extracted his hand from hers, raised his arm to her neck and guided her by the nape toward Grey and the eager-looking vendor.

"I'm getting slightly dizzy here, Toni. There's topaz and there's royal blue and there's navy."

They were gorgeous. Delicately embroidered. Flirty strapless dresses to wear over your bathing suit or just around the house. God, *every*where. "I love them."

"We'll take the three blues, then."

Heath stepped up and he and Grey discussed something, first between themselves and then with the vendor. Heath pulled out his wallet and spared her a glance, grinning like a boy. "Grey gives you the world; I give you three dresses."

"In different shades of blue," she teased.

"Exactly," he agreed.

"Thank you." She surged up on her toes, intending to kiss those strong, mobile lips she'd been aching to taste, but he swiftly angled his head to the side so her mouth hit his whiskered cheek. She frowned and dropped flat on her feet, realizing she could benefit from curbing her enthusiasm now and then. "I'm sorry. I didn't think you might not . . . want that."

The glimmer in his eyes was disconcertingly intense, his face unsmiling as he gazed at her mouth in a way that made her nervous enough to lick her lips. He swiped a big palm across her forehead and smoothed the creases with his thumb. "That's all right."

The thing with Grey was that the man could go without talking for hours. And Heath appreciated peace and quiet as much as the next man, or maybe more, which was why they'd both sat in silence under the shade of a thatched-roof terrace while Toni mingled with the partygoers. She had an avid conversation going on with the married couple, and when Heath caught himself straining to overhear her laughter, he squirmed in his beach chair and let his mind run away with other thoughts. How-to-get-Toni-out-of-his-head-after-Cabo thoughts.

Grey was engrossed in jotting down numbers and executing brisk sketches over a tower of napkins he'd procured, when Heath said, "I'm thinking of getting a dog."

Yeah. A dog. A *puppy*. Who'd lick his hand. Who'd be all grateful and excited when Heath fed him. A good little mutt. He was fully convinced he'd need one to get his mind off a particular kitten.

Grey flipped the napkin over to continue, and it seemed to take him a moment to realize Heath had been speaking to him. He glanced up, his eyes lost, as though his thoughts were drawn inward. "What for?"

"Company."

Look at her. Toni, ankle-deep in the pool, wearing that silly mariachi hat Grey had just bought her, her hands holding her skirt high to keep it dry. Her legs were slim and toned, and with this glance alone Heath had them memorized. Damn. She didn't have to be so cute. And look at him, sitting here with her blue dresses folded on his lap so they wouldn't get wet, guarding her feminine things. He must look ridiculous.

After perusing him in silence, Grey went back to sketching. "You'd need to get a small sissy dog, one you can travel with easily."

"I don't want a sissy dog; I want a big dog." Heath mentally listed all the breeds he knew existed, which weren't all that many. "I was thinking more of a Saint Bernard or . . . something."

Grey canted his head as if listening like one, grinning in amusement. "Why a Saint Bernard?"

"I don't know. They're big and they don't seem too playful. A playful pup would just piss me off."

"Cleaning up after him would irritate the hell out of me."

Heath considered it might piss *him* off, too, but damn, he needed a mutt. She'd wanted to set him up on a date, damn her. Paddling her behind for that would be ecstasy.

Keeping a vigilant eye on her, he watched her curvy calves emerge from the pool, and he followed them up slim hips, a small waist, breasts made especially—*especially*—for Heath's hands. He went higher, up a slender, elegant throat, smiling lips. . . .

Shit, she was watching them. Waving them forward and mouthing something indiscernible.

Grey's head jerked up instantly, as though he had some Toni alert system, his attention immediately homing in on her. His eyes went all shades of gold possible, then settled to a heated glow.

He folded the napkins and jammed them into his shorts. "A Saint Bernard isn't you. People look like their dogs. Try a black one. A Rottweiler. I'll give you two months, tops."

"I can take care of a damned dog."

Pulling his shades out from his shirt collar, Grey slipped them over his eyes and rose. "Get a fish, Heath."

"I want to kiss her." The brusque words checked Grey's stride. His shoulders stiffened, and Heath added meaningfully, "On the mouth."

Grey shook his head, not turning.

"Why not?"

He spun around. "Because the thought makes me green. Satisfied?"

"Not even nausea could turn you green." Pushing to his feet, Heath slapped his back in a companionable, come-on-I'm-you're-friend gesture. "One kiss."

"Don't push it."

"Aww, Grey, come on!"

"I said no."

Heath glowered at his retreating back. That massive, broad-shouldered, impenetrable fucking back.

What Grey needed was a cock up his ass, to dislodge the stick he had perennially stuck in there. Sheesh!

Collecting Toni's dresses, he ambled up the walk while the bride and groom shoved a pair of newly delivered drinks into their hands. He heard Toni's excited "To the bride and groom!" and Grey's mumbled curse as he grudgingly tossed back the shimmering liquid.

And he explicitly heard Grey's "Son of a bitch!"

⌒

"So they're from Chicago, and the groom has a daughter he says looks just like me."

She caught the moment Heath and Grey rolled their eyes heavenward as Grey helped her dismount, but she was so excited she didn't let that stop her.

"Well, he said so! He said he thought I was her. Seriously. So, anyway, I gave him my phone number, and maybe when you're in the city . . . Heath?"

Heath looked ready to choke, his eyes wide and incredulous.

"Feel free to stop her at any time, Heath," Grey said, a corner of his lips raised as he walked the horse and tied it to a nearby palm tree.

"Are you kidding me? I'm loving this. This is funnier than *Sein-*

feld. Do go on, Cat. I'm thoroughly entertained." Still on his mount, Heath urged the black beast forward.

She shot him such a furious frown that he let go of the reins and lifted his hands to placate her. "All right, tell me about my date."

"You're interested? Really?"

"I'm not, but tell me anyway." His eyes flicked past her shoulders for a second. "You're looking a little nauseated, Grey."

"I'll shove that shit down your throat and I'm sure you'll look your best, Heath."

"Not all of us drink champagne."

"That was rat piss, honest to god. I need to wash it down with something."

"It wasn't that bad," Toni defended, out of respect for the married couple. But in truth, it hadn't been bad—it had been awful.

"I did catch that feminine little sip you took," Heath offered, sliding his sunglasses over his forehead. "But Grey here tossed it all down like a real hombre. You should have seen his face." He looked directly at him. "May I borrow her for a second?" He turned those debilitating black eyes to hers and extended his hand. "We're going to work on this fear of horses for just a bit."

Instantly wary of the devilish sparkle in his eyes, she took a backward step. "Oh no. No no no."

"Grey's too cautious to push you, but I'm not. You'll be happy to master it. Get over here, seriously." When she didn't hop to, Heath shifted his inquiry. "Grey?"

Visibly tense, Grey curled a hand around his nape and cranked his head to one side, then the other. His face was screwed up in thought, and Toni felt a sweet stab of tenderness when she realized he was preoccupied.

His protectiveness evoked a sudden, wishful image of Grey as a father, of them having a little girl. She could picture a young, spirited, golden-eyed teenager asking her father permission for a first date. Would Grey wear that thoughtful face? For sure he'd be stern and want to meet the boy and know who his parents were. And

Toni would have to team up with their little girl and plot and plan together in order to convince Daddy it was all right.

"If it's me you're doubting . . ." Heath said, letting the words trail off.

His hand fell at his sides. "It's not you, Heath."

Toni was brought up to her full height, her pride instantly smarting. "Well, if it's *me* you're doubting—"

Grey smiled reluctantly. "I don't doubt you for a second." He took a breath as though to speak but fell pensive again, until finally he assented. "You'll be fine."

His sudden, startling encouragement made her balk. "But what if I—"

"I'll kick the shit out of him."

The men were smiling now, sharing looks only they could understand. Toni wasn't smiling at all. She was rooted to the spot, debating whether to rush for cover and admit her cowardice or engage in a decent display of bravery and meet her maker.

The wind whipped her hair around her. It got curlier at the beach—it got impossible, frankly—and as she contemplated her dilemma, she got sick of it. She gathered it in one hand, twisted it into a rope, and tied it in a loose bun at her nape, leaving a few strands still flying across her eyes as she raised her face to Heath's.

"If I want to get down . . . ?"

He inclined his head in agreement, and she could tell he was making an effort not to smile. "I promise you."

Before she could screw up her courage, Grey caught her hips and boosted her up. "Up we go, pretty lady. She gets the stirrups," he told Heath.

"Of course."

Grey unbuckled the straps and then pulled the leather up three holes from its former setting. "Heath," he warned when he was done.

"I got it, Grey." Heath deftly steered the horse around. "We'll walk around for a bit, and then we'll trot," he told her once they were on their way.

Her nails dug in to the pommel of the saddle. "First we *walk*, Heath."

"Whatever you say, Cat. And you could ride this baby from here to Alaska. All you need is your thighs to hang on. If you let the animal know you're afraid, it senses it."

"I'm terrified."

"You need a new experience, that's all."

Just talking about trotting had her stomach in a grip. She gazed out at the sea and tried to think of something relaxing. "Around March, you can see humpback whales here. They swim back north with their babes, and they're so close to shore you can spot them from here sometimes. Especially when they jump. Once, Grey and I took a boat up to see them, and they were so close I dipped my fingers in the water and touched one. The skin was so smooth, with little calluses formed by the . . ." Realizing he probably wasn't really interested in whales, she promptly shut up. "Did I put you to sleep? Hello? Heath?"

His forearm was a hairsbreadth under her breasts, where he held her secure, and his hold strengthened when he said, with unmistakable annoyance, "Why in the hell do you want to set me up?"

She was startled by the genuine outrage in his voice. Her mouth opened, but no reply came forth.

"I'm *fucking* you. That you're going around matching me with someone else ticks the hell out of me."

She went completely stiff. She'd never expected this attack, but perhaps she deserved it. "I didn't mean to offend you," she admitted tightly. "I'm sorry if I'm overstepping."

"I'm not going on a date with anybody, all right?"

"May I know why?"

"I suck at them. I suck at small talk."

"You do not; we're talking fine just now. I think my friends would love you. If you'd only tell me what you look for when you meet someone . . ."

Heath kept walking the horse, making soft clucking noises that caused the little hairs on her arms to rise to attention like the horse's ears. His sullen silence lasted until he said, "All right. I'll tell you what I like. Pretty eyes. Pretty smile. Pretty lips. Pretty—"

"Yes, I think I get it, Heath."

"Well, good for you," he said good-naturedly.

Her eyes fell on the vast, endless expanse of white sand before them. "And how am I supposed to know what *pretty* is to you?"

"Pink is pretty." In a move too slow not to be sensually deliberate, he traced the shell of her earlobe between his lips. "Did you know you're pink all over, Toni?" She caught her breath when a moist flick of his tongue teased the area behind her ear. "Your lips are rosy as your nipples, and down there, you're bright and moist. So damned pretty my eyes hurt."

She wanted to close her eyes and swim in his words; then she wanted to wail in frustration when he stopped weaving his magic on her foolish, susceptible self. He straightened behind her, and getting down to matters, said, "I want a good woman. With a good heart and feelings. Someone who enjoys life and who enjoys the things I'd like to do to her . . ."

"You're deliberately making this complicated, aren't you?"

"Ahh. Perceptive, and pink all over. I like you, señorita. But the truth is, I don't need relationship troubles, and I don't *need* a woman."

"Then would you like a date with a guy?" she countered.

"Crap, no! Why would I want to date a guy?"

"Well . . ." *Let's see, now. How to phrase this delicately?*

"Because I've enjoyed fucking a few?"

So much for being tactful. "Yes." And the visual made her just a tad wet in the panties. "Have there been a lot? Men, I mean?"

"A couple."

"And do you prefer . . . well, you know. What role do you prefer, the woman's role, or the—"

He guffawed with laughter, slapping a hand on his thigh. "Oh, Christ, Cat!"

"I'm sorry," she quickly burst in. "Don't unsettle the horse! And I know I'm prying. I'm too curious for my own good sometimes. I'm sorry. Really."

"It's okay. I like that." The laughter faded from his voice. "If it gives me pleasure," he explained matter-of-factly, "I can take it and I can give it."

Like the waves on the shore, a crash of liquid flooded her panties. She should not be discussing this with Heath. She needed to change topics—to one that did not have her sex organs clenching so tightly. She said, "So, you meet someone and have your fun; then you just leave forever?"

"Right."

"You never, ever come back, or want to?"

"Right again, gorgeous."

"You'd never come back to Cabo San Lucas?" *With us . . .*

She wrinkled her nose, instantly resenting the thought. She didn't want any more threesomes and already she was planning on a second trip?

He reached between her spread legs and boldly trailed his thumb down to her sex. "What would you want of me if I came back?"

He burrowed four fingers under her body and used his entire hand to grind. The strong heel of his palm bit into her hardening clitoris. "Please don't," she cried, stiffening.

But he continued, massaging her entire pussy with strong, sure presses. "Do you enjoy our sex together, Cat?"

Her spine curved helplessly. "I don't want to do this on a horse!"

"I won't let you fall." He spoke against her temple, where she felt his tongue snake out for a lick. "Grey told me to be careful. In his own words. And he *has* kicked the shit out of me before."

"Don't. I don't . . . I don't want to do this without him."

"It's all right. I'm just caressing you. We're making out on a horse—isn't it fun?"

"No," she lied, and prayed her dampness hadn't seeped into her clothes so fast.

"All right." He easily relented, leaving her pussy a furious throb between her legs when he released it. "Let's ride, then. Here. Take the reins." He caught her hand in one of his and began to settle her fingers where they should go.

The sight of her small porcelain hand and his large tanned one moving together sent a jolt of sexual awareness through her. "You tackle all your fears this way?" she asked meekly.

"If I can."

"And the flying?"

His fingers faltered over hers, then continued to lace the leather reins through her fingers. "I haven't quite figured that one out.

"Now, to ride the horse, you just need your thighs. You've got lovely toned thighs, so that won't be a problem. To steer it, you use the reins. You don't kick the horse to a run and tug on the reins at the same time or you're sending mixed signals, and it gets confused or pissed out of its wits at you. Understand?"

Her heart pounded. His palms went to her thighs, and as he bent his head, she felt an unfortunate escalation of her arousal. This was *so* not the place to be melting. . . .

He urged her legs into the horse's flank. "Close your thighs tightly around the horse. You grip it with your inner thigh. And I've got you with one arm, see? I won't let you go."

"Okay."

"And now we trot."

"Okay."

But nothing happened. He said, "Cluck to it, beautiful. Send it a kiss. You're the boss here; ask it to trot for you."

Beautiful . . .

She did as he instructed, and the gelding began to trot, and she bounced up and down in the saddle with absolutely no control of herself. "Heath!" She was panicking.

"We're doing fine; don't get scared. Use your legs to rise a bit before your ass hits the saddle and you won't bounce. Very good, that's it! You're getting it. Now, steer this fellow in a circle, and go with it. Be one with the horse. That's right, Cat. That's just right."

They found a stride, and she began to smile. It did feel good. A sensation of freedom and bliss flowed through her. She moved with the horse, and Heath moved with the horse; their bodies moved like a single entity. Like when they moved during sex, or when they'd once danced so close.

"I'm going to let go of your waist now, and you're going to do it by yourself, all right?"

"Yes," she gasped, and steered the animal around, trotting it back the same way they'd come. The animal's rhythmic breathing was a rough, heady sound coming out through its nose, echoing their pace. Toni could *tell* the gelding was loving this; his ears pricked, head up and alert, his awesome, capable body straining with attention for her commands. The horse looked so content trotting; he did not look inclined to turn his head and bite her leg or throw her off his back at all.

With that realization, coupled with Heath's massive chest such a reassuring support against her back, she was getting *so* into it. She wanted more of this awesome sensation, this feeling of accomplishment, of freedom. "And to get it to gallop I just . . . ?"

He chuckled. "All right, we graduate to galloping. Just kick with your heels a bit, send him more kisses, and let him find his stride."

She felt exhilaration when they took off. "We're galloping!"

"We're galloping."

"Yay!"

He was chuckling, and her own laughter was welling up in her throat. After a few minutes they slowed to a canter, then galloped more and trotted again. By the time they rode up to the house, Toni was wearing a smile so wide it was almost painful. The chestnut mare stood waiting by the curved, willowy palm tree. On the second stone step leading up the cliff, Grey waited cross-armed, his glasses tucked into his polo.

"There's your Grey," Heath said.

And she said, breathlessly, "He's smiling."

"He's proud of you."

With a smile that made her all the more breathless, he strode up to help her dismount. Toni fell into his arms, her limbs winding tight around his strong, solid body.

He gave her a fierce squeeze and brushed her tangled hair out of her face, running his eyes over her cheeks and lips and eyes. His face worked with emotion. "Look at you. All smiles and laughs."

"Did you see me?"

"You're a sight, Miss Kearny." He cradled her face between his two hands, his eyes like molten amber. "We should've done this months ago."

"Why didn't we?" It felt so good!

"You know why," he said quietly, and caressed her cheekbone with the pad of his thumb.

"Because you saw me fall?" she asked, reaching out to brush a blond lock from his forehead. "Would you miss me terribly if something happened to me, Grey Richards?"

Grey either didn't like the question or the thought it conjured; she'd never seen that strained look on his face. "Don't even think it," he hissed, and crushed her lips with his. When he pulled away from that slow, stirring kiss, he spoke over her shoulder.

"Heath."

"Grey."

There was a wealth of satisfaction in their voices, giving her the impression the words meant more than just their names. Rather than say *thank you*, Grey had merely said *Heath*, and judging by Heath's reply, he'd known exactly what Grey had meant. How oddly they communicated!

Turning, she noticed Heath was returning from tying up the

gelding, smiling directly at her as he closed the distance between them. Her legs trembled with adrenaline—and something else. A need to kiss him, hold him, make wild love to him.

"Hi . . . ," she lamely whispered as he came within touching range. Belatedly, she realized there was a multitude of meanings behind that single word, too. *Thank you, kiss me, touch me, don't ever stop looking at me that way . . .*

Slowly, he bent to place a chaste kiss on her cheek. His lips lingered over the spot for a pulse-stopping moment, where he breathed raggedly against her skin. "How about you ride me now?"

⌒

In the master bedroom, Grey pinned Toni against the nearest wall and kissed the breatn out of her.

Slamming the door shut, Heath jerked his shirt off, his clothes an untenable scrape against his skin. He'd never had such a need to be naked, to feel free, to take and be taken. His tongue throbbed in his mouth, the sound of their sloppy, wet kisses making him thirst.

He'd have given his soul to the devil to open her mouth and feel it welcome his. Instead he watched, trembling in his hands, his legs. He was a mass of aching. His cock felt leaden under his shorts, his balls blue with pain. Her laughter still sang in his veins, and her smile . . . god, you'd think he'd given her light, a rainbow, something special and magical.

No one had ever looked at him with the open, innocent admiration she had. He would never forget those wide green eyes, those pink cheeks, and her airless *Hi . . .*

"Get over here, Heath," Grey growled, and fisted his hand around her shirt to jerk Toni back to his thickened mouth. He kissed her, shoving his tongue in for a quick, demanding sip, and Heath could almost taste her on his own tongue. Against Grey, her body undulated softly, plush and pliable like clay. She breathed short, shallow pants and he found the delicate suction of her lips on Grey's tongue arousing as hell.

Heath flanked her from the back, letting her squirm between both of them. Grey loosened his fist on her shirt and grasped the tiny point of a nipple with his thumb and index finger. He pulled it and she shuddered with hot, debilitating desire. "Grey."

He circled the peak as it pushed up into her T-shirt, then scraped the balled point until it quivered. His voice was broken with need. "Grey, what?"

Her mouth worked, but nothing came out. Heath saw as Grey reached between her legs, flattened the pad of his thumb to the throbbing flesh of her clitoris, and rubbed. Toni dug her fingers into his shoulders, her spine arching. "Grey."

"Easy, kitten," Heath purred close, raising her arms above her head in one hand.

Her ass cradled the bulge of his penis. As she wormed against him, he felt the tiny frissons of need overtaking her body. Sweat broke across his temples, his back, his forehead as he fought to keep from splaying her wide and taking her backside like he itched to do.

He was so turned on he could come on her clothes, all over her, on her backside, her thighs.

With a primeval noise Heath understood as urgent, Grey hooked two fingers into her capris and folded them to her ankles, leaving her in only her tank top. Without barriers, the touch of Grey's thumb on her clit made her throw her head back with a strangled sob.

"Oh, god."

"Is that good?" he cooed, leaning forward to lick one hardened nipple. "Hmm? That good, darling?"

Heath ducked and desperately French-kissed the silky curve of her nape. His tongue was wild on her skin, tasting a path to her bare shoulder. He wanted her to mount him, ride him harder than the horse. He wanted to watch her hair fly and her breasts jiggle, and he wanted her to have him.

"I crave something juicy," Grey murmured and moved to suckle the opposite nipple, swirling his tongue across the tip right over the stamped Y of the word JUICY. He captured the peak and took it into his mouth.

The helpless sound of her whimper sent a current of electricity down to Heath's crotch. He grabbed at the breast Grey suckled and wrested it higher up to his mouth, and Grey buzzed the breast in hunger and continued to devour.

"Guys," she gasped, twittering in ecstasy. Her sexual scent was powerful in the room. It shredded at Heath's control, had him leaking against his shorts.

Dispensing with her shirt, Grey tossed it aside and her hair tumbled in a shimmering cascade down her back.

"Someone told me patience was a virtue," he teased her. Heath peered over, and past her newly bared rosy-tipped breasts, he caught sight of Grey's thumb on her wet, pearly nub as he pressed slow, relentless circles to it.

She twitched her wrists in Heath's grip above, trying to break free. "Please don't make me wait. . . ."

Heath made a strangled sound when her ass stroked against his fabric-covered erection. *I hear you, gorgeous. I hear you.* . . .

Relenting his hold, he trailed his hands down her sensitive inner arms. He smiled at her shudder, then traced her ribs with his fingertips while Grey laved a wet circle around her navel. Her stomach was flat, the skin flawless, leading down to that morsel of a pussy. A sheen of sweat coated her skin, but the gleam was nothing compared to the glistening labia between her thighs.

She was pink and hot, and she was all Heath wanted.

Her breasts rose and fell quickly as she labored for air, as though her body were an empty cavern without their cocks inside her. "Grey, I want . . ." She paused to take a quavering breath.

"We know what you need, don't we, Heath? Get your shorts off, Solis."

Grey steered her around as Heath climbed onto the bed. Leaning back on a tower of pillows, he deftly plucked open the button of his shorts and yanked them down before both their watchful gazes. His cock sprang free, slapping against his stomach.

"Is that what you need, baby?" Grey asked.

She swallowed audibly. Heath took his erection in his hand and swiped his thumb across the dripping slit, inviting her to it. Fuck, he needed her bad.

Her tongue darted out to lick at her lips, and his blood sizzled in his veins as Grey urged her forward. Slim and agile, creamy and feminine, she was climbing on top of him, straddling his hips with her slim, toned legs.

Grey held her hips, and Heath's words barely got past the tightness in his throat. "Ride me, beautiful." *Ride me to hell and back, and then ride me all the way to heaven.*

He cupped her ribs, just above Grey's hands on her, and they both spread her down over him. He thought he would tear her, he felt so thick, so freaking rigid it hurt to push the head past her swollenness.

"Sit on it, Toni. That's right, sit on his dick, baby," Grey told her.

Above Toni's rolling gasp, the men's gazes met. Grey's eyes were red with wanting to pleasure her. And Heath felt the chip fall off his shoulder when he recognized his same old friend as before. Grey's eyes glowed with trust, not hostility. They were one in wanting to drive themselves to ecstasy in Toni.

They groaned with her when they simultaneously impaled her on Heath. Heath's head whipped to the side for a blinding, lust-seared moment. Then Grey began to move her. Heath tossed his head again, struggling for control as she clamped and milked him; then Grey lifted her once more.

Seconds passed, their breaths warring in the silence.

A part shriek, part whimper caught in her throat when Grey said "Fuck him!" and pushed her low again, embedding Heath in her, embedding him long and rock hard inside the juiciest, tightest, wettest place he'd ever been in.

"Oh, god!" she cried, head thrown back.

"Ride him," Grey barked. "Fuck him hard."

Like a wild animal just liberated, she rode him with purpose. Heath wanted to capture her every move in his eyes, and he wanted to fling his head back and roar with ecstasy. He'd never thought a liberating experience like the one they'd shared could be such an aphrodisiac.

For him, for Grey, for her.

Moving her hips, she mapped his chest with her hands, her eyes dilated and heavy on his face. She was wild, free, untamed, and moving over his cock like crazy. And he was loving the feel of her fingers, her palms as they made love to his skin, loving the dewy patches she left on his abs, his pecs. When she flicked his small brown nipple, he groaned, and his hands went to her hair.

He rubbed his fingertips through the silky tendrils and pitched forward, sheathing himself up to the balls in her, and still it wasn't quite enough. "Damn, I want you so much." He raised his head to nibble on a rosy breast. "I want to kiss you all over." He laved it with his tongue and imagined he was tonguing her mouth—that mouth she'd offered so openly at the party hours earlier. "I want to kiss your mouth, your breasts, your belly button, your feet."

Her grip was blazing tight around him, and she was such a sight to behold. Her features were mellow with arousal, and her shoulders were shaking, as were her thighs draped over his hips. The adrenaline of her ride and the lust—they were galvanizing things. "Toni."

"Heath."

"Oh, fuck, Toni." He moved in her with single-minded purpose, making a rumbling sound deep in his throat. Sensations ricocheted inside his body. The sight of her over him seared into his brain.

Their skin scraped as they fucked, the bed rocking, her breasts jiggling for his eyes. She mewed in relief when he gave a jarring thrust that stretched her vagina to the limits. He set a wild, animalistic rhythm.

Her pussy was soaked and burning around his penis, the juice falling like a drizzle of rain to coat the curls under his cock. Her hand groped the air nearby for Grey, and Heath sensed she needed him.

Grey stood by the side of the bed with his juice-slicked dick in his hand, his eyes alight with fever.

Heath *knew*, all of a sudden; Grey would have given him anything for having made Toni smile the way he had. And Heath would have granted Grey anything for allowing her to ride him like this. Heath had hungered to have her; now he hungered to be included in what she and Grey had. Something palpable in the air, something that charged their looks, their touches. And he felt *part* somehow, right now. He was not the addition, he was . . . among. The thought was stimulating as hell.

Grateful, hungry, he reached out at the same time Toni did, and their hands simultaneously enveloped the veined column of Grey's cock.

Grey was everything that was strong, everything that made Heath bold; if he screwed up, Grey would fix it. Grey would make it happen, if Heath took the risk. And Grey was also everything that made Toni vulnerable; she was open and soft and giving of love to him. They needed Grey in this.

"I'm starved for you, baby. Let me drink you up." Toni's plea to Grey brought him a step closer. And he let his head fall back as her lips enveloped him and she took him in her mouth.

Heath could see Grey's contorted expression; the man was in nirvana. He was gone as he dipped the crown into her mouth, swiveling his hips, his abdominal muscles tightening and loosening. He was being sucked by the woman he loved, and in all the times he and Heath had shared, Heath had never seen Grey surrender like this. He was lost to her mouth, to his lust and his feelings for her.

Heath had never known sex could be like this. Something emotive. Something that moved not only your body, but your soul.

As Toni grabbed the base of that penis and bumped her lips along the head, kissing it with a tenderness only a lover could kiss with, Heath reached under Grey's glistening, sliding cock and began to stroke his balls. Grey hissed out a breath but didn't stop him; instead he reached for the back of Toni's head to hang on to. Heath and Toni began to move their hips, mating hard as they worked Grey. They fucked until the sounds in Grey's throat began to spill out without control, until Heath's eyelids fell shut and he was whipped into a storm, until Toni's hoarse cry of ecstasy exploded in the room, bringing them all to orgasm.

Chapter Nine

"But you did notice it wasn't just me. Touching you?"

Inside the dimly lit kitchen, wearing one of Grey's long-sleeved button-down shirts, Toni was draped against his sweat-coated torso, drawing figure eights along the back of his biceps. She stood between his thighs as he sat atop the kitchen island, where they'd been feeding each other cheese and fruit.

"I noticed," he replied evenly.

"And?" she encouraged, ignoring the sound of Heath's knowing chuckle in the background. With heavy-lidded eyes, like those of a man who'd just spent hours in his woman's bed, Grey gazed into her face with a combination of indulgence and amusement. He'd slung on his khaki shorts but hadn't bothered to zip them up. Through the parted zipper, she could see the damp arrow of hairs dipping into his crotch. It took an effort not to insinuate her fingers inside and take him out, touch him with her hands, her mouth. "So you noticed," she repeated, "and you liked it?"

"I was too hot to care." His lips curved as he feathered them across the length of hers. "All I knew was your lips were on me."

A tremor ran down her spine. Lust rampaged inside her even when she had just had the best sex of her life. She simply could not erase the memory of Heath's hand around Grey's thickened, slickened cock. The sounds of pleasure Heath had made when Grey let him touch him . . .

Grey, I want you to do that again, she thought wantonly. It was embarrassing to think it, maybe even to want it this bad, but she was certain nothing in her entire life had made her so out-of-her-mind horny as that scene she'd witnessed.

"Toni here has been curious about male-on-male action," Heath said from behind her, shoving the fridge shut with his hips. Privately, Toni still couldn't get over the amount of food that man ingested. She doubted there was a slice of ham left in the refrigerator for a sandwich.

"Has she?" Grey cocked a brow, and she felt a telling heat swamp her neck and cheeks.

"I was just asking," she admitted, dropping her lashes under his intent scrutiny. What would he think if he knew?

But something odd had happened today. It was as though Grey and Heath had become one. Whatever tension they had brewing between them had ebbed away, and suddenly their strengths seemed magnified as they united forces. The sex they'd shared had been so agonizingly delicious, so complete between the three of them. It was almost surreal.

For the first time it had felt like a *threesome*—not two gorgeous hunks having their way with her at once.

"What is it that makes you curious?" Grey asked as he fed her an apple slice.

The juice exploded in her mouth as she munched. She swallowed before admitting, "I don't know. It's sexy."

He bit off half a slice and then popped the rest into her mouth, watching in lazy male interest as she nibbled. "You think so?" he asked.

He seemed only mildly curious, but she was fast to nod. Oh yes, she thought it was sexy. Grey being done by a man was so, so sexy. Heath's long, blunt-fingered hands on Grey were so damned sexy!

Rising on tiptoe, she framed his jaw in both hands. "You're

beautiful, Grey Richards." *You're so beautiful when you let go. I want Heath to help me suck your cock, and I want to watch you love it. . . .*

"Why do you do that?" Heath interrogated. "Say your names like that. Grey Richards, Antonia Kearny. It's Grey or Toni. Period."

Grey lifted her up to his lap and shifted her sideways to face Heath, his arm curling possessively around her waist. "She *is* Antonia Kearny," Grey said.

Studying her with a dark-eyed look that felt almost as possessive as Grey's arm around her, Heath propped an elbow on the closed fridge door. "Will you take Grey's name when you marry? Toni Richards?"

The blow was so unexpected, Toni actually heard the air whoosh out of her lungs.

Heath had *not* just said that.

She tried to summon a giggle in order to laugh off the words. She couldn't.

The warmth deserted her face and a cold wind slid across the back of her neck. She felt horribly, *horribly* humiliated for some reason, as though the seconds she sat there—speechless, stunned, perplexed—were telling Grey more than she'd ever wanted to let on about her evolving thoughts.

"Grey and I don't believe in marriage," she said with an impressive attempt at self-recovery. She breezed away from Grey. "We think it's . . ." She seemed to have forgotten all the bad things they thought about the institution, so she waved a hand and said, "We just don't believe in it. So I am Antonia Kearny, and I will continue to be Antonia Kearny until I die." She patted Heath's raspy, stubbled cheek, her chin up and haughty. "Satisfied, Heath . . . Solis?"

It took her every ounce of willpower and then some to meet Grey's gaze head-on. He sat in the very spot she'd left him in, thoroughly quiet. He was smiling, but he didn't look amused.

She shot him a brave smile, and when it faltered on her face, she knew she needed a moment to herself. "I'll be back."

⌐

Grey reached into the fruit bowl and thwacked Heath with a flying banana.

"What the . . . !"

"The next time you have an idiotic thing to say, *don't* say it in front of Toni."

Heath swept the fruit up from the floor and wiped it across his T-shirt. "You mentioned marrying her, so I thought you'd at least discussed it with her. Sheesh. What were you planning?"

Grey crossed his arms, his forehead furrowed in annoyance. "It's called a surprise, Heath. You're fairly good at them yourself."

Casually peeling the banana, Heath took a bite and leveled him a look. He said nothing. But he didn't need to. He'd fucking said enough already.

Grey glared. "And now that you've fed her stories of Heath's Life as a Bi, she wants you and me to go at it—is that it?"

"How should I know?" He ate the last of the banana in one big mouthful and crossed the kitchen to toss the peel into the trash. "Toni's just curious about men."

"Good. She can watch *me* screw the devil out of *you*. I can think of a lot of ways to shut up that big mouth of yours."

"And I can think of one very good way to make you squeal like a girl."

"Who's going to squeal like a girl?"

Appearing through the hall, Toni steered around the kitchen island, still wrapped in Grey's shirt. She had rolled the cuffs up to her elbows, and the cotton fabric was wrinkled across her hips. Grey had thoroughly disliked it when women he'd slept with had taken the liberty of wearing his clothes, but the sight of Toni in his shirts had the opposite effect on him. It stirred a wildness in him, made him want to sniff himself on her, made him want to brand her with his tongue.

With a quirked brow, she directed a questioning look in Grey's direction, then at Heath. "Who's going to squeal like a girl?"

"Grey is," Heath said.

Grey caught her before she could pass, flanked her between his thighs, and wrapped his arms around her shoulders from behind. "Antonia Kearny," he said. "Who would want to change such a pretty name?"

Grey would. Fuck, he was dying to. But all of a sudden, Toni didn't seem too thrilled. Her words were as stiff as her back. "Nobody. I like my name just fine."

He fell silent, and part of him wished he could see her face to gauge her expression. It had never occurred to him that she might not want to marry him. The possibility perturbed him. No, it *ate* at him. It would kill him. Not having her. Not making her entirely, irrefutably his.

"Toni Richards isn't pretty?" he asked uneasily, and to that he got a shrug in reply. Heath's intentional smirk didn't help matters. Heath's *presence* here didn't help matters. Grey wanted to turn Toni around and go searching in her eyes—he thirsted to find the answer he needed, *craved* seeing her *yes* to that unspoken question in his gaze.

He couldn't have asked for a more inopportune moment to seek it.

Now, in all honesty, he could not stop wondering whether she wanted to be his wife or not.

It would all have to wait.

Leaning close to the top of her head, he twined a hand through the soft coil of hair at her nape, caressing the curve that led to her shoulder. "Do you want to play?" he breathed into her.

"Like Monopoly?"

She tipped her head way back to meet his gaze. He smiled down at her, and his lower lip met with her top one when he huskily confessed, "A grown-up game, baby." *One where I'm all over*

you, sweetheart. Where you moan my name over and over and show me
I'm your man . . .

"What's it called?" she asked.

"It's called, Heath Watches While I Take You Like a Caveman."

She laughed, and Heath sauntered forward, his eyes smoldering with intent. "Or we can play Let's Watch Grey Take It Like a Man. Doesn't that sound like fun?"

Laughing once more, she turned in Grey's arms to regard him. "Does the idea disturb you?"

"Sex between guys?" He met Heath's gaze over the top of her head, then admitted, "I've seen Heath with men. We had an orgy once."

"Oh, really?" Toni gnawed at her lower lip, not quite successfully hiding her enlightened smile. "You *have* been around, Mr. Richards."

Chuckling, he kissed the tip of her nose. "To hell and back, sweetheart."

"And what did you think about . . . what you saw?"

"I think I wouldn't want to be the unfortunate bastard on the bottom," he said, pretty severely.

Her soft, quiet laugh faltered when her eyes snagged on his erection that was starting to swell for her. She wet her lower lip as her eyes lingered on the flesh exposed through the V of the zipper.

"And . . . the one on top?" she ventured, trailing a hand up his knee.

"Do you want us to get it on? Is that what you're saying?"

She turned bright scarlet at his directness, and he knew right then that she did. Want it. A hell of a lot.

"Would you enjoy it?" she whispered.

He wasn't entirely sure, but while he weighed the matter, he countered, "Would it be enjoyable to *you*?"

Her breasts pressed into his shirt at each of her rapid breaths. Just the thought of it seemed to have her verging on a climax. Grey had *never* seen that particular shade of red on her cheeks. "This is embarrassing," she murmured under her breath.

He angled her face up and stared directly into her gaze. "I'm not sensitive. Tell me. Is this something you fantasize about?"

Her eyes flared wider with hopefulness, and the forest green around the pupils was the darkest he'd seen them. "Would you like to, Grey?" she asked, almost in a plea.

"Not without you," he admitted. But with her it was anything, everything, anywhere, anytime.

"But . . . with me?"

A little arrogantly, he signaled down at the thickening flesh rising up against his abdomen, the head stretching, the veins filling darkly. "This cock is yours. If you play with me and if you touch me, then tell me where it goes. Do you want me in your mouth? In your pussy? Where do you want me? Do you want me to push it into Heath's mouth? Maybe he'll stop breathing if I push hard enough."

Heath chuckled, watching their exchange with eyes that were alight with interest. "Grey, your sadistic side is very amusing."

"I own you?" Toni baited, dragging a fingertip around the sensitive folds that circled the crown.

"I'm yours," he agreed.

She pulled the zipper farther aside, edged it under his balls. "Every inch of you."

"Every inch."

"These nine inches of the most beautiful cock I've ever seen?" she continued, and folded her right fist around the middle of the stalk.

"All yours."

He was thrumming for her caresses, his blood boiling as it coursed through his veins. "So if I tease you," she began, fluttering her hand up and around his cock in a way that had his teeth clenching, "you and Heath would have some fun . . . with me?"

"If Heath's a good boy." When Heath inched closer, an arm

stretched out with purpose, Grey barked, "Wait up, asshole. We haven't decided."

Heath engulfed her in his arms, shifting so he stood behind her. "Bah, discuss, discuss. Do I get to vote?" he asked her.

"Yes!" she said.

Heath's hand came down and in a clean, easy stroke, he ran his fist up Grey's erection. Grey sent his arm flying. "You touch me before I say so and your teeth are going to collide with my knuckles. We're discussing here." He spread his legs wider apart, then grabbed the base of his cock. "This fine apparatus is Toni's."

She shot Heath a crooked smile. "Maybe I'll share." At Grey's scowling look, she laughed. "I'll share all of him you want, Heath."

"Nobody wants Grey—he's a wuss." His hands delved under the hem of her shirt and Grey watched him massage her delectable cheeks. "It's your little dent here I'm craving, kitten." He nipped her earlobe. "I promise you you'd love it."

"You're not getting that this weekend. I'm not kidding," Grey warned.

"Look at her. Toni's all squirmy and blushy." Heath sampled the spot behind her ear as he reached out to palm Grey's crotch. "Don't even pretend this isn't turning you on, Richards, 'cause I've got cum all over my hand to prove it." He brushed up nice and swift, and Grey's cock jerked. "Your dick wants my hand. It likes my stroke just fine."

"Then shut up and let me enjoy."

Grey closed his eyes, aware and aroused that Toni watched him. As his dick expanded in Heath's hand and those big fingers slid down to stroke his sac, Grey considered what it would take to push his dick into Heath's mouth. Not very much, actually. He could ram Heath's face down into his hips and order him to eat him, then sit Toni over his face and have her sluice her juice all over his mouth as she came.

"I know it turns you on," Heath murmured to Toni as he slid a finger under Grey's nuts and stroked into his seat. "You want Grey on all fours, don't you? Do you want him to be the woman?"

"The—" Grey's eyes flew open and he burst out laughing. "Please tell me Heath did not get that from you?"

Toni looked ready to hide. Mortified, she began to nod, then shake her head; then she seemed to give up, flushing up to her pretty little ears. Her curiosity and innocence about the male-male matter made Grey itch in his seat to satisfy her.

Self-consciously pushing a strand of hair behind her ear, she said, "I just asked . . . well, you know how they say one is the . . ." She sighed, turned up those beseeching green eyes to his. "Is anyone else getting excited or is it just me?" She lightly touched her fingers to his jaw; they trembled. "I'm so turned on just thinking you might do it."

"That settles it," Heath said. "Talk is over, Grey."

She'd never been so drenched.

Grey lay on the bed, seemingly endless yards of sinew and muscle stretched across the mattress. His neck was strained, his eyes shut in a grimace. He swiveled his hips, and between his legs was Heath, a large, hunched figure sucking Grey's long, damp cock, making gruff sounds deep in his chest. Grey's hand was on the back of his head, urging him down, and he was mumbling, "That's right. Milk it dry. Take it all in."

Oh, god, she was positively dying.

She hadn't realized, had never considered, that Grey wasn't physically all that reserved. Though he was emotionally unattainable, her Grey was no pussy in the sex department—he was giving Heath cock, and looking quite calm about it. Her organs felt near bursting. Witnessing this, something bloomed in her chest—a tenderness, a longing.

If she could freeze this moment to play over and over in her mind, capture every detail of their rippling bodies in her memory, she wouldn't have asked for more.

Heath's dick was so long between his folded legs, untouched and oozing with precum as he milked Grey. The plum-shaped head shone red and ready, blood filling up his length. The muscles in his jaw worked, and he sucked so hard, tasting Grey, savoring Grey.

"Lick my head—ahh, right there, suck it in."

Grey's shaft glistened like varnished bronze as Heath moved up, then went so low that his mouth hovered over the thatch of silky blond curls at the base. He took him all the way down to his throat.

Grey angled his head to rest his jaw on Toni's parted thigh, and his tongue snaked out to flick at her pussy, his fingers insinuating inside.

"You've never been this wet, darling." He spoke against the wetness, moving his head as he worked her with his mouth. "You taste like peaches and spice, and I want to drown in you. . . ." His words turned to a groan when Heath ducked his head between his thighs and nuzzled his balls, lapped the sac with his tongue while fisting him with one hand.

Her muscles tensed against the sensations pulsing through her, the visual stimulus, the men, the pleasure, too much. She came with Grey's tongue, tossing on the bed as her orgasm tore through her. She struggled to sit and gasped at Grey's ear while he ran his thumb around her soaked clitoris. "I can't stand this. . . . I picture you fucking together and I . . ." She convulsed, coming all over his fingers. She couldn't stop coming. Crying out and coming.

"You like it, my love?"

"*Yes!*" He plunged one, two, three fingers into her soaked sheath and twirled her clit with the tip of his tongue, his breath caressing her pussy. She splayed her hands on the bed and arched for a third, earth-shattering climax, head tossing sideways while she pumped her hips up to his fingers and mouth.

When she collapsed on the sweat-soaked sheets, Heath rose to his full height at the foot of the bed. Tendons lined up the front of his neck, and the cords along his forearms seemed to stick out as he braced his legs apart, his bloated penis pushing up like a lance.

"Go on, Grey," he said. "You know you've wanted to. Pleasing our woman together, watching our dicks slide inside her. It turns you on, watching me with her."

"First of all," Grey said, sitting up and bearing his weight on outstretched arms, "she is not our woman. She is *my* woman. Second of all, she turns me on the second she's in the room, and it has nothing to do with you. But I'm feeling generous."

Grey brushed Toni's hair back and skimmed his lips across hers before he rose.

Toni scooted mutely up to the headboard as Grey stalked to Heath's place at the foot of the bed. They looked impossibly larger all of a sudden, their bodies taut and vigorous and deliciously close to each other. Her walls clenched heatedly at the sight of their erections.

"Bend over."

Planting his hands on the edge of the bed, Heath bent over slightly, his thick, packed torso unyielding and motionless, *waiting*. Grey reached around, touched his cock with one hand. He fondled him as easily as he would himself—as though it were his own cock he was fisting. He caressed upward, engulfing the reddened head in a big, loose fist. Heath's abdomen rippled when Grey tightened his hold, then released him, sending his cock slapping hungrily against his stomach.

As Grey rolled on the rubber, Toni thought he was long enough to sink it right up to Heath's throat. He lubed himself, then he gripped Heath's hips and grunted as he nudged him.

A strangled sound welled up in Heath's throat, his body stiffening as though in pain, and Grey said, "Ahh, that's what you crave. Hmm? A cock in your ass? Are you watching this, sweetheart? This show's just for you."

Toni hadn't realized she had so many nerves in her body, and that they could all quiver at the same time. Her pussy throbbed, a river of lava, her lips so turgid she could barely ease her fingers inside. Through eyes that shimmered blindingly with passion, the sight of them was visual ecstasy. She was wiggling in her seat, her nipples screaming to be touched, her skin scorching on the inside.

Grey became rough with Heath, pistoning his hips without mercy, not gentle like he was with Toni—because Heath wasn't breaking for anything. He was locked in his place, taking Grey in with straining muscles, his frame powerful and unbending. Heath engulfed the tip of his own erection in one big hand and smoothed his fist upward, closing his eyes. Grey's skin glistened, his chest laboring for breath, and then he was shoving his mouth at Heath's ear, hissing, "Are you touching yourself, Heathcliff?"

"Yeah."

"Did I say you could touch your dick?"

"Shut up and give it to me."

Heath's hand expertly worked up and down his length. Toni climbed to her knees and seized him, and he bucked in pleasure, his breath whistling through his teeth. "Shit, yes, like that. Oh, baby, just like that." The black eyes he fixed on hers were stormy with lust, and the hand that reached between her legs unerringly found her.

She purred while he fingered her, and in the meantime Grey was on him, his mouth on his ear, tonguing him, his cock carving into him.

"Make noise for Toni."

Heath groaned. And it was a rousing, concentrated sound that went straight to her head. Perspiration gathered on their flesh, their foreheads. Their balls slapped as they moved.

"Tell me how much you like being fucked, Heathcliff."

"When you tell *me* how hot my ass is and how you're loving this."

"You're not getting anything from me but cock." He thrust deeper, his jaw bunching tight. "Take her while I take you, Heath. I want her coming with me."

"Come here, Cat." Heath grasped her by the ankles, dragged her down the length of the bed until she was splayed beneath him, and pinned her arms at her sides. Grey looked down at her as Heath swiped his tongue around the puckered tip of a breast. "You're trembling," Heath spoke against the nipple. "You're so excited. Do you like it?"

"I love it," she whispered, stroking his face, meeting Grey's liquid gold gaze as Heath spread her thighs wide and entered her. She gasped as Grey shoved hard into Heath, his powerful thrust simultaneously digging Heath deeper into her. It was like being fucked by Grey with an extension, or like being possessed by both of them at once—it was like being *possessed*, period. She was awash with sensations, with pleasure, with the sheer carnality of what they were doing.

"How are you doing, sweetheart?" Grey asked.

"Good, so good." God, so very, very good.

"One more whimper out of you, Heath, and I think we'll firmly establish who the girl is."

And he was coming. This fucking Heathcliff while he worked his cock into Toni's drenched sex seemed to undo him. He exploded with a muted sound that worked his mouth open, and Heath's cum gushed into her as he bucked his hips. He hadn't worn a condom, and she felt the warmth of him bathe her tissues and slide down the insides of her lips. Hovering on the brink, her womb bursting with tension, she saw Heath extract himself from her pussy and guide his still-hardened cock to stroke her clitoris. He circled the taut pebble with the slick-coated head, caressing both of them with their sexes and juice, and her orgasm took her with such power she came off the bed with a cry of bliss.

For minutes she lay in a tangle of limbs with Heath's heavy body against hers, the sound of a faucet running filtering through her haze. Grey moved around the room in silence, until Heath looked over his shoulder.

"Aww, come on, don't look so serious. We fucked. I don't see a problem."

"Heath, you're really something—do you know that?"

"I do." He pushed himself upright and slapped Grey's shoulder. "Welcome to being bi. Embrace it, buddy."

And then Grey came over, scooped her up like a limp, sexually sated doll, and carried her into the bathroom. She sighed when he set her into the tub, the warm water seeping into her muscles. She relaxed when he settled behind her, stretching his legs down the length of the tub.

"I am so blown away, I can't stop thinking about it," she murmured, gazing up at the bright light fixture and wiping her eyes with her hands.

Heath joined in on the other end of the tub, resting his head against the glossy ivory surface. His eyes were weighted and smoky as he gazed at her.

"You all right, Heath?" Grey asked after a moment.

"Dandy. You're the best I've had, Grey."

Grey released a quiet chuckle and began to massage her scalp with one hand and slide a sponge between her breasts with the other. She fitted her back to his front, tucking the back of her head under his chin with a dreamy sigh. "What are you doing?"

He lifted one leg and gently lathered her calves, the soft skin on the back of her knees. "Washing you diligently." He was thorough, soaping every inch of that extended leg, dipping the sponge into the water to clean her inner thigh. "Can you get the toes for me, Heath?"

"I'm on it." Heath propped her toes on his chest and traced the arch of her foot with his thumb, causing a tingle up her leg. He lathered his fingers and stroked in between each toe, the gentle pressure of his fingers relaxing her.

Even as she floated limply under their ministrations, heat pooled between her legs in such a way that she thought the water smelled more of her scent than shampoo and soap.

"Grey . . ."

He had leaned back in the tub and was absently stroking her stomach. "Hmm."

"I want us not to get dressed. I want us to touch each other all afternoon and all night, and I want to come a thousand times."

He chuckled, a lazy hand coming up to fondle a breast. "We can arrange that."

"And I want you and Heath to play with each other."

Heath's smile was crooked. "Are we little toys for your pleasure?"

Grey followed a drop of water up her temple with his tongue, lapped it up, and under the water, he cradled her pussy in his hand. "Heath and I want to play with you."

Her lips curved at the deliciously decadent thought. She pushed her pussy into his hand. "I can arrange that, too."

After a silence, Grey ran a finger up the curve of her hips. "I used to play with airplanes in my bath when I was little. They couldn't withstand the thunderstorm of the showerhead, and they'd crash and burn and sink deep into the ocean."

She smiled. "So that's what it takes to wreck your plane? A little rain?"

"Not the Citation X."

She laughed, curling her arms around herself while her toes played with Heath's stomach under the water. "I used to wash my dolls, and they'd squeak for weeks. Mom hated that."

Toni waited for Heath to offer a story. He lifted one brow when he seemed to realize she expected one; then his other brow rose. "I didn't have a tub. But if I'd had one, I'd have played with my wang."

She splashed water into his face. "Heath!"

He laughed and wiped his face with one hand, then let his head drop. He propped her legs up on his chest, caressing the arches of her feet with his thumbs.

Her mind flickered with naughty images of licking their cocks together. She had images of Grey's mouth being filled with Heath's sex. She had vivid thoughts of Grey bending over, his face twisted as he was penetrated by Heath. She sighed. "I'm so horny."

Grey's fingers spread across the inside of her thighs. "So am I."

"There's not even an order that covers all the things I want to do between us." She felt frantic, sick with need to have more sex with them, push their limits, push her own. She ought to be concerned, but shamefully, she wasn't.

"Let's get you dry first—and you can tell us about it in bed."

Minutes later, she lay bare-assed, stomach down on the bed while the men dried themselves. When the phone rang, Toni dove across the pillows to snatch it up.

"Hi, Toni. May I speak to Grey?"

"Hey, Louisa. I thought he wasn't working this weekend." Quickly she noted it was five p.m. in Los Cabos, and much later in Chicago.

"It's sort of an emergency. The Dallas construction has been halted, and we can't find Mr. Solis."

Toni held the phone up and away from her ear. "The Dallas construction has been halted, and they can't find Heath." Grey snatched it up with a none-too-pleasant frown. "Grey." After listening, he gave a long put-out sigh. "We sent a message that Heathcliff wasn't making it to Dallas until after Canada, and that's next week. Send Parsons to look into it."

Toni rolled onto her back and smiled at Heath. *Heathcliff*, she mouthed at him.

He made a face as he edged closer. She laughed, and he followed suit, but his laughter died when he propped his hands next to her head and stared broodingly at her mouth.

"Oh no. Don't stop; it's a nice laugh," she encouraged.

The way he stared at her lips made her think he was memorizing every crease and dent in her mouth. "I'd rather shut up and hear yours," he admitted.

She ran her index finger over his raspy, darkly shadowed jaw. "Heathcliff. I happen to like your name very much. I've been in love with Heathcliff ever since I read *Wuthering Heights*." At his blank look, she effusively explained, "The passionate love affair, so dark and stormy and poignant. And a haunting." She smiled when she got a reaction. "See, I can tell you liked the sound of that."

"No. I liked your big, wide, scared eyes when you said *haunting*."

His smile was holding, and Toni felt giddy at how beautiful it was. "Seriously, why don't you use it? Your name?" she asked.

"Why don't you use Antonia?"

She pulled a face, and he chuckled.

"Ahh, I pressed a button. Antonia."

"Heathcliff."

"Antonia."

"Heathcliff."

What began as play made their smiles fade, sensual awareness creeping over them. His eyes clouded as he bent his head. He gazed at her lips once more, then wet the corner of her mouth with the tip of his tongue. "You're very beautiful, Antonia." A wet flick of his tongue caressed the other side of her lips. She opened her mouth, but he only breathed into her. "Has Grey spanked you?"

"Yes." *Kiss me, Heath.*

"Tied you up?"

"Yes." *Lick me up—oh, god, please kiss me.*

He slipped his hand up her tummy. "Do you have little toys?"

"Just a-a dildo."

"What does he do with a dildo, Antonia?"

"I put it inside her." She closed her eyes when Grey captured her arms above her head. Heath continued stroking her torso, his hand velvet, skimming up to her throat.

"He watches when he puts it inside you?"

Grey's mouth was on her fingers, nipping the tips. "I watch her take it all the way into her sweet, wet little cunt, then come all over it."

Heath studied her breasts. The nipples were wet and puckered tight, and he seemed to like watching them jolt when he brushed his thumbs across them. "He likes control, and you like to lose it?"

She squirmed. "Maybe *I* am going to torture you men for a

change and—ooh, oh Heath!" Her hips rose when he buried his thumb inside her pussy.

"Ooh, what, Antonia?" He withdrew to tease her clit with his index finger, his midnight eyes watching the folds spread and wet for him. The tendons in his neck worked as he swallowed.

"Ooh yes, ooh yes," she said, moving to his hand.

"Not until you tell Grey what I did to you."

"Grey."

"What did he do to you, Toni?"

"I touched her on the horse."

"Did you let him touch you on the horse, Toni?"

And Toni, burning, confessed, "A little."

"Did you love it?"

"I . . . well . . . yes."

"I'm thinking you probably want to spank her. I'd paddle this rear if she were mine," Heath offered.

"And right you are, Heathcliff, right you are."

She squealed when Grey flipped her around. "Am I getting spanked?" she cried.

"Were you naughty?"

"Yes."

"Then I'm going to have to smack your ass. Get over here."

Biting back her smile, she let him set her across his lap, his desire stabbing into her abdomen. He smoothed his hand across the curve of her ass, his palm warm and dry. When he hesitated, she lifted her head, cocked it to the side, and kissed him.

"Give me that little tongue," he growled.

When she pushed her tongue into his mouth, he suckled it with relish. No sooner had he let go of her mouth than a slap landed on her left cheek, making her stiffen. "That is for not waiting for me." A second slap stung across her left cheek, tearing a squeal from her. "That is for letting him touch you."

She heard one of Heath's more cynical snorts. "You spank like a sissy, Grey. Oh, wait. You *are* a sissy."

Grey chuckled against her nape, rubbing the places he'd abused. "I don't want to hurt my baby." He kissed each of her round cheeks. "This is my little baby and I need to take care of her."

"For your information, I'm a big girl and I can definitely—oooh!"

He slapped her so hard she felt the sting in her clit; then he grabbed her wrists and yanked them up over her head, trapping them with one powerful hand as he shoved her flat on the bed.

"You want rough?"

A twinge of excitement skittered up her spine. "Yes."

He scissored her legs open and stroked her entry. His cock rubbed every inch of her lips and every fierce pulse in him resonated between her thighs. The sensitive bead of her clitoris received delicious stimulation from the contact with the sheets.

"Heath's been a bad boy," he growled, nipping the small pearl earring at her ear. His breath burst out of him in hot, furious pants. "Now he gets to watch. Are you watching, Heathcliff?"

"I'm watching."

"What are you going to do?"

"I'm in my hand, I'm so hard."

"Good. You're not getting any yet." Grey screwed into her damp pussy, and when he started expertly circling his hips, she felt herself contract. Ready to come again, ready to explode.

He pushed her to the limit and then retracted, and when he growled, "Eat Heath's cock," Toni was thirsty to oblige.

Heath moved over and knelt before her. The next second he was ramming down to her throat. She struggled to take all of his hot flesh inside her, unaware that she was rubbing herself against the sheets until Grey continued pushing into her with fierce, hot jabs.

She whimpered in heat, clutching the sheets in her fists to hold herself in place, stomach and pelvis rubbing against the bed at his impacts. Her tongue traveled, flat and hungry, under Heath's thick penis, then around the head. Her nerves quivered, her muscles contracted, and she felt herself get pulled inward, crammed tightly, impossibly tightly, in the very pit of her, and her orgasm crashed into her. . . .

"I got you."

Grey's arms enveloped her as she bucked in ecstasy, his weight coming on top of her as he continued to move inside her, riding her passion, prolonging her tremors, whispering dirty words about him, about her eating Heath.

Gasping for breath, Toni tipped her head back to Heath, and his eyes blazed as he watched her. Something wild flashed inside the pupils, primitive, thrilling and scary. Roughly, he pulled out of her mouth, fisted himself in his hand and pumped, angling his cock to her face, her lips, her mouth. His eyes were fevered.

His cum exploded across her face with one pull, blasting her skin with warmth. He spurted it across her lips, her chin, her cheeks and delivered several final, unbridled strokes, groaning a long, deep sound of contentment as he coated her with him.

Toni was still gasping from the shock when Grey tensed and released in her. In the aftermath, he propped himself up on his elbows to ease some of his weight off her as he rolled her over, smoothing one hand across her damp forehead.

"Look at this mess," he said smilingly, but as his eyes coasted over her face, they became glazed, hungry. "Let's get you cleaned up." And then Grey bent, and his tongue began to lap at all of Heath that was on her.

Chapter Ten

"Did I fall asleep?"

Toni canted her head back and blinked. Fading sunlight filtered through the window of Heath's room, and she guessed she must have dozed off before dinner. That was *after* the men had cornered her in the hall, backed her into Heath's room, hoisted her up on the bed, determinedly opened her legs, and lapped at her pussy in unison—alternating their thrusts into her. She had come three times, once while they both speared their tongues into her sex. Then she had watched them come against each other.

She had never had sex like this.

The sight of the males rubbing against each other, their penises coated with each other's cum while their bodies rocked in the aftermath, their mingled tastes when she went in to lick them side by side, drop by drop . . .

She shuddered at the memory, afraid that she was getting high on their sex, too dependent and drunk on it to think straight. She could only think of touching them, being touched, or baiting them to touch each other.

She was so lost in her reverie, it took her a second to realize Heath stared into her eyes with a singular look on his face, as though she were something priceless and riveting. Her jaw rested

on his warm chest, and snuggled against his side she felt unexpectedly . . . comfortable. She had no inclination to get up, but instead
found her fingers too eager to sift through the little hairs between
his pecs. "Where did Grey go?"

"Phone." He gave her an enlightened smile. "Or cleaning out
his closet. I don't know. The guy's a freak."

Her lips curled in the ends, one playful fingertip going to circle
his nipple. "I love my freak."

He chuckled, the vibrations humming through her. "I know
you do." He skimmed his knuckles down her cheek with tender
familiarity, his arm tightening around her shoulders. "And I'll have
you know I can be very freaky, too."

"Oh, really?"

"Be afraid, Toni. Be very afraid."

Her eyes crinkled. "I'm shaking in my undies," she teased. When
he subjected her to a thorough scrutiny, she shifted up on her elbows and asked, "What's your favorite color?"

"Black?"

"Why are you asking *me*?" At the uncertainty on his face, a
laugh escaped her. "It's either black or it isn't," she good-naturedly
explained.

"All right. It is. Black."

"Favorite band?"

"U2?"

"Why are you asking me!" She laughed again, both bewildered
and enchanted. She was under the impression he'd have changed
his answers just to please her. From such a dark, big, raw man, it was
so endearing. Who would have thought Heath Solis would give a
damn about what Toni thought of his choice of band? Really, what
woman on earth would not want him?

"Tell me yours," he encouraged, stacking his hands behind his
head.

"I like blue and green. Fresh colors. And I like . . . well." Her forehead furrowed as she considered. "I think I like solo singers better than bands. I like girly music."

"Of course."

"Madonna, Céline Dion—ooh, and I like Shakira."

"Ahh, can you move your tushy for me like Shakira?"

"I can move my tushy all over you, Heathcliff."

Laughing, he hauled her up so she straddled his hips, and her body responded to his nearness. The lazy smile that had been tugging at his lips faded while a sensual awareness began to creep into his gaze. His eyes shimmered like onyx as he took in her face, her shoulders, her breasts. His cock pushed into the apex of her thighs.

He wanted her.

And she wanted him. She wanted him not less than before, but more. It was slightly worrying. Before, maybe part of her attraction had to do with what Grey had told her about him. It was like being told Paris was beautiful, full of shops, romantic. It was like listening to a motivational cassette or even a doctor working you in a hypnotic trance; suddenly you wanted Paris with your entire being. It had all been Grey . . . what he said . . . and Heath had been an eclipse, a dark mystery Toni had begun to ache to unravel. But now he was less a mystery and more a real human being to her, and he was marvelous. He and Grey together were marvelous. The three of them. This trip. It was *all* marvelous.

Eyes hot as he raised his hand to stroke her face, he thrust his thumb into her mouth, dampened her lips with her saliva, then ran his thumb across her mouth with a brusque, desperate swipe. He covered her cheeks with his hands and rubbed his nose against hers. His breath seeped into her lungs when she parted her lips. "I want you all the time," he whispered.

"I want you all the time, too."

She slanted her mouth to his in offering, but he buried his lips in her arching neck. Her lashes fluttered shut as he tended to the area, her head tilting to give him better access. "Heath, when are you going to kiss me?"

He kissed her neck—wetting her skin, lapping it with his tongue. "I am kissing you."

"My lips. Don't you want to?"

"Yes." He didn't stop at her neck, but his warm, moist lips ventured up to nibble her chin.

"Don't you like kissing?" she insisted. Because she was *dying* for his kiss. She had pictured it in her mind, had decided he would taste of beer and mint, and every atom in her body craved it like life.

He went to her earlobe, ran the tip of his tongue up the tender backside. Through the irregular sound of his breaths, she could barely make out his gruff words. "I have a feeling I'd like kissing you very much."

She dropped her face and searched for his mouth with hers. "Then kiss me now."

"No."

"Don't you know how to kiss?" she hissed, her leg getting tangled on the sheets as she rolled away. Grinding her teeth together in sheer frustration, she pushed at his shoulders with the heels of her palms and rose to her feet, ready to spit nails at how annoying and impossible he was.

"Son of a bitch!" He was on his feet the next instant, his hands plunging into his hair.

In a black pair of boxers, chest heaving up and down, he watched her stalk around the bed, grab her pillow, and storm out. And she stormed out of there knowing *precisely* why he was all alone in the world. Knowing exactly why no woman wanted to be with him. All that man wanted was sex!

She quickened her steps down the hallway, cursing him and herself. A part of her had hoped she'd have the nonchalance not to care whether he wanted her kiss or not, but there was no denying the awful pressure in her chest. His denial hurt.

Pushing her hair back, she stopped in the living room and wrapped her arms around her chest, trying to stifle the furious tremors shuddering down her spine. She felt so . . . so . . . so unwanted. Her lips were not at all bad to look at, and yet he tore his eyes away from them every time he saw them. She didn't know of a man who would do the kinds of things Heath did to her and not want to kiss her!

She tensed her shoulders when she heard him breathing heavily behind her.

"Come to bed with me."

When she didn't respond, he curled his hand around her elbow. Though she didn't extract her arm, she made no move to touch him, either.

Whispering, "It's not what you think, Toni," he caught her by the waist and pressed his lips to her neck. And he rocked her. To and fro against his body. Rocked her so she wanted to dissolve against his strength. She stiffened against the impulse.

"I don't think you even know what I think."

"Then maybe you don't understand." The fact that he was speaking to her like a child, not patronizingly, but with an odd, gruff tenderness, only wrenched the knife in her further.

"I understand perfectly. I'm your weekend screw. Not good enough to talk to and not to kiss."

"I can't fucking . . . argh, this is ridiculous!"

He thrust his hands up, and she shoved past him when he did. "You're right—it is."

Ludicrous. Ridiculous. Why did she even *care*? Why couldn't it *not* matter whether he wanted to kiss her or not? Why didn't Heath *feel* like just sex to her, like he was supposed to? Like she was to *him*?

"Are we having a fight?" he asked as he followed her down the hall.

She didn't know what to reply, so she swiftly closed the door behind her. Lounging on the bed, Grey glanced up and immediately set down his Sudoku as she plopped down on the bed. "I thought you'd fallen asleep. I didn't want to disturb you."

She curled up against his side, cheek to chest. "I woke up with the Grinch."

"What did that blockhead do?"

She made a grimace of distaste, not even wanting to get into it. "He's just sour company."

A knock came, and the door opened before anyone could invite him in. "Cat."

"Stop calling me Cat."

"She's very moody when she hasn't eaten, Heathcliff. Didn't I warn you?"

"It's not the goddamned food." He stared from the door, a hand on the doorframe. His neck was flushed, his eyebrows drawn low into a furious scowl. "Kitten, I've never *done* pillow talk before. Can we try this again? I really want you in my bed. We can nap and we can . . . do things."

Toni snuggled to Grey's side while throwing Heath her fiercest look to date.

His lips turned into a thin, uncompromising line as he slapped a hand on the doorframe. "Look, I don't know what to do with a woman if it's not . . ."

"Take some of your own advice, Heathcliff. 'Women like words and shit.'"

"Toni," Heath said, ignoring Grey. "Come on."

Grey rolled his eyes, groaning to himself. "Heath, I'm feeling really, really sorry for you."

Toni snuggled closer to Grey, mumbling, "Just bring your pillow."

Less than a minute later, he stormed inside with a look that dared anyone to contradict him. He fluffed up his pillow beside her, snorted when satisfied, and then he spooned her. The room started to darken as the sun set.

"Anyone up for dinner?" Toni queried.

"I'm up for sleeping," Grey murmured.

Cuddling between the two men, she was about to drift off to sleep when Heath snagged her earlobe between his teeth and rasped, "I'm up for sex."

Chapter Eleven

The next morning she found them having breakfast in silence, and although she said good morning, they didn't seem to hear. She went directly to the coffeepot, noticing across the counter as she poured a cup for herself that they'd already filled their cups.

Two large males at the breakfast table could've been incongruous, but it felt so right, like a family. She warmed all over as she watched their hands. Both long, Heath's more callused than Grey's as he cradled his cup in one hand. She walked over, snatched the bread crust from Grey's plate, and rumpled his hair on her way to her seat.

"Didn't your nannies teach you to clean your plate?"

He looked up, smiling. "I was always a very good boy. I ate all my spinach."

"You hate spinach."

"They made me hate it." He folded the morning paper, ran a finger across the back of her ear, tucking a chestnut curl back. "How do you feel?" he asked thickly.

She leaned back contentedly, taking a sip. Outside, the day was clear, the skies blue—a day that promised to be special. "I feel great."

"Get over here." The chair legs screeched as she obediently rose, and he drew her down to his lap and kissed her lips. "Good morning."

She petted his morning stubble and whispered, "Good morning."

"Do I get one of those?"

Her eyes flicked to Heath's. Unlike Grey, he was unsmiling this morning, intense, his eyes liquid coals. "Of course."

She made her way to him, her attention zeroing in on those pink, luscious lips of his. Just when she was going to give him a peck, he hauled her down on his knee and lightly bit around her chin. "I think I'll have you with my pancakes."

The way he looked at her lips made her tremble.

He was a great listener, he was a great lover, he was great fun in bed. Why didn't he kiss her?

"What's your favorite breakfast ever, Heath?" she queried, linking her fingers behind his nape.

"I think it's going to be you." He glanced up at Grey. "May I?"

"Bon appétit."

Toni squeaked when he jumped to his feet. "Heath! Señor Gonzalez is somewhere around the house, *mopping*! You'll have to wait for dinner."

He winked. "Or breakfast in bed."

She stuck her tongue out and wiggled free, then went back to her seat and coffee. "I thought we could do something interesting tonight, since Heath is leaving tomorrow," she said with as much nonchalance as she could muster.

She didn't like it when she thought of him leaving, of never seeing him again, never having sex like theirs again.

Trying to determine the impact of her words, she peered up at him through her lashes, but he'd dropped his face to his plate, uncharacteristically pensive. Grey was reading the newspaper—looking at the pictures, actually, and making his own deductions, because she knew he didn't speak Spanish.

"Do you want to go clubbing?" she insisted.

Heath forked up several slices of pancake and shoved them into his mouth. Grey sipped coffee.

"Heath?" Grey finally asked, lifting an eyebrow at him.

Heath shrugged. "Whatever Toni wants."

The fact that he did not meet her gaze made her shift restlessly in the chair. She stroked the length of a spoon. "Well, we could have drinks," she said, "and we could dance, and then we could . . . come back and have more fun."

Grey made a face Toni had seen plenty of times before. "Dancing."

"I know you hate dancing, but maybe Heath will dance with me. We've danced before, remember, Heath?"

Heath said nothing, did nothing but scowl at his food. They were both being sour, and she bristled with annoyance. She wanted tonight to be special, and they were ruining all of her plans with their surly dispositions, particularly Heath.

"Will you dance with me, Heath?" she insisted. "It'll be fun." *I want you to remember this forever.* Selfishly, she thought, *I want you to remember me.*

All she got as a reply was, "If I'm drunk enough."

⌒

Music blasted within the four walls of the nightclub. Lounging back on a red velvet upholstered booth, the three of them sat facing the dancing crowd, which consisted mostly of tourists—young and in the mood to party.

Grey drank wine, Toni Baileys, Heath beer. Grey had an arm around her shoulder, his wine idle in his hand, while Toni's left hand rested firmly on Heath's thigh.

Heath felt restless.

Like when he was about to take a flight, he wanted to numb his senses, to not hear or feel or think. It was the people. The noise. It was Toni, with a drop of perspiration trickling into her cleavage, with that skintight dress the color of whipped cream, with her scent suffusing his nostrils.

She was horny. And a little drunk. He could tell by the wanton drape of her body against Grey, the way she put her mouth up to his lips, the way she let him kiss and kiss and kiss her. Fuck, he was tonguing her so hard. Heath shifted on his seat. His lap was hurting, his balls drawn up tight enough to choke him. Every inch of his cock was pulsating. Anxiety ate at him. He had the horrible sensation of wanting to gorge on her, like a man about to move to the desert and who desperately needed to pack himself with food. He did not want to be in a club; he wanted to fuck her. No. That wasn't entirely true. What he most wanted was to *kiss her*.

She rolled her head and gazed at Heath with half-mast, hazy green eyes. That sultry gaze dropped to his lips, and he could not tear his eyes off her mouth, enlarged and wet from Grey's kiss. An invitation to kiss her beckoned to him as she shifted her torso discreetly toward him.

His tongue felt anxious. He wanted to lick. Go searching deep into her mouth. Fuck her mouth with his. She'd taste milky, of Baileys. He'd never been one for kissing, but it was all he could think about now. What she offered were kisses he could not take. So when he went back to his beer, his eyes on a young blonde dancing nearby, Grey reached out and grabbed her back to him and took more of those kisses.

He made love to her tongue. Their mouths opened wide in a lazy tangle. Grey knew and Heath knew that Toni wore no panties tonight, and by god, through the smoke, booze, and vodka, Heath could smell her. Grey fucked her mouth and his nostrils, too, flared as though he wanted no breath that didn't smell of creamy wet Toni.

Both their drinks were forgotten on the table as Toni massaged Grey's chest with her palms, his hands on both sides of her head, pinning her for his onslaught. Heath gazed out at the crowd, his gut twisting painfully inside him; then his eyes went back to them again.

He saw Grey's groin, a mountain of need against his trousers, and Heath knew he was going to come just from kissing her. His hips made the slightest, barely perceptible swivel, and his fingers moved up and down the back of her head as they slanted their heads, their mouths red and sloppy with saliva.

He'd never find a woman, and he'd thought Grey never would, either. They were each impaired in their own way, and yet . . .

Heath had been wrong. Grey had found Toni, and Heath would never have that kind of pure, sweet, beautiful love with her. *Face it: you don't inspire love.* Across the smoky room, a group of women stared. They scanned the three of them—Heath, Toni, Grey—and their attention returned to Heath. They gauged him as the third. Grey and Toni the couple, Heath the third wheel looking for a mate.

He did not want to be the third.

He caught the sight of Grey coming, his fingers flexing on the back of her head, hands tensing into fists. His body shuddered, and a wetness seeped through the fabric of his slacks.

No kissing, damn him. Heath would give anything to feel the heat of Toni's lips. Take something sweet from her, not wicked or dirty or blatantly sexual—just a kiss.

"Darling." Grey chuckled as they drew apart, smiling down at her as she lifted her head to his.

She caressed his jaw with those little magic fingers, speaking huskily to him so that Heath barely overheard. "I love it when you do that, let go with me like that."

To her words, Grey just said, "Hmm," and kissed her lingeringly, and she whispered, "I love you."

Heath blocked their conversation, took his eyes to the dance floor and lifted his beer to his mouth. He took a long swig. Set the glass down and moved his thumbs up and down. Drummed the fingers of one hand on the table.

Grey said something about having to go clean up, and within seconds he disappeared into the crowd.

Toni straightened in her seat, and an awkward silence settled in the booth. Her eyes landed on Heath's hands cradling his beer. She wanted them on her. She wanted to make out with and French-kiss Heath, too.

He knew it, *felt* her wanting him. His heart thundered with this knowledge, louder than the music, ramming in fast, vigorous beats against his ribs.

"You're so quiet tonight." A cool hand was on his cheek, turning him. "Are you all right?" Green eyes studied him.

"Yeah."

She didn't buy it and scrutinized him for a moment more, but then she smiled. She was so sweet, so female and caring. "I thought we were going to dance?"

Dance with her. Like they danced in the buff and in bed. Touch her without Grey there. *Want her more, more than yesterday, more than before*. Shit.

When they got home . . . he was going to tear off her dress . . . he was going to unleash this beast and he was going pour all this need and jealousy into her. . . .

"I don't like that song," he bluntly stated.

He signaled to a waiter for another beer and asked for her Baileys to be refilled. The smoke stung his eyes, tickled his nostrils. And through it all he could still smell her pussy under her dress. A pussy that was wet for Grey, wet for Heath, just plain wet for cock.

He cupped her bare knee and tried feeling his way up that toned, creamy leg, but Toni began flirting, evading, clamping her hand on his wrist to stop him. Her teeth shone white behind her smile. "Where do you think you're going, Señor Heathcliff?"

"Let me touch your pussy."

"But that's the game. You know I'm wet under my dress, but you don't touch until we get home."

"It's torture for me." *Tomorrow I can't see you or feel you, and I can't goddamned kiss you.*

He was not in the mood to be played. He tried again, inching three determined fingers under her skirt, consumed by a wildness to touch her. "I need pussy and I need it now."

"Heathcliff, behave!" she chastised, extracting his hand with force before she rubbed her palms up his chest and whispered, "We can kiss, Heath." She placed those lips of hers right within an inch of his. "Kiss me and I'll make you come like Grey, I promise." He could smell sweetness and alcohol on her breath, and he didn't know how he could stand not taking that mouth. He yanked his head away, assessed the crowd with a disinterested glance, and then noticed a pretty brunet coming over.

"*¿Quieres bailar?*"

Dance? Fuck. *Yes.* Dance with another woman, one who did not belong to someone else. Heath could kiss her, slam her against the wall, and fuck until his dick bled. This was Heath Solis underneath it all—underneath the face and the eyes and the many kinds of smiles. He was as unstable as he'd ever remembered being. He was that angry, rebellious kid who'd told the world to go screw itself.

Except he did not want to ditch Cabo, or Toni, even when leaving was all he knew how to do.

And yet *nobody* would want him to stay.

Toni watched him wide-eyed, lips parted in surprise as though she couldn't believe this girl had had the nerve to ask him to dance. But Toni had Grey. And her little game. And Heath needed something Toni could not give him. He wanted her, damn her. More of her, all of her. He needed her out of his freaking system!

Maybe his ploy would not work. Maybe he would make out with this pretty olive-skinned stranger and still want Toni, still have this hard-on, this perennial ache just for *her.* Maybe he would come back and smash Toni on the table and kiss her right in front of Grey and to hell with his word and Grey's fucking rules and to hell with everything. Maybe rather than finger-fuck this brunet's little pussy on the dance floor, he could have hot, painful hate sex with Toni. And he would tell her, in excruciating detail, how he would fuck a million pussies after hers. He would tell her how other women had meant more and how many times he'd kissed their mouths. He would tell her what a decent screw she'd been, and *hasta la vista, baby*. He wanted to *hate* her.

So Heath wiped his hands on his jeans, set his drink down and rose. And he said—"Let's dance."

⁓

Excuse me?

Toni blinked twice. With disbelieving eyes, she watched Heath's retreating back as he blended into the lively crowd, a big, dark, handsome thing, while the brunet with him began jumping up and down only inches away, waving her tits, dancing her heart out. The muscles of Toni's stomach gripped.

"Heath's dancing," she whispered to no one in particular. He was dancing, and it wasn't with her. His hands were grasping the woman's hips, his eyes were . . . they were taking in the sight of her jiggling breasts and he was . . . *smiling* down at her, and damn it, it *mattered*. Her eyes stung. All she could think of, with an unexpected hurt and confusion, was—

Why didn't he want to dance with me?

The warm spot where he had been sitting felt vacant. Like a black hole in the universe. And now his huge hands were almost on that woman's butt. He towered above her, inches taller than the entire crowd. There was just no way Toni couldn't look at him. She gritted her teeth as anger surged through her.

He was not hers. Somewhere in these marvelous, decadent days, she had started to think of Heath as *hers*. Hers and Grey's. Theirs.

A part of them. The fact that she had no right to feel this blinding, staggering wave of jealousy did not help to diminish it at all.

They danced one full song—the longest song in worldwide history. Toni didn't so much as twitch in her seat; she was too angered and appalled to do anything but stare. In her mind, she pictured doing violent things she'd never dreamed of doing to both him and that . . . that *twit*, and then she felt childish and immature for having relished those images.

Her frown was biting into her face by the time Heath returned. He plopped down beside her and took a long swig of his beer. For three seconds, neither spared the other a glance. He took a few breaths, and then just like that, moved his hand in her direction.

She stiffened when he pawed her knee with one squeezing palm and brazenly made his way up her thigh.

"Do I get pussy now?"

She pursed her lips, grabbed his hand, and threw it back into his own lap. He grabbed her hand tightly and set it crudely on his fly, pressing it to the iron-hard bulge at his crotch.

"Then grab that, will you?"

Under her hand, he was a huge, tight, enormous bulge, and the thought of him aroused because he'd been dancing with that . . . that . . . bitch made her want to smash her Baileys into something. She closed her palm and squeezed into his groin hard, so hard she heard the air tear out of his lungs. "Go show it off to whoever gave it to you," she snapped, yanking her hand back.

He snatched her wrist and forcefully pushed her palm to his crotch again. "You. Gave it to me."

It was a struggle to remove her hand, but somehow she managed. "Your girlfriend might disagree," she said tightly.

"Girlfriend." He engulfed her cheeks with his palms, his face a mask of pure black rage. "You're the woman I'm fucking tonight. You're the woman I fuck *in my sleep*." He pressed her hand between his legs again, commanding, "Leave it there."

Through the denim, his wetness seeped into her skin. Toni was

just as wet between her legs, and she was tense and angry and confused. He'd hurt her. How he had gotten to her enough to hurt
her, she wasn't sure. But he had. The turmoil raging through her
was frightening. She wanted to ride him until they screamed, and
by god, she wanted to smack him. Lust-filled anger had her digging the heel of her palm into the head of his cock so hard his hips
rose from the seat cushion and his head fell back with a muttered
curse.

"Why didn't you want to dance with me?" she demanded.

He clutched her face almost violently and scraped her lips with
his thumb, his expression vicious. "I'm in the mood to fuck you
very hard tonight." He showed his teeth in a wolfish snarl. "I'm in
the mood to make you scream."

"And I'm in the mood not to fuck you at all!"

He let go of her with a curse and stopped the first girl who
passed, wrenching her down to the bulge on his lap. "You look
good enough to eat," he growled, and crushed her lips with his. He
startled the woman, startled Toni as he gave the woman an angry,
devouring kiss on the lips and set her on the table, turning her into
a feast he gorged on. It was a kiss that must've hurt, in which Toni
could see his tongue plunging, venturing deep. His mouth slanted,
opened wide, the girl whimpering as she tunneled her fingers into
his hair and seemed to wiggle against his body for more. Toni didn't
stay to see the rest.

She wanted to throw up.

Stumbling out of the booth, she dove across the crowd. Her
vision was blurred as she shoved her way through the throng of
people, her mind spinning with images, obscene images of that kiss,
of Heath.

She hated him. She hated his eyes and his smiles and all of
Heath Solis. She hated that her eyes stung and tears of frustration
threatened to spill. She went straight for the doors, unsteady on her
blasted four-inch heels, until a hand on her arm seized her.

"Where you going, pet?"

"Home!"

"Where's Heath?"

"Heath can go to hell!" She stormed outside with Grey following, a cool breeze blasting her face when she hit the sidewalk.

"What did he do?" He whirled her around, his eyebrows drawn menacingly low. "What did he do to you, Toni?"

"Apparently, Ms. Kearny here thinks I'm only good for seconds."

She bristled against the sound of his voice coming up behind her, near the bouncers by the entrance.

"I didn't know I was for her exclusive use this weekend," Heath went on in a sneering voice she instantly hated as much as the rest of him.

"Exclusive use!" she scoffed.

With his usual grace and self-possession, Grey spoke to the valet and guided her forward. Seconds later, their driver pulled up with the limo. She wrestled her arm free. "He's crass and embarrassing. He practically violated a poor girl on our table. Before she knew what hit her, she'd been ravaged by this . . . this . . ."

"Bastard," Heath said wryly.

"Heath," Grey warned.

She gritted her teeth as the three of them got into the car. She'd hoped this evening would be special, something the three of them would remember as fun and sexy and cherish in their memories. What a nitwit! Romanticizing her dirty little ménage weekend with a perverted, horrible jerk like Heath.

Sitting across the limo from her and Grey, Heath gazed out the window, his jaw flexing. Toni couldn't believe she'd once thought nice things about him. She wanted to take her shoe off and fling it at him—and then at herself because it should not even matter!

"She's pissed because it wasn't her I kissed," Heath told Grey as the car lurched forward into the streets.

"Hah! Like I'd want your tongue in my mouth."

"You're dying for it."

"By all means, keep deluding yourself."

They fell silent, and Heath's barely leashed fury was like a tangible force around him. Toni could feel it calling to hers, daring her to fight, inciting her to a death match. The shadows in the interior of the car flickered with passing lights as Toni directed her attention at Grey, who seemed to be assessing the situation. "He almost drew blood from that girl's mouth—he kissed her like some demented wild man," she told him.

"Did he?"

"Yes! She was just some stranger. I doubt he'd even remember her face if I showed her to him. He just grabbed the first thing that came strolling by. He's not even selective."

Grey had been stroking her hand between both of his when he paused and without inflection said, "I asked Heath not to kiss you, Toni. If that's what's bothering you."

"Of course it's not—what do you mean?"

Grey's words were so unexpected that for a moment she didn't register them. She glanced from one man to the other, humiliation spreading through her. Her voice was full of indignation when the meaning sank in. "You mean he could do all sorts of dirty things to me, and the most basic—"

"Yes," Grey interrupted.

"Why?"

He wore that cautious, assessing look he got when she was starting to get pissed and he was determining what to do with her. "To keep it under control," he said calmly, reaching for her hand.

She was stupefied and folded her arm protectively around her chest to avoid contact. "What else did you give him—lines to rehearse?"

Grey groaned.

"What did you offer him—a medal for obedience? Instructions on how to fuck me like a robot?"

"Work yourself into a fine temper, Toni, why don't you?"

"Oh, I am. I definitely am, Grey. Do I have your permission to do that, or will this display of emotion be too much for you to bear?"

"You can do anything you want. You always do, and I sure as hell have never stopped you."

"Of course you haven't. I'm not Mr. Loyal Dog of the Year right over there."

She watched Heath's jaw bunch, his entire body coil as if to spring, and she was not yet satisfied. She didn't recognize this person: a woman who wanted to tear her nails into him. The twisting sensation in her stomach seemed to intensify in the closed confines of the car, because she was acutely, angrily aware of him. He'd wanted to hurt her. The realization that he had done it on purpose only intensified the blow.

"Well, Grey? Can I kiss her?" Heath asked without a hint of emotion, turning to meet her accusing gaze.

Grey stared rigidly out the window, tapping a finger restlessly on his knee. Whatever he was thinking of, it did not seem pleasant, but Heath seemed to take his silence as a yes. He patted his lap, his voice deceptively serene considering the bright, eerie lights in his eyes.

"Come here, Toni. I'm more than ready to give you exactly what you're itching for."

She fisted her hands at her sides. "I'm itching to slap you. Both of you."

"You're itching to have my mouth on yours, and I'm going to give it to you. Come get your kiss, kitten."

"Not with the same tongue you put inside that . . . that . . ."

"That juicy pussy of yours."

She tensed in her seat.

He stretched an arm out, palm up. She had never heard him speak so harshly, had never fully understood how dangerous he could be until he stared at her this moment. He looked uncivilized and ready to do damage—the gleam in his eyes was as grim and brutal as the iron edge in his words. "Come here. I'm going to tongue you so hard you won't be able to breathe, much less continue to speak."

"Fuck you, Heath."

"All right, that's enough! Both of you."

"Fuck you, too, Grey!"

All those times she had begged for a silly, stupid kiss from Heath, he'd been playing Grey's obedient little dog. And Grey! The control freak. So calm. Like a god. Nonchalantly notifying her of the fact: *I told him not to kiss you.* Damn them both, and damn her for letting it hurt so bad.

When they arrived at the house, Grey pulled her into a shadowed nook down the corridor.

"Toni . . ."

"Don't 'Toni' me!"

"You're getting too worked up over a kiss, princess. Take it if you want it."

She yanked free of his hold, her gaze shooting bullets at him. "Don't talk to me, Grey."

"Antonia."

"I don't care if you want to control your schedule, the room temperature, and the way you organize your freaking clothes, but don't ever try to control me again! I may like it in bed, but I assure you I don't like it outside of it."

"I know," he said with a solemn nod that only served to increase her anger tenfold.

She bumped into a rigid chest when she spun around. A straining blue vein trekked up Heath's throat, his body motionless as a statue. He was so tense, so still, so vividly *craving* her kiss, she could feel the waves coming off him like blankets of fire. It had festered between them, this elusive, stupid, silly kiss, and now the need for it felt violent. It would be a kiss that would bleed, and Toni would bite her tongue before she let him have it.

She tried going around him but he lifted a hand, sank his fingers into her hair as he lowered his lips. "Give me my kiss."

She slammed her palm into his chest, aware of his hand trembling. "No!"

He tightened his hold on her hair, muscles flexing on his face. "Give it to me."

"Don't touch me, Heath, or I swear I'll get sick all over you."

"Give. Me. My fucking. Kiss."

"I said no."

He let go of her and left his hand open in the air, as though it itched, as though he couldn't close it. And he gritted, "Then give it to Grey."

Heath wanted to pound something. The wall. The mirror. Oh yes, the mirror—seven years of bad luck. He welcomed it. Any other kind of pain except this one.

He adjusted his nuts inside his pants, feeling pain when he touched them, then grabbed the phone on the nightstand and punched some numbers, checking for flights to Chicago. He had to get out of here, get a grip on himself, get far and fast and away from Toni.

When he hung up, Grey stood by the window, his profile chiseled with shadows from the night.

"Booking a flight?"

"Yes."

His friend. His only friend. Heath did not like the fact that he was *considering* hurting him over a woman. He did not like questioning his loyalty to him. Heath had always known, in his heart, that the day he went against Grey, life as he knew it was over.

Grey tucked his hands in his pockets and spared a distracted glance at the room in general. "So."

With that single word, Grey waited for Heath to speak. It was an opening. Heath took it.

"She's nothing to me. Nothing. I can goddamn kiss whoever the fuck I please."

When Grey remained pensive, Heath slapped his wallet on the nightstand. He wanted to punish her for not being his, for calling him a loyal dog, for pushing him until he felt like cracking. He

wanted to pound and pound and pound Toni until she screamed
Heath!

"Do you want to go grovel with me?" asked Grey, regarding
him as though he thought Heath might actually say yes. "It's not
that bad. Once you get a smile, you know you're safe and feel such
a sweet victory."

Heath met his gaze in stony silence. Apologize. For what? For
wanting her? For not being able to have her? "I am not fucking
sorry."

"I am," Grey admitted, raking a hand through his hair. "She had
a right to know what I asked of you." He flexed his shoulders, visibly restless. "I had no right to set terms she didn't know about."
He fixed Heath with one of his most commanding looks. "Let's
apologize, Heath. Then we can make love to her."

No. Not make love. Heath would fuck her. He would rape her
lips with his, force his kiss on her, force his tongue right into her,
search everywhere in her mouth. And even then he wouldn't be
done with her—oh no, not nearly. He'd just be getting started with
his pillaging, because then he wanted the rest of her, every inch
his.

The sound of slamming drawers from the other room echoed
within the walls of his.

Heath kicked his shoes off, heard them plop against the marble.
"She's all yours, Grey," he said, lying back on the bed to stare at the
ceiling.

Another slam reverberated, followed by Grey's long, lingering
chuckle. "Ah, I do like a good handful." From the threshold, he
sent an admiring look in his friend's direction and said, "You know,
sometimes I envy you, Heath. You don't need anything but yourself.
You don't crave money; you don't depend on luxury for comfort.
You don't give a shit what people think."

Heath managed to keep his grunt to himself, all while thinking
Grey was wrong. Heath had nothing. His days came and went. His
life came and went. All because he kept leaving, avoiding rejection.

He left, he moved on, the few acquaintances he made forgotten. If he didn't want anything, he wouldn't care if he wasn't wanted. But he wanted Toni. He wanted that rosy-cheeked girl, and even fantasized at this very moment about tearing her away from the one person he'd always cared for—Grey. Nobody, *ever*, had made Heath want to hurt Grey.

When Heath did not reply and continued dwelling on his grim thoughts, Grey said, "The door's open, Heath."

Heath propped a pillow behind his head, bracing himself for the sounds of their lovemaking. Soon they filtered through the hall. Murmurs. Words. Heath dropped his arm over his eyes and drew in a breath.

Then he heard it. A little moan. His chest caved in on itself. Another one. So tiny. Only in the dead silence of the house could he hear it. Grey's deeper, pleasured groan. He squeezed his eyes shut, furious at the jagged sound of his own breathing.

She could never be his. The knowledge destroyed him, frustrated him, made him feel helpless. He cursed and lunged to his feet. She was his for this weekend, damn it.

Out in the hall, he pushed at the slit of their bedroom door, widening the opening.

Grey's body covered hers on the bed. He was still dressed in his dark shirt and slacks. His hips circled between her parted legs, his head moving over hers. He was kissing her lips—those lips Heath wanted—and then he was draping one of her legs around him, his hand stroking her ankle. "Kiss me back, Antonia. . . ."

A whimper. Of protest.

"I've admitted it: I'm a greedy bastard. I wanted this mouth to be just mine."

Heath pushed a bit more at the door to enter, and the hinges screeched. Everything went still. Even Heath's heart.

In a smooth, startling move, Grey rolled on the bed and sat her up, facing the doorway. She squeaked as though stunned and her eyes fluttered open. They glowed in the shadows. In the light streaming from the hall, he saw every luscious inch of her. She wore a gauzy white peignor buttoned from her neck down that showed her nipples and had a bit of lace around her neck. Her hair tumbled down her shoulders in a shimmering cascade, and in a swift jerk Grey pulled her arms above her head. She gasped, her breasts stretching the sheer fabric, pushed up and into it. Her nipples created two tiny, dark bumps.

Her eyes were glazed, and she didn't look angry but lost. So lost. So well-kissed.

Heath could not breathe.

He came forward, watched his sun-roasted hand engulf her soft cheek. What could he say? *I'm sorry? For being rough. For wanting more than what you can give. For losing my mind. Sorry you belong to Grey. Please give me my kiss.*

She stared at his throat. His pulse beat there; he couldn't control it. He let go a breath and flicked one button of her robe open. Then a second one. Her breasts moved with her breaths. Heath wanted her with every burning cell of his body, but suddenly he could not unbutton more. He felt beaten and pummeled and defeated. He burned and throbbed, but inside he was nothing but a mass of aching.

Nevertheless, he clamped his jaw and yanked up his shirt. It fell at his feet, and his hands went to his belt. "How do you want it? Hard? Soft?"

She straightened her spine, shoulders firming. "Don't bother."

"If you two will just relax," Grey injected lightly. "Come on, darling. I've got to make some points with you. Let's have fun tonight. It's our last night in Cabo."

"You get three points if you leave me alone," she said petulantly.

With a quiet laugh, Grey bumped his nose along her neck, lowering her arms at her sides and stroking her wrists with his fingers. "Not the number I was aiming for."

How easy that she loved him, that she would forgive him anything. Grey could screw up, and minutes later be touching her. And chuckling. And everything would be all right. He wouldn't feel ripped or beaten. He wouldn't feel like shit.

He wouldn't leave tomorrow and never see her again.

"As far as I know, I'm still in the doghouse until Heath kisses you," Grey was saying.

"Think only of yourself, Grey, why don't you?" she accused.

"Eat your words, Toni; you know I live for that little smile of yours. Be a good girl and kiss and make up."

Heath clenched his hands tight. There was no order to what he wanted to say, to what he felt. So many emotions, he didn't know what to do with them. He wanted to spill them all back into her and to be left alone. Like he was before. Before the first time he'd ever heard *Toni*.

"Do you want me or not?" he demanded.

Her silence grated on him.

His temples throbbed when he ground his teeth, his legs tensing with predatory power, ready to tumble her down. "Grey, I'm feeling a little viperous."

"*Viperous.* Is that your new word of the day? Must use *viperous* in a sentence."

Heath no longer tried to hide the fact that he was panting. "Take off your robe, or I'll tear it off with my teeth."

"I like this robe very much, Heath, and I do believe I paid for it. Toni loves La Perla."

"I'll pay you back."

Toni wrapped her arms protectively around herself. "Don't you dare!"

Heath manacled her hands and moved them aside so fast she gasped. "Take. It. The fuck. Off. *Damn you!*"

It was an almost imperceptible movement, Grey sliding from behind Toni, rising to his full height, saying in a low, dangerous voice, "Heath?"

It was all the warning he got. The next second a fist smashed into his gut, and when Heath doubled forward, he was being yanked back by the arms until Grey's lethal murmur poured into his ear. "Apologize."

Heath bucked his arms up, ready to tear free, but Grey tightened his hold, his voice once more ringing in his ear. "Fucking. Apologize."

He made a strangled sound, his tormented mind registering that it was Grey speaking, his voice of reason, his common sense, and it demanded he calm down. Another voice spoke, this one soft as a whisper.

"Let him go, Grey," Toni said.

The breath tore out of him when Grey rammed an elbow into his back, pain shooting up his neck as he dropped him down a notch. "He apologizes first."

"Fuck you."

"You either get yourself under control, or I take care of it for you, Heath."

Heath slammed his head back, intent in breaking his nose, but Grey was fast, ducking to evade the blow while Heath managed to yank free. A wide distance crept between them as they faced each other, their gazes colliding with conflict.

Heath clamped his jaw tight. Grey was not what he wanted. "I'm not going to fucking hurt her," he snapped, his attention shifting to Toni.

Heath glared past Grey's shoulder, his lungs burning for air, his eyes holding a pair of vivid green ones in the darkness. In a hoarse, broken voice, he said, "I still want to fuck you until you scream."

Her reply was what he'd expected, but her words held no force. "I still want to claw your eyes out."

Grey stood guard beside the bed, his tension palpable as Heath approached her. Deliberately slowly, he lifted her hand and set it against his cheek. "Do your worst to me," he whispered.

She was panting softly. God, would his cock stop coming up for her? How many times must he screw her? A dozen, two dozen? Her hand lay motionless on his jaw. He was trying to be calm, drawing in big gulps of air, taking her fingers and raking them across his face. "Hurt me."

She was staring at him.

"Hurt me."

She tried drawing her hand back, but he flattened it to his skin, digging his fingers into the back of hers until her fingertips bit. "I'm asking you to hurt me."

"Stop it."

And he groaned in anguish. "Fuck, do something to me."

"Heath." One second she was staring up at him; the next she was grabbing his face and crushing his mouth, and he was growling, opening, stealing inside.

Like taking a bite from a ripe peach, her taste exploded in his mouth. He tasted Baileys . . . mint . . . *Toni.* His chest expanded, his lungs stopped functioning, and he poured every ounce of himself into that kiss. It soothed his soul, all of the anger in him, and left in its place something mellow and supple and hers. And for the first time in his memory, he wanted to weep in joy. He had never felt so connected, so free. Through his rioting mind, amid the hunger and longing spreading like a firestorm through him, he held on to one thought alone: *I'm home.*

⤳

It was for all the times he hadn't kissed her . . . and it lasted an eternity. It lasted until her lips felt puffy and red and violated. It lasted as he grabbed her pretty La Perla robe and tore at it. And she whimpered when he did, no longer caring about the gown, only wanting to feel his hands on her, his mouth everywhere, wanting to feel Heath . . . one last time. Heath. His hands shook as he pulled at the tatters, yanking every scrap of fabric off her. And then he was grabbing at her head again, delving for her mouth. "Fuck, Cat, forgive me. I'm losing my mind."

She fondled his face, his mouth so forbidden, so delicious, so hungry on her. "I'm losing mine, too."

His tongue blistered her lips, her tongue. He was so hot. His hands were hot, his mouth, his skin. Sweat coated his every lean inch, smearing her with his fever.

Then she was lying back on the soft bed, and it was Grey in her mouth. The taste of wine and the cool, fresh savor of Grey invaded her. Her heart soared with love for him. She was in a daze, floating, dying, living. Her hands clutched at his hair, holding him to her while she plunged her tongue into his sweet mouth. Heath bit at her breast, stroking wetly across her nipple. Then hands rolled her to her side, bodies flanked her. Hot, naked bodies. And Heath was behind her, stroking a finger down the crevice between her buttocks, his voice terse. "I feel like deflowering you. Right here. Right in this tight, warm little passage. Give me something that's mine, Toni. Something just for me."

Grey was snaking his tongue into her mouth even as she breathed, "Yes."

Grey's hands traced the contours of her hips, his cock rubbing up her thigh. "Can you take us both, princess?"

Toni undulated between them, wanting to be as close to them as she could. "Yes."

"Slowly, Heath," Grey said, shushing her noises. Petting her pussy with his hand while she heard the slick sounds of Heath lubing himself. Heath's hands clamped her waist like manacles. His cock probed. The breath shuddered out of him, fanning the back of her neck as he entered. Pain sliced her, stretching her. A burn flared from her core and she sobbed. She wanted it, wanted more. It was a startling pain, a sweet pain. She wanted to give it to him.

"More," she gasped. Grey wound her leg around his hips, bringing his column against her pussy. The position opened her ass to Heath.

Heath pulled out, and her heart protested with a jarring beat. She cried out when he came back in. She cried into Grey's mouth as Heath thrust deeper. She slid her hand around Grey's waist, clutched at his buttocks, mewling helplessly against him.

Grey's thumb circled her clit, then searched deep into her pussy. Two fingers parted her, probed, and readied her engorged opening for another cock. "Think you can still take this?" Him. Grey. Fat and long. Easing inside.

She gasped and flung her head back, agonizing in pleasure. Heath stopped moving, his cock pulsating within her anus to give Grey entry. Their exerted breaths echoed in her ears. She did not seem to be breathing herself when the two of them were embedded deep. Grey groaned when she bit his neck, and he began to move. A careful slide that brought a staggering wave of ecstasy through her.

"Move slowly, Heath. See if she likes it."

Heath moved. Slowly. His fingers sank into her skin at her waist and his rocking motions gained pace as he set a rhythm. It was merciless; each time he was fully seated, he was tearing her apart. She liked it. She wanted it. Grey licked her lips, his breathing arduous on her face. "I can feel every little ripple of your pussy."

She tossed and wormed and bucked, pushing at Grey with her hips, her noises. "Fuck me. Fuck me like Heath." He thrust faster. Both of them plunged faster. Heath in. Grey out. Then together. Fattening her, spreading her, swelling her. She had never thought it possible to feel so full. Her body tensed. Heath's mouth was on her shoulder, moist on her ear. "Cat, baby, you're so tight here."

Toni writhed, her mouth finding places to lick, her hands searching, one behind her, one in front, one for Heath, one for Grey, and she was chanting, chanting in doughy, breathy murmurs, "I love you." A chant to Grey, to Heath, to what they did to her and to how they made her feel.

Heath was hammering, grunting as he took that tight, hot, dirty place, and Grey went taut when she began to scream. Coming, Heath twitched inside her as he was drained of air and strength and his juice. Toni bellowed exultantly, her orgasm overtaking her, tremor after tremor. Heath continued to push into her ass, stimulating her nerve endings, while Grey went motionless inside her. He grabbed her head, bracing himself for climax. He gave his cry into her mouth, his body spasming, three shots of milk blasting against her walls, drenching her with his heat. And finally, they fell, and swam into a deep black sleep.

Chapter Twelve

She woke with the sheets tangled around her ankles, and the bright sunlight pouring through the parted drapes. The room was cheery and quiet—and the bed was empty except for her.

Pushing her hair back, she brought her knees up beneath the blanket and sat up. Physically, she felt comfortably relaxed, but inside she felt like she'd been punched. She could not shake the sensation as she stepped into the shower, lathered her hair, scrubbed her body. One thought alone seemed to overtake her mind: Heath was leaving today.

She'd known him so little, and yet at the same time, she knew him so much!

How could things change so fast? How could you meet someone and give so much of yourself so soon?

Petulant, selfish, or greedy as it may seem . . . she did not want him to go.

When she stepped out of the shower, she dressed in one of the embroidered cotton dresses he'd given her, hoping he would remember her in it. She knew she was not going to forget him.

Emerging from the closet, she spotted Grey out on the terrace, his posture relaxed, arms crossed as he scanned the blue horizon. Water lapped at the dark ocean rocks, morning yachts floating in the distance. The breeze played with his hair, and she felt a wrench of longing so deep she had to pause to take a breath before leaning on the banister next to him.

Grey, don't ever let me hurt you. It would be my suicide, my death. . . .

He eyed her profile with a furrowed forehead. "You all right?"

Her smile was weak, but at least it was a smile. "Of course."

"Heath's gone. He took a commercial flight, wanted to get a head start."

Something fragile and new threatened to break inside her. Hiding the bleak expression on her face, she circled a pattern with her finger on the banister. "I expected I would get to say good-bye."

Grey watched her with a calm but intent gaze. She wished he weren't so perceptive. "He doesn't like good-byes. That's Heath."

Her arms went tight around herself, almost meeting at her back as she tipped her head to his. "Where is he flying?"

"Chicago, to pick up his things. Tomorrow to Vancouver."

She turned away, attempting to clear her thoughts. Down on the beach, a couple strolled past, holding hands. She clung to their image like a lifeline and watched them in silence. "And what time do we arrive in Chicago?"

"Late afternoon."

Perhaps he didn't ask why, because he knew, or perhaps because he didn't want to know, but Toni offered it, anyway. "I want to say good-bye, Grey," she said in an odd croak.

The broken admission didn't mean anything else, except that she couldn't bear to part like this. They had shared moments, and they had shared lovers, and though they had been joined by Grey at the beginning, now they were joined in ways she couldn't fully comprehend.

But the anger in Grey's eyes flared bright, though fleeting. As soon as it appeared, it faded into coolness; his eyes became like fog. He seized her elbow in his hand, a dangerous muscle ticking in his jaw. "Fuck him well and hard, Toni, 'cause that's the last time you'll

be fucking him." Toni was ready to shout and deny his accusation, more than ready to fight with him, when he tonelessly added,
"Here. He left this for you."

Her stomach constricted when he draped the familiar shimmering red around her neck. The cool material slid sensuously across
her nape, making her heart hammer against her ribs.

When Grey stepped away and disappeared into the house, the
tip dangling across one shoulder was all Toni could hang on to.

Clutching it on an end, she yanked it off and gathered it in
one hand. She'd never thought the sight of such a soft, pretty thing
could ever render her so wretched.

Heath had left her sash.

⌒

Out in the hallway, Toni thanked the cleaning lady who opened the
door for her and stepped into the small hotel room. A faint smell of
tobacco lingered in the air, and the bone-colored tapestry on the
wall seemed peeled in places. At the end of the room, leaning over
an open suitcase propped atop the bed, a shirtless, jeans-clad vision
went utterly still at the sight of her.

Shutting the door behind her, she leaned back against it, drawing in breath after labored breath.

"So you're not that good at good-byes, huh?"

The atmosphere was charged with electricity as black eyes met
green. Through the silence, the bitter wind outside blasted across
the city and stormed across Lake Michigan. Rain pelted against the
sidewalks, gently smacked the windows.

With a hard, bitter, uncompromising thinning of his lips, Heath
wadded a shirt in his hands and shoved it into the rumpled suitcase.
"Does Grey know you're here?"

"Yes."

His head fell forward as though it weighed too much; then he
sifted five restless fingers through his hair and made a low, cynical

sound. "He must think me more saint than devil." He stalked over to the window and shoved his hands into his jeans pockets, his posture rigid. In silence, he watched it rain outside.

She'd wanted to say good-bye, and yet a part of her was reluctant to do so when he seemed so distant. With a mounting sense of despair, she took a step forward, finding it hard to imagine that she'd clawed at that broad, ridged back only yesterday and had taken tiny bites of those beautiful square shoulders. They had been hers for a weekend, and a wealth of resentment filled her over not feeling free to touch him now. "You leave early tomorrow?"

"First thing."

She paused behind him and inhaled a breath. His earthy scent was so powerful in the little room she thought she'd be intoxicated by it. "Canada?"

"Yes. Vancouver."

Her control deserted her, and she pressed her cheek to his muscled back. He stiffened under her lips as she whisked them across his skin, but the yearning in her was so great, she did not care that he did not want her touch.

"Cat, I don't know what rules we're playing by here." His voice was coarse and broken as he shifted his weight to his left side— away from her.

Did he feel they'd been playing a game? It had felt so real to her, fun like games, but serious like . . . life.

Putting space between them, she circled the room even though there wasn't much to see. A TV cabinet, a floor lamp, a landscape painting behind the bed. "Your flight from Cabo all right?" she asked.

He splayed one tanned hand on the windowsill, unwilling, it seemed, to face her. "Yes."

"Heath, about last night . . ."

"I'm sorry, Cat."

"No, I'm sorry. I had no right to . . . expect anything from you."

"You had every right." When he looked at her, his expression bleak with meaning, the shining light in his eyes made her heart leap in a strange forlorn joy. "You have me by the balls," he admitted.

She wrung her hands, not entirely sure what he meant, but certain he wasn't too pleased about it. "W-we were both tense. You were leaving, and things were so intense."

For one long, tantalizing moment, he seized her chin and ran his thumb along her lower lip, and an aching tenderness both bloomed and died inside her. She had to forget Heath. . . .

"Heathcliff . . ."

"On your lips, I love my name." He tipped her face up to his scrutiny and slid all his fingers into her hair, cradling her so gently she felt like porcelain. "Can I kiss you one last time?"

"Please." *Oh, please.*

"This is your kiss, Cat, and I swear I've never kissed a woman the way I'm going to kiss you." He whisked her mouth with his, scorching her with that fast pass. A sea of anticipatory ecstasy surged inside her. "It's going to last forever, kitten. I'm going to take it with me."

She sucked in a breath when his lips whispered across hers. A flood of wanting drowned her words when his mouth opened and he leaned in to kiss her. His tongue massaged hers softly at first; then it raked across her top and bottom lip.

She sobbed his name, and he whispered hers, and then he delved and delved and delved his tongue into her hungry mouth until his lips closed fully around hers. His kiss was like the storm outside, starting with a drizzle and then bursting with passion once unleashed.

She felt his teeth behind his lips as his tongue pushed and then as he caught her lips between them. She could only moan when the pressure of his hands on her back glued her against him. Their sexes rubbed as hungrily as their mouths, their entire bodies.

Their tongues tangled and melted against each other, their mouths slanted, their ravenous kissing sounds echoing in the room.

They kissed until her mouth felt swollen, until her tongue felt numb and she was hardly moving her mouth. She just let him plunder, take it, take it all. He panted against her when he withdrew, leaning his head against hers as they tried to recover.

"Go now," he whispered, setting her away.

She couldn't bear to, held herself between both her arms. "Talk to me a little."

He expelled a frustrated breath. "Cat, go."

"Just talk to me; say nonsense."

"Nonsense." He smiled for the briefest, most enchanting instant; then he sobered up and touched her nose with a fingertip. "Did you sleep well?"

His palms were rough running along her cheek, and she found herself tucking her chin into his hold. "Like a baby."

"I woke up, and you were curled on my stomach like a kitten." He smiled fondly as if remembering. "Grey had nearly tossed us out of the side of the bed."

Her smile didn't quite make it. She felt so wet. So achy. So trembly. She made an ugly sound and choked, "I'm so wet, Heath." *And I'm so sad you're leaving us.*

"Argh, Christ, don't. How many times do I need to fuck you to make you not want to anymore?"

She sifted her fingers through the fine hairs across his torso with her fingers, then bravely traced his right nipple. It was so small and dark, a temptation to her lips. "I had the most amazing time of my life."

He drew her closer and seized her lips again, growling when she pressed her breasts against him. They nibbled at each other's lips and continued kissing, tonguing, the bulge of his erection pressing insistently against her belly swamping her pelvis with heat.

When he pulled free at last, he expelled a ragged breath and pressed his hands to his temples, as though his hands were all that kept his head together. "Go."

She was shaking, couldn't seem to make her legs move. "I'll

miss you." *Come home with me and Grey. . . . We'll make love until morning. . . . We'll laugh and eat and sleep. . . .* "I'll really miss you, Heath."

His beautiful black eyes ran over her face, taking in her anguish, mirroring it with a spark of pain in his own. "Shit, come here." He wrapped his arms around her shoulders and pulled her close, burying her face in his neck in a protective way much like Grey's.

Against his throat, and reluctant to move from the circle of his arms, she whispered, "Maybe you can come to the city more often and—"

"No."

It was a chore to speak, but she forced the words out of her dry throat. "Why?"

"Grey's not comfortable with it."

"But why?" She drew back to stare into his eyes. "He was fine in Cabo."

He lifted one challenging brow, then two. "His dad's not in Cabo, is he?" At Toni's confused frown, Heath explained, "Lucien Grey Richards has spent his lifetime tailoring a perfect son. Grey's not going to do anything reckless. Not where the old man can see, anyway."

"But Grey *is* perfect," she countered, anger raising her voice. "No matter *what* that old fart thinks."

"I know." With tenderness shining in his eyes, he rubbed the gooseflesh off her arms. "He doesn't want to expose you to anything that may harm you. You're his everything—do you know that?"

"I adore him." *And why do I feel this strange other thing toward you?* "So even if you wanted to come back, he wouldn't let you?" she questioned.

"I leave because I want to. He doesn't send me off."

When he noticed she wasn't convinced at all, he chuckled and reached for her arms. "Come here, my sentimental little bit."

"I'm sentimental?" She scowled, but still allowed those thick arms to wind snugly around her. "Tell me you wouldn't like to be with me again, Heath," she dared.

He did not deny it, but stood embracing her in silence. She shook her head, realizing how selfish she was. She had never realized how much so until she couldn't stand the thought of letting him go.

"Heath, you deserve to be loved. You deserve to have anything you want. . . ." She smiled brightly, even though her every expression seemed like pain on her face today. "Don't settle for less."

"I never planned to settle." He held her at arm's length and delivered a meaningful look. "Now I might never. You make me want things, Toni. Things I cannot have."

She did not want to hear more.

She wanted to hear it all.

"At the benefit, did you want to get to Grey through me?"

"No. Cat. No. I wanted *you*. I still want you. I'd spent months dreaming of you, and the moment I saw you . . . I needed to have you. I'd have taken you for myself if you weren't his."

"But I am his."

Their eyes locked for an electrifying moment.

"Don't make me hate him," he said hoarsely, and, jerking his eyes away, raked a frustrated hand across his hair.

"Heath, what if—"

"No what-ifs. Only what is." Her stomach muscles clenched as he fixed her with a black, tormented look, his profile as hard as granite, and said, "Go home to Grey."

That was all the good-bye she was going to get; Toni realized she was being dismissed when he went to the closet to fumble around with more of his clothes. He did not glance back at her, didn't so much as give her another view of his face.

Some emotion demanded justice, but she could not speak it, could not even name it. Impulsively, crazily, maybe desperately, she pulled the sash out of her bag and buried it deep in his suitcase, and thought, hoped, prayed before she made her way out of his room, *Come back, Heath Solis.*

⁓

Grey waited in a cloak of obscurity, sprawled on the couch among the shadows. His thumb steadily clicked the ballpoint pen in his hand. Click. Click. Click. The tip went in and out, in and out. A panel of light from the hall streamed into the entry when the front door opened. He sucked in a breath, his finger frozen on a click.

Toni shut the door behind her. By the cautious way she advanced, he was certain he'd been spotted.

She flicked a lamp on, her eyes landing on him. So rumpled. Her hair was tangled, her mouth swollen. She had just been fucked.

She moved to him and stopped a few feet away, her eyes never straying. He let the pen fall on the cushion, roll to the back.

"Grey." It was there in that tearful tone—oh yes, she'd let Heath fuck her.

He shoved his pants and underwear down to his knees and the pink rod of his cock popped out, slapping his abdomen. "I've had this for hours," he rasped.

Glimmering green eyes followed the pronounced veins pulsing up the lengthened flesh. The crown was bloated, stretched taut as a drum, and it quivered painfully.

Her purse fell to the floor, her shoes were kicked off, and she fell to her knees between his thighs, as though helpless to stand. "Grey." Her fingers trembled as she reached out to grasp him, and he lifted his hands to stroke his fingers down her cheek.

"Kiss me."

She pressed her lips to the tip and kissed once, twice, then licked down the length. Groaning hurt. Just sitting here, wanting, hurt.

She cradled his balls in the bowl of her hands, using her thumb to stroke the seam where they joined. He sifted his fingers through the tangled silk of her hair, fisting a handful at her nape so he could pull her head back.

"Did you come?" His voice was terse and gruff, and the air felt dense with his arousal. The scent of him wanting her.

"I didn't fuck him, Grey."

Something let loose in him. A breath. He grazed her temple with the pad of his index finger, then smoothed her hair gently back. "Thank you."

She peered at him through her lashes, her gaze both needy and coy, as though two hours being separated had grown into hundreds. As though they had more between them than time, more than mere inches.

"Make love with me?" he asked as she kissed the bloated head again, tenderly, lovingly using her tongue to draw the milky drop at the tip into her mouth. "Just you and me, like before."

Good-bye. No more Heath touching her. No more hands on her other than Grey's. No more Heath haunting her.

He fought to keep his head from rolling back, to keep his eyes open, but her mouth was so warm, so sweet around his cock.

Fabric rustled as she guided his pants down the rest of his legs and tugged them free of his ankles. He watched her, feeling too big for his skin, near bursting at the chest.

"Suck me," he whispered. "Take me in your mouth and eat me like there's no tomorrow."

She drew his dick up from his stomach and her mouth enveloped him fully at the tip, her lips sliding down. He stretched his arms on the couch back, bracing himself with his hands.

"God." He bucked up, and a shuddering breath tore out of him. He pumped up again, and she moved her head down, her tongue flat under him. Delicious.

They established a rhythm that gradually increased in speed. He groaned through a strained throat, blind, glassy eyes staring up at the ceiling. His every cell thrilled, his penis an oversized stick gliding in her silky, wet mouth.

"Ride me."

The sound she made was muffled by the engorged width of his flesh. She let it slip out of her mouth and rubbed her face against him, nuzzling his balls, his penis. Her words quivered against him. "I love you."

He let his eyes drift shut, tightly shut. Maybe he hadn't really heard it before. Or maybe he hadn't heard it in a while. Maybe he just needed to hear it more than he needed air. Maybe that's why his chest throbbed. Why it cramped and released at just hearing it. Maybe that's why he needed to hear it again.

Almost violently, he grabbed her hair and lifted her face up, his words exploding out of him and into her moist mouth. "I adore you. *Adore* you. I love you passionately. Completely. With all my heart and my soul."

Trails of wet tears met his palms on her jaw, and as though to hide them, she buried her face in his neck as she took his penis inside her. She clutched at his shoulders and he wrapped his arms around her, groaning when they were one. Why was she crying? Why was she crying?

For Heath. He knew it was Heath. He nudged her face to the side and rubbed his lips over the tears, salty on his tongue. "I'm sorry I don't say it." He wiped the drops with his hands, his mouth. "You make me weak, and I fear that you can hurt me. But you like hearing it, don't you?" She choked on a little sound. Oh yes, she did love it, she wanted it. "I love you—god, you *know* I do."

She clutched his face, kissing him passionately, the taste of tears on her lips. "You won't stop loving me?"

"Never."

"Ever?"

"Toni." He shifted her, still inside her as he lay her down the length of the couch and made love to her so, so softly. Dying a little. Dying a little more. Tracing her collarbone with his nose. Tracing her cheek. Inhaling her. "You're like my skin—how could I feel without it? Like my blood—what would my heart pump without my blood?"

And she cried more. And Grey didn't know what to do but move. Fold her legs around him and move. And move and move and forget. And tell her how good she was. How sweet. How warm he felt inside her. How she was his home, his heart, his everything living. Until she whimpered. And she forgot Heath, too. And she came. And Grey came. And there was no one else coming but them.

Chapter Thirteen

Mr. Carstairs wanted his money back. He did not like Toni's design.

"He's right—it sucks." Toni grimaced, dropping the proposal atop the rest of her clutter. Dinner had been awful. She had never been so unprepared and unfocused. She braced her hands on the edge of her desk and tried to calm down, gather her thoughts.

From his position lounging on the couch, Grey scrutinized her in silence. She sensed him waiting for her to offer more, and she rubbed the tense muscles at the back of her neck and sighed.

"I just can't understand why I can't come up with anything original. It's like my muse completely dried up. Now I have no pending clients, and of the appointments I rescheduled, two of them canceled. I'm going nowhere with the Viscevis logo, either! If I hadn't been gallivanting around Mexico so irresponsibly . . ." She went quiet, flipped open her proposal, and fingered the design.

"So how is Heath?" The casualness she tried to inject in her tone was not evident when the words came out a little high-pitched.

A long, dreadful silence followed before Grey answered. "He's fine."

Fine. Of course. He was fine. Why wouldn't he be? He was big and dark and determined. . . .

She needed to stop thinking of Grey and Heath and Mexico. She needed to reclaim her life, her work, to land more business.

The Viscevis logo. It would be such a coup. She shuffled a pile of papers until she came across the two logos. One a sleek cylinder inside a vine forming a circle, the other a solid gray ball in motion. How to integrate the two . . . ?

She sighed within minutes. "I'll never do this."

Grey was on his way to her when she pivoted around. He framed her cheeks in his hands and touched his nose to her forehead, then kissed her so gently she sighed. "It's all in here. In this brilliant brain of yours. All you have to do is find it."

"It's not that easy. . . ." she protested. Things weren't always so simple. Not all designs could merge.

When he captured her lips with his, she whispered his name in a reverent breath, allowing him access to every recess and nook of her mouth.

"I didn't say it was easy, sweetheart. But I do know my Toni can do that and more."

⌇

After checking in at the hotel, Heath rode out to see the land that had caught Grey's eye. A rolling hill with a partial view of the English Bay and the imposing Art Deco–style Burrard Street Bridge. Lush and green, it was an impressive place, from any standpoint.

Grey wanted to build a hotel here. The wider, sweeping hill next to it offered more. A view of the entire city skyline. But it wasn't for sale, of course. The most beautiful never is. The most beautiful is taken. Always taken.

After a leisurely walk around, smelling the dampened earth and maple, lost in his thoughts, Heath got in a cab to go to their construction site at a residential area in Cole Harbor. He'd been gazing out the window for what felt like hours when he spotted her.

She stood with a group of women at a corner—women dressed

to entice a man; women ready, it seemed, to get down to the dirty. She was dressed like a nurse. A nurse. Someone to lick his wounds. Someone that wasn't *her.*

Heath halted the car, popped his head out the open door. "Get in."

All heads swiveled in his direction, and she stepped away from the group and righted her little white hat, her heels tapping on the sidewalk. "Can you afford me?"

"I said get in."

Raven-haired and willowy, she shouted something at the "girls" and slid into the cab. She pulled a piece of gum out of her mouth and jammed it into the ashtray, rolled out a couple of sexy words to him, finishing with the word *lover.* She had glossy red lips and vivid red nails to match the tiny cross on the breast of her dress.

She would do. Anyone would do.

He didn't speak to her as he let her into his hotel room. She had been talking during the ride, but he hadn't listened to a word. His eyes were blurry. They stung. His throat felt cramped and his heart numb.

A fuck. That was all he was. A fuck. Grey held her, stroked her, supported her. He bought her earrings. He washed her hair. Heath just fucked her.

I want to be Grey. Dear god, I want to.

The nurse kicked her heels off and he felt her arms go around his neck. "What's it gonna be, tough guy?"

Her fingers were fiddling with his hair, and it bothered him. Pulling them back, he leaned on the door, swallowing back the bile as he unfastened his jeans. "Blow it, fuck it, or play with it. Just do me."

Helping him slide his jeans partway down, she weighed his newly bared testicles, fondled his dick. "Oooh, you're big. Try to get a little hard for me, huh, big guy?"

Heath clamped his eyes shut when he felt the stinging moisture there. Good god, what was this? The pills. The plane. Leaving her.

"I'm not feeling well," he said thickly.

"Oh, honey. Sweetie. Let Nurse Tina help you. I'll make you hot for me. What do you like? Let's get these off you first."

Her hands got busy and he let her strip him fully of his shoes, his jeans, his socks. Her hand moved to stroke at his penis, trying to work it up. He felt her lips graze the tip.

With his head back against the wall, he tried to suck air into his lungs, feeling suffocated. He tried to picture this woman's breasts. Her red mouth around his cock. Something to entice him, arouse him.

His cock was a limp, heavy weight in the nurse's hands. *What have you done to me, Antonia?*

He cursed as he grabbed her cap and a handful of hair, noting that it was dry and stiff, unlike Toni's virgin tresses. "Don't," he said and hauled her up.

"Let me try a bit—"

"Just don't. Here. I'm sorry." He bent to his jeans and slipped several large bills into her hand. "Go."

"We could try something—"

"Go!"

She fumbled with the door, and she was gone. A woman he could have had, even if paid for, even if only for an hour. Gone. He gritted his teeth. "Fucking *fool*!"

He'd been curious? He'd wondered what it felt like to care for someone? He was an *idiot*. Caring was not for him. He had stopped caring years ago, *years ago*, and now he remembered why. Nobody wanted him to give a shit.

Storming to the tiny closet, he jerked off his shirt and rummaged through his suitcase for his boxers.

And saw a flash of shimmering red among his jeans.

The sash.

His heart leapt up to his throat. He fished it out from the bottom and touched the satin with his fingers. His body responded to its texture, its scent, his cock distending, stretching until it was jut-

ting out of his body in a painful lance. He brought it to the bed and
lay on his side as he spread it across the center of his palm, folding it
around himself. He gave an upward stroke, the silk gliding, gliding
around him. He tightened his fist and groaned.

And he saw the rosy nipples he'd suckled raw. The light little
hands feathering across his body. Green eyes, forest dark with passion. *Toni*. He tried the word out loud, a low, guttural murmur.
"Toni." His mouth made love to it, and he turned his head to the
coverlet and muffled his next words. "Cat . . . oh, kitten, this is me
making love to you. This is me loving you." And he rocked his hips
and pulled his heart out.

By the time Louisa Fairchild arrived at the quaint café only blocks
away from the RS Corporation building, Toni waited for her by a
quiet corner table at the far end. She had been fidgeting with her
napkin and utensils, and the relief she felt when she spotted her
friend was immediate.

She'd had nonstop anxiety for a week. The feeling wouldn't
leave her, not for a second. It was a heaviness. An anxiousness. Like
when she had something to do but couldn't remember what it was.
Like when she and Grey fought. It was there, always. This thought
of Heath. This wondering about Heath. This wish that the weekend had never happened, and another that it would have never
stopped.

Her smile spread as she watched the slim, sexy blonde slide into
the seat across from hers. A friendly face. A familiar face. A female
face. God, she was happy to see her.

"Corporate life suits you, Louisa," Toni said teasingly.

Louisa's blond hair tumbled lustrously behind her back, and she
was dressed as sexily as if she were going out to a nightclub. Toni
felt a momentary pang of jealousy at the thought of Grey seeing
her every day, especially when Toni sometimes waved him off to

work in her pajamas, but she quickly dismissed her concern when her friend laughed. Like they used to laugh in college.

"I'm still such a nervous wreck, but getting better." Louisa smoothed her napkin on her lap and, remembering to do the same, Toni followed suit.

"How's Grey treating you?" Toni asked her. "Not too bad, I hope."

Louisa lifted her gaze, startled. "Oh, no, he's . . ." Her gaze drifted to the window as though a passerby had caught her eye. "Grey's wonderful."

Dreamily, Toni propped her chin on her linked hands. "I'm glad. He's really a softie, isn't he?"

The moment she spoke the words, she had an image of Grey cooing at her, touching her, and what went soft was her own body.

"Soft?" Louisa said testily. "Not in appearance *or* personality. Not with me, I mean."

Toni smiled. Yes, of course. *Soft* was the last word you'd use to describe him. *Greek god*, more likely. *Sex with Midas eyes.* The only thing soft in relation to Grey Richards was the way Toni felt on the inside when he looked at her. And the way he was when he coddled her. And the way he—

"Well! What are we having?" Louisa surveyed the offerings on the menu. Toni already knew what she would order—the Caesar salad and the chicken parmigiana—but she waited until Louisa finished her perusal and set the menu aside.

"So," Louisa said. "How was Cabo?"

"Fabulous. We went to a Mexican wedding. It was so lively and interesting. I wore my first mariachi hat, too. Grey said it was wonderful, but Heath said it was ridiculous."

The waitress interrupted to inform them of the daily specials, and while Louisa inquired about the soup of the day, Toni warred between spilling her guts and attempting to have a normal meal.

Once the waitress jotted down their food orders and left, Louisa fished into the bread basket the waitress had left behind. "So you mentioned Heath. You mean Heath Solis, the—"

"Grey's partner, yes." When Louisa made a face, Toni was compelled to ask, "You've met him?"

She munched with a thoughtful face. "Once at the office, yes. He's rude. Gorgeous and rude."

"Oh, really? Why?"

"He's just rude. Everyone says so at the office. He gives me the creeps."

Heath smiling . . . *No. I liked your big scared eyes when you said* haunting. Heath encouraging . . . *Cluck to it, beautiful. Send it a kiss. You're the boss here. Ask it to trot for you. . . .*

Her stomach vaulted, and she dropped her face to hide the color flaming in her cheeks. Absently, she circled a pattern on the linen with the tip of one finger. "What else do they say about him?"

"Well." Louisa took a sip of water. "That he's Grey's attack dog. One of the funny guys calls him the Mastiff. They say he growls like one, too. That he sniffs out lots for Grey, does all the dirty work, that sort of thing."

"A dog?" Toni slumped back in her seat, flabbergasted. "That isn't a nice thing to say about someone."

I'm not your Mr. Loyal Dog of the Year right over there. . . .

The thought of her speaking those words made her furious at herself, furious at these people.

"Hey, I'm just passing it on. I don't know the guy," Louisa said defensively.

Toni had a staggering urge to punch these people. No wonder Heath was always on the defensive. Did anyone want him close? He was obviously intimidating to men, and maybe a little too much man for some women. But if only one would take a good look up close and open her heart to him, she was sure Heath Solis was a man to love a woman forever.

He would love so surely and determinedly, steadfastly . . .

Why couldn't it be *her*?

Frowning at the despairing turn her thoughts had taken, she asked, "Louisa, does Grey know that's what these people call Heath?"

"Of course not, no!" Diving across the table, Louisa clenched Toni's hand between hers. "You aren't going to tell him, are you?"

Worry shone bright in her friend's eyes, and without hesitation Toni turned her hand and squeezed in reassurance. "I won't. But I don't think he'd appreciate it. Much less Heath."

"So how do you know him?" Not entirely concealing her curiosity, Louisa went back to the rolls, spreading butter on a piece.

Memories threatened to surface, and Toni fought to keep them inside, to push Heath away. But it felt like he was knocking from inside her, living in her, *breathing* in her. "I just told you he said my hat is ridiculous," she said, as if that explained it all. Why she couldn't sleep. Why she and Grey did not speak of him. Why he had become their ghost.

"But he's never in the city, as far as I know. Except that once when he stopped by the office a few weeks ago. Some of the workers didn't even know what he looked like!"

"I met him a few weeks ago, too," Toni admitted, and gathered her breath. "He was with us the whole weekend in Cabo, actually. Remember arranging his schedule?"

"Vaguely, yes."

"Well, he's not a dog," she defended, still smarting over it. "He's . . . Heath is . . ." How to explain Heath to someone? To anyone. He was a mystery, a beautiful, damaged box with all kinds of novelties and goodies inside. "He's just as wonderful as Grey is," she admitted. "Different, but wonderful. Rough on the edges. A little bad." And fun and rebellious and enchanting.

Alarm skated through Louisa's eyes. "Toni . . . don't tell me—"

"We had sex, all right! We had a threesome."

If a waitress had come by and dropped a tray fully loaded with icy beverages, she doubted Louisa would have been more paralyzed. The shock and horror on her friend's face made Toni sigh in de-

spair. She shouldn't have spoken about this to her. Threesomes were
not discussed with regular people, period. "I'm sorry to dump it on
you like this. I needed to talk to someone."

"What do—exactly what did you do? What do you mean, a
threesome?" Louisa's color had risen, and her voice was an octave
shy of a shriek.

"The three of us had sex." She said it simply, matter-of-factly, as
she figured one should deal with these situations once they were
done. As if they happened every day. Yes, yes, *yes*. That was her problem. She should just say it, deal with it, and let it go. "There!" She
impulsively slammed a hand down in mock celebration. "I've said
it, I feel great, and I really needed to get that off my chest."

"And whose idea was it? I can't imagine Grey would be so
kinky. He's so . . . he's so . . . reserved."

"On the outside. And it was our idea." Toni refused to look directly into Louisa's stunned blue gaze as she dismally added, "Sometimes I wish we could do it again and again, forever and ever."

"What does that mean? Are you dumping Grey?"

"Never! No! I love Grey." Her hands trembled, and she plucked
at her straw, frowning into the depths of her iced tea as she twirled
it. "I sometimes feel Heath belongs with us, that's all."

"As in, you three?"

Toni spread her arms aside. "It's just that I've lately wondered . . .
well, we have two legs, right?" She smiled wanly, lifted her shoulders. "Two eyes. Two hands. Why can't we have two lovers?"

Two lovers who also went at each other, two male lovers who
also understood, cared about, admired, and complemented each
other. . . .

"Okay. This conversation has turned from normal to creepiest
ever. I don't know what to say! The extent of my sexual experience
ranges from missionary to woman on top, and that was weeks ago.
Now you tell me you have not one hunk in your bed, but two?"

"Oh, god, and I want them both!" she groaned in a strange
combo of mirth and misery. "What does that make me?"

"A bitch!" Louisa said with such force Toni felt electrocuted in her seat. "And you're speaking nonsense," Louisa continued, calming herself with a breath. "I mean, who's ever heard of that?"

"It's not that unusual, Louisa." Toni angled her head and assessed her friend, a little surprised by the sudden, overwhelming ire Louisa was trying and failing to control. "I've Googled it. And some people make it work."

Even while the rest of the world thinks they're crazy . . .

"But, Toni, you have Grey! How can Grey Richards not be enough for any woman in the world?"

"He's enough. I adore him! One has nothing to do with the other. Having four children doesn't mean you don't love all four of them. *Anyway.* Enough about me. Tell me about you."

"You'd be asleep in minutes. No. Explain this to me, because I'm finding it difficult to come to terms with all of this. What would your parents think? I mean, do they even know?"

"I don't care what they think. I don't care what anyone thinks except Grey . . . and Heath." She went red remembering them in Cabo . . . their hands . . . their mouths . . .

Glancing over her shoulder, Louisa scanned the expanse of the restaurant and dropped her voice to a whisper. "How did they . . . Was this at the same time?"

"Sometimes." Toni cooled her palms with her glass and placed them over her cheeks, refreshing her burning face. "This is a little awkward. Can we talk about you now?"

Louisa sat back, nodded, and for a while they talked. They ate. They laughed. Then an odd, strained silence came, and Louisa said, "No wonder."

"No wonder what?" Toni asked, munching the last bit of her chicken.

"No wonder Grey has been so distant since his return. He stares blankly off into space, or dictates something while staring at the window. He rubs his face with his hands. Today he hadn't shaved when he came in. I've never seen him looking so scruffy. I thought he was stressed. The wheels in his head never seem to cease, and you know he always seems to be thinking something, evaluating, analyzing? Now I know what he's . . . stressing about. He's stressing about *you*."

When the words hit—and they took a stunned moment to—her heart clenched awfully tight. If she'd thought she could feel no more anxious, no more confused and miserable, she wasn't counting on this last. The thought of Grey unhappy . . .

"What do you mean?" she said weakly. "At home he's . . . at home he's fine."

He'd been fine with her all week. At night he whispered to her, told her he loved her, and by day he showered her with attention and welcomed her own eager attempts to be with him. They couldn't seem to stop calling each other, wanting to be together. She and Grey were fine!

"Really?" Louisa pursed her lips in distaste. "Maybe it's work stuff, then. I hear there's an IPO of the company coming up."

Toni's eyes dropped to her plate, and she frowned at the remains of her food in puzzlement. Was he closing himself to her? Was he pretending to be all right for her sake? And if he was, could she blame him? Wasn't she doing the same, desperately attempting to restore their lives as they were before?

As soon as the bill had been paid and they stepped out into the sidewalk, Toni asked, "Want to hit the shops?"

Louisa glanced at her watch. "I need to get back. Lunch hour's over—"

"Do you know where he is?" Toni whispered, running a hand down her skirt as they hit the busy sidewalks of Michigan Avenue.

"He?"

"Heath."

Louisa stared at her, then briskly answered, "Oaxaca." She added meaningfully, "It's in Mexico."

Toni waved a hand. "I know where it is."

"You do? I had to look it up."

"Louisa?" Pausing as though to think straight, Toni stared at a window display, her eyes on the clothes but her mind far away. "Do you think you could get me his phone number?"

"Might I ask what you want it for?"

"I want to talk to him," she admitted. *To know he is all right*, she told herself. "And I want to know if he's talking to Grey."

"Give me until this afternoon."

"Thank you."

Minutes later, Toni followed her to the impressive marble lobby of the RS Corporation building. All eyes across the nineteenth floor seemed to zero in on Toni when they stepped out of the elevator.

Louisa settled behind her desk and fidgeted around before she announced her to Grey. It took only a second for six feet three inches of handsome and magnificent to fill the doorway. That smile. From her desk, Louisa looked like she had never seen it. It was wide and devastating, it was so dazzling. Toni felt tiny butterflies race down to her toes when he jerked his head toward his office. "Get in here, Miss Kearny."

Toni did.

He leaned back against his desk and crossed his arms, looking displeased. "You steal my assistant for two hours and dare come here without something for me?"

"I've got this." She lifted her skirt, and Grey peeked at one of her newest acquisitions: a sheer pink thong that was barely there. He palmed her ass, his hands huge and tanned on Toni's creamy buttocks as they squeezed.

"I like that." She squeaked in delight when he massaged deeper, his chuckle echoing in her warming body. "Hmm. I like that more."

She dropped her skirt and whirled around to trap him by the collar. "I thought I could steal *you now*."

"I'm afraid that's going to cost you," he drawled in deceptive casualness.

"Oh? And do you take body as payment?" She signaled to all

five feet four inches of herself with what was, hopefully, a tempting
sweep of her hands.

Brows quirked in interest, Grey moved around his desk and
punched an extension from his desk phone.

"Louisa, what does my afternoon look like?"

It seemed to look busy, because Louisa spent a long time on the
other end of the line. But what mattered to Toni, what gave her the
opportunity to be with the man she loved and talk and make love,
was Grey's arrogant smile and the husky command, "Empty it."

Chapter Fourteen

It was a hotel room number, and the two times she tried there was no answer. She didn't dare to leave a message. With a sinking heart, she grabbed the Post-it and tore it.

Enough of him. Forget it. Forget Cabo!

Plopping down on the couch, she covered her face with her hands and groaned in misery. It was no use; she couldn't forget. And all she wanted was to know how he was doing. Whereas before their weekend, Grey would mention him all the time, the subject of Heath had been carefully avoided for two weeks. Toni was desperate to know something about him. Anything. Was he all right? Was he with someone? Did he at least think about her?

She was in that same sulking position when Grey got home, and as she rose to greet him as she always did, she gathered her courage. She worked on his tie and jacket and rumpled his hair, and whispered, "Grey, I want to talk to you about something."

He placated her with a kiss. "Ten minutes, then I'm yours."

And he disappeared into the bathroom, where she heard him running the water for a shower. Normally she might have joined him, but she was too anxious for anything except running her thoughts through her mind. So she waited on the bed, knees curled under her, fingers drumming on her thighs. Talking was the best way to go. If only he would express his opinions more openly, and he would listen to hers . . .

The phone rang, and when she lifted it, she answered to silence. "Hello?" she repeated.

"I'm calling for Grey."

The low, gruff sound of thunder gripped at her chest. "Heath?"

"Yeah."

Inside her a feeling went loose, wild and untamed, like a deadly tornado. She began to shiver, her hand trembling, her lungs straining for air. She wanted to weep with joy and to cry with sorrow at the distance she sensed between them. "You could at least say hello to me," she said, more with longing than accusation.

And briskly, almost coolly, he said, "Hello, Toni."

His voice . . . it was almost too much to bear. A breath shuddered out of her.

She wiped her free hand on her lap—it was clammy, and suddenly she didn't know what to do with it except tug at the fabric on her waist. "H-how have you been?"

"Working."

"Oh."

"Is Grey there?"

"He just got in. He's in the shower." She lowered her voice, pressed the receiver closer to her lips, her voice betraying her emotion. "Why won't you talk to me?"

"I'll call back later."

"Heath, please." Why didn't he talk to her? Was she the only one who felt this?

The tomblike silence was deafening.

When she spoke again, she sounded desperate even to her own ears. "Please. *Please.* Talk to me, Heath."

For a wrenching heartbeat, she thought he would hang up, but then his terse, emotional hiss charged into her ear. "I'm losing my mind. I get hard just listening to your voice. I hurt all over, all day.

You're in my mind, in my dreams. I try and try to forget you, and just knowing you're with Grey is driving nails into me."

She squeezed her eyes shut as she fell back on her pillow, the sheets cold against her nape while her body felt so hot. "I hurt, too."

"Cat, baby." His sharp inhale skittered through her. "Where do you hurt, tell me?"

My heart. Toni hesitated before saying it. Grey would hear. He would see. He would know. It didn't matter. Nothing mattered. It was all wrong, it was all terribly, unbearably *wrong*.

"I hurt all over."

"Where?" His voice dropped to a coo that might have been meant to soothe her but wreaked havoc on her rioting nerves. "In your little pussy?"

"Y-yes."

"Oh, Cat, what I wouldn't give to be there now. I'd kiss you until I don't know who I am anymore, spread those long, silky legs and . . ."

Planting her heels on the bed, she spread open her legs, sliding her fingers into her panties, imagining it was *him* searching her body to find this place he'd been before. This place that missed and wanted him so badly. "And?" she asked when he stopped. "Please tell me."

"I can't do this."

"Heath, tell me!" She pinched her clit so hard she winced in pain. It was nothing, that pain. Compared to the other. Nothing. "I'm wearing your dress."

"Oh, baby."

"I'm so wet just hearing you. My cream is all over me. I'm touching my clit and I'm desperate; I want your fingers in me."

He made a strangled sound,

She found her slick folds and gentled her strokes, pleasure radiating up to her tingling breasts. "Heath." She moaned as she circled. "Oh, Heath."

"I can hear you panting for me," he said in a terse rasp. "Are you touching yourself? I want to hear what you're doing."

"I'm touching my pussy. I want it to be you."

He made another sound, full of agony and frustration, then croaked, "Where are you?"

"On the bed, with my legs open. And I ache all over."

"If I were there, I'd be licking that wet, syrupy puss—" He trailed off when she slipped two fingers through the slit and cried out, moving them fast. The pleasure whirled around her walls, piercing up to her nipples, her pussy rippling with wanting.

"Heath, I miss you so much." She rocked against her hand, seized by the sound of his voice, the rampaging need that listening to him unleashed in her.

"Toni." She heard it then, in the sound of his voice, the quick scrape of flesh; she knew he was touching himself. She imagined him pulling from root to crown, humping, sweating, and her blood felt sluggish with arousal.

"Heath, I don't want you to be with anyone. I think of you going to some prostitute somewhere and I feel sick. You belong with us."

He didn't reply. She heard his grunts, his sounds of pleasure. A fever broke in her, merciless, racking her with shudders inside and out. She moved her fingers in her, wishing they were the fat, blunt-tipped fingers of Heath.

"Heath . . . what are you doing?"

"I'm fucking you," he rasped, and as though he couldn't think of anything else, "I'm fucking you, Cat."

"Don't stop. Please don't stop." Her hand was drenched with cream and his voice in her ear struck her womb like a thunderstorm. "Fuck me harder."

And she heard him—him coming, the breath tearing out of him so that even the phone seemed to vibrate—and she closed her eyes and pushed deeper into her cleft.

"Want some help with that, princess?"

Her eyes flew to a bare-chested Grey, exiting the bathroom with a towel around his waist, his face impassive as he propelled himself forward.

As though in slow motion, she watched with a thundering heart as he pried the phone from her fingers, his free hand curving on her hip as he set it back into its cradle. He was so . . . calm.

"Want to explain to me why you're having phone sex with . . . ?"

She chewed on her lip, embarrassed, angry, desperate. "Heath."

"Heath. Of course."

"Grey . . ."

"How long?"

"What?"

"How long has this been going on?"

She tugged her skirt back down and swung her legs over the side of the bed. While she spoke, all she could face were her own bare toes. "I've never done it before. He was calling for you. I just heard his voice and . . . I wanted to talk to him. You used to tell me everything about him, and now that you don't, I've felt so thirsty for just a little news."

"But you weren't talking just now, were you?"

She shrugged, swung her legs back and forth. "I miss it. I miss . . . him."

When she dared look up to gauge his reaction, there wasn't so much as a flicker of his eyes to betray him. Flooded with relief that he was so self-possessed, she plunged on, wanting to get this out in the open.

"*You* talk to him," she explained. "He's your partner. With me . . . I shared things with him, personal things, and suddenly all ties have been severed."

"*I* talk to him?" As though she weren't safe around him, or him around her, he stalked across the room, gritting his teeth. "Heath and I are fucked. *Fucked*, Toni. We barely speak three words to each other."

"But why?"

"Because you still want him and it is tearing me *apart!*"

"No, Grey, no!"

The phone began to ring and ring and ring. Incessantly.

When Grey saw her glance at the phone, considering answering, an icy veil settled over his eyes, making the hair on her bare arms rise. For the barest of seconds, pain ravaged his features as if a flood or wildfire swept through life and civilization and love. Then there was nothing on his face at all.

The idea that he thought he wasn't important to her, that he thought she didn't *care*, made her break out in a sweat.

"Grey." She took a step toward him, but was quickly halted by his stare. Grey never lost his temper. The only time she'd seen him out of control was after the benefit, when he'd been so jealous. But the walls he put up now to obstruct her seemed as effective as a roar. She cringed under his eyes. The gold in them was glacial. Freezing her to the spot.

If she hadn't experienced the fire within him firsthand, seen his face crumple when he came in her, his every wall shatter when he looked at her, she'd have thought him inhuman.

His mellow tone and his lack of emotion as he regarded her was no less chilling. "Am I failing you in some way, Antonia Kearny?"

"No! You're perfect. I love you." She dared to step up to him and rise on tiptoe to kiss him. She'd never felt such unmoving lips under hers. She tried coaxing them open with feathery movements of her mouth, catching his lower lip between hers, giving hot little tugs. She slid her hands around his strong neck, caressed the damp hairs at his nape. "Grey, I love you."

"Do you?"

"I'm passionately in love with you."

"I used to believe you were." He extracted her arms from his neck and set them at her sides before walking to the window to peer out through the blinds.

The muscled back he revealed to her was so taut and rocklike that it proved successful in keeping her from approaching, from *reaching* him. She wrung her hands, tried to explain. "Grey, somehow it's as though he's always been a part of us. Like a ghost, but he's alive."

He stroked the back of his head with one hand, his frustration so tangible it caused her throat to squeeze. "One weekend, Toni. It was supposed to be just that. But it's not enough for you, is it, princess? Nothing's enough for you. I can't fill you. I can't make you happy. I can't—"

"That's not true!"

"You *call* to him. In your sleep, you say our names, you say my name, *his* name." At his sides, his knuckles jutted out of his fists. "You've been . . . god, you've been pining away for him."

Fury and a dispiriting frustration seized her, and her voice trembled with both. "You're the one who invited him!"

He whirled. "Like hell I did!" he roared, his scowl ominous.

"You did, Grey!" she cried, as confused and hurt as he was. She wanted to slap him. She wanted to hug him. She wanted him to understand. "You planned the trip, you took my sash to dinner. You thought it would go away just like that? What do you think everything you told me about him felt like? *Foreplay*, Grey. You wanted me to like him, to accept him, to want him—you even wanted me to fuck him to rid yourself of that guilt of having it all while he had shit. You wanted me to care, and guess what. It worked!"

"I wanted you to appreciate a man whom I appreciate and nobody else seems to—that's far from wanting you to screw him behind my back!" He was shaking, the ice melting within hot, volcanic anger, and Toni felt his pain like a suicide, like driving a dagger into her chest that she was twisting herself.

"Grey, I promise you we're not doing anything behind your back. You thought I would have sex with him that day I went to say good-bye, and you *let* me."

He was breathing for control, fighting for it as he advanced. "He's been like a brother to me. The most important person in my

world, until you came along. You wanted him, Toni. You wanted
him, and I *gave him* to you."

"Why, how generous of you! You, the Almighty Grey Richards,
took pity on us both and let us fuck! And for your information, *he*
gave himself to me!"

He slammed a fist to his chest. "*I* gave myself to you! I am . . . I
am *humbled* with you. I've stripped my soul bare for you! Does that
even matter to you?"

Her eyes stung and a tear leaked. She brushed it off with a hand
that shook violently, her words strangling her. "It means the world
to me. At first I lived to live, and now I live for you to love me and
for me to love you."

He put a halting hand up. "Don't." The torment in his eyes was
unbearable to her. He didn't want to believe that she loved him. He
didn't want to love her. She could see it hurt him, and she wanted
to choke in her pain.

"I didn't ask to feel this," she said brokenly, dropping in a heap
of misery on the edge of the bed.

"What do you want, Toni?" Leaning a casual outstretched arm
on the bookshelves, he delivered the words without inflection, as if
he were tired of everything, tired of *her*. "A ménage every Christmas? Do you think that's fair to him?"

"Grey, I've been reading about relationships with more than
two people. Permanent ones. We could make it work. You and
Heath are amazing together and—"

"You're *mine*!" He closed the distance between them, the possessive red sparks in his eyes skinning her alive. "I'd give my life for
him, but not my girl. You're mine, Antonia Kearny. I'm not a man
who shares. I'm not a *fool*." He caught her arm and hauled her
up from the bed. "I take back every good word I ever said about
him."

"You can't take them back. You can't take Cabo back—not
even *you* can!" Impulsively, she tore the towel from his waist and
grabbed his cock, the stalk rigid and standing impressively tall

in her hand. Her throat dried, a surging heat instantly spreading through her as she fondled him. "You're excited," she said in a hoarse purr. "It excites you that I get hot when I talk about him. It excites you that I want him and get aroused wanting to have you both again. Your cock is wet, Grey. You're ready to explode right here in my hand."

He grabbed her face. "My cock knows *shit*, Toni. I haven't been myself since Cabo, and my life has gone upside down. I feel out of control, and just the thought that I may be losing you is driving me insane."

"Never, Grey. Never. Oh, baby, you know I can't even breathe when we fight. You're my rock; my first thought in the morning and my last thought at night. Grey, please. The idea is strange to you, but if you wrap your mind around it a little, Heath belongs with us. He's so loyal and truthful and so lonely."

"Setting up a charity foundation, Toni?"

"It is not charity. I want . . . I want him. I need him, too. I need you both. If I could have you both, I would! The three of us, close, so close."

His voice changed as she fondled his erection to a straining point, almost giving the impression he was subdued by his desire. Tamed by it. "I don't want him close, and I don't want him near you," he said gutturally.

She lightened her caresses along his cock, letting her voice fade to a whisper. "Why? Because of what others would think? You liked sharing me with him. You loved watching us together, and you loved playing with him, too. You liked giving him to me, and giving me to him, and enjoying our bodies between the three of us. You want to come, don't you, just listening to me? Remembering what he did to you, what he did to me. I feel like that when I remember, too. I get so excited, and in my chest it hurts because I need it. I know you need it, too."

His cock was leaking in her hand, twitching at each stroke, and his neck was flushed and strained as he tried to fight it. "You want it, and you feel restless and out of control. . . . But what if you gave in, Grey? What if you gave in like you do when you come? Doesn't it feel good? To come? To let go and find that you won't lose me after all, that I'll be right here, still wildly, desperately in love with you . . ."

"Arghhh. Goddammit."

"That's all right, baby. Come for me, Grey."

"Grab my balls."

"Like this?"

"Squeeze. Damn it. Yes."

"A little harder, Grey? Did Heath fist you like this? What if I squeeze the head just like this and twist my hand around your balls just . . . like . . ."

When he recovered from a powerful racking tremor, he clamped his teeth together and snared her wrist in his hand. He'd regained himself. His control.

Trembling from frustration and lust, Toni leaned to flick her tongue across a taut brown nipple. A muffled sound wrenched up his throat at her hungry suckling, but then he took her in his grip and dragged her to the bed.

He deposited her there and walked to the nightstand, his stance a warrior's challenge, demanding submission. His voice was a dry rasp as he pulled something out of a drawer. "You know what I think? I think you just want to be full. Every little crevice in you." She sensed his need to control something, to control her, her lust, and she appeased. Appeased him, appeased her own need and turmoil.

She lifted her embroidered dress up to her ribs and waited on the bed on all fours, ready, so ready, totally open to him. Grey came over to slip the dildo into her panties, and she gasped as he pushed it inside her pussy. How easily it went right in. How cruelly he smiled, mocking her shivers of bliss when he slapped the panty back in place. The fabric held it inside her. The silicone balls of the toy were upside down and nestled against her clit, and then

Grey aligned himself behind her and shoved aside her panties at the back.

"I keep forgetting you want this all day, every day. If you want cock, sweetheart, that's what you're going to get. Every minute of the day, I'm going to give you cock."

She wrapped her arms around her pillow, opened her mouth on it, licking it as though it were something else as she waited for him to take her. Then he was there; hot, hard, long. Opening her.

"Take it up your ass, Toni—and screw that dick in your pussy."

She made an *mmm* sound, because his flesh tearing through her felt so good. Good pain. Delicious, straining pain. Her breath grew choppy, his grip tightened on her hips as he pushed, but his turgid flesh left her all too soon.

"Don't!" she protested.

When he burrowed in again, he advanced through the tightness with ruthless purpose, wrenching a yelp from her that was part pain, part ecstasy.

"Tell me whose stick you have in your pretty derriere, Toni."

Pain ricocheted through her body, spiraling a million other sensations of pleasure in her. She panted, the silicone balls giving delicious ease to her clit as she wormed back her hips to take more of him, more in her ass, more pain, more of his punishment. "It's yours, Grey. You're inside me."

He thrust all the way in. Her pillow muffled her scream, a scream of rapture and agony, and it made him pause.

"Am I hurting you?"

Her body hugged every inch of his—it squeezed, clamped, sucked greedily at his flesh. It made him jerk inside her. It made her want to explode with heat.

"I want it," she sobbed, clutching the pillow tighter to her neck and face, "I need this from you." She was wild for it, craved this tearing pain from him, for it brought the sharpest pleasure.

"Then squeal for me." He withdrew, stabbed her fast and deep, and a whimper tore out of her.

He eased up a little, retreating to the head. "I wanted to be here." His voice was like ice on sandpaper, his hands warm, slipping downward and kneading her ass cheeks. "I desperately wanted to be here. In this hot, tight, sweet little ass."

She had wanted him here. She'd been frightened out of her wits, but Heath had taken care of that, too. And now she enjoyed feeling crammed up to her throat, gloried in the blinding, deafening pressure of him moving along the tight passage. "Grey—*oh, god!*" she cried as he rammed her hips with his. They both jolted with pleasure, their heads rolling helplessly; his went forward to hers, hers went back to him.

Making a grating sound of ecstasy, he swiveled his hips, extracting himself. He plunged next with a growl, making her scream as he plugged her with his long, rigid extension so thoroughly she thought he'd embedded himself inside her forever. But then he moved—in and out, in and out.

They had never made so much noise.

They were drowning in pleasure; both of them in pain, both of them experiencing excruciating pleasure, both of them torn in two by this mating and by their changing circumstances.

Grey needed it; she needed it. A pain of the body that matched their insides.

He splayed his hands over her ass cheeks and pushed the flesh closed around his erection as he slid and slipped and worked himself in. And when he wanted to make her scream, he fucked in so hard that a shout of pleasure would explode from him as well as her. His shouts were so agonized, hers so deep and wrenching, it felt like they each wanted to be killed by the other.

Shuddering, feverish with heat in a way that frightened her, suspended in the pinnacle of orgasm while she creamed all over the dildo, she panted, "I want Heath to fuck me, too. I want his dick inside me. I love it; I love him there."

Grey groaned. She bit at the pillow, her face rolling against it in delirium. Her vagina rippled around the silicone shaft, but the pain, the pleasure, the torture, came from Grey, and the slow, hard way he mated her. And Heath. Heath was somewhere right now, slick and wet from coming for her. No. No. He was here. Inside her. He and Grey were inside her. And it felt so right—so, so right. Bone-deep good, the pleasure seeped into her marrow, whacking away at bone, turning her flesh liquid. And she was licking Heath's mouth and whimpering and thinking, *Don't go away again. Don't leave me again.* "Call him back, Grey. Give me Heath."

Grey was thundering to the brink, body taut as he stabbed her body erratically now, his fingers digging into her hips.

"Give us Heath, Grey. Let him be with us."

"Ahh, god!"

"Grey, please."

"Fuck. Fuck, fuck, fuck, *fuck!*"

He roared, and she felt the hot jerk of his penis inside her, the spurts triggering her orgasm. They shuddered together, her scream and his bellow of ecstasy coming one atop the other. And with his heart thundering against her back, her own breaths still a roar, she whispered, "I love you." She sagged into the mattress and turned her cheek into the pillow. "I love Heath, too."

⌒

I love Heath, too.

No, she did not, *could* not, love Heath, too. Goddammit.

Toni. She was like holding water in your hands; it slipped through your fingers. He could feel her slipping, ebbing and flowing away from him, his hands, his order. He was torn between wanting to flow with her and wanting to contain her; to keep her where he was comfortable.

Driving to work the next morning, he tried assimilating everything she'd said to him, some words striking a chord more than others, but all he could really focus on was her feelings for Heath.

This was all Grey's doing. Building up his character, letting him into their bed because he trusted him. Foolishly, stupidly trusted him. Had he thought he could control their attraction by yielding to it and keep it at that? How wrong he was. How stupid. How *fucked*.

With this . . . with this, Heath had his fucking dick up Grey's ass, and as long as Toni professed her devotion to him, Grey was utterly, *supremely* screwed by them both.

Pulling into his front slot at the basement parking lot of their building, he yanked the gear into park and punched Heath's hotel number. The bastard answered at the first ring.

"Asshole."

"My thoughts exactly."

"Mind telling me what the fuck I'm doing in Oaxaca?"

"Doing what I told you to do."

"The business is shit. You cannot tear it apart and sell the pieces. It's not good enough to burn."

"Then see the sights, Heath. You're staying put until something new comes up."

"I've seen the mummies, which, incidentally, look like you, you fucking bastard. I'm coming back to Chicago."

"You're staying put. Do your job."

"You sent me to the only place I have no cell phone signal. I know what you're trying to do."

"Leave Toni alone. Understand?"

"She doesn't want me to leave her alone, damn you."

"Why do you want her, Heath? Because she's mine?"

"I want her." He dropped his voice to a menacing whisper. "I either take you with her, or I take you down if I have to."

"Try it, Heathcliff. Just try it." Ending the call with a press of a button, he pitched the phone into the backseat, gritted his teeth, and shouted, *"Son of a bitch!"*

He didn't know how long he sat there, his fingers digging into the wheel, and he didn't know how long the phone's rhythmic vibrations took to filter through his fury. Irately registering the call, he flung himself across the back and grabbed the phone, ready to crack it in two. Ready to take the call and tell Heathcliff *all* the nasty things Grey planned to do to him. But the name of the caller blinking on the display screen was someone else entirely.

Lucien Grey Richards.

Grey did not answer. Could not, *would not*, deal with his father right now. On each of the phone's subsequent vibrations, he crammed the device in his fist until its motion ceased. By the fourth attempt, he cursed and turned the damned thing off.

The entire nineteenth floor stumbled into silence when he stepped out of the elevators. He stalked down the hall directly toward the tall rosewood doors of his office, barking for his messages as he passed Louisa. Behind her desk, she raised a halting hand and quickly pressed a button on the phone, holding the receiver away from her ear. "Your father. It's the third time he's called."

Damn him. What did he *want*?

"Put him through," he snapped, slamming the double doors behind him.

He fell into his chair, picked up, and easily said, "Father."

"Explain."

"Explain *what*?"

Tiptoeing inside with the expression of someone about to be hanged, Louisa held out the day's paper. Grey homed in on the social column headline as she set it on the surface of his desk.

GLACIER TOO COLD FOR THE SUN?

Spotted vacationing in Cabo San Lucas recently, sexy "ice" millionaire Grey Richards showed no signs of thawing as longtime girlfriend, Antonia Kearny, got cozy with a dark-haired stranger on the beach.

Icicles pricked him on the inside. The chills of Antarctica *paled* in comparison to the sweeping cold that spread through him. He didn't continue reading. The picture said it all. Toni smiling, Heath crowding her with his body, cupping her breasts from behind, whispering something in her ear. And Grey. Nonchalant as could be, and right behind them, speaking to the Mexican with the dresses.

"I said explain."

His father's angry voice snapped him back. With characteristic remoteness, Grey waved Louisa off, and only when he was sealed inside his office—alone—did he put his forehead in his hand and rub. His thoughts tumbled one after the other—one in particular, one that prevailed. *Toni*. His baby. His lively, mischievous little imp. In the eye of the storm. Subjected to public speculation and scorn.

"I don't know what you're looking for, or what you want to hear," Grey said levelly.

"I want to hear that my son, with my name, isn't engaged in some strange type of business. I warned you against men like that one. I know who that good-for-nothing is. How do you expect your mother to face her friends at the function today?"

The function. Yes. Of course. How inconsiderate of Grey. "Just like she always does, smiling wide and bright. Dad."

"If you can't control your own woman, you're not the man I thought you were."

The anger he felt was sweeping, blinding, cramming his mouth with poison he wanted to spit, but even then his voice remained passive. "Like you control your wife? Who's she sleeping with now, the gardener? I have another call. Have a good day, Dad."

⌒

"... Now, your father and I are very certain there's a good explanation, so I propose you both come over for dinner and talk to us."

Toni was so stunned by the article she could barely make sense of her mother's words. A rabid, vehement anger flared up in her, then a profound, wrenching hurt. It seemed she wasn't even breathing, nor her heart beating, while a single thought slammed into her brain—Grey.

She was portrayed as the harlot and he like the ... the *fool*. How many people bought this paper? Exactly how many people would read *this*? What was this paper's circulation? He would be crushed. He would be. Oh, god. She stuck the phone between her shoulder and ear and fell on her knees, frantically spreading the paper on the coffee table and flipping the page, where the words continued. More words. Malicious, cruel words. Hurtful words about them. And her mother's voice droned on in her ear like an annoying noise that never stopped. That made you want to scream and scream and scream.

". . . couldn't possibly be what I'm thinking . . ."

"Mom, please. *Please.* I can't talk to you right now."

"Just tell me who is this man? What is he to you?"

And through her mother's fraught words, she heard her father's furious rant in the background. "I don't want to be hearing this. That is not my daughter right there. These people are scammers. I tell you, they put ten pictures together to come up with this stuff!"

Dad. Who still thought her to be faultless. With unsteady arms, she pulled herself up to the couch seat, barely registering that the person speaking in that peculiar, toneless voice was her. "Mom, I'll call you later."

She hung up and dialed slowly, an alarming calm settling over her. She was livid, she wanted to scream, and here she was . . . sitting. Hanging on to the phone as though for dear life! *Oh, god!*

"Grey Richards's office. May I help you?"

Her heart jumped at his name. "Louisa, I need Grey."

"Toni." Louisa's abrupt, startled pause lasted only a second. "He's on the line with some PR person."

"Did you read it?"

"Yes. I—" Louis paused, and Toni became aware of a perturbing silence behind her friend. As though the office were dead. As though everyone had stopped in their tasks in order to overhear this particular phone call. "I'm so sorry, Toni," Louisa finally whispered.

"They turned me into a . . ." *Whore.*

She couldn't say it. While she had been experiencing her first Mexican party, having a wonderful time, with her two men watching her like the most adorable bodyguards on the planet, these people had taken it and turned it into something horrible. They'd turned her *life* into something horrible. Her *men. Her loves!*

"Oh! Hang on. I've got Grey. He's asking for you."

She wasn't left waiting. His voice immediately poured over her; a salve for her wounds, a blanket for her quaking, breaking heart.

"Toni."

She had an insane urge to apologize, say, *I'm sorry, Grey! I'm so sorry!* But really, why? To *whom* was she apologizing, and for *what*? Apologize to the world for something three consenting adults did?

"You've seen," he said with such quietude, she ached.

"Yes."

Their pause was dense with repressed words.

His sigh clenched around her stomach, crowding her with even more cutthroat pain. "Are you all right? Is anyone out there hounding you?"

That was all he could think of. If she was all right. She had ruined his life. Something was wrong with her. And all he wanted was to know she was all right.

"I'm all right."

"I'll be right over."

"I'm fine, Grey." She spared a preoccupied glance at the front door, eyeing it as though she could see directly through the slab of wood. "Nobody's here. Don't worry about me. I'm a big girl." *And if I see someone, I'll break their cameras in two!* "I'm worried about you, Grey."

"I want to hold you in my arms."

The longing his words evoked was so great, her limbs trembled. "I want to be held."

"I'm sorry, Toni. I should have protected you, I should have——"

"Don't be! If anyone should be sorry it's me. Your public image——"

"Don't."

"This would never have happened if I hadn't—"

"Baby, don't. Don't do this."

She twirled the phone cord with one twittering finger, inhaling one breath at a time. One short, unfulfilling breath at a time. "Grey, I don't want them to make us regret it. We had amazing moments, and if we let them take that from us, we're so screwed."

His chair creaked, and she pictured him leaning back in that massive thing, rubbing his hair, frowning as he thought. "Your mom and dad?"

"Want us over for dinner. Which, of course, I will refuse until . . . I don't know. Your dad?"

"For the first time in my life, I wanted to tell him to go fuck himself."

The melancholy in her laughter made her regret having let it out. "Maybe you should. Not care what he thinks anymore."

"It makes no difference." His voice changed, became authoritative and businesslike. "I want you to put on something very pretty for me. We're going to Tiago's tonight, and I've got Louisa making sure every reporter will be there to see we're fine, and kill this right off."

Kill the rumors. Smile for the camera. They'd never taken an interest in Toni before. Grey's plain little girlfriend. But as soon as the water looked murky, the press was all over them. And she would pose for them?

"To deny it," she said, choking in distaste.

"To stop it before it gets worse," came the stern correction.

She shook her head many times, continued shaking it as she spoke. "Grey, I hate not having explanations for my parents, but you know what? In a week, some starlet will come out with her skirt up to her waist and nobody will even remember us." She almost prayed that one of them was already doing mischief now, and then felt miserable for wishing such bad tidings on someone just to get rid of her own pain.

"They *will* remember. It's in print. They'll have a field day with this."

"I don't want to play their game! In fact, I wish Heath were here and the three of us could pose, with each of you grabbing one of my breasts while we tell the entire universe. YES. Big deal. We had a freaking *threesome*!" Okay, she was really losing it, and most surprising of all, she was really loving it! She wanted to do something reckless, and she wanted to scratch everyone's eyes out for attacking Grey.

"But Heath is not here, is he? This is about you. And me. And me needing to fix this."

"Heath would say they should go fuck themselves."

"Not. Another. Word. About *Heath*!"

"He's your instinct, and sometimes you need to trust it, Grey. How can we be happy trying to please the entire world? I'm not going anywhere," she said in an emphatic rush of rebelliousness. "I'll be home and I'll be waiting for you just as I always am, but don't expect me to pose. I'm not living the life of everyone; this is *mine*. If I listened to what everyone thinks I should be doing, I'd be looking for a sperm donor, since it's clear there won't be a husband coming to me!"

"What in the hell does that have to do with anything?"

"Nothing! The point is . . ." She sighed. What did a baby have to do with anything, damn it? Was she growing desperate? Was she so without dignity that she'd propose to Grey herself now? "The point is, all I care about is what you think. And Heath. The rest is not important."

"Then would you care to know that I have our IPO coming up next week? RS is going public. We can't afford something like this. Not now and not ever."

"And what did your fabulous PR person suggest?"

Silence.

"What did he suggest would be great for your IPO?"

More silence. Not a peaceful, serene silence, but the kind that made you aware of just how many things you did not know, did not hear, were not aware of.

"What?" she fragilely demanded. "Did he suggest you pose with some other bimbo so the world thinks you broke up with me before Cabo and we were both there by accident, *me* with my new fling?"

"Yes."

She gasped, the thought that everybody, everybody in the world, including her parents, did not think her fit for Grey devastated her. Because maybe they were right. Because no matter how much she adored him, she might not be worthy of him after all. She had hurt him, and maybe she truly didn't have a clue about what a man like Grey needed.

With a serenity that belied the pain in her very bones, she mumbled, "Do what you have to do, Grey Richards."

In her mind, she hung up—no, she *slammed* the receiver into the cradle—and yet a second later she remained in her same spot, anxiously clutching it to her ear.

"I fired him."

She blinked in surprise, stuttered, "You did?"

"On the spot."

Her laugh was feeble. Of sadness mingled with relief. "Oh, Grey." He was chuckling, too.

And she conceded, "One picture. That's it. Grey, this is none of their business!"

"I know," he appeased. "But I need the ball on my field. If they write about me, it'll be what I tell them to. If I hide or keep silent, they'll find out who Heath is and dig in our pasts until that one time we smoked marijuana only god remembers where . . . I can't have that."

"I know," she ruefully agreed.

But she knew Grey couldn't have anyone knowing who Heath was and what he meant to them.

It was over before she even knew it.

They sat undisturbed in a shadowed nook of the restaurant, and all Grey said, a second before they strolled out of the place, was, "Smile." And she smiled. Blinding flashes exploded before her eyelids. Then Grey was tucking her into his Porsche, and they were driving off, the camera lights fading in the distance.

Neither spoke a word until they got home.

Toni went to her vanity, plucked off one diamond stud earring, then quietly set it down and said, "Why did we just do that?"

Without a backward glance, Grey whipped off his shirt and threw it in the hamper.

"Because of the IPO? Grey, people will buy a piece of your company because it rocks. You *make* it rock, Heath makes it rock. They'll buy it because you make them money—they won't care if you're the craziest person on the planet or not." When his hands went to his belt, the concentrated frown on his face spurred her on. "And it's not about money, either. I hear you talking about off-shores all the time; it's like you have so much, you don't even know where to put it."

He made neither acknowledgment nor denial, but he was listening, so she shimmied out of her cocktail dress and plunged on.

"So why is it?" she insisted.

He yanked off his belt while Toni grabbed his old T-shirt and popped her head inside. "Is it that you can't stand that people may think less of you?"

He thrust his legs into his cotton drawstring pants, then turned his back to her as he hung his slacks.

"Or is it him, Grey?"

He crossed the room toward the bed, leaving a lamp on by the nightstand. His long, strong arm was already waiting for her by the time she lifted the sheets and slipped into his embrace. "I don't feel like discussing my father tonight," he said, kissing the tip of her nose as though to gentle the directness of his words.

She gazed into his golden eyes, noted the low set of his eyebrows, the worried crease on his forehead.

"Grey, look at you," she marveled as she sat up, her heart exploding with love for him. "Look at this incredible man you are! I swear I quiver every time I see you. Not because of these eyes, this hair, this body, baby, but because of the mesmerizing man that you are! If you haven't proven yourself to your father by now, there's nothing you'll ever be able to do to please that man."

"I am aware of that, Toni."

"Then why do you still try to please him? All these people?"

The rigidness in his body increased tenfold, and as the silence lengthened, Toni figured he was not planning to answer her. He clicked off the light, his hand stroking up and down the back of her head when she lay back down, and then he let go a breath.

"I don't want to *please* him. I want to be a better man than he is."

Chapter Fifteen

Duffel bag slung over his shoulder, Heath shuffled among the line of people boarding the aircraft. He sank down in the window seat on aisle eleven, stuck his bag under the front seat, and rubbed his sweaty palms over his jeans. No drugs. He could do it, of course. Pop them at any time. But he wouldn't.

For the first time in his life, he wanted to *kiss* an airplane. This was the carrier that would take him to her. And he would not leave again. He would not fucking leave her *ever*. Whatever Grey said, he was staying. If he had to eat shit, he'd eat shit. If he had to fight Grey, goddammit, he didn't want to, but he would.

He patted his right pocket, his two pills neatly tucked inside. Next he went to his left pocket and produced the red sash.

The fabric slid like a familiar skin against him, its scent memorized in his lungs. What did it mean, this present she'd given him? Why had she given it to *him*? She wanted him. She wanted him *with* her. Did she feel what he felt? Did she care about him?

Whatever she wanted, he would not say no. Oh no, he would not say no to his Cat.

"My, how pretty."

He frowned, and it took him a moment to realize someone was speaking to him. Normally he would snore or ignore his flying companion. Why people loved to tell their life stories inside an aircraft was beyond him. But this time, he found himself turning his attention to the elderly woman who'd just settled in her seat beside him.

"It is," he said cautiously as the plane doors slammed shut.

"Your wife's?" she inquired.

He hesitated. "Her name is Antonia." God, it was such a relief to tell somebody. Have someone to talk to about *her*. This little lady with the silvering hair and the crooked teeth was so sweet to ask.

"How long have you been married?" she asked, her wrinkled hands motionless on her lap.

"We're not married." He blinded her with a smile, a smile meant to make a woman even of her age blush. "Do you think she'd have me?" he baited.

He was so distracted watching the heat creep up her dainty neck that he didn't notice they'd taxied until they took off. He cursed under his breath, tensing when the plane soared, the ground falling away beneath him.

His heart raced—not with dread this time, he realized, but with anticipation. The captain spoke, and when the speakers fell silent, Heath told the old lady, "So, was that a yes?"

She lowered her glasses to the tip of her nose and eyed him speculatively above the rims. "Yes." She patted his cheek, her smile thin but honest. "You look vigorous."

He propped his head back on the seat and gazed absently up at the head compartment. "I haven't seen her in . . . well, hell, it's almost three weeks." He frowned. Only three weeks? It felt like forever.

"Three weeks is a long time. I'm going to see my grandsons, and I haven't seen them in two years."

Heath whistled through his teeth. "Two years? Really? Wow, that's tough."

She righted her glasses on her nose, her eyes lingering on the sash. "What are you going to do with it?" she asked.

Ahhh, that was easy. "Tie her to the bed with it and make her mine?"

Her eyes widened under her lenses, and he realized he shouldn't have said that to a sweet old lady. So he smiled and did something unthinkable. He grabbed her hand, soft and wrinkled and looking like it would disintegrate in his, and said, "I'm going to tell her I love her."

⌒

"Four-carat, E, VVS-one round brilliant."

Inside a sumptuous jewelry store on Michigan Avenue, Grey grasped the tweezers being offered by the middle-aged jeweler and brought the loupe up to one eye. He gazed into the rock—a massive, blinding sparkler—and then looked up. "Am I supposed to see anything?"

"No, sir—it's a VVS-one; it would be impossible to see the inclusions with a regular jeweler's loupe."

"Ahh." Grey lowered the loupe and turned the tweezers around to glance at the diamond's glinting tip. "It's a bit too large for what I had in mind."

"Nothing screams *money* like a big rock."

"I don't want it to scream *money*; I just want her to like it."

"With a four-carat rock like that, the world will know your woman is loved by a rich, powerful man."

Grey set it down on the black velvet-covered tray. "Is there something more subtle?"

The man tucked the stone back into a small, crinkling blue paper. "We could go to fancy. Colored diamonds are appreciated only by the finest connoisseurs. The ladies love the pink."

Grey waited for the man to produce one. The bubble gum pink rock he revealed, although decently smaller than the last, struck him as perhaps a bit too girly for a woman. "She's not that much of a pink lover," he said pleasantly.

"Ahh, I have just the thing." The jeweler fished into a discreet leather briefcase and presented another rock, one that was darker, brilliant. He secured it with the tweezers and handed it over. "We call it the Chameleon. Natural diamond. Will change color depending on the lighting. You'll get colors ranging from the brightest green to a dark gray."

"Gray?"

"Yes, sir."

"A gray diamond. I've never heard of that before."

"Usually, sir, one never hears of these things until one is wanting to marry." The old man smiled placidly from where he stood behind the low display case. "I take it she's your first?"

"My only." Grey studied the rock.

"That's a two-carat, internally flawless oval cut. That baby is as pure as they come."

Grey assessed it from every angle, admiring the way it refracted the overhead lights, taking in the color, the size, its flawlessness. He set it down. "I need a moment." He pulled out his phone, dialed on automatic, and lifted it to his ear, casually eyeing the other patrons in the store as they peered into the jewelry cases while he waited for Louisa to answer. "Louisa. Can you come down to Fried's for a moment? Michigan Avenue; a large, very fine store. I need your opinion on something."

When he hung up, he smoothed his tie in place and paced the length of the store, his eyes roving the glass cases, occasionally pausing on a particularly brilliant jewel that caught his interest. *Patience, Grey, it is a virtue. . . .*

His lips curled when the words popped into his head. He could be the most patient man when it came to business deals; he could take weeks, months, years, to tailor matters to his specifications, shape them just as he wanted them. But in personal matters—more exactly, in *this* matter—he wasn't feeling particularly at ease. Much less patient.

The memory of them posing three nights ago, smiling for those blasted cameras, Toni's smile so stiff on her lips—a sad, forced smile she'd placed on her face because he'd *asked* her to put it there . . . Grey hated it. Loathed himself for having asked her to do it. Hated forcing Toni to bend to these people. She was right; it wasn't their fucking business. And Grey *did* want to tell them to screw themselves. Them *and* his father.

She was so brave, so spirited, a fiery creature of passion and life. . . .

She'd have rather chowed on cement than placate the press, but she had done it for him. Out of love for him. Though he'd thought it impossible to love her any more than he already had, he did. He cherished her. Adored her. Wanted to, *needed* to, marry her.

By the time Louisa appeared through the sliding glass doors, flushed and excited and dressed indecently like always, he was simmering with impatience. Charging across the store to lead her to his corner, he sat her down on the upholstered chair next to his and briskly lifted the tweezers up to her line of vision. "It's a gray diamond."

Louisa's expression was an interesting mix of awe and confusion that looked almost painful.

"Do you think Toni would like it?" Grey pressed.

She raised stunned blue eyes to his; she didn't seem to be breathing. "Are . . . are you going to propose?"

"This is between you and me. What happens at . . ." He gave a meaningful glance at the store logo. "Fried's, stays at Fried's. Until the ring is on her finger."

"Yes, of course."

"Do you like it?"

After a timid moment, she took the tweezers between awkward fingers, gave the stone an expeditious look, then lowered her hand. "I just don't believe Toni ever intended to marry."

"Nothing is set in stone." Grey turned to the jeweler, who'd been eyeing their exchange with a benign look on his face. "And this is?"

"Two hundred seventy-five thousand."

Louisa's hand flew to her mouth, not quite in time to cover her gasp; then she coughed and patted her chest with the other.

"It's a GIA certified diamond, sir."

Pleased with this new important detail and unfazed by the price, Grey raised his hand to the jeweler's inhumanly devoid gaze and tapped the base of his wedding finger. "Would this include it being set in a band?"

"A setting, yes. I'd suggest platinum, with white pave diamonds surrounding the central stone to bring out the color in it, and a very delicate band."

"Could we arrange for a wire transfer to be made to the store today, Louisa?"

She was on her feet, twisting a bracelet around her wrist. "Sure, it's— Yes, anything is possible."

"Splendid," the man said.

Grey drummed his fingers on the glass in a restless gesture, studying his fidgeting assistant. "How should I give it to her, do you think? The old-fashioned way, roses, dropping at her feet?"

Louisa's sudden laugh had a raspy, unattractive quality to it. It almost sounded cynical. "Toni isn't that old-fashioned."

"You're right. Hmm." He considered his Toni in all her dimensions, caring and funny and explosive. "Something fun, maybe. Balloons and a mime?"

"A mime?"

"Something she won't expect." Grey smiled at his own ingeniousness, his mind racing full speed. "Yes. I like that."

⌒

Stubborn, stubborn Grey.

Toni had been sitting at her workstation all morning and had accomplished nothing but a headache.

Dropping her pencil, she pushed her chair back and wound her way around the living room, plumping the pillows. How would she get him to admit it, to stop being so hardheaded? She knew that *he* knew deep down she was right. Heath belonged with them. Grey adored him in his own way, and not talking to him was tearing him apart, too! They couldn't push Heath out of their lives. He was all instinct and passion and courage, and Toni wanted him, needed him, with them. How would she make him come back? How could she make Grey accept him?

While she set the kitchen into a semblance of cleanliness and order, she heard a knock. She was so lost in her thoughts, she didn't hesitate to stroll over and open the door, thinking it might be one of her neighbors.

Instead, she came face-to-face with the same pair of twilight black eyes that haunted her dreams, her nightmares, and all her daydreams in between.

Looking tired, Heath Solis ran a hand through his rumpled hair, and his lips slowly, slowly, curved into a devastating smile.

Her stomach tumbled to the floor. Her breath went with it. "Heath?"

"The one and only."

He lifted his right hand and held up her satin sash like a white flag announcing the end of a battle.

She didn't realize she was clinging to the door until her knuckles protested in pain. She loosened her hold, trying to stand upright. "I wasn't sure when you'd find my sash . . . or that you'd even want to come."

He dropped a duffel bag at his feet and took a step forward, prying the door from her fingers and shutting it behind him. He did not let go of the sash. "When have I not come when you wanted me?"

She sucked in a breath when he reached out to trace the boat-neck collar of her shirt with his free hand. Gooseflesh broke out along her skin as his finger trailed the edges. Her heart could not beat any faster and she survive it.

"Heath."

His hand journeyed higher, up the curve of her throat. His eyes tracked the caress up to her lips. Her mouth opened, her eyes drifting shut as he pushed his thumb into her mouth. "Heath . . ." She tilted her face higher, drawing his digit inside and wrapping the heat of her mouth entirely around it. Longing spread through her veins, stretching her system taut. He tasted salty, and she wanted to continue licking until she had tasted every part of his skin.

"Oh, my god, Heath." She tore her eyes open, pressed her breasts into his chest and tangled her fingers in his hair, and then his arms were unyielding vines around her, squeezing out the little breath that remained in her.

"Christ! You feel so good, you smell"—he sucked in a breath of her hair—"so good."

She clutched the cotton of his shirt in her fists and smelled him, too. Earth. Sweat. Heath. She flattened her hands over his pecs to encompass as much of him she could. The drum of his heart beat strong and steady under her palm. "I missed you, Heath. It's been horrible without you. Everything's been just horrible lately," she confessed.

His eyes were weighted, the lashes silky, almost resting on his prominent cheekbones. Framing her mouth with his thumbs, he studied her lips with the hunger of a wild man, but seemed hesitant to take them. "Fuck, Cat, I'm so screwed."

"No. No." She clutched his face between her small hands. "You're home. You're home, Heath."

He drew back a little. "Do you mean that?"

She bit her lip, nodding.

"Shit, come here."

He crushed her mouth with his. His tongue pushed inside, demanding, insistent, voracious, twirling against and around her. "I want you, Cat." He lifted her off the floor and spun her around. "All of you, the good and the bad."

She laughed. "Oh, it's all good."

And they were laughing, kissing, when a closing door broke through their merriment.

They swiveled their heads to the entry. And there stood Grey. With an enormous black gorilla at his side. The gorilla grasped a bunch of colorful helium balloons in his meaty hand.

"Grey?" A puzzled noise rose up her throat. "W-what is a gorilla doing here?"

Grey wasn't listening to her. His gaze was riveted on Heath, his unguarded expression registering shock. Pain, *anger*. His lips hardened. "Heath."

"Grey."

With a strained move, Grey rubbed his two index fingers up the bridge of his nose, whispered something into his hands before he dropped them at his sides.

Toni gulped. In her anxiety and desperation to reunite the men, she had failed to predict the sheer enormity of the blazing hostility between them. It was suffocating. Her lungs burned for oxygen, her knees wobbled, and she could not seem to move.

"Unbelievable," Heath muttered as the gorilla proffered the tangle of balloons ceremoniously before her. "Where on earth did you find that thing, Richards?"

Grey looked ready to explode in some kind of internal combustion, and Toni felt the turmoil in him as if it were her own. The guy in the gorilla suit was jumping with glee, either too stupid to realize what was happening or too frantic to do his job to care. But the stark emotion in Grey's simmering gold eyes was so vivid, his face seemed to grow black with his pain.

Releasing a freakish king-of-the-jungle sound, the hairy black beast lumbered forward and dropped to one knee, extending a gift to her. A dangerous weakness crept up the back of her legs, loosening her spine. She took the small box with trembling hands.

Grey cursed and went to stare out the blinds.

And Toni flicked the box open. A beautiful diamond ring sat nestled at its plush velvet center. The stone was brilliant, dark and different and sophisticated, and so beautiful it robbed her of her breath. It was Grey. And it was heartbreaking.

"Grey, what is this?"

He was seething with energy, frustration and anger sharpening his words, each piercing her like a needle. "You know what it is."

"You said . . . you said we wouldn't do it. Ever."

"Well, I want to do it now."

The gorilla was punching its chest, doing goofy stuff around the room; then it made a silly noise and tooted a little horn. That was all it took to make Grey lose it. What had not happened in thirty-five years happened when the gorilla tooted that little horn.

Grey threw himself at the man, grabbing him by the shoulders. In the oversized suit the guy was no match for him. In a flash of fury, Grey jostled him out into the hall, yelling, "Out, out, *out!*"

The slam of the door made the walls vibrate. Motionless as concrete, Heath and Toni regarded him with caution as he returned, but Grey only had eyes for her. Wounded eyes. Eyes full of accusation and torture.

He stared at Toni with those eyes. Toni, with the box in one hand. With her sash in the other. With her heart in her eyes and no oxygen to speak with.

Out in the hall, she heard voices. Doors. The elevator dinging. But the inside of her apartment was dense as a coffin; there was no life here.

"Did you give Heath your sash?" Grey asked in a voice so taut it sent prickles of unease down her back.

"Yes."

"May I know why?"

Her throat felt dry as sandpaper as she swallowed. "So he'd come back."

Plunging a hand into his hair, Grey circled the room. And circled. And circled.

Toni stared hopelessly at the ring again. Oh, how she'd wanted this ring. How she wanted to marry Grey. Vow her love for him before the world and god and a roomful of people. What she would give to be his wife! But how could she? How could she *now*, with Heath here, humbly asking to be part of her, too? Her eyes clouded with tears. Her throat worked as she tried to speak.

"Grey, about the ring . . ."

"Forget it," he said blandly. And as though this were any ordinary day, with that confident, take-on-the-world stride of his, he disappeared into their bedroom, pulled open the closet doors, and very carefully began to draw out his clothes.

When Toni realized his intentions, she hurled both the ring and the sash on the bed and rushed to stop him. "Grey, what are you doing? No!" Panicked, she seized the hangers in his hands and frantically tried to shove the clothes back inside. "Don't do this—don't leave me!"

"Grey," Heath said in a threatening voice from the doorway.

Grey pivoted, his face taut with rage as he pointed a commanding finger at him. "You stay the fuck out of this, Solis."

While Toni struggled to return the armful of shirts to his side of the closet, he reached for his laptop on the nightstand. He unplugged it, shoved it into his leather briefcase, strapped it inside.

Toni rushed to him, her eyes stinging, the words barely getting past the painful obstruction in her throat. "Grey, don't you dare leave me. Don't you dare!" She grabbed both his biceps and pushed her face into his neck, shaking her head a thousand times, certain that she was falling, torn by not knowing what to do, and fearing that this time Grey wouldn't catch her.

He cursed under his breath and dropped his forehead to her shoulder. His chest heaved so roughly she thought his clothes would tear. "Grey." The word was a shaky plea against his collar. "It would work, you *know* it would. The three of us . . . the three of us love each other."

Even as she began to speak, he was shaking his head, shaking his head faster, blocking her out, blocking out her words. She trapped his jaw in her hands, her voice almost a shriek. "Please, please, listen to me! We can be together. All three of us. Grey! Please listen."

The fury and misery in him raged rampant in his eyes. "*No*," he hissed. Grabbing her throat in his hand, he lay his thumb on her pulse, a hairsbreadth from pressing. "You," he said in a savage snarl she had never, ever, heard before. "*You* listen to me." His hand trembled and he let go of her. "It's him or me." Snatching the sash from the bed, he rammed it into her chest, where her clammy hand came up to cradle it against her. "You've only got one of those. You get *one* pick!"

Heath narrowed his eyes. "You're going to regret this, Grey."

"I already do."

Toni laughed. That nervous, she's-lost-her-mind laugh, and it was mingled with tears. She brought her fist to her mouth, trying to strangle the laugh, but the sounds that came out in the attempt were even worse, and it made both men stare at her incredulously.

Grey's expression transformed from ominous fury to a twisted, pained grimace as he caught her face, streaming with tears, in both his hands. And then he was hauling her to him, crushing her in his arms. "Don't cry on me now, Antonia. Don't fucking do this to me now!"

The raw agony in his plea battered her. She tried sucking back the tears, but her sobs came from somewhere so deep and wretched. She couldn't even say from where; only that she couldn't stop them. The tears flowed unchecked and her body spasmed, racked by the force with which they tore from her. She had never clutched his shoulders so hard, so violently.

Then something happened. His arms tightened surprisingly harder around her, and Grey buried his face deep in her hair and choked on the most awful, heart-wrenching sound she'd ever heard, and she knew he was sobbing, too.

He had never held her so hard, hard enough to crush her bones, and she wanted to disintegrate right there in his arms.

But instead, a moment later he was transferring—*transferring* her, fast and not gently, to another pair of arms, and his footsteps sounded across the room. He was leaving. So fast. So surely. Like he couldn't wait to get out of there. Out of her life.

Toni sagged at the definitive click of the door. She fell in a heap at Heath's feet, tears rolling down her cheeks in rivers.

Heath kneeled before her, collecting her—all limp bones and muscles that felt lax with grief—against him. "Cat. Sweetheart." He gathered her close and rocked her, and she knew by the way his hands shook that he was at a loss, that he'd never handled a woman in this situation before, and no matter how she tried, she could not seem to compose herself for him, either.

"Toni, I've ruined your life. Jesus, I've ruined your life." The way he spoke it as he rocked her, like a chant of hatred, a curse at him-self, made her wipe at her tears with furious hands.

"No, don't say that."

"Yes, I have. Yes, I have. Oh, baby, I have."

Tenderly, she filled her palms with the tightness of his jaw, cry-ing softly. "I love you. Grey loves you, too—you're like his brother. He's too stubborn to admit it."

He was gripping at her, rubbing against her. "Use me." He was pulling at her hair, ravaging her neck. "Use me for what you need. I can be Grey for you. I'll make love to you. I'll tell you all the things he—"

"Heath, stop it, stop!" she cried anxiously, and locked her eyes on his. "You're my Heath. Stop this."

"Oh, Cat, this is killing me." His back against the wall, he shifted her onto his lap and petted her hair so roughly, she thought he'd tear it out at the roots. His voice was gruff and affected. "I've never felt like this before, did you know?"

"I know."

"Look at me."

She did. She looked into those eyes, luminous on hers, expres-sive and meltingly tender. She grazed her cheek across the familiar calluses in his palms as he cradled her. "I missed you, Heath Solis."

He was drinking up her face as though it were his only sustenance. "I missed you every day, Cat, every single day. Christ, I don't want to leave. I swore to myself nothing would make me leave this time. But if I stay he won't come back."

"He will, Heath, he will!"

"He won't, Cat. He's stubborn as they come."

"But he *loves* me," she said brokenly.

The grim set of Heath's mouth and the bleak look in his eyes had her wildly shaking her head in denial before he even spoke his thoughts out loud. "If I stay, you lose him."

"Don't say that—that's not true!"

"I'm no match for Grey, Toni."

"You are! You make me smile—I adore being with you, I want you in my life, and Grey adores you, damn him. I *hate* him!"

"Fucking *look* at you!" Heath roared as he gestured down at her, at this heap of clothes that she was, tear-stricken, trembling, someone she would pity. "Look at you without him! And did you get a fucking good look at *him*?"

"Well, I was a little busy at the moment!" she screamed.

"Then I can *tell* you what he looked like. I can—goddammit, *it's killing him*!" Frustrated, his throat hoarse with agony, he smashed her body to his. Her thighs opened for closeness, their bodies fitting together, heat to heat. He ducked his head to hers, his mouth furiously nipping, biting between words. "Take me in, kitten. Take me in your body one last time."

He kissed her rampantly, a good-bye kiss, as intense as the first but tasting of anguish and pain instead of eagerness and thirst and lust. It took all her effort to tear her lips free.

"What are you saying? Stop talking to me like this, Heath!"

"Baby." Panting against her, he dragged his lips across her face. "Oh, baby, can't you see? I love you too much to break you." He dropped his head and buried his face in the softness of her breasts, releasing a low, tortured sound. "I can't see you like this, I can't . . . see Grey like this—*fuck*."

She trembled, feeling very cold even as he groaned and wrapped her in arms of steel and warmth. She wanted to make love to him, to celebrate his arrival with joy. She wanted for her eyes to dry up so she wouldn't have to cry anymore, and she wanted to marry Grey and Heath and have children together, and she wanted world peace and no one to ever die. . . . And yet all she could do was clutch Heath tight until she finished wanting and wishing and crying. Heath held her, told her he loved her, that he would understand. He was painstakingly gentle when he scooped her up in his arms and tucked her into her bed.

When seconds turned to minutes and minutes to hours, and she remained alone in it, in a bed that had been warm with someone else's heat for more than two years, she realized Heath Solis had left her, too.

Chapter Sixteen

For three days, she poured her heart into her work. She sat at her workstation and crumpled paper after paper, sketch after sketch. Balls were littered around the wastepaper basket and her pencils were at their last inch.

Viscevis. It was all that held her together. Kept her sane. She thought about Grey and a knot formed in her throat. She remembered how she'd been stressing about this logo night after night, and he'd held her head in his hands, kissed her forehead, centering her over and over, telling her again and again, "Here's your head. You have it in there somewhere."

But it was not there; instead she found her answer in Mr. Preston's words.

Your work has heart, Miss Kearny. I like that. . . .

Staring at the two logos, she isolated each of the elements first, then began to play with them. That gray ball in motion. The vine shaped into an oval. The sleek brown cylinder.

She set the cylinder at the bottom. Unyielding, all alone. Empty. She set the ball an inch above it. It would roll and roll and roll and never stop without that cylinder to hold it. And the vine . . . she sliced it open. She made it fluid. Rather than an oval, it slithered into an *S,* and she wrapped it around both the cylinder and the top ball, so that the two other elements were embraced by it, joined by it.

Viscevis.

For six hours she concentrated on creating a clean copy to show the clients, and by the time her neighbor took her poodle out early in the morning, Toni lifted the logo up to her admiring gaze. Yes.

Yes.

Calmly, she crossed her apartment and went to her bed, pulling her sash from under her pillow. She had slept with it and cried over it, and cursed and thrown and stomped on it.

The sash had taken her places she and Grey hadn't meant to go, and there was no undoing what had been done.

Her men were strong men, and in the most hopeful corners of her heart, she thought if they were the men she *knew* they were . . . if they were men who loved with the force and passion she did . . .

Without further thought, she recalled that vine, the solution to holding together two elements too strong to combine, and she grabbed a pair of scissors and sliced the soft, shimmering fabric in two.

⌣

Drunks.

He'd held a private distaste from them for some time. They lacked character, strength of will, an instinct to push forward no matter what blows life brought.

Drunks were fools. And Grey had never thought of himself as either until now; as he sipped more brandy, and sipped and sipped and sipped, and grasped for that numbness he'd sought for three days. Three long, never-ending days in which he warred with himself not to call her, go to her, drive past her place and spy on her. Take that freaking sash from her.

Instead he stood in the living room of his penthouse like a fixture, one of the many artifacts of this vast, lonely, cold place. There was no clutter here. No dying plants, since there weren't any plants at all. No balled-up papers around the wastebaskets.

Things were just as he liked them.

The apartment covered the space of an entire floor—every square foot furnished by a renowned New York decorator who'd later begged to take pictures for *Architectural Digest*. The fabrics, the woods, the rugs; they were the finest money could buy.

It wasn't home.

Not even Toni's place was home. It was *her*—and he'd uprooted himself because he was proud and stubborn and more. So now he was alone. Waiting. Still not hopeless, but growing desperate.

A sensation he did not welcome. *At all.*

He heard the loud ding of the elevators, rolling open directly onto his foyer, and it was followed by the unmistakable tap of Louisa's high heels gradually advancing toward him. At nine p.m., he was still dressed in the suit he'd worn to work that morning. There had been no green-eyed, chestnut-haired woman to undo his tie. Rumple his hair. Slip his coat off. Kiss his throat, his jaw, his forehead.

"I've got your suitcase," the feathery whisper came from behind him. "I couldn't quite make everything fit, but I could make another round tomorrow."

He spared a fleeting glance at the tall black suitcase sitting on the limestone floor and said, "Never mind. That's fine."

"Your colognes are in a Ziploc bag. I rolled up your ties so the silk wouldn't snag. Also, I had to leave a few shoes behind—the Guccis and two or three pairs of Prada."

He scarcely heard her. Across the room, through the window, distant city lights began to blur, blink, flutter before his eyes. The glass in his hand felt weightless. Empty once again. "Did she send anything?"

Hope was a strange thing. It had wishes in it and it had fear, and he was bursting with it.

Louisa drew up to his side, her eyes riveted on his face. "What do you mean?"

"Did she send me a message? Anything?"

She wavered noticeably between speaking and remaining quiet; then her attention shifted to his throat, his shoulders, arms. She crawled one hand up his biceps. "Let me get this off you," she purred. "You look tired."

He didn't want her to remove it, but he was powerless to stop her. He was taken by the fantasy, rashly creating a little pretend moment for himself, and he closed his eyes and imagined those were *her* hands on his chest. Small, loving hands pushing his jacket off his tired shoulders. She didn't smell like Toni. No peachy scent fluttered about her; instead, Louisa was surrounded with the scent of a flowery perfume. He heard the slap of his jacket across the back of the couch. She tugged on his tie, first touching a finger to his Adam's apple, and he opened his eyes, seized her chin, and forced her head up.

"Did she send anything?" he repeated.

In the dark, he could almost pretend her eyes were green, an aroused, dark forest green, with the sheen that made his heart kick into his ribs. She was staring back at him, lips parted, but even drunk he couldn't mistake those lips for those ones he loved. These were thin red lips that gradually, distinctly, in a voice that was decidedly not *hers*, said, "No."

No. She hadn't sent anything.

Briskly stepping around Louisa, he wrenched off his tie and tossed it across the back of a nearby chair. "Was she alone?"

He was about to repeat the question when she said hastily, "Yes."

The relief he felt was instant, causing a shudder to run through him. He'd never thought he'd ever feel grateful to Louisa Fairchild.

Rolling his cuffs up to his elbows, he admitted, "I was wrong about you. You have proven useful, and I apologize for misjudging you. My gratitude to you."

"I'm . . . I'm glad I please you, Grey."

She did not take the hint of his dismissal, and Grey wasn't certain if she'd been standing so close two seconds ago. "I'd say it's time you call it an evening, don't you think?" He signaled toward the bronze elevator doors and stalked across the room to refill his glass with brandy. "I'll be sure you're properly compensated for your time."

"I was just over at Mr. Solis's hotel," she offered, her bracelets tinkling on her wrist as she tucked her hair behind one ear.

His entire body went rigid. Glass full, he had to force his legs to walk him back to his place by the window. "Were you?"

"I had something to deliver."

His heart hardened. It closed, *protected* what was there. He brought the brandy to his lips and gazed disinterestedly out the window. He saw nothing now. No buildings. No lights.

In a voice so balmy even he scarcely heard it, he said, "A red sash?"

"Why, yes, how did you . . . ?"

His hope was pulverized. "You delivered her red sash to Heathcliff?"

"I didn't know his name was—"

"Did you?"

"Yes."

When the word sank into his gut, it shot up to his chest to annihilate his heart. It was a massacre. His stomach lurched, and when the impact sliced through each and every one of the walls he was struggling to maintain, the bottom fell out of his world so hard that he had to brace a hand on the window and face the floor. "Thank you, Louisa. That will be all."

"Would you like me to fix you something?" She made her way around the place, her footsteps an unwelcome, annoying sound that made him realize just how desperate he was to lash out at someone. "I make a killer apple martini," she said—and the cheery note grated on his nerves.

He heard her putter around the bar area, heard glass tinkling, Louisa asking him something. And then all he could hear was Toni. Sobbing in his arms. Clutching him with all her might, crying for him, for her, for Heath. He'd come *apart* holding her. Because he was afraid that was the last time he'd have her in his arms. He was afraid he couldn't be the man she wanted him to be. She was bursting with life and passion, rebellious against the world and its rules, and he had made her stand there and be photographed . . . and he had made her smile . . . smile for all of them . . . and hold his hand while they were breaking in two.

Don't. Grey, don't leave me . . .

But he'd left. Even when he adored her, even when he knew— in his gut, his heart, his every cell—he was *adored* by her. He had landed the last blow needed to shatter them. He'd tried holding the pieces of them together, but he'd quit. He. *He* had ripped them apart. He'd left when she needed him. When she was confused and frustrated and still fighting for that stupid, foolish idea of hers. When those incredibly green eyes of hers had been flowing with tears in a way he'd never, *ever*, seen before.

He'd broken her heart for making him share it with Heath.

Now Heath would take care of her, fix her low tires, live in that annoyingly small place with all her frustrating clutter. And he would get all of her smiles. He would fight with her, make up with her, drink her lousy coffee, and wake up with her.

His throat was clogged to words. His eyes burned as if the brandy simmered inside them. His jaw wouldn't work as he tried to speak. He struggled with it, forcing himself to form the words, "I said, that will be all, Louisa."

He didn't expect her to launch herself at him when he turned. The soft, dry kiss she planted on his lips came as an equal shock to the feel of her breasts pressing into his chest. "I'm here for you,

Grey." She rubbed her hands up and down the plackets of his shirt, breathing fast. "You're a strong, vigorous, incredible man—"

His ire came so viciously, so fast and potently, the glass flew from his hand and crashed into the wood-paneled wall in a deafening explosion. Glass rained down on the floor. Drops of liquid slithered down the tapestry. The color drained from her face as she stumbled back a step, her hand at her throat.

Grey sucked in a gust of oxygen, striving for control, for patience, for *anything* but this devastation. He ground out the words: *"I said that will be all."*

When she left in a startled, fumbling hurry, the room fell so silent he could hear his own breathing echo within the walls. It was a spiked, shallow sound, like he'd imagined the breath of a monster lurking in a cave would sound. His were even more terrifying.

His hands shook violently at his sides. The muscles of his face trembled. He leaned his forehead on the window and shoved his hands into his pockets and released a low, frustrated noise instead of the savage wail he wanted to let out.

In his mind, he imagined himself storming into their apartment—*her* apartment—and shaking her, cursing her, having punishing, violent sex with her.

The thought made him feel even more repulsive. More bitter.

For the first time in his life he frankly, wholeheartedly, wished he were dead.

And Grey Richards, with all the wealth he had amassed and a name that would make any foe tremble, stood alone by the window of his penthouse, willing his heart to grow as cold as it was rumored to be.

⌒

He'd never thought he'd see the sash again. Or that Louisa Fairchild would deliver it to his hotel room. Or that the red satin strip would be half its normal size.

Heath did not care if it was a millimeter square; holy mother of god, he'd been out of his mind waiting for a sight of red.

He almost knocked Louisa over in his rush to go to her. *Toni.*

Heath rapped on her apartment door exactly eighteen minutes later.

Toni wore the same sexy, strapless red dress she'd worn the first moment he'd seen her, and all the words of love and devotion he'd practiced fell out of his lips when the door swung open to reveal her.

"Christ." He swept her into his arms and twirled her around. "Where do you think you're going with that?"

"I'm going to seduce you," she said laughingly as he set her down.

"I'm seduced." He could not keep his hands to himself, so he had them on her butt, the small of her back, then her breasts. His mouth dragged across her face, desperate to go everywhere at once. "I was waiting like a lovesick fool to hear from you. I was half-convinced I should leave the city, and half-convinced I should take you with me."

"Kidnapping, you mean?" Her lively green gaze shone like emeralds, but there were still lines under her eyes.

"And Grey?" he asked, sobering.

Her smile faltered, but then appeared once again as she guided him into the living room. "He'll be here," she said, shooting him a sidelong glance. "I cooked for you two."

He grinned. Nobody had cooked for him before. "Ahh, kitten, you don't have to go through that trouble to please me." But shit, he was more than pleased. He would be pleased if she just sat there and stared at him; he was so crazy about her.

He plopped down on a couch seat and yanked a stiff cushion from behind his back, then thoughtfully set it across his lap. She'd made dinner. She'd dressed up. And Heath was freaking embarrassed that he was already so eager to fuck.

He'd had this pain for days.

Innocent to his dilemma, Toni stared into his eyes as she lowered herself to take the seat next to his. "I wanted to," she admitted, reaching out to clasp his hand and link their fingers on the pillow. "I wanted to cook for you. I want to make you and Grey so happy, Heath."

He was so aroused, he could not suppress the pained sound in his throat as he stroked his hands through the silky tendrils of her hair. "You do, sweetheart, you do." The satiny mass fell across her bare shoulders in wavy tresses he wanted to wrap around his face and hands and cock, and he could barely think straight when he buried his nose and inhaled its sweetness.

Ahh, buddy, get your butt over here now.

It was all he thought of as he took her lips and kissed her. *Get the fuck over here now.* It was all that kept him from coming when she stroked his erection over his jeans, and it was all that kept him inserting one finger rather than three under her dress and into her weeping cleft. *Get the fuck here now, Grey!*

And yet minutes became hours, and Toni's arousal began to dim with worry. Attempting to salvage her pride, Heath ate Grey's portion of her meat loaf and potatoes, but while he ate he was quietly hurting for her.

And he was hurting for himself.

Because it was *Heath* that Grey did not want here. It was Heath that Grey would never take.

Toni's eyes kept straying to the door.

Heath's eyes kept straying to the door.

Neither spoke.

Well into the small hours of the night, they settled in the couch and she fell asleep in his arms. By then, it was more than clear to Heath.

Grey was not coming.

The office fell into a cadaverous silence when Grey strode across the carpeted floors the next morning. People began whispering as he quietly shut the massive doors of his office behind him. What nobody expected was the appearance of Heath Solis a few minutes later. They knew it was him, and he was everything he was reputed to be. Dark, big, and menacing, he crossed directly to Louisa's desk. He was not smiling.

"Heath Solis to see Grey."

He didn't sit down on the chair Louisa offered, but waited standing, arms crossed, his hip propped on Louisa's desk as she shakily dialed Grey's extension. "Mr. Solis requesting to see you."

Three seconds later, the doors were thrust open to reveal Grey. The men assessed each other, then Heath pushed himself away from Louisa's desk and strolled into the office behind Grey. Inside, the air crackled with hostility. Heath's arms lay rigid at his sides, and his knuckles jutted out of his fists.

"She's miserable."

If Grey thought he couldn't feel lower, more contemptible, he had been wrong. He felt the pressure of Heath's words in his chest, crushing into his heart, and it irked him that he cared. Releasing a tight, broken breath, he turned back to his desk, to the pile of papers he had yet to get to, the million things he wanted to do, one on top of the other, to keep from thinking of her. Of them. Together.

"She made her choice."

He shuffled the papers on his desk, then rearranged the pens by color. Blacks, blues, reds. "Heath, I've got Parsons in Atlanta, but he's an imbecile with the zoning commission. I need to know your plans."

Heath gaped at him, then shoved his arms up high. "Toni needs you, and you sit there and talk to me about Parsons?"

"She made her choice!" he snapped. *She made her choice, and she chose you. My baby chose you.*

"I can't fucking replace you. I can't fucking make up for your half, and you can't fucking make up for mine. She adores you. What is it that you can't stand—that she loves me, too? That I want to belong to someone, to her?"

He only half listened; his brain was pounding. His temples throbbed and he knew, without a doubt, if Heath did not leave, he was going to lose it. He was on the verge of smashing someone's head into the window, a hair away from turning back into his ancestral ape and roaring out with pain. He wanted him for breakfast. He wanted his *blood*.

Searching for the last vestiges of control, he looked Heath directly in the eye and said, "If you ever mention her again—"

"What?" Covering the distance to his desk, Heath dug into his jeans pocket and slammed his palm into Grey's chest. "Where's your half?" Grey's eyes burned at the sight of red. "Did you tear it up, throw it away?" Heath nabbed Grey's wrist and forced the sash into his palm, anger making his teeth show. "We waited all. Fucking. Night for you!"

Trancelike, Grey ran three fingertips across the cool fabric, then dropped his face and buried his nose deep inside. Oh, *fuck*. Her scent clung to the satin like perfume, and he wanted to suffocate in it. He wanted to hear her, see her, touch her. In that instant, while the fruity scent of her feathered across his straining lungs and the sight and texture of the sash made him long to burn in hell rather than stand this, Grey could not summon any anger. Not for Heath. Not for her. It just hurt. Like nothing in his life had ever hurt before.

"What did you do with yours, Grey?" Heath tightly pressed.

It struck him then that the sash was different. Shorter. The edges tattered on one end. One *cut* end. The bile rose up in his throat, his stomach churning with acid. In his mind, he fit the puzzle together. In his mind, he calculated one plus two and added the three and the four and a thousand other inconsequential inconveniences that alone did not matter but together made a whole.

Setting his face into a stoic mask, he lifted the phone receiver, his voice surprisingly mellow considering the storm brewing inside him. "Miss Fairchild, can I see you for a moment?"

He did not address her as Miss Fairchild often, so naturally when Louisa peered through the doors and stepped inside, her eyes were wide and guilty, and she was pale as a sheet. Oh, she knew. She fucking *knew*.

Grey signaled at a chair. "Sit down, please."

She sat.

Anticipating a show, Heath accommodated himself in the nearby sitting area, leaning forward as though not to miss a word. Grey stepped around the desk and came forward, letting the sash flutter to her lap.

"You've seen that before?"

Head bent low, Louisa Fairchild wrapped her arms around herself as Grey began to circle her.

"You took it to Heath." He paused behind her, leaning closer. "What I want to know"—he enunciated each word carefully into her ear—"is where my half is?"

"I–in the glove compartment. In my car."

"Your car." He straightened, disarmed by her quick admission. "Good. Very good. Bring it."

Neither Heath nor Grey communicated during the time it took her to fetch the sash. Heath sat motionless on the couch, while Grey remained rooted to the spot, bloodthirsty for the sight of that red silk, silent, burning, hoping, wishing.

When Louisa reappeared, she handed the sash over with trembling hands. Grey clasped it in his fist, and his heart exploded at the feel of it, his breath tearing out of him in a hiss of bliss and ecstasy.

Mine.

"I didn't mean any harm," she burst out in pale-faced anxiety, taking a step forward in appeal, "but Toni was being so unreasonable. You can do so much better. I don't think anyone, much less you, should settle for those odd terms!"

"That would be my business," he stated. "And Toni's. And Heath's."

"But I just wanted you to notice there are other women who would have you. Just you. I wanted . . . I just wanted a *chance*."

His smile did not reach his eyes. "You know what I want?" he asked placidly, running his knuckles over his desk as he circled his way around it. "Your resignation. On my desk. Tomorrow morning."

She sucked in a great deal of air, then gripped the back of the chair as she jerked her head up and down in a nod.

Grey pinned her with an admonishing look. "I don't think you're a very good friend, Louisa."

Flushing bright crimson, she stumbled back a step, eager to leave. "I'm not," she choked, wiping at her eyes before she stormed outside.

As Grey watched her leave, his train of thought barreled forward.

Was he judging himself through the eyes of such people, people like Louisa, because he was different, his girl was different, their relationship was different? What was he afraid of that he would let go of the two people he cared most about in his life, the two people he needed?

She had made it rain for him.

Toni had made it rain, and Grey wanted to crash and burn his plane into the ocean, surround himself with the peace and tumult of her water.

He wanted to break every rule with her, make her every wish come true. He wanted to take the world by storm with Heath and her. This was not a decision for his mind, but his heart.

And his heart said *yes*. Yes to the sash, yes to her, yes to his partner, his brother, his friend—yes, to hell with everyone but them. Fuck, he was losing it.

Grey admired the sash once more and tucked it tightly into his hand. This. This strange three-way relationship that everyone would frown upon, that would most probably send his father to his grave and make for an interesting discussion at Toni's parents' dinner table, felt undeniably . . . right.

"Heathcliff."

"Yeah?"

He met Heath's gaze. "Let's go get our girl."

Chapter Seventeen

Toni almost jumped out of her skin when she heard the front door. She'd been jittery all morning, and anxious and a hair away from institutionally depressed. Her fingers froze on the keyboard as muffled footsteps approached behind her. There was more than one set coming. . . .

Spurred to her feet, she turned and was arrested by the sight of Heath, smiling a lazy, toe-curling, heartbreaking smile at her. Like a formidable statue, Grey stood beside him, his tie perfectly in place, his sharp black suit sharper than ever, not a hair out of place. And that face . . .

Vaguely, she remembered she was in her sweatpants, without a drop of makeup and with purple bags under her eyes. And Grey looked wonderful. Odious, stubborn, beloved Grey.

They were here. Both of them. Heath was smiling. Grey was not. His eyes were alight with emotion.

Her vibrant red sash hung from his right hand.

A wave of relief flooded her, but with it came a sharp, startling pain.

Hurt and anger churned in her belly. Her eyes filled up, and Grey became a blur. She rounded the desk and began to back away into the kitchen, trying to swallow back tears as she said in breathless shriek, "H–how could you!"

"Toni."

He started toward her, and she impulsively grabbed the empty coffee cup from the corner of the desk and flung it. He ducked and it fell on the runner with a low *thunk*.

"You jerk. You pigheaded son of a bitch, you've put me through hell!"

She changed directions when he almost caught her, still backing away, then grabbed a couch pillow and sent it flying at him. His hand shot out to derail it, and he seized her arms before she could go further, his eyes crinkled, full of laughter. "Come here, darling."

Her treacherous heart leapt at the fact that he called her darling again, and a sob wrenched her throat as she fought weakly against his grasp. "Don't you dare laugh at me, don't you dare!" she screeched. "Y–you say you love me and the s–second you don't get your way, you're out the f–fucking door!"

He pulled her to his body, engulfing her in his arms, his voice full of despair as he sifted his fingers through her hair. "Baby." He captured her lips, not tenderly, but with shattering desperation, his moist, warm mouth everywhere at once—on her eyes, her lips, her cheeks, his hands cradling the back of her head.

"You call that l–love, t–turning your back on the two people who love you most, who love you just as you are, Grey Richards!"

He clutched her face with no finesse, his eyes feverish and reckless as he met her accusing ones. "I was in hell. Oh, baby, you have no idea. I was *in hell!*" And he kissed her more, his mouth ravenous, opening so wide around hers she felt swallowed whole. When he drew back, his gaze covered every inch of her face and made every bit of it burn from the intensity. "I love you. I have from the first moment and I've never stopped. I love you more and more and more."

More tears sprang into her eyes, one leaking past the corner. He tracked it with his eyes, then caught it with his tongue and groaned.

He kissed her hard, a dry, tight kiss on the lips. "We're home now. We're not going anywhere. Heath is not going anywhere. Neither am I."

Nodding, she choked on a part sob, part laugh. "I'm not going anywhere, either."

He let out a frazzled breath, as though he'd been holding it forever; then his fists were on her track jacket, pulling down the zipper and pushing it off her shoulders as his lips descended with purpose. "Fuck me. Hold me. Love me. Don't let me go."

"Oh, Grey, yes, yes." She busily shrugged off her jacket while their mouths locked, melting together. Grey yanked roughly on his jacket, his tie, his shirt, as though the fabrics were everything they needed to shed so they could once again be one.

When they were bare-chested, she jumped on him and he caught her by the ass, and they were skin to skin, her nipples plastered to his chest, her legs coiling around him as their ravenous mouths slanted and their moans poured out of them.

Desire invaded her in a flood of molten lava as he carried her to the couch, laid her back, and slipped off her sweatpants and panties. "I want you writhing. I want you moaning. I want you screaming *Grey.*"

Oh, god, yes. Knees folded on the seat, she opened her thighs wide for him. Naked, he lowered himself above her, and she locked her ankles at the small of his back a second before he impaled. She moaned. So did he. He felt huge inside her, sliding his hands under her and lifting her higher to take him. The upward angle of her hips sent the blood rushing to her head then back to her pussy as he started pounding and hitting her walls with every deep, plunging inward stroke.

"Oh, baby . . . oh, god . . ."

He closed his eyes briefly, and when he opened them, his simmering gaze greedily feasted on her. She could feel the jiggle of her breasts, noted the complete exposure of her body to him.

He bent over her, pumping red-hot pleasure into her body,

holding her hips in those large, capable hands. He kissed her lips and captured her debilitated sounds with his mouth, their tongues brushing, tangling.

"Say *Grey*."

At the unexpected suction of his mouth on her breast, her spine curved into a dramatic arc. "Grey."

He growled and took the pearl between his teeth, tugging gently, then suckling hard. "I want it on your mouth when you come, Antonia. I want you to never fucking forget it. It's Grey."

Yes, yes, yes, and he was *hers*.

Her orgasm was building, swelling inside her at each slide of his shaft, each pull of his scalding mouth on her nipple. "Grey!" she gasped, the pressure building to a peak. "Heath, don't leave us."

"I'm right here, Cat. Right here with you."

She pried her eyes open and found his rigid, powerful legs beside her. When her eyes traveled up their long, bronzed length, his cock was fully erect above her head, rising up toward the muscled squares of his stomach. His balls looked full and tight and she raised her head and gave them a teasing lick, satisfied when he groaned. "Oh, baby, lick me right there."

She licked him there again, in that smooth place where both balls met. Then she stroked them gently with her hands on her way up to his cock, and caressed the long length of his shaft with her fingers. "Heath."

He emitted a husky sound that hitched in his throat, and, encouraged, she lowered her mouth to lick a wet path up his erection. The gleaming, musky rod jerked under her tongue, making her tummy constrict.

Nearly salivating for more, she wrapped one hand around the base and slanted his cock lower to her mouth. She teased her tongue around the head, gently swiping up the creamy moisture, and he made that sound again, the raw, strangled sound of a man in pleasure. Her body felt it vibrate like an electrical surge rising from her core.

She trembled from head to toe, powerless against the insistent throbbing of Grey, slowly, slowly rocking inside her pussy. One of her palms came to rest on Heath's stomach as she used her mouth and fist to set a rhythm. The muscles in his abs contracted when she sucked him in as deep as she could, until his crown touched her throat and her suctions were milking him fast.

He groaned again, deeper this time, as if farther away. As if lost now. Laboring for breath and thirsty as she'd never been, she used her fist to stroke his length up and down, her hand following the fast motions of her mouth.

"Yes," he hissed, tangling his hand into her hair as her head started to bob, her mouth frantic. She sensed Grey's smoldering gaze on them. He was watching Heath's cock slide in and out of her mouth, wet and rigid and marked with veins.

"Can you take me, Cat?" Heath purred, caressing his fingers through the bun halfway undone in her hair. "You know where I want to be."

"Please. I need you."

Grey hauled her up, still inside her, and she waited in excruciating, anticipatory bliss as Heath knelt behind her and positioned himself.

Grey went still as Heath entered, groaning, "Kitten, oh, kitty Cat, you're tiny."

"All right?" Grey strained out.

She assented with her head, bit at his shoulder. Grey began plunging. "Toni," he rasped, his body vibrating with tension. "I needed this. You."

The men slid in perfect accord, one in, one out, the friction unbearable. "I feel you, Grey," Heath rasped, even as he nipped at her ear, "I feel your cock against mine. Fuck, I love it."

Toni made a sound, torn in pleasure, and Grey grabbed at him past her shoulder, growling, "Come here, Heathcliff." He slammed his mouth against Heath's and they fucked each other with their tongues.

Tearing away, Grey seized her waist and began moving fast, his every effort now on his hips and the powerful slide of his cock into her snug grip. She was awash with sensations, her every nerve attuned to him and Heath, to bringing them pleasure, to taking the pleasure they gave. Nothing else existed. Grey was sweaty, rippling with tension, and fucking her like mad. Heath was going slowly, carefully, the burning driving her to a fever pitch.

"Yes, yes, oh, god!"

Grey brought one knee up, his leg folded, and angled his hips so he'd graze her clit as he stroked. A shudder racked her, the stimulation delicious, poising her orgasm at the very top of that pearly nub.

She rolled her head and gasped. "I'm almost there. God, I'm almost there."

"Jesus, look at you. I'm crazy about you." Grey gained momentum, then suddenly he called something to Heath, and he rolled over, bringing her with him. And she was mounting him. So ready to come. Quivering down to her bones. Riding him.

She bit her lip, unable to keep her eyes open, and Heath was adjusting behind her, her ass being stuffed with his flesh, his slab of a chest on her back. The whistle of his breath whispered across the top of her head. Her undone hair now tumbled past her shoulders as she rolled her hips, moving fast, searching for release, that instant of pure, white pleasure. The instant the spasms in her vagina would drain Grey dry inside her, make Heath spill in her.

Grey's hands fluttered up her stomach and grabbed the globes of her breasts. And his face. Dear god, it was twisted with ecstasy, his eyes sizzling as he watched her. "Ooh!" she cried when he tweaked her nipples, then rolled them between his thumb and forefinger. Her eyes fluttered closed.

"Look at me, Toni."

She opened her eyes, stared into his as they screamed out his love for her, and her body clutched his in a long, tight orgasm. When she cried out his name, he bucked under her, coming with her name on his lips, too. His head twisted to one side as a tremor racked him.

When her shudders subsided, she fell on him with a gasp of delight. Their chests heaved in unison, and Toni made a humming sound at the amazing sensation of having Heath, still aroused, inside her, waiting.

She disengaged herself and whispered into Grey's ear, "Touch him, Grey. Touch Heath."

She wanted to see them together. For Grey to remember how much they'd enjoyed each other's bodies. For Heath to feel wanted.

And Grey rose, his body glistening with sweat—still primed.

"Heathcliff."

"Grey."

They eyed each other like predators, their size alike, their strength alike. Heath was grim-faced. He stood stock-still as Grey began to circle him, his twilight eyes tracking Grey's every move.

Grey spoke first. "If you want Toni, you get me."

Heath's erection was at its fullest length, his muscles flexed as if for a fight. A vein throbbed at his right temple as he answered, "I'll take you both."

"And we'll take you."

Grey pressed into his back, and Heath lifted his gaze to hers, hot and smoldering.

He said nothing else, but a powerful shudder rocked him when Grey said in a silky murmur against the side of his head, "Are you sure this is what you want?"

The tendons in Heath's neck rippled as he swallowed and looked at her with those intent black eyes. His breath was soughing in and out of his chest. And she ached for him. For that big, proud man who had suffered for years in silence. Because she understood Heath in a way Grey never would.

She knew Heath Solis, and that his heart and hers were twins.

And she knew when Grey entered him because his whole body

stiffened, his jaw clamped, his hands fisted at his sides. Grey's tongue darted into his ear as he began to move. Heath was solid, barely moving except for his abdomen and the sounds welling up in his throat.

"This is me," Grey rasped. "Making you ours."

Heath hissed through his teeth, his eyes rolling back. He moved his head, making himself accessible for Grey's tongue on his ear.

"This is me making you Toni's."

Another sound. The sound of someone in pain. Heath's slit leaked and leaked, his cock twitching at each thrust.

"Say you're mine, Heath."

"I'm yours."

"Say you're Toni's."

"I'm yours, Cat. All yours."

"Then bend over and please her. I won't have Toni unhappy."

Heath charged forward as though he'd been waiting for permission, and when he caressed her throat with his lips and tongue, she said, "Hmm."

His callused hands settled on her breasts and fondled the sensitive peaks. "Cat."

"Heath."

"I love you, Cat."

"And I love you, Heathcliff."

His cock was wet with precum and his balls seemed bloated, as though they'd doubled in size. She was entranced watching him being taken. Her hands came to rest on his shoulders as he ministered to her breasts, leaving Grey's torso in full view: sweaty, flushed, rippling sexily. Grey's eyes sizzled as he locked gazes with her, his face contorted with pleasure.

Heath pinched her erect nipples.

Her spine lifted from the couch, her throat bowed in an elegant curve as she dropped her head back, her eyelashes sweeping down to her cheekbones.

He feathered his lips across hers, latching on to her plump bottom one, then the top. He pushed his tongue inside, made a noise, and huskily whispered, "Open your legs for us."

He didn't let go of her breasts as she followed his order, spreading all the way open on the couch. He stroked a hand down the supple silk of her hair, his nose grazing her jaw. "Touch your kitty. It's so wet I can see it from here."

Toni heard the slick sound of her pussy sucking her finger in, and Heath groaned as they both watched it disappear through the lips. "How does it feel?"

"Good."

"Tight? Does it feel tight? Slick?"

"Y-yes."

"Move it for us, move it inside you."

She did as he asked, the rhythm she set causing her to break into a sweat.

Soft, gurgling, mating sounds rose up to her throat, and she slid her hand up her drenched entrance so she could stroke her clit in fast, urgent little circles.

He pressed her nipples with his thumbs, then tugged them out with a hard pinch. "You masturbate thinking of your men fucking?"

A whimper tore out of her as she restlessly moved in her seat, pushing her breasts up to his hands and her pussy to her toying finger. "Yes."

The fast flick of his tongue across a rigid nipple felt like an electric shock coursing through her. "What do you think about?" he demanded.

She yelped when he gripped the heavy globes in his hands, her crested nipples crushed into his palms, and gasped, "You eat each other and you touch each other and . . ."

"We rut with each other."

"Yes."

He pinched her extended nipples with two fingers and watched them jerk and darken as they swelled.

Breathing hard, he caught the curve of her earlobe between his lips and tugged. She relished hearing his breath in her ear—almost no breath at all, he breathed so brokenly. "Don't stop touching yourself. That's right: fuck that kitty and tell me who it's for."

Her hand moved at a frantic pace between her legs. Her middle finger infiltrated her pussy, coming out glistening, plunging back in, then back out to slide up to her clit. Her head rolled senselessly on the couch back, her nostrils flaring with her frenetic breaths as she strained to get the words out. "You and Grey."

He smoothed his tongue into her ear, and desire threatened to overflow her veins. "That's right. It's ours."

"Heath, please."

She was riding her hand fast, and her soft breasts were bouncing in his hands as she whimpered, "Oh, god, I want to come. I want . . ."

One second he was before her, kneading her breasts, and the next he was boosting her up. Holding her flush against him, he subjected her mouth to a violent kiss charged with carnal hunger. "You come when I come. I come when Grey comes."

She framed his face and shifted in his arms so she could wrap her legs around his hips. And Grey was there, his abs at her ankles, and he was lifting up one leg and licking at her toes.

"Please." Their sexual scent was powerful on their bodies, filling her every breath. She was wrapped in it, in them.

Heath snaked his hand between their bodies to secure the base of his stalk, melting her with the slow surge of his body into hers, strong and slick into her fiery heat.

"Kitten."

"Heath." Her fingers were at his shoulders, keeping him close as her cunt clenched around his cock.

"*Shit*. So tight and slick. So perfect."

Gasping sobs tore out of her as he pushed and retreated. She saw in his face, in his constrained expression slowly disintegrating into pleasure, that he could feel the spasms in her pussy already starting to ripple around his cock. His slanted eyebrows cast shadows over his eyes, but they glowed like lightbulbs on his face.

He fought against her hot grip, his thrusts becoming erratic, his fine white teeth bared to her as he threw back his head in abandon. Her thumbs and index fingers went for his nipples. She tugged the beads tight, imitating what he did to hers, and the caresses made his body jerk with pleasure.

"Heath," Grey gritted. "Come *now*."

Clutching at his hair, she let out a mute cry as Grey's great body bucked in orgasm. Heath tensed, then jerked, head twisting as he began to convulse, coming with Grey. Her vision blurred, heat piercing through her as Heath filled her and her orgasm hit. Heath roared, charging for one breast, sucking fiercely as his hips pistoned against hers.

He grabbed her ass, pulling her to him as he hammered her with harsh, animalistic strokes meant to catapult her into her earth-shattering climax. And as she came, he came and came and came in her. Every muscle—even those in his face—tensed and contracted and then burst loose as he drilled her pussy with his cum.

And when he was finished, her body wrapped around him as the aftershocks shook her, he held her tight.

Gently, he kissed her mouth. A third mouth joined, and both men were kissing her. Their tastes combined as she opened wide, their three tongues curling and tangling hungrily, creating an ambrosia of flavors that overwhelmed her senses and flooded her heart.

Truly, she'd suffer through the past three days all over again, if she had to, just to get to this heaven.

Minutes later, they were settled on the king-sized bed, transfixed by the sight of the ceiling. More minutes passed while all they did was breathe. Outside, the afternoon traffic was getting noisy, while inside, Toni lay docile and pliant between the two naked men while Grey absently stroked her hand on her bare stomach, his expression lost in thought.

"We need a bigger place. Two bathrooms."

A smile came automatically to her lips. "Grey," she chided, a playful scowl on her features.

"I'm serious. We should move to my penthouse. If you manage to clutter it like this place, we'll feel right at home. I can't fucking live here with Heathcliff. He's breathing my air."

"You're breathing mine, Richards."

"There's plenty for us both at my penthouse," Grey assured.

"All right. Fine! Penthouse it is," Toni burst, pushing herself upright.

Shifting to his side, Grey directed his solemn gaze at Heath. "We want you here. We can hire someone to do what Parsons can't, which is plenty."

"I love my land, Grey. I like scouring it."

"You can scour it, but your ass will be right here where Toni wants it. Isn't that right, princess?"

She nodded. "That's right, Sir Richards."

"I'm not going anywhere, Cat," Heath said, lifting an arm to caress her jawline with one hand. "If there's land to see, I can do that in a day. Or we can do it together during the weekends. I'll supervise on and off during that time."

Remembering how Grey trusted Heath's instinct above anything, she smilingly asked, "What does your gut tell you?"

Lifting himself up on one arm and bringing his chest tangibly close to her breasts, he smiled a lazy, full-of-it smile. His lips stretched even more as he whisked them across hers. "It tells me I'm home, kitten."

Moved by his admission, she stroked his whiskers with the tips of three fingers, and suddenly Grey caught her hand with his. "You're wearing it."

After registering the awe and pleasure in his words, Toni knew exactly what he was referring to. "Yes." She grinned at him. "I thought whatever happened, I wanted my gray diamond."

He was up in an instant, taking her shoulders in his hands and drawing her close to him. Their mouths locked swiftly as they sought each other's heat, taste, essence. "It's yours." His voice was a throaty rasp. "In my heart, you're my wife. If you want papers, we'll draw papers."

"I don't need papers." As she held her hand up to ogle, sunlight played across the mysterious gray stone, making it sparkle on her fingers. "But I'll keep the ring, thank you!"

"I've got something for you, too."

Both she and Grey turned to Heath in surprise. He had stalked out and was scouring his clothes out in the living room, and when at last he returned, he looked decidedly uncomfortable. First he stood by the door uncertainly; then it seemed to take an effort to approach.

He held his fist out to her and grudgingly uncurled his fingers. "It's black. It's not as expensive as Grey's, but I thought you might like to wear his on your left, and mine on your right."

Her heart did not fit inside her chest, and for a moment she thought she'd burst with emotion. She belonged to two men. Two amazing, stubborn, wonderful men belonged to her. The three of them belonged to one another. To hell with convention—this was awesome!

"Do you like it?" Heath looked so unsure, like a little boy. "Will you wear it?"

With eyes quickly welling up with tears again, she took the plain white gold ring between her fingers and gazed into the black rock. It was like looking into Heath's eyes, it was so captivating.

Her fingers were sure and steady as she slipped it on her right hand. "Come here, Heathcliff," she whispered, imitating Grey. She drew him down to her lips and kissed him, and Grey bent his head to join. Their three tongues tangled lazily, their bodies rubbed together, and as Toni felt them get primed to be together again, she breathed, "You'll both have to wear mine."